Framed...

When eighteen-year-old Methusal Maahr is framed for the murder of her oldest friend, she will do anything to expose the true killer and clear her name, including team up with her arch rival in the Kaavl Games, Behran. But all clues point to her guilt...and appear to tie into a conspiracy regarding the new peace talks with their oldest enemies from Dehre.

While peace looms on the horizon, Methusal doesn't trust it. Mentàll Solboshn, Chief of Dehre, is not what he appears to be. Her determination to discover the truth soon pits her against the formidable Chief. Not only is he the best kaavl player in the land, but he is determined that the peace plan will pass. Can Methusal's rare kaavl skills possibly outmatch him, and stop him from succeeding with his devious plans?

Methusal is ready and willing to do anything to protect her community of Rolban—even put her own life on the line to expose and defeat a dangerous political foe. But little does she realize the true danger may lie within her own community...

KAAVL CHRONICLES
(Book One of Quadrilogy)

KAAVL CONSPIRACY

Jennette Green

DIAMOND PRESS

Kaavl Conspiracy

A Diamond Press book / published in arrangement with the author

ISBN: 978-1-62964-011-2

Library of Congress Control Number: 2016904289
Library of Congress Subject Headings:
Paranormal—Juvenile fiction
Paranormal romance—Juvenile fiction
Courage—Fiction
Individuality—Fiction
Sisters—Fiction
Families—Fiction
Paranormal—Fiction
Fantasy fiction
Young adult fiction

Diamond Press
3400 Pegasus Drive
P.O. Box 80043
Bakersfield CA 93380-0043
www.diamondpresspublishing.com

Published in the United States of America.

To my friends, who have always encouraged me.

You know who you are.

Also by Jennette Green

ROMANCE NOVELS

The Commander's Desire
Her Reluctant Bodyguard
Ice Baron
The Pirate's Desire

YOUNG ADULT/NEW ADULT

Kaavl Conspiracy
(Paranormal, Book 1 of Quadrilogy)
Beyond the Rapture
(Christian Apocalyptic)

Castaways
(a novelette)

SHORTER WORKS

Toot of Fruit
(a children's story)

Murder by Nightmare
(a novelette)

Koblan

Quasr
Var
Tarst
Ilgnon Region
Aestoff
Eerpor
Nelph
Dehre
Rolban
Wyen
Linn
Sasrin

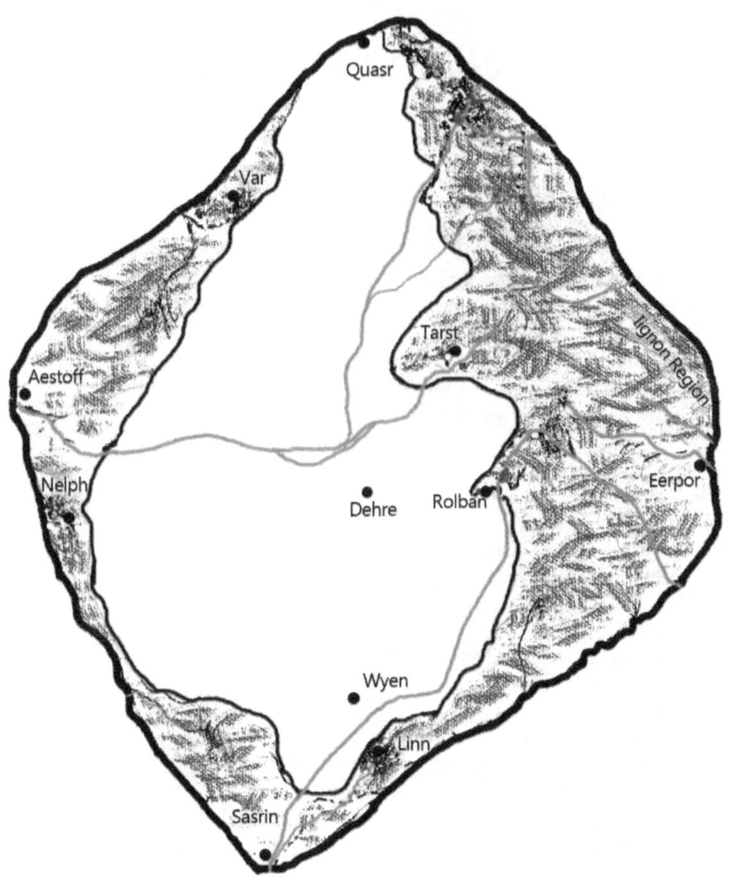

Pronunciation Guide

Kaavl (Kah' vl)

Kaavl levels (from highest to lowest):
Ultimate level (only Mahre ever achieved)
Primary level
Bi-level
Tri-level
Quatr-level (Kwah' tra level)
Quint-level (Kint level)

Places

Aestoff (Ay' stoff)
Carachki (Ka ra' chki) capitol of Zindedi
Dehre (Deh' ree)
Dehrien (Deh' ree un)
Koblan (Koe' blun)
Koblani (Koe blane' ee)
Rolban (Role bane')
Rolbani (Role bane' ee)
Quasr (Kay' zer)
Quasrian (Kay zar' ee un)
Tarst (Tarst)
Wyen (Why en')
Zindedi (Zin deh' dee)

Characters

Rolban

Aalicaa (A lee shaw') (Aali (A' lee)) Deccia's sister/cousin,
    Methusal's cousin, Quatr-level
Barak Mehl (Bare' uk Mel) Kitran's brother
Behran Amil (Bee' hrhun/Beh' rhun Uh meel') Tri-level
Ben Amil, Behran's father
Deccia (Day' shuh) Methusal's twin sister
D'Wit (Duh wit') Elderly Rolbani doctor, Petr's political advisor
Erl (Earl) Methusal's father
Goric (Gor' ik) Tri-level
Hanuh (Han' nah) Methusal's mother
Kitran Mehl (Kih' trun Mel) Barak's brother, Primary level
Liem (Lee' um) Renn's father, Chief contender
Mahre (Mah' ree) The Old Kaavl Master
Matron Olgith (Ol' gith) Petr's aunt
Maxmil Verdnt (Vernt) Bi-level
Methusal Maahr (Meth u' zul Mare) Tri-level
Motr (Moe' tr) In charge of water systems, Behran's boss
Petr (Pet' r) Deccia and Aali's father, Bi-Level
Pogul (Poe' gull)
Poli Amil (Pol' ee Uh meel') Behran's mother
Renn (Liem's son)
Sims Nalg (Sims Nalg) Supply room supervisor
Timaeus (Tim' ay us)
Vogl (Voe' gl)

Dehre

Hendra (Hen' druh) Quatr-level
Jascr (Jas' kr) Bi-level
Mentàll Solboshn (Mn tall' Sole' bah shn) Chief of Dehre, Primary
    level
Wortn (Wor' tn) Dehrien, Tri-level

Tarst

Aenill (Uh neel') Pan's wife
Dastn (Das' tn)
Pan Patn (Pan Pat' tn) Tarst Chief, Primary level

Zindedi

General Greisn Rohasch (Gree' shun Ro' hash) (brother of Zindedi
    Presidente)
Presidente of Zindedi

Prologue

CARACHKI
CAPITOL OF THE ZINDEDI CONTINENT
Sixthday

THE PRESIDENTE OF ZINDEDI fingered the sharp edge of his sword, and smiled as the blade caught his skin. Red bubbled up. War. He loved the taste of it. He loved the smell of it.

Hadn't he unified his continent with one ruthless, bloody stroke? Now the entire continent of Koblan would fall, too.

A hard knock sounded on the wooden door of his office. "Presidente."

"Enter, General." The Presidente smiled as a stocky man strode into the room. "Brother. Sit." He plucked a plump red fruit from a bowl and turned it in his hand.

General Greisn Rohasch smiled, and his teeth gleamed a pale yellow beneath his mustache. His black General's cap fit tightly on his spiky black and silver hair, and his amber eyes, which were set in his square, florid face, appeared a bit unfocused, as usual. "Presidente. You have a report?"

"Yes." Thoughtfully, the Presidente stroked the fruit over the blade. "Hatred is stirred. Vengeance is sought. Soon the village of Rolban will fall to her enemies, as we have long planned."

"And the ore?" General Greisn's voice sharpened. "It will be ours?"

"Ripe for you to pluck. Only a few more weeks until the fruit is ready for harvest." The President tossed a dull, silver lump of metal to the General, who caught it with whip-like swiftness. "A specimen."

The General turned it over in his thick fingers. "Nearly perfect."

"Yes." The Presidente smiled. "And victory is assured."

"What about Koblan's kaavl?" General Greisn's soft-jowled smile disguised his well-known core of cruelty.

The Presidente snorted. "Mind games cannot win wars. Neither will Koblan's crude weapons. I warned the spy to focus on his job. Not kaavl. Soon we will bring the Koblan continent to her knees." He stroked the fruit over the blade again, and smiled. "It will be as simple as taking a toy from a child. They are ignorant of our existence. I might pity them, if they were not so stupid."

The fruit's skin split, and red juice ran down the Presidente's skin.

The General giggled, and his eyes gleamed amber, like the fires of hell. "I am ready to lead the charge." Spittle formed at the corners of his mouth. "I anticipate plucking their ripest fruit."

"Patience, my brother. All in good time. Rolban must first fall, and the three communities become weakened. And then we will invade the Koblan continent." The Presidente bit into the sweet delicacy. "Raping ore from that fertile land will be a pleasure. And the fruit of her womb will deliver to us the world."

△ △ △ △ △

ROLBAN
KOBLAN CONTINENT
Same day

THE VELVET NIGHT CLOAKED RENN. Only his harsh, unsteady breathing broke the silence. His moccasined toes curled deep into the soft earth of the crop plateau.

He stood only a step from the edge. Far below, the cliff crashed into a jumble of rocks, and then the plains stretched on, black beneath the star-pierced sky. Running to eternity.

Why had Methusal asked to meet him here?

Renn's trembling fingers clenched around the cold metal object in his pocket; the proof he'd risked his life to find. A parchment crinkled next to it.

He had to warn the others, and soon. Unfortunately, he knew the identity of the traitor, but little else. What was the traitor's mission? What else did he plan to steal from Rolban, and why?

Methusal's necklace was the key.

A cool breeze kissed his cheek and he breathed greedily, trying to calm the nervous gallop of his heart.

Surely Methusal wasn't involved with the traitor.

Why hadn't she arrived yet?

Releasing the heavy object, he pushed a shaky palm across his brow. The thefts from the supply room hadn't seemed like much, at first—only a hint something was wrong. The stolen ore was another matter.

Now he knew the threat ran deep, and originated in a foreign land—Zindedi. A land far from the Koblan continent's shores. And no one knew this but him. And the traitor. And possibly Methusal. He believed he could trust her. He hoped he wasn't wrong.

It was dangerous out here. His gaze slid to the plain floor. The wild beasts were out, but that didn't explain the apprehension licking through him.

Scuff.

Footsteps whispered over the earth. He jerked around, his shoulders rigid, and heart pounding.

A dark form stalked toward him. It wasn't Methusal. It was a man. A big one.

No. How had he found out?

Renn's eyes darted, seeking a way to escape.

"It is time we talked." The familiar voice was a hiss.

"Where's Methusal?" To his disgust, his voice trembled.

"She didn't receive your note. I followed you and stole it."

"But..." Bewildered, Renn uncurled his fist. Pale parchment glowed in the starlight.

"Give it." The dark form grabbed his wrist and ripped the paper from his fist.

Horror crept through him. "She never got my note?"

"Soon, she will." Another soft chuckle. "An edited version, anyway. And this note," he crumpled it in his fist, "is one I wrote."

The traitor had written the note that Renn had received. Not Methusal. The hairs on his neck rose, like the hackles of an apte beast.

A knife appeared in the traitor's hand and glinted in the feeble starlight.

Renn choked back a terrified cry. He'd always been so careful, and so neat and logical in everything he did. But he had never foreseen this. Never. He couldn't seem to think clearly. "I know what you've been doing!"

"You know nothing."

"You've been stealing."

"A few pots. A few skins," the soft voice scoffed. "And...oh, yes." The black form stepped closer, knife glinting inches from Renn's throat. "Give back what you stole from me."

"You're the thief."

"Give me the ore."

"Leave me alone." His chest felt tight, clamped by fear.

"Sorry. You know too much."

"I know nothing!"

"You know who I am. You found the ore. And the letter to my Presidente. Can't allow that."

"I won't tell!" Backing up, Renn's heel hit solid rock. It was the lip of the cliff, a handbreadth from the edge. His brain felt fogged. He needed to escape. But how?

"The ore." The voice sounded cold, now. Determined. "I'll give you an exchange for it."

"Exchange?" Would he be allowed to live, after all?

"Now."

Renn pulled the chunk of metal from his pocket and thrust it at the other man. A pale smile glimmered through the darkness, and then a smooth, flat rectangle with cut surfaces jabbed into his palm. His heart hammered. "Where did you find this? You've been in my compartment!" Since he wanted his hands free again, he quickly shoved it into his pocket.

"As you have been sneaking through mine. Did you find your answers?"

Why hadn't he been more careful? Renn's eyes darted left and right. He needed to buy time—finally, a rational thought. "Tell me then...why? What's this all about?"

A chuckle hissed. "Power, ore...and so much more. And kaavl is the key."

"Key? Key to what?" But he was no longer listening. He was ready to make his move.

"Everything."

"Traitor!" With a snarl, Renn lunged to the right, but out of the corner of his eye the knife slashed through the inky black. Pain ripped into his neck. And then the dark form pushed him, hard.

His heel tripped over the stone lip, and wind rushed by his ears, soaring with his unending terror. Falling...falling.

And then nothing. Blessed darkness.

CHAPTER ONE

ROLBAN
KOBLAN CONTINENT
Seventhday

TAGMA LEAVES WHISPERED, and Methusal Maahr quickly swiveled her head, her heart pounding.

Nothing.

A cool breeze swept the small, sun-kissed plateau. It was still light outside, and too early for the dangerous wild beasts to creep from their caves. All the same, she sharpened her senses. *Kaavl* would help her spot the beasts before they charged within attacking range.

Concentrating hard, she stared at the far bluffs, which were stamped in black against the pale blue, eastern horizon. Where were the flying beasts now?

There! Eyes sharpened by the rigid practice of kaavl discriminated the outline of black wings against the black bluffs.

Bluffs. Renn had fallen to his death from a cliff last night.

Tears stung her eyes. This morning a runner had discovered the remains of Renn's mangled body at the base of Rolban's nearest cliff. Wild beasts had licked half of his bones clean. His death had shocked the community. It had devastated her.

What had happened? Why had he visited the crop plateau last night?

His funeral this morning had been surreal. To Methusal, it had felt like the memorial service had happened much too quickly, but funerals always took place immediately in Rolban. In the past, disease outbreaks had been a problem, and so the community had passed a law requiring that the dead be buried as quickly as possible.

At the gravesite Renn's only living parent, Liem, had stood as still as a stone, his features blank.

Grief still felt like claws shredding Methusal's soul.

Stop it. Concentrate. He'd want it that way.

Renn had been pragmatic. A careful thinker, with unexpected flashes of wit. They'd been good friends for their entire lives.

She let the hot tears fall. Surely he was in a better place now. He wouldn't want her to cry over him, either. If he was here, he'd probably say, "Life goes on, Thusa." Then he'd smile. "Remember that baby whip I hid in your jacket? Almost bit your finger off. Count your blessings I'm gone."

Methusal swallowed against the ache in her throat. *Kaavl.* Kaavl would deliver her from the grief. For a while. Maybe running would help, too.

She climbed down the rocky hillside, fiercely trying to concentrate into a kaavl state of mind. Soon she'd be ready for the Kaavl Games, which would take place in a few days.

Even better, she'd soon deliver an unpleasant surprise to her arch rival.

As she focused, Methusal became *kaavl*; intensely aware of the late afternoon sun toasting her skin, and the sharp stones biting into her thin, multi-patched moccasins. Tall, thick tagma bushes dotted the plain, networked by thick gnarled roots that rippled across the surface of the flat, dry brown earth. A whisper of movement tickled her ears, and dry leaves rustled.

A whip beast was stalking a round, furry apte. Muted gasping noises interrupted the peaceful quiet.

The sounds of struggle, and of death.

Death. Again, thinking about Renn stole the breath from her lungs.

Concentrate.

An innocent animal fought to live. She could help it.

The squeaks sharpened, and she slipped closer.

There. Behind a low scrub bush. A whip beast, as long as Methusal's leg and two handbreadths wide, clenched a small apte's stubby leg between its large, triangular teeth. The whip beast wriggled, readying for the final, lunging gulp. Although whips had no legs or arms, they could spring as high as a man's waist. They could kill an adult human.

Methusal couldn't bear to see the apte suffer and die. No more death. Not today.

Ignoring her fear, she plucked up two large rocks and analyzed the situation.

The apte's markings looked familiar. In particular, the thick white stripes bisecting its black ears dredged up an old memory. Had she nursed this apte to health three years ago? That one had broken its leg.

It didn't matter. The whip would lose its supper. Silently she moved closer and slipped behind a thick, prickly tagma bush that was nearly as tall as she was. Concentrating into pinpoint focus, she flung the first stone.

Whack. It connected with the whip's snout. The animal's jaw slackened, but not long enough for the apte to scramble free.

Mean, rock-like black eyes swiveled to Methusal. Fear stabbed her. She ignored it. With swift precision, she hurled the second rock. It *thwacked* hard between the whip's eyes. The leathery, worm-like creature jerked and fell. It lay motionless, its mouth still clamped around the apte's leg.

Suspicious that the beast was playing dead, Methusal grabbed the kaavl stick from her belt. The weapon was as long as her thigh, two fingers thick, and made of dense, strong hardwood. She poked the whip beast. It didn't move. The apte whimpered.

"I hear you." Methusal wiggled the stick between the whip's teeth and levered the locked mouth open. The apte scrabbled free, dragging his injured leg behind him.

Using the stick, Methusal rolled the whip further away. When she stepped closer, to give it one final push, it convulsed in half and sprang at Methusal.

She gasped, and jerked up the weapon to block the attack. The whip's heavy weight hit the stick, and Methusal staggered. Automatic kaavl training kicked in, and she whipped the stick right and left, repeatedly smacking the beast's head. Its sharp teeth snapped empty air, and its body convulsed, preparing for another spring. Panic slid into the corners of her mind. Trying to block it out, Methusal struck the beast again and again, focusing on the cold precision needed.

The whip stopped moving. Blood trickled from its mouth.

Trembling, she stepped back a few safe paces. The whip beast lay inert, but she didn't trust it. It was probably just stunned. Its hide was thick.

The apte had stopped a length away, perhaps to watch the drama. Or maybe because its leg hurt. He stared at Methusal.

She knelt and murmured, "Come here." Extending one hand in a loose fist, she used the other one to pull a healing coltac leaf and leather kaavl strip from her pocket. She always carried medical supplies, just in case she injured herself while practicing kaavl. Or in case she came across an injured beast, like today.

The deadly whip, on the other hand, could fend for itself.

The apte hopped closer, using his good leg as a spring. "That's it. Come on," she whispered. The animal stopped. His fur brushed against her knee. She smiled and said softly, "Know what? You remind me of my pet. His name is Chup Chup."

Few animals feared her, and it was a gift she cherished. Only once had she been bitten, and that was by a feral wolmite which had been crazed with pain. He would not let her touch him. A week later, she'd found his carcass licked clean by the wild beasts. She still wished she had tried harder to save him.

With firm, gentle fingers, Methusal grasped the furry apte and examined his short leg. No breaks, thankfully. That would require longer care, and her parents had forbidden her to bring home another animal. Although she'd turned eighteen a few months ago, Methusal would live at home until she married. She snorted softly. If that ever happened.

No men had shown the slightest amount of interest in her so far. Although that hurt, she valued her freedom far more.

She broke the coltac leaf in half and dribbled thick juice over the bloody mess. After adhering the leaf on top, she swiftly wound the leather around the leg and tied it closed. There. By the time the apte gnawed off the bandage, the wound should have healed.

The apte nosed at the leather and scurried away.

With a sigh of satisfaction, Methusal stood and gazed north, across the desert plain, studded with scattered, thick bushes, to the cave entrance into the mountain. The metal gates were flung wide to drink in the last fingers of sunlight. Home. Rolban. The sun hung low over the western plains. Twilight would arrive within minutes. And so would the wild beasts. Her flesh prickled, and she slipped back into kaavl to listen for scrabbling claws.

A whisper touched her ears. Flying beast wings sliced the sky far overhead. And a faint rustle of stones tickled her ears. Too late, she sensed a presence behind her.

"Practicing, Methusal?"

She spun. "Behran." How had he managed to sneak up on her like that?

"Looks like you need more practice." Deep blue eyes grinned at her, and familiar annoyance surged. However, she made certain her expression did not betray it.

But he knew. The tall young man continued to grin. "Need pointers?"

"No. Thank you." The words ended in a snap, which she regretted. Kaavl contenders needed to remain self-disciplined and courteous at all times. *To everyone,* and that included her arch rival, Behran. She'd be disqualified from this year's Game if she didn't meet that high standard.

"Fair enough." His straw colored brow flicked up his sharply cut face. "So. Think you're any good yet?"

She silently counted to three, which wasn't anywhere near long enough. "You still don't think I have what it takes, do you?"

Behran opened his mouth.

"You still think I'm that silly thirteen-year-old..."

"Who worshipped the ground I walked on?" A grin twisted his lips.

"Until I realized how conceit..." Methusal shut her mouth. Why was she allowing him to provoke her?

Jaw set, she turned and strode for the wide, dark cave which lead into the heart of the mountain. For five years she'd endured Behran's condescending put downs. But no longer. Soon she'd surprise him with her kaavl skills.

He easily kept pace. "I'm sorry about Renn." His serious tone surprised her.

"Me, too."

"I didn't know him well, but he seemed like a good person."

"He was." Methusal blinked back stinging tears and wished Behran would stop talking. She didn't want to cry anymore, and especially not in front of her adversary.

Renn. Renn was nothing like Behran; neither physically, nor, more importantly, in character. Stocky Renn had been dark-haired and brown-eyed, whereas Behran was blond, blue-eyed, and whip lean. Renn grew up in Rolban, but Behran and his parents had immigrated from Dehre five years ago, when he was seventeen. Renn was a steady friend. Someone she could trust. Behran Amil was nothing but trouble.

"Thusa?" She became aware that Behran was watching her, one brow lifted in that familiar, annoying manner.

She frowned.

"You look lost."

How was she supposed to respond to that comment?

Behran continued to watch her. Was he making fun of her? Or, based upon their history, needling her? Methusal would not allow him to provoke her again.

And then a welcome memory made a tiny smile tug at her lips. She remained silent, however. He'd learn about her step up the kaavl ladder soon enough. Surprise would give her the edge in the Game a few days away.

His next words turned her smile upside down.

"Congratulations on reaching the Tri-level." His eyes gleamed at her surprise. "I have the right to know my competitors at the Tri-level. Remember?"

"Of course." Although her voice sounded calm, inside she felt anything but. Another point for Behran. How had she forgotten that vital piece of information?

Behran's mouth twitched, but finally his gaze turned serious. "I look forward to competing against you."

"It'll be interesting," she allowed, and managed, just in time, to squash another small, anticipatory smile.

"Probably." His grin reemerged.

What was he really thinking? They'd never competed against each other in the Kaavl Games before, because they'd ranked at different skill levels. Did Behran consider her a serious threat yet?

If not, he soon would. Methusal slipped back into kaavl, and tried to ignore Behran and his attempts to aggravate her.

She took in every nuance of her environment. A cool breeze kissed her skin, and licked up swirls of dust from the tan, cracked surface of the plain. Fading sunshine glinted off of the tiny, gray-green tagma leaves that rustled in the strengthening breeze. The cool, rainy season had ended three passes of the full moon ago. It had not rained since. They had another pass to endure before the hot season, sprinkled with a few rain showers, began.

Behran interrupted her thoughts. "Almost forgot. Petr wants to talk to you about Renn."

"*Renn?* Why?" Like a fist, grief again gripped her heart. And whispers from this morning slid through her mind. *A bloody mess.* Renn's body had been shredded by a pack of wild beasts. Methusal hadn't seen it. But she couldn't stop herself from imagining it, and it made her feel sick to her stomach.

Behran shrugged. "It sounded urgent. I'm supposed to make sure you arrive in a timely manner."

"Message delivered. I'll go on my own." She'd rather not go at all. Any meeting with her uncle boded ill—for her.

"You don't want to enjoy my company?" His lips twitched.

Methusal couldn't summon the willpower to smile at his small joke.

"All right." Behran' serious blue gaze bored into her, as if evaluating the heavy grief weighing upon her soul. "I really am sorry, Thusa."

Behran finally sprinted off for Rolban's entrance, but the tension coiling in Methusal's gut did not ease. She tried not to think about Petr, and what he might want. Instead, she assessed Behran's fast lope. His speed would be difficult to beat in the Kaavl Game. But skill would help her win it, she told herself. Not speed. Behran was right about one thing, though. She'd made a major slip, not detecting him earlier. She did need to practice more.

It felt cooler than it had just a few minutes ago. Methusal walked faster for the entrance hall. Soon the sun would dip below the horizon, and the guards would close the gates and thrust the ceremonial sword through the center lock. The clanging screech would signal lockdown until dawn. In the past, the blade had warned off invaders. But after 200 years of peace, the only danger to Rolban's security were the wild beasts.

An icy breeze brushed her cheek. She glanced left, toward the setting sun. Fingers of darkness sped from west to east across the lonely, flat landscape.

Only a cloud, covering the sun, but a shiver slid down her spine. She glanced over her shoulder. Bright swathes of sunshine still lit most of the landscape. The dark shadow only enveloped her body and the entrance to the Rolbani mountain community...and stretched west, in a straight line, as far as she could see.

One long, lingering swathe of darkness. Another chill rippled through her, reminding her of Renn's death. Of the burial service.

The darkness felt like a bad omen.

Methusal gave herself a mental shake. Ridiculous. After all, she wasn't empathetic, like her mother and sister were.

She slipped into the Great Hall, past the empty reclining day chairs used by young mothers and the elderly to soak up the warm sun, to the end of the Great Hall, where it curved right and led to wide, steep stairs hewn out of solid black rock. The huge cavern was naturally formed, as were all the caves in the Rolbani community.

Sounds of laughter and clinking dishes drifted down from the dining hall, and she quickened her pace upward. Her stomach rumbled, and she wished again that she didn't have to visit Petr before supper.

At the top, she crossed the passage and glanced through the arched entrance into the dining hall. Tantalizing smells of savory cooked meat and freshly baked bread teased her nose. Gray streams of light illuminated the good natured, jostling scene. The dim light filtered down through carefully preserved cracks in the dining hall ceiling. When it rained, special leather tarps covered the holes and collected the rain water.

Methusal didn't see her family at their table yet, and the line at the buffet was short. Maybe if her meeting with Petr ended quickly, she could still find a choice piece of meat for supper.

She turned right down the passage, and stopped at the third wooden doorway. A burnt image of a three-peaked mountain range, over-crossed by three stalks of grain and encircled by the outline of Koblan's coastline, signified the Chief of Rolban's office. Methusal knocked.

"Come in," her uncle boomed. Then, when she complied, "Sit."

Petr Storst settled his big bulk back in his chair, his white, bushy brows furrowed in a deep frown. Surprise, surprise, he wasn't pleased with her. What had she done now? In her uncle's vocal opinion, she was a stubborn, willful, outspoken young woman, all three of which were true, and all three of which he thoroughly disapproved. However, he most especially disliked her kaavl influence over his youngest daughter.

Petr lifted his hand. A silvery metal object rested in his palm, and a fine chain spilled between his fingers. "I suppose you recognize this."

With a shock of surprise, she automatically reached for the familiar object. "Where did you find it?"

Petr let her take it. Smooth and flat, it was a finger-breadth thick, and shaped like a rectangle, with the longest sides nearly as long as her palm. It was made of solid ore, and heavy. A carved border outlined the object and a large, flourished capital letter "M" was embossed upon the tablet necklace.

Her fingers rubbed its familiar lines and edges. "I've been searching for it all week." She flipped it over and traced two familiar scratches on the back—a large, crude "M" in the center, and on the bottom right, a small "r." Some ancient child ancestor of hers had scratched those in long ago.

"I found it on Renn's body this morning."

"On...*Renn?*" Methusal gasped. Why had Renn had her necklace? He'd known it belonged to her. Everyone did. After all, the necklace had been passed down to the oldest Maahr child for centuries. Why hadn't he returned it?

Petr's frown deepened. "Nothing to say?"

"What do you mean?"

"Fine. This might loosen your tongue." He shoved a scrap of paper across the table. "Read it."

She smoothed out the wrinkles and read the small, cramped handwriting, which looked messier than normal, as if Renn had written it in a rush.

4/10

Methusal, I found your necklace. I'll have to tell Petr, but I wanted to warn you first. Meet me on the crop plateau tonight. I know you've been in the ore mine, because that's where I found your necklace. Are you the ore thief? We've always been friends, so I wanted to give you the chance to explain to me first. Renn

The message left her speechless. At the same time, she couldn't help but touch the parchment.

Renn had written this note to her. Why hadn't she received it? Her bewilderment grew. "This doesn't make sense. I've never been to the ore mine."

"Mmhm. Then how did he find your necklace?"

"I don't know. It's been lost..."

"Lost in the ore deposits!"

"But how? I don't even know where the ore mine *is.*"

"Don't lie. Renn's letter proves you've been there."

"*No.* I haven't." Exactly what point was her uncle trying to make? Methusal scrambled to make sense out of something...*anything*...in this strange line of questioning. "Isn't the mine closed? That's why we can't make more weapons, right?"

"No. We choose not to mine ore. It's a condition of the Great War Peace Plan. Surely you know that. Just as you know the Rolban Mountains house the biggest deposits of ore on the Koblan continent. Maybe in the entire world."

"Yes. But..."

"Don't play dumb, Methusal. You *knew* Renn was an ore mine guard!"

"No. I didn't. I thought he was Sims' supply room assistant."

"He had two jobs!" Petr's fist crashed onto the table. She jumped. He lunged to his feet. "*Why* were you in the restricted area? *How* did you get back there?"

"I didn't!"

"Obviously, you did. We have proof. You stole ore! Who did you give it to?"

Methusal gaped up at him. "*What?* I didn't steal ore! What are you talking about?"

Petr leaned over the table. "We know you're involved, Methusal. Renn found your necklace in the ore deposits. He sent you the note. You met him on the bluffs last night. He confronted you about your ore thefts, and you pushed him over the edge."

"*No!* I would never," Methusal exclaimed, horrified. "How could you *think* that? And...and I've never seen that note before, either!"

Petr sat down again. His hard eyes resembled gray stone. "We searched your compartment this morning. We found that note hidden under your pallet."

Methusal felt overwhelmed, and more than a little scared. "I didn't put it there. I didn't receive it!" she insisted. "And why would you search my room in the first place?"

"Renn left a detailed letter in his compartment. Apparently he was afraid for his life. For good reason, it appears."

"I didn't receive that note. And I certainly didn't kill Renn!"

Petr seemed convinced that Renn's death wasn't an accident. That someone had murdered him. Her muddled mind tried to make sense of the facts Petr had just presented. Renn had found her necklace in the heavily guarded ore mine. How had it gotten there?

Petr glared. "I knew you would be difficult. Until we get to the bottom of this, you won't leave the gates of this community. I should put you in jail, but I don't have enough proof. Yet. And count yourself lucky you're my niece. But know this: when we do find solid proof against you, you will be tried, and severely punished."

"But I didn't kill Renn! And I can't stay inside. I have to practice for the Kaavl Games."

"You won't take part in the Kaavl Games." He stood, dismissing her. "Consider these charges seriously. I want the name of your accomplice. Much as you've proven yourself to be a rebellious and undisciplined young woman, I don't think you are stealing ore on your own. I want to know who's behind it all, and where that ore is going."

In a daze, Methusal stumbled for the door. "You're wrong. You're accusing the wrong person."

"Prove it."

Chapter Two

DEHRE
KOBLAN

HENDRA SAT AT THE SUPPER TABLE in the Chief of Dehre's tent. Through the open tent flap, daylight had faded into dusky nightfall. A lamp illuminated the food, as well as the only other occupant of the room: her cousin—the Chief of Dehre, Mentàll Solboshn (Mn tall' Sole' bah shn). Although he was her first cousin, he'd always behaved more like a brother to her than any of her natural ones.

The lamplight softened his harsh features, but its shadows emphasized the intimidating size of his lean, broad-shouldered body. He was only eight years older than she was, but the tenuous bond that had developed between them during childhood appeared to have broken when he moved away from home at sixteen. Although he protected her now, they weren't close. In truth, Mentàll never let himself get close to anyone. Still, Hendra loved him as if he were her own brother.

She swallowed her bite of meat and tried to squelch the worry that had been eating at her over the last few weeks. Tonight she would ask the question.

Just not yet.

She cast a quick, apprehensive glance at her cousin. Their mothers had been identical twins, and although both she and her cousin possessed the same white-blond hair, and had grown up in the same house, there the similarities ended. Mentàll had grown into a hard man, and he'd become hard to read, too.

Although Hendra barely understood him anymore, she was grateful to him. Four years ago, when she was sixteen, Mentàll had given her one of his tents to live in after her father died and her real brothers threw her out of the house. Casting off a family member was an unthinkable act in Dehre, but Hendra would never dream of complaining to the elders. Her shame would only increase if the community learned the truth of who she really was.

Even Mentàll did not know. He had asked no questions; he'd just taken her in.

As Chief of Dehre, providing Hendra with a tent was a luxury her cousin could easily afford. Still, she felt grateful. Without his shelter and provision, she'd be dead now. Or wish she was.

At the end of the long table, Mentàll ate silently. He'd made little effort to speak to her tonight. What was he thinking?

Did she want to know? She bit her lip. Lately, her cousin's attitude had become even more off-putting. He didn't encourage questions, or idle chit chat. To Hendra, it seemed like a wall of impenetrable ice guarded him. The caring cousin she'd once known lived somewhere inside that ice. Or perhaps his heart had frozen solid within the cold and—she suspected—ruthless man he had become.

The worry that had nagged Hendra for the last month could be ignored no longer. Gathering her courage, she said, "I've been smelling smoke at night. Not the fires protecting the town," she clarified. "It smells different. Bitter...like burning metal." In the daylight, she'd seen no evidence of unusual fires. So the smell must be drifting to Dehre from the low lying hills to the north.

Mentàll sent her a cool look. "All is fine," he said in his low, harsh voice. "Do not speak of it again."

Still, she dared to press further. "What about the Alliance with Rolban and Tarst? Don't you want peace?"

"I desire everything Rolban will offer me." After a pause, he grimly finished, "And even what it will not."

She softly gasped. "*Mentàll.*"

His ice blue gaze flayed into her. A warning. He would never hurt her, but she must heed him now. "I seek peace, Hendra. Do not be afraid. Everything will be safely delivered into my hands."

What did that mean? She didn't like the sound of it, but fell silent. Clearly, he would tell her nothing further. What was he planning? What burned outside the town at night? It meant nothing good, she knew it. Metalworking—except for fixing hunting and kitchen utensils—had been banned two hundred years ago by the Great War Peace Agreement.

Hendra was afraid for Mentàll. Although she barely understood him, she loved her cousin. Growing up together in that horrible house had bonded them.

She did understand one thing clearly, however. Fury simmered deep in her cousin's soul.

Mentàll hated Rolban. True, Rolban always had plenty of food and Dehre usually had little, especially now, after the poor harvest last year. But she didn't think starvation alone fueled his lifelong hatred for the Rolbani community.

Mentàll was plotting something. She knew it, and it scared her. It must have something to do with the upcoming Alliance with Rolban. Whatever it was, she hoped it wouldn't end in bloodshed. Or his death.

CHAPTER THREE

METHUSAL ESCAPED from Petr's office. In a daze, she leaned against the lumpy rock wall and took several deep breaths. Renn was dead, and Petr thought *she* had killed him.

Had Renn really been murdered? Plenty of other questions tangled in her mind.

After drawing a few more trembling breaths, Methusal entered the dining hall, grabbed a plate, and stood in line at the buffet. Without really seeing it, she stared at the counter, which was sculpted from an outcropping of rock and loaded with succulently cooked meats and vegetables. The freshness of the food normally would make her smile. The first spring logne leaves and wildberries, both harvested high in the Rolban Mountains, had arrived. For the first time in months, no dried food was being served. But she barely noticed.

Balancing her filled plate and drink, consisting of a nutritious mix of powdered tagma berries and water, she slipped to her family's empty table. She picked at her food, her thoughts jumbled. She felt faintly sick.

Her parents soon arrived with loaded plates.

Her father's plate clattered onto the table. "Petr is wrong, Hanuh! He's desperate to win this election. He's grasping for the wind."

"Erl." Methusal's mother curled a slender hand around his arm. She stood a few inches shorter than her husband. Flyaway gray hair wisped about her tanned face. "I'm not sure how I feel about it yet, either. It's the first we've heard of it. But an Alliance with Dehre could benefit us. Wait until you've read the treaty. Then decide."

He scowled. "Tell that to Petr. He hasn't read it yet, but he's ready to sign. How can he trust a Dehrien?"

"The Great War ended two hundred years ago," Hanuh reminded him. "Perhaps it would be wise to hear out Dehre's Chief."

Erl snorted. Methusal had never seen her calm father so upset before. "Petr is afraid Liem will win the election. So he thinks a big move now with the Alliance will win him votes. What he needs are good ideas. Liem knows that." Erl's frown eased when his gaze fell upon Methusal. "Thusa."

"Hi, Papa." She glanced at her food again. It didn't look any more appetizing than it had a moment ago. And she couldn't summon up interest in her parents' argument, either. Her problems seemed far more urgent than a hypothetical alliance with Behran's home village, which was their closest neighbor and only a half a day's run from Rolban.

"Methusal?" A small frown drew Hanuh's brows together. "What's wrong?"

Her throat felt tight. Swallowing didn't help matters. "Petr just accused me of murdering Renn."

"*What?*" Erl exclaimed.

Her mother gasped. "*Why?* Why would he think such a horrible thing?"

"It's a long story. Apparently, Renn found my necklace in the ore deposits."

"Really?" Behran slid onto the bench across from Methusal. Since their parents were friends, they frequently ate together. "How did it get there?" Suspicion sharpened his gaze.

She frowned. "How am I supposed to know?"

"Thusa." Her mother's warm hands covered Methusal's cold ones. "Tell us the whole story. Start from the beginning."

"Petr found a note from Renn in my room." She searched her parents' eyes. "Did you know? Did you receive it? Or put it there?"

"No."

Erl shook his head. "I've been on the plateau all day."

"Petr searched my room. He found the note under my pallet."

"What did the note say?"

Methusal explained the main points. "Now Petr thinks I met Renn on the crop plateau and pushed him over the edge."

Hanuh's grip tightened on Methusal's fingers. "That is nonsense!" She glanced at Erl. "We'll get to the bottom of this, won't we?"

"I will definitely talk to Petr." His tone was grim.

"He won't listen. He hates me, you know that. In his mind, I'm already guilty."

"He doesn't hate you. He's raising your twin sister, Deccia. He cares for you both."

"No. He thinks I'm a bad influence. Especially on Aalicaa. He doesn't approve of girls learning kaavl."

"He doesn't hate you for knowing kaavl," her mother said. "That's silly."

"Well, he doesn't like me. He never has. And he's convinced I'm guilty."

"Be logical, Thusa," Behran said. "He's found evidence..."

"*Planted* evidence. How else could that note get in my room?"

Behran said, "Renn is dead, and Petr needs to solve the case. Especially if it was murder."

"Right. He wants to close the case as quickly as possible. Then he'll look good. Maybe it'll help get him reelected as Chief."

"Prove him wrong, then." Behran forked up a logne leaf.

Methusal bit her lip. Behran was right. Then a new thought struck her. If Petr thought the case was closed, would he look for the real murderer? At least Petr believed she had an accomplice. Maybe he would still look for that person—possibly the true murderer?

Murder. She still couldn't believe they were talking about murder. Was a killer roaming Rolban right now?

One thing was for sure. Renn would never have "accidentally" fallen off a cliff. So someone must have pushed him. But *why?*

The whole thing seemed crazy. Rolban was a peaceful community. Although it had had over 300 people living within the mountain, the last violent crime had happened almost a decade ago.

"I know you and Petr don't get along, Methusal," her father said. "He and I don't see eye to eye on the Alliance, either, but he's a good man. I'll talk to him."

"Thank you, Papa." Unfortunately, she didn't hold out much hope for her father's success. Reversing the seasons would be an easier task than changing her stubborn uncle's mind.

So it would be up to her. She'd have to find the evidence to clear her name.

And what about the Tri-Level Game? A sick feeling twisted in her gut. She'd practiced for *five years* to earn the right to play in that game.

"I may not be able to play in the Tri-level," she mumbled.

"Why not?" Behran's tone was sharp.

"Petr said so. I can't go outside to practice, either."

"Kitran has the final say in the Kaavl Games. Not Petr."

"That's true." A bit of hope took root. "I'll talk to Kitran, then. Before Petr has the chance." She swiftly scanned the dining hall, but didn't spot her dark-haired kaavl instructor. Her gaze lingered on Renn's empty seat. Even his father, Liem, was missing. He probably wanted to be alone tonight.

How could someone ever get over losing a son...a friend? The familiar ache tightened in the back of her throat. Renn shouldn't be dead. As much as murder seemed unbelievable, based upon the sketchy, but suspicious facts, it could very well be true.

I'll find out who killed you, Renn. I promise.

Another scan of the dining hall did not locate Kitran. She'd find him after supper. Surely Kitran wouldn't ban her from the Tri-Level Game. Not after she'd spent five grueling years in training. Not after she'd finally earned the chance to challenge Behran, face to face, for the first time in her life.

In the meantime, she must clear her name. Her necklace had been found in the ore deposits. Ore was missing. Both clues tied into the ore mine. Unfortunately, she knew little about the mine. Where was it? And who had access?

As a council member and former Chief, her father would know.

"Papa, where's the ore mine?"

"It's restricted."

"I know, but where is it?" She knew of several passage-ways that had been locked off for security reasons; one of which was a collapsed hallway. She'd never been able to explore them as a child.

Her father just looked at her. "You're not allowed back there. Don't do anything rash, Methusal."

She turned to her mother, but after a glance at Erl, Hanuh shook her head. "I'm sorry, Thusa."

She felt frustrated. After her parents cleared away their plates, Methusal eyed Behran, who was forking up the last bites of his food. She offered him a winsome smile. "What about you? Do you know where the ore mine is?"

Of course he did. His job required it.

His eyes narrowed. "You know I help Motr with the water systems. I have to know every tunnel and cave in this mountain."

That was no answer. "Have you been to the ore mine?"

Behran shrugged. "Occasionally."

"Petr said Renn was a guard. Did you ever see him?"

One straw-colored brow flicked up. "Lot of questions."

"Well, have you?"

"No," he admitted. "They change the guard every few hours."

"Guard? So only one man guards the ore deposits?"

Humor sharpened Behran's gaze. He popped his last bite of bread in his mouth. "Didn't realize we were such good friends. Should I be flattered you want to know so much about my work?"

Methusal's patience slipped, and she glared. "*Where* are the ore deposits?"

"Ahh, now we come to the heart of the matter."

"Well?"

"You know I can't tell you."

"Thanks for nothing."

One corner of his mouth twitched. "Any time."

Methusal gritted her teeth and stood. She'd been a fool to think Behran would help her. Kitran. She needed to find her kaavl instructor before Petr did. She'd search for him right now.

"Have a good night." Behran's mocking smile was back.

"And you." Whirling on her heel, she marched away.

She stacked her plate and utensils in their proper tubs, carved deep and wide into the flinty rock, and hurried for the dining hall entrance.

"Thusa! *Thusa,* wait." The quiet, urgent voice and the sound of running footsteps made her pause.

When Methusal turned to smile at her best friend, who'd just come to a breathless stop beside her, her own face smiled back. Her identical twin, Deccia (Day' shuh) Storst, had green eyes, tanned skin, and long, dark brown hair caught back in a ribbon. She was slim, and tall for a Rolbani woman. Each of them matched their father's height, and only two differences distinguished the two: Methusal's eyes were spaced a bit wider apart, and her skin was a faintly darker hue. And she wasn't wearing a ribbon in her hair.

A rueful smile tugged at Deccia's lips. "Aalicaa says your name got switched to the dishwashing roster tonight."

"Thanks for telling me. Matron would have a fit if I didn't show."

"No problem."

The path to the dishwashing chamber led past the Storst table, so Methusal followed her sister, who walked with her slim shoulders held gracefully straight under her leather tunic. Colorful pieces of dyed fur, sewn in patterns, decorated the back and front of the garment. So similar to what Methusal wore today, and yet so different. Just like their personalities. One or two decorative bits were enough for Methusal's more spartan tastes.

Methusal averted her gaze as she neared the table where Petr Storst, Deccia's adoptive father, sat. Maxmil Verdnt, one of Petr's competitors in the election, sat across from him. She would have passed by, except her uncle thundered, "*What was that all about?*"

Petr's gaze bored into Deccia, who now wore a conscience-stricken look. Petr's white brows bristled together. "Running,

Deccia? Shouting across the dining hall? What sort of an example is that to your sister?"

Methusal felt compelled to point out the obvious. "Aali's not here."

Deccia cast her a grateful glance. "It's okay, Thusa."

Petr glared at Methusal. A faint flush mottled his features. "Aalicaa needs the best role models she can get." His tone made it clear that Methusal's example lacked in every quarter.

"I'm sorry, Papa," Deccia murmured, and settled onto the bench next to the dark-haired Verdnt.

Methusal struggled to ignore her sparkling temper. Not for the first time, Petr was being unreasonable. How did Deccia or Aalicaa stand it? Again, she wished her parents hadn't allowed the Storsts to adopt Deccia so long ago. And she wished she didn't have to deal with Petr right now. Her impulsive tongue unfortunately spoke before her better sense prevailed. "Deccia helped me out. Isn't that a fine example for Aali?"

"*Thusa,*" Deccia said. "See you tomorrow. Bright and early, right?"

Methusal bit her lip. She'd almost forgotten that tomorrow was Firstday. Breakfast duty. Wonderful. Could life get any better?

Methusal felt Petr's glare follow her through the kitchen doorway. She knew her uncle believed she was a mouthy, willful young woman, and maybe he was right. Disciplining her tongue and emotions were twin mountains she'd struggled—and repeatedly failed—to master her entire life. Her first impulse was to speak out, or *do* something to right an injustice. But now she was an adult. It was time she grew up.

Walking that fine line of insubordination just now with Petr had been stupid. Did she need to give him more reasons to throw her out of the Kaavl Games? Even worse, he held the power to throw her in jail.

She ran her finger down the kitchen duty roster, which was posted on the stone wall. Deccia was right. It was her turn to wash dishes tonight. Young Aalicaa, the Chief's only natural daughter, and also Methusal's sole cousin, would dry.

A low, howling moan drifted into the cave, through the stove's chimney. It sounded eerie and plaintive. Wild beasts roamed outside right now, hunting their prey.

Just like they'd devoured poor Renn last night. She swallowed hard, and again tried not to think about his mangled body. With a shiver, she slipped over to the mammoth sinks, where dirty dishes were piled arm deep. The starving wild beasts had become more vicious lately. Last week, a hunter had been killed. His friends had managed to kill the beast and harvest the meat, oil, and skin, but at such a terrible cost.

"Thusa!" Her thirteen-year-old cousin grinned. "I'm glad you're helping tonight. Matron was s'posed to help, but she had another attack." With an unconcerned head toss, she flipped her long, pale gold braid over her shoulder.

Methusal managed a faint smile. Matron Olgith was known for her "spells." She only did the work she wanted to do—mostly ordering others about.

Methusal pulled the metal water pump lever, and sprayed cold water onto the dishes. Then she scrubbed them with a foaming ball of lynnte weed. The mindless task soothed her troubled thoughts.

Aalicaa carefully dried the clean dishes and stacked them on nearby ledges. Kitchen duty fell to the young and the very old. Neither of these groups performed vital tasks, such as raising food, relaying messages between outlying communities, or being a teacher or hunter, so they performed lower tasks to fulfill their role within the community.

Only two weeks of school remained for Methusal. Soon she would have to choose a formal vocation. In fact, the apprentice mentors were already pressuring her to make a decision. She hadn't told them why she felt so reluctant to commit.

Out of the corner of her eye, she glimpsed Behran dumping his dirty utensils in the tubs. He glanced at her, but she pretended not to see. After a second, he strode out of her line of vision.

She thrust her hands into the cold, soapy water and attacked a large metal pot. Behran might think he held the winning hand in kaavl, and that he had succeeded in ambushing her attempt to discover information about the ore mine, but she'd prove him wrong. Petr, too. In fact, if Petr wouldn't let her practice kaavl outdoors, she'd find a way to practice indoors. And she'd find the ore mine, too, and soon. Somehow, she'd find Renn's killer.

△ △ △ △ △

As Methusal rinsed the last, squeaky clean plate, she watched Petr leave the dining hall in deep conversation with his political advisor, D'Wit. The shrewd, elderly doctor was Petr's uncle and confidant. She wondered what they were talking about. The election? The Alliance? Or maybe Renn's murder. She'd love to find out.

Kaavl. With a smile, she wiped her hands on a towel. Petr would certainly disapprove of her newest plan, but he wouldn't find out. She followed them out of the dining hall at a discreet distance, and she watched them slip down the Grand Staircase, and into the entrance hall. It was deserted at this time of the night, so obviously they wanted to have some privacy.

Little did they know she didn't need to be near them to hear their whispers. This was thanks to one of her new kaavl talents that was uniquely her own—the last person who'd possessed it had been her ancestor Jotham, 200 years ago.

She sat on the topmost stair and pretended to retie her moccasin while she slipped into kaavl. Concentrating hard, she forced all unnecessary thoughts from her mind. Then she ran a quick test, to make sure her mind was solely focused into kaavl, and then, one by one, determined that she had gained complete control over her senses. Satisfied, she concentrated intensely on her environment.

She became sharply aware of the smooth stone of the stairs, the flickering lights down in the entrance hall, and then Petr and D'Wit's faint voices tickled her ears. She focused harder, concentrating on the sounds, while at the same time trying to ignore her annoying conscience, which questioned the ethics of eavesdropping. Their voices grew distinct.

"Are you sure this is a good idea?" muttered D'Wit.

"I've seen the outline of the document, and it will work out in my favor."

"Can't trust those Dehriens."

"Kitran's with me. The Dehrien can bring a lot to the table. It will help me build a stronger..."

A snarl, and the sudden scrabble of claws broke the quiet downstairs.

"What the..."

"Beasts!" D'Wit gasped, and screamed, "*Wild beasts!*"

Methusal scrambled down the stairs. Her flying feet slowed when she reached the bottom of the stairs. Other people thundered downstairs after her.

Beyond the metal gates, a pack of wild beasts, each one more than a length tall—the height of a man—paced, snarling. They stood on their hind legs, and their powerful haunches flexed as they slunk back and forth. Their shorter arms, which were punctuated by three fingered paws and long, vicious claws, twitched, as if wanting to reach inside the cave and yank out a warm body to devour. The animals, one by one, alternately lunged for the gates and then, whimpering, whirled away to protect their fiery red eyes from the entrance hall's dim lights.

Wild beasts only slunk out of their gloomy caves at night. Never during the day, and never during a full moon, because their eyes could not tolerate bright light.

The moonless night made it difficult to count the number of animals skulking beyond the light that pooled beyond the gates. But Methusal guessed there were ten or more.

"Blood hungry," growled Barak, a short distance away. The massive, dark-haired man was Kitran's brother.

More men crowded around Methusal. The small crowd allowed a healthy distance to remain between them and the metal gates, and the beasts roaming beyond.

"Last night whetted their appetite for fresh blood," agreed another man.

Methusal shuddered. As if sensing her horror, a huge beast—at least a length and a half tall—lunged for the gate, and roared. She jerked back. Streams of saliva dripped from razor sharp fangs.

"I'll get us some wild beast tonight." A hunter strode forward, threading an arrow onto his bow.

"Fool!" D'Wit blocked his path. "The beasts feed on their own. They'll be here all night if you kill one."

"We should light more torches." Methusal was surprised to discover that she had spoken. "It'll scare them off. It'll keep them away from the gate." Although the gate had held strong for centuries, she, for one, didn't want to find out what would happen if a whole pack of wild beasts attacked it now.

Petr frowned, but nodded to the hunter, who reluctantly lowered his bow. "And the rest of you get upstairs! The beasts see you and smell you. If they think they can eat you, they'll try harder to get inside."

The beast roared again.

Although the beasts frightened Methusal, they also fascinated her. They looked like her imaginings of the primordial beasts of ancient legends. Those carnivores had terrorized men all over the earth. In the present day, the wild beasts were the only natural predators of humans.

"Methusal!" Petr glowered at her.

When she turned to go, another snarling roar made her stride a little faster for the stairs. Unease prickled down her spine. Would the wild beasts stalk Rolban's gates every night now? Would the gates hold?

She ran up the stairs, and when she reached the top, she remembered that she needed to find Kitran. Barak lumbered past her and entered the passageway.

"Barak! Have you seen Kitran?"

His brown gaze rested upon her. "No." His brows bristled into a frown. "Made your decision yet? Going to work with me?" Barak was the chief crop tender for the plateau.

Exactly a subject she'd rather ignore for a few more days. But Barak's frown made it clear she'd put him off long enough.

"I'll decide tomorrow."

"You'd better." He strode down the hall.

Great. Now she was committed to make a decision.

But more important right now was finding Kitran.

A glance down into the entrance hall proved he wasn't there. She slipped back into kaavl and headed down the main passageway, heading for the family compartments. Her moccasined feet whispered silently over the smooth stone floor. A kaavl skill she practiced at every opportunity.

Nonsmoking lamps lit her path, and were placed every four steps down the hall. Though the domed passageway was deserted, noisy laughter echoed from a cave branching to her right. She cast a quick glance into the gathering chamber as she passed.

A group of families sat huddled together, playing an intense, laughter filled game of *whaal*. A man leaped up and flung the winning, gold mottled card onto the stone table. Applause burst out. Methusal hurried on. Whaal was fun, but tonight she had no time for it.

To the left branched a dim passageway which led to the garment room, where her mother and Behran's mother worked during the day. The supply room lay just beyond it. Old Sims managed it, and Renn had worked for him. Sims would be needing a new apprentice soon. Much as she didn't want to face the reality of finding a job, she was about to graduate from school, and would need to decide upon an occupation soon.

She concentrated harder into kaavl, listening for Kitran's distinct, gravelly rumble. Another gathering chamber lay ahead and one corridor over. She fanned out her hearing, searching for sounds. Quiet voices drew her attention in a northeasterly direction.

The voices grew distinct as she concentrated on the gathering room where women often met and stitched decorations onto garments and bed coverings. It wasn't likely Kitran would be there, but still she should check...

"Hmmph!" That sounded like Petr's aunt, Matron Olgith. "He'll win the election, you can be sure of that."

"He will if Liem drops out," Behran's mother, Poli, replied dryly. "Petr's worried about losing. Haven't you seen it?"

"He'll *win*," Matron Olgith asserted.

A small silence fell, and the tiny sound of needles poking into leather pricked Methusal's ears.

A quieter voice said, "I understand why Liem would drop out, but I hope he doesn't. He has so many great ideas. Like rotating schedules for guards..."

"Nonsense!" Matron Olgith's strident voice echoed in the rock chamber, and the decibel made Methusal wince. "If guards needed rotation, Petr would see to it. Rolban has never been run better. Last thing we need is a Chief distracted by petty issues."

Silence fell. Apparently, no one wanted to speak against Petr's aunt.

A moment later, someone gasped softly. Maybe she had pricked her thumb.

Methusal wondered if Liem would step down from the election in order to mourn his son. If so, Petr would surely win, and become Chief again. Verdnt was his only remaining opposition. The teacher had presented a few good ideas too, but he was a former Dehrien. He probably wouldn't receive many votes for his first election.

Well, Kitran clearly wasn't in the gathering chamber. Her steps slowed. So now what should she do? She didn't really want to go to his private compartment, especially if he wasn't alone. The good news was, if she hadn't found him, then neither had Petr. And the wild beasts would probably keep the Chief busy for quite a while tonight. Finding Kitran first thing tomorrow morning might be her best bet. Well, after breakfast and class...

Methusal relaxed her concentration. Maybe she hadn't found Kitran, but she had accomplished another goal. Twice tonight, she had successfully practiced one of her two secret kaavl skills. The other skill—carrying—she'd practice on another day.

No one knew that she could hear conversations corridors away, blocked by rock. Certainly Behran didn't. The talent was rare, as was carrying, which was the feat of mentally placing herself in a physical location, and then hearing everything around her as if she actually stood right there. She could extend her extraordinary hearing from that point. In fact, her ancestor, Mahre, the Old Kaavl Master, was the first to possess both skills at the same time. Mahre was the founder of kaavl, and was revered as the most brilliant kaavl player of all time. He'd written the honored kaavl texts, *1st Book of Kaavl*, and the missing *2nd Book of Kaavl*, and had lived 300 years ago, during the First Great War.

Jotham, an ancestor who had lived 100 years later, had possessed a few of Mahre's skills, but he had died young, during the Great War with Dehre and Tarst. No one knew how great he might have become in kaavl, if he had lived. Since Jotham's death, no one in Methusal's family had possessed any of Mahre's legendary skills. Methusal was the first. This fact both thrilled and troubled her, because legend also said that extraordinary kaavl skills only manifested themselves in times of war. But legends were fables, right? War was nowhere in sight. Instead, a peaceful Alliance with Dehre loomed on the horizon.

Methusal hoped, more than anything, that her unique kaavl skills would help her win the Tri-Level Game against Behran.

Where the passageway forked she turned right, and headed down a narrow wing which led to her family's living quarters. The door handle to her compartment pushed down easily, and she slipped inside the Maahr's living quarters and shut the smooth wooden door behind her.

Cold air swirled into the cave from the unshuttered ledge across the room. Methusal crossed to close it, but a small *chirrup* made her look down.

Round, furry Chup Chup pressed up against her foot, and his imploring dark eyes stared up at her. "Oh, Chup Chup." She dropped to the floor and hugged him close. The soft, fluffy animal snuffled at her nose. She'd rescued the apte from a flying beast six winters ago. He'd suffered two broken legs and terrible, deep cuts, but he'd survived and thrived. He was old, gray, and chubby now, but he was whole-heartedly devoted to Methusal.

As a rule he didn't like being held, but he forbore it now. He seemed to sense that she was upset. All of a sudden, she wanted to cry. All of the horrible things and obstacles pressing in on her seemed overwhelming: Renn's horrible, awful death, Petr's accusations, maybe missing out on the Tri-level...

"Sometimes life is so hard, Chup," she whispered.

The beast *chirruped* softly in her ear. He didn't wiggle at all. Tears slipped down her cheeks. Chup Chup knew how tough life could be. Did he understand how she felt, even a little? The improbability that he understood what troubled her brought a wry smile to her lips. But even if Chup Chup didn't understand, he did sense how she felt, and he cared.

She rubbed her cheek against his fur. The animal's love was so simple and uncomplicated. He, more than anyone else in the world, accepted her, just as she was.

After a few minutes passed, she felt a little better. Sensing this, the apte wriggled free and waddled to his food dish. Empty, of course. "Poor thing." Methusal took down a bag of dried red tagma berries and shook the treat into his bowl. He ate eagerly and glanced over his shoulder with a satisfied, approving look in his eyes.

"I'm glad I can make you happy, Chup," she smiled.

The cold breeze again swirled through the open ledge across the room. The soft green night beckoned, so she stepped out for a moment. Resting her elbows on the stone wall which enclosed the ledge, she glanced to the right, up the steep cliff to the top of the mountain. The green glow intensified as the large moon, Ryon, peeked over the mountain ridge. Without thinking, her hand slipped into her pocket and curled around her tablet necklace.

Renn had carried this in his pocket last night.

Renn. Tears blurred her eyes. She still couldn't believe he was gone. His body, at least. What about his soul? Was it gone forever, too? Or had God, The One she'd been taught to believe in as a child, take him to heaven, never to die? She wanted to believe this.

Methusal swallowed back the ache in her throat and studied the heavy, silvery object in her palm. Where had she lost it? How had it ended up in the ore mine?

Its silent surface reflected back green moonlight. A dark fleck in the corner caught her eye. Dried blood?

Horror choked off her quick breath.

She scrubbed her fingernail over it, and the fleck flew out over the wall and into the still night. It drifted in sweeps and swirls toward the plains floor. Kaavl kicked in, and her eyes followed the speck down the sheer bluffs until it disappeared into the black, bush dotted plain.

The dark landscape was still. Unnaturally so. It felt as if nature held her breath, waiting for violence to shred the peace. Methusal sharpened her hearing and listened for the snarl of wild beasts on the other side of the mountain, at the entrance gates. Claws scrabbled and an apte screamed.

With a shudder, Methusal retreated back inside and banged the shutters shut. She latched them. At least the beasts couldn't climb the cliff to her home. As a child, that had been her most terrifying fear...until the night she'd seen them for the first time.

She still remembered those fiery red eyes glowing through the darkness, as the pack of wild beasts had leaped and clawed at the cliff that night. Specks of foam flew from their snarling mouths, which were illuminated by cave lamps, five lengths above them.

Her father had instructed her to watch, so she would see that the animals couldn't climb to their rooms. Terrified, she had obeyed. And learned she was safe.

Thankfully, wild beasts were poor climbers. They hated moving water, too.

Methusal struck a brittle piece of firestick against the wall and lit several lamps. The mountain dwellers could avoid the wild beasts if they were careful. Rolbanis rarely hunted the nocturnal beasts. Even though bright lights blinded them, the beasts viciously attacked anyone who entered their dark lairs. Hunting parties who met a wild beast pack always brought home a dead hunter.

With a shiver, Methusal wrapped her arms around herself. She thought about Renn's death again. The crop plateau was safe from wild beasts. A rushing stream separated it from the mountain, and sheer cliffs dropped away from two sides, and the third side was extremely steep, and no beast had made it to the crop plateau before. No, a wild beast probably had not attacked Renn on the cliff. Someone definitely must have pushed him.

But who? And what about the note in her apartment?

Something about the note had struck her as odd when she'd read it, but the shocking contents hadn't allowed the impression to solidify into anything concrete. Now she couldn't put her finger on what exactly had disturbed her, besides it being messier than Renn's usual handwriting.

Too many questions, and no answers.

Even worse, the fact that her necklace was somehow linked to Renn's murder made Methusal feel sick to her stomach, as if she was somehow partly responsible for his death. That was illogical, of course, but it didn't make her feel any better. If she hadn't carelessly lost her necklace in the first place, would any of this have happened?

△ △ △ △ △

Honorable Presidente,

My mission proceeds on course. A menace was neutralized and blame placed on a kaavl threat. This trick was accomplished by using kaavl. I am able to roam Rolban at will, virtually undetected, by using kaavl techniques. The more I learn of kaavl, the more I fear it is Koblan's only weapon against which we have no defense. As I have previously reported, their other weapons are so primitive as to be laughable. In fact, I am beginning to suspect kaavl may be as valuable as Rolban's ore. However, I will not know this full truth until I find the 2nd Book of Kaavl. Legend says that book explains all kaavl mysteries.

Are Dehrien legends to be believed? My ally is convinced—as I am—that the necklace is the only clue to the book's location. Engravings in the necklace indicate the book must be hidden in Rolban. I will find it soon, and will bring this volume to Zindedi after I successfully complete my mission. Kaavl means power here, and I am convinced it will also strengthen our military, once I bring its secrets home.

Never fear; your multi-pronged attacks are prospering on all fronts, and will soon fester seeds of distrust and doubt within and outside Rolban. Soon Koblan will be yours. I will finish this report tomorrow, and send it to you.

△ △ △ △ △

Methusal struck a fire stick against a rough, rocky wall in her room, and touched a flaming tip to a lamp positioned over her low, cushioned bed pallet. She couldn't stop thinking about kaavl, or the upcoming games. Since today was Seventhday, only two full days remained for her to practice, since the Kaavl Games would take place on Thirdday.

So far, she had kept her unusual kaavl skills a secret. She hoped they would give her an edge over Behran in the Tri-Level Game. Once and for all, she wanted to prove herself equal to him. How stunned he'd feel if she beat him in their first competition! At last, he would have to admit he'd been wrong to sneer at her all these years.

A flash of temper warmed her cheeks when she remembered his insults today. He *still* thought of her as that pestering thirteen year-old he'd first met ...*who worshipped the ground I walked on.* Behran's mocking words echoed through her mind.

What she wouldn't give to rewrite history!

Unwelcome memories of the mortifying afternoon that had changed the entire course of her life scorched her mind.

She had been infatuated with the new Dehrien boy. And yes, a pest.

That horrible day, she'd followed Behran to the plateau on top of the mountain, where he'd retreated for solitude. Perching beside him, she'd begun to chatter, hoping to impress him with her knowledge of Rolban.

At that point Behran had scowled. He'd bluntly told her that he was sick of being followed everywhere, and although she was a nice *kid*, he was not interested in her, because she was too young, and because (he implied) her intellect was sorely below his.

Methusal had been stung to the quick. And furious. How dare he think he was better than she was?

She'd known Behran practiced the ancient art of kaavl—the process of highly sharpening the senses, coupled with intense concentration of the mind. Anger had pushed her to take the first step toward learning kaavl. She was not stupid, and meant to prove it to him. Better yet, she wanted to beat him squarely, one on one, at his own kaavl level.

Although only talented people could progress beyond the beginning kaavl level, also known as the Quint-level, or fifth level, Methusal soon discovered she was gifted in the art, and had caught up to her peers within a few short years.

Now she was an adult—eighteen—and her childish hurt at being rejected had of course healed. But she still burned to beat him in the annual Kaavl Games. Especially since Behran still held such a patronizing attitude toward her, and her kaavl abilities.

Changing into her thick, warm pajamas, Methusal blew out the lamp and slipped beneath the coverings. Tomorrow she'd ask Kitran to allow her to play in the Kaavl Games. Surely he wouldn't disqualify her, like Petr had threatened.

△ △ △ △ △

Low, arguing voices roused Methusal from deep sleep a few hours later. Her parents rarely disagreed, so the intensity of their voices made her sit up on one elbow.

"I don't like it!" Her father sounded vehement.

"We have to give him a chance. This might be a wonderful opportunity," her mother murmured.

Were they still arguing about the Alliance? Methusal stifled a yawn.

"Petr's going too fast. Why didn't he bring this issue up earlier?" A firestick cracked against the wall. "He wants to make every decision by himself!"

"Erl, you're going to wake Thusa."

His voice lowered, but was still intense. "Something has to be done, don't you see? Petr's selling us out! Mark my words, Hanuh, this will be the end of Rolban's freedom."

"It might be a good thing. Rolban's been independent for two hundred years. Maybe it's time we developed a closer Alliance with Dehre and Tarst. It could benefit us."

"It'll benefit *them*," he growled. "The Dehriens are decades behind us, always scavenging for their food, and preyed upon by the beasts! If they weren't so lazy and shiftless, they wouldn't need an *Alliance* with us."

"We've heard reports that they're starving. Shouldn't we help them?"

"I'm not against helping them, if we had extra food, which we don't. I'm against *trusting* them. This is just how the Great War started. Dehriens were starving, and a drought had gone on for three years, just like it has now. Their Chief decided to attack us, with Tarst's help, so they could steal our water and croplands for themselves."

"We're friends with the Tarst now," Hanuh pointed out. "You're good friends with Pan Patn, their Chief, for goodness sake. And we trade with them, because they're so close—only a day's run from here. What difference would an Alliance make?"

"I trust Pan," Erl said grimly, "but not the Dehriens."

"Because you know Pan. You messengered together for years. Maybe if you got to know Dehre's Chief, you would come to trust him, too."

"The Dehriens haven't changed. I tell you, Hanuh, I don't trust them. We're safe now. Let's keep it that way."

"What are you afraid they'll do?"

He gave a sharp laugh. "Soon as that treaty is signed they'll send more Dehriens to Rolban. Security is an issue. And what about thefts? If I didn't know better, I'd think it had already started—skins missing from your garment room, and plates and utensils missing from the kitchen. Too many strange things are happening, and I don't like it." Agitated pacing reached Methusal's ears. "I don't like it one bit. Sounds just like Dehrien tricks!"

"Erl. You're being judgmental. Look at the Amils, for goodness sakes. They're from Dehre, but they're not dishonest or..."

"That is exactly my point!"

"What is your point?" She sounded bewildered.

"The Amils left the plains *because* the Dehriens are so lazy and backward. They knew our community was more advanced, so they wanted to move here. And they were willing to work hard to do it. Petr's making a huge mistake. Haven't we learned from the past? How can we ally ourselves with those dirty, stealing scoundrels? And their Chief is coming here Secondday? Who arranged that? I don't like any of this one bit..."

"Erl," Hanuh broke in. "If you're so worried, then call another Council meeting."

"Maybe I will," he muttered. "The Council needs to realize that if we sign that Alliance, that's it. We've given our word, and we'll be honor-bound to keep it. We can't agree to it too quickly."

"I agree," Hanuh said. "But don't you think the fear and distrust from the Great War have gone on long enough? Maybe it's time for a change. Just think about it. Maybe the new Alliance will benefit us all."

"What do you sense about the Alliance?"

A long silence elapsed. "I don't know. I'm trying to be logical, Erl. But I've honestly been having a bad feeling about something else all night."

"Like last night, when Renn died?"

"Yes. But I think it's because Petr accused Thusa of murder..." Hanuh's voice caught.

A rustle of movement, and Erl murmured, "Everything will be all right."

"How?" she whispered. "You *know* the penalty for murder is death."

Chapter Four

Dehre
Firstday

Hendra had smelled the acrid, burning fires again last night.

As dawn streaked the far horizon red and gold, she tossed the leather bucket down into the well. It was one of the few wells still working in Dehre. It fell a long way, and then she heard a faint splash.

Her cousin hadn't answered her questions about the fires last night, and that made her feel uneasy.

Hendra tugged on the rope. The bucket felt light. Hand over hand, she pulled it up. Half full. And dirty. The food situation was worse. How would the orphans ever survive? How would she? Still five passes of the moon to wait until the cold, rainy season began again. If they were lucky, the nearing hot season might bring a few rain showers.

Water still flowed in the Rolban Mountains, runners said. And Mentàll had recently used Tarst's timber to construct a dam to divert a portion of the Tarst River south. If only that Tarst River offshoot wasn't a half day's walk north. But at least now they wouldn't die of thirst, anyway. And if Dehre had seed grain, they could grow crops near the river, too. But Hendra feared they had none.

Rolban had seed grain. If only they weren't still enemies with Dehre... Not for the first time, Hendra hoped Rolban would accept the Alliance her cousin would present soon.

Hopefully, the suspicious fires would play no part in it. Should she confront Mentàll again about the fires? Or trust him, as she had done for all of her life?

She trudged toward the orphanage, where she helped every morning, and paused to let a skinny child pass. Last year's hot, dry summer and the apte beasts had decimated their grain crop. And the cold winter had killed the new seeds they'd tried to plant. Now summer was about to begin again, but the remaining grain was long gone. Had any been kept for planting crops? If so, it must be hidden, or the starving people would have found it and eaten it long ago.

Hendra and the children survived on wild beast meat and the sparse tagma berries the hunters searched for days to find. Not for the first time, she wondered if they would eventually starve to death. The Alliance had to pass. It just had to.

"Hendra!" She jumped at the sudden shout.

Jascr, her oldest brother, loped to catch up with her. Everything in her urged her to run, and she walked a little faster.

Jascr tried to grab her arm, but she instantly spun out of reach, thankful for her rudimentary kaavl training at the Quatr-level—a giant step above the Quint-level, which she had struggled for years to master. A shudder rippled through her; a reaction to his brief touch. Jascr saw it. Pleasure glittered in his eyes. With his black hair and black, cruel eyes, Jascr looked just like their father and two other brothers. Hendra looked nothing like any of them, and felt both blessed and cursed by that fact.

"Time to listen to me, little *sister*."

She prayed for the emotionless wall to wrap her heart in ice, to freeze her emotions; to protect her, as it usually did, but nothing happened.

Hendra struggled to harden her features into a dead, expressionless mask. "You have no authority over me, Jascr. I don't live in your tent."

His lips curled into a sneer. "You cannot live in our cousin's tent forever."

"I have my own tent."

"Wortn will take you in marriage."

Horror made her blink. "I will not take him." Outwardly, Hendra was glad she sounded cool and confident, but inside, she quaked. It took every shred of courage to meet her brother's gaze and stand her ground.

Jascr snarled, "If you lived in my tent, you would do as I say!"

Childhood memories stabbed like a thousand knives through her heart. Much as Hendra tried to forget, she could not. Not ever. But if Jascr sensed how deep her terror still ran, he would seize that power, and rule her by intimidation; she knew that very well.

As steadily as she could, Hendra said, "You would not allow me to live in your tent when Father died. Remember?" How grateful she'd been for that rejection! Although Mentàll may be a cold, and quite possibly dangerous man, he left her alone. She would live no other way.

"You *must* marry!" Jascr's voice rose into an ugly shout. "It is natural. The way of women."

Hendra shuddered at the thought of a man possessing complete control over her. "I will *never* marry."

A violent cuff caught the side of her head. Pain exploded, and with it overwhelming, choking terror.

Jascr grabbed her shoulder, but Hendra twisted free. She cringed back like a defenseless apte, forgetting all of the basic Quatr-level kaavl skills she'd learned.

Her brother kicked the bucket out of her hand. The meager amount of water spilled into tiny rivulets over the dry, cracked earth. In less than a second, the dusty earth sucked it dry. "I am your oldest brother and closest kinsman! You *will* marry Wortn."

Hendra wanted to run, but refused to give her brother the satisfaction. With a hard gulp of fear, she turned and walked away as fast as she could. Helpless tears slipped down her cheeks. Her brother had won, once again. His vicious chuckle followed her. Gasping, she strode faster for her own tent now, instead of for the orphanage. In her cousin's tent, under his protection, she would be safe. She ducked inside and huddled into a dark corner, despising her own frightened sobs, and yet unable to stop them.

Wortn was Jascr's friend. And she knew Jascr owed him money and pelts. No doubt he wanted to trade her life as payment for his debts. But she would *never* submit. She would rather die.

CHAPTER FIVE

METHUSAL HADN'T SLEPT well after her parents' argument. *The penalty for murder is death.* The words wouldn't quit circling through her mind. She didn't want to die.

Fear twisted her gut into tight knots as the slow, dark hours of the night passed. At least Petr hadn't thrown her in jail yet. He'd admitted he didn't have enough evidence. It had also surprised her to learn he was treating her with a bit of leniency because she was his niece. But what did that really mean? If "evidence" was found against her, would he order her imprisonment? Her death?

In the early morning hours, she finally fell asleep.

"Methusal." Her mother's soft voice came through the painted leather curtain. "It's dawn, and it's Firstday. Time to get up."

Methusal pried open her eyelids. The first day of the week. Breakfast duty. A groan escaped.

Doggedly rolling herself from her warm bed, Methusal rubbed her sleepy eyes and pulled on cold stiffened breeches and a leather tunic. Last night's fears swirled in again like a dark, suffocating cloak.

After class, she'd talk to Kitran, and then she'd investigate the ore mine. It seemed her best chance to find a clue. She needed to find out who could have left her necklace there. In order to narrow down the suspects, she'd first need to discover how easy it was to break into the mine. If that was impossible, then the murderer had to be one of the few people authorized to access the mine.

It also might be a good idea to investigate the cliff from which Renn had fallen, in order to see if Petr had overlooked any clues.

As Methusal slipped from her room, she noticed that her mother sat alone on the outside ledge with a cup of hot water, steeped with tagma leaves, warming her hands. Her face looked troubled, and her eyes blank as she stared out at the pink streaked dawn.

"Are you okay, Mama?"

Blinking, Hanuh Maahr faced her daughter. A small smile touched her lips. "I'm fine, Thusa, thank you. Better hurry, or you'll be late."

"See you later." Softly, Methusal closed the door behind her. Was her mother upset because of last night's argument with her father? Or was something else wrong?

Quick footsteps carried her down the silent hallways, through the empty dining hall and into the large kitchen. Dawn's gray light streamed down through the narrow rectangular skylights. Matron Olgith and Deccia were working in the large cavern.

"There you are!" Matron Olgith's strident voice echoed in the chamber. Apparently, she was none the worse for her "attack" last night. Her heavy arm motioned Methusal toward the enormous wood burning stove. Three large metal pots, filled with boiling water, rested on them. A triangular pattern was stamped under the top lip of each pot. Centuries ago, the triangular symbol had been adopted by Rolbanis to remind them of the three most important things in life—The One, family, and their mountain home. Two of these pots had been stolen within the last two months. Many more, and they wouldn't be able to prepare meals.

"You'll make the cereal this morning," Matron ordered. "Deccia will prepare the drinks and set up the dining room. I," she abruptly sat on a stool beside the counter, "will supervise." This small amount of exertion had caused beads of sweat to break out beneath her white hairline, and her breath came in sharp gasps. The widowed Matron was past the age of productivity—but only just. She enjoyed the new role life had thrust upon her: supervision.

Methusal shot Deccia an amused glance. Both of them were used to Matron Olgith's work patterns. She kept her job only because she was Petr's aunt.

Deccia restrained a fleeting smile, and measured red tagma powder into metal pitchers of water. Most of the kitchenware was made of precious ore, fashioned two centuries ago from the weapons of the Great War—as ordered by the Peace Plan. Metal working was banned now. The rare metal was highly prized, for Rolban was the only place on Koblan's continent where it was not layered too deep for retrieval.

A new thought hit Methusal. Why would a thief go to the trouble to steal bulky kitchenware, if he just wanted ore? Pots would be harder to conceal than compact lumps of ore. Then again, why steal leather from the garment room?

The weight of the heavy tablet necklace around her neck drew Methusal's attention again, and she touched the cool ore with her fingertips. Had she truly lost it? Or had the thief stolen it? Had he left it in the ore deposits by accident...or to implicate her in his crimes?

The endless questions made her tired head hurt.

Time to focus on the job at hand. After breakfast she'd get to work on clearing her name.

A squat sack of grain hunkered next to the pots. *Grain.* Not again! Every day, for the past six months, they'd suffered through the same breakfast. Surely yesterday the gatherers had found eggs, or a few fresh berries...

"Water's boiling, Methusal," Matron Olgith said sharply.

Gritting her teeth, she grasped the measuring bowl and dipped out the appropriate portions of grain, crushed nuts and dried wildberries, and stirred them into the roiling cauldrons.

"Make sure you stir that."

Methusal managed not to roll her eyes. "I know, Matron." She was careful to keep her tone neutral.

"See you do, then. I need to check on Deccia." Matron Olgith heaved herself from the stool, and lumbered through the arched doorway and into the dining room. In that large cavern, Deccia busily stacked towers of dishware on the serving counter and filled the utensils tray.

The next half hour passed slowly. Methusal stirred the beige glop in the huge pots, and counted her blessings that she wasn't her twin. A glance through the oval serving window revealed a lecturing Matron dogging poor Deccia's footsteps as her sister moved from table to table, wiping down the spotless stone surfaces.

Although identical twins, Methusal and Deccia had not been raised in the same home, and Methusal often wished things had been different. Their mothers, Hanuh Maahr and Juni Storst, were sisters, too, but when years passed by and neither bore any children, both became deeply discouraged. Methusal had learned in school that difficulty conceiving children was not only a common problem in Rolban, but also in all other communities on the Koblan continent. Finally, Hanuh became pregnant, and when she gave birth to twins, it seemed only natural to give the extra child—in Rolbani culture seen as a double blessing—to her sister and her husband, who were sure to remain childless.

However, six years later Juni gave birth to Aalicaa. By then the Storsts were too attached to Deccia to give her up, and the Maahrs did not ask them to—even though Juni died a few years later, leaving harsh, autocratic Petr to raise the two girls alone.

The mixture was becoming hard to stir. Mouth curled in distaste, Methusal watched the way the goop, speckled with black berries, plopped in clumps from the wooden spoon. It was done.

Wheezing mightily, Matron Olgith waddled back to the kitchen and collapsed onto the stool. Fanning herself, she puffed, "Get ready to serve, girls. The early risers have arrived."

Methusal grasped several thick, layered leather squares and carried the cauldrons, one by one, to the serving window. They were heavy, but her arms had long ago grown accustomed to the weight.

A few breakfast diners stood in line now. Timaeus Rolnnt was first, as usual. Deccia poured his drink, her eyes bright beneath her lowered lashes. Timaeus smiled as he accepted the cup from her hand and hesitated, as if about to say something. But he didn't. After a moment, he moved to Methusal's station.

Methusal glanced at the dark haired, brown-eyed young man as she ladled a sticky ball of cereal into his bowl. No doubt about it. The tall, well-built messenger was handsome, and nice, too, and she understood why her sister liked him so much. The trouble was, the two didn't speak much to each other. A situation Deccia would like to change, Methusal knew, but shyness often caught her sister's tongue.

With a smile, Methusal handed him the steaming bowl. "Have a good breakfast."

Timaeus grinned. "I would, if we were having something different."

Behran's irritating grin met her next in line. "Good morning." His blue eyes zeroed in on the necklace draped about her neck. "So, you're wearing it."

"No reason not to."

His gaze sharpened. "Isn't it evidence?"

"Not that it's any of your business," Methusal felt irked by his question, "but Petr *has* no evidence."

"Didn't he find it in Renn's pocket yesterday?"

Methusal didn't recall telling him that information. "Why are you so interested?"

"Thefts keep happening. Renn was murdered. Any intelligent citizen would want to know more."

"Great! I'm pleased you're so curious. Maybe you can help me find the real murderer. Then Petr will let me play in the Tri-Level Game. Or...maybe you don't want real competition."

"Ouch." Behran pretended to wince. "Not good at encouraging support, Thusa."

Methusal realized her attitude bordered on the obnoxious. "I'm sorry. But I don't know how Renn found my necklace in the ore mine."

"Did you really lose it?"

Her jaw dropped. "Do you *really* think I broke in and stole ore?"

The question seemed to surprise Behran. Her adversary hesitated, bowl still held out, as if for more gloppy cereal. Obligingly, Methusal flung in another sticky ball.

He scowled, but didn't move on, as she had intended. "What I meant was—do you think someone stole your necklace? Like Renn, maybe."

"How could Renn be the thief? The thief murdered him."

"You don't know that. You said yourself that Petr has no evidence—except, of course, the note Renn left in your room."

Methusal glared. "The note was planted. Are you accusing me of something?"

"Touchy this morning, aren't you?"

Methusal had no opportunity to respond, for Matron Olgith thwacked her shoulder with a spoon. "Stop jabwacking and move the line along!"

Tears smarted, and she scowled at Behran. He frowned at Matron Olgith, and after a moment her supervisor lumbered away. Behran leaned closer. "No. I'm saying you don't have all the facts. Try to think outside the lines." He moved on.

Methusal took several deep breaths to cool her temper, and ladled goop into the next person's bowl. Behran's advice wasn't unreasonable, she admitted after a few minutes. No, what bothered her was his attitude. Mr. Kaavl. Mr. Know Everything. Clearly, he still labored under the illusion that his intelligence far surpassed her own. Her desire to beat him in the Kaavl Games intensified. To take him down even one notch would be pure bliss. But to win, first she had to be able to play.

After she finished ladling out one caldron of goop, she carried it to the washroom to soak. When she returned to the serving counter, the breakfast line had doubled.

A shout drew her attention. "There you are!" A silver-haired man charged toward the counter, glaring at Methusal. Red mottled his face, and he clenched a narrow, leather wrapped object in his fist. It was Liem, Renn's father.

People parted to make room for the stocky man.

Methusal eyed him warily. "What's wrong? Are you talking to me?"

"*Yes*, I'm talking to you!" He shoved the object across the counter. The leather flopped open, revealing a knife covered in congealed blood.

With a gasp, she stepped back. "What's *that?*"

Liem leaned closer. "Is it yours?"

"*What?* No!"

Deccia slipped next to Methusal, and stood there as a silent source of support.

"I found it on the cliff, under a bush. *Right where my son fell.*"

"So it *was* murder," Methusal whispered.

"Of course it was murder," Liem shouted. "And *you* killed him! With this." He shoved the grisly weapon closer.

Methusal shuddered. "No! I didn't. Petr's wrong. I never..."

"What's going on?" Petr's burly figure pushed through the growing throng of onlookers.

Methusal's face felt hot. She felt trapped and helpless. How could she make these people see that she was innocent? "It's not my knife. I hate knives! I don't even own one."

"And that's supposed to prove you're innocent?" Liem sneered. "Arrest her, Petr. Now. We have proof she lured Renn to the cliff. Now I've found the knife she used to kill my son."

"I *didn't* kill your son," Methusal cried out. "And I don't own a knife. That looks like a kitchen knife. Anyone could have stolen it. And...and I never met Renn on the bluffs!"

His face an alarming purple shade, Liem glared at Petr. "Well? Are you going to stand there? Arrest my son's murderer!"

"What's happening?" Erl appeared.

With relief, Methusal turned to him. "Papa..."

"I found the murder weapon," Liem interjected. "Your daughter is going to jail."

"But I didn't kill Renn." Methusal was near tears. "I would never do such a thing."

"Not by yourself," Petr agreed grimly. "I believe that. You had help. Tell me who's behind this whole plot, and I might go easier on you."

Liem's eyes narrowed.

"I don't know what you're talking about! I'm innocent," she protested.

"Let me see that knife." Erl pushed forward and carefully inspected the weapon. "Matron Olgith, is this one of your kitchen knives?"

Matron Olgith shuffled forward. Her gaze shifted suspiciously between Methusal and the blade. She only got close enough to give it a quick peek, and then quickly backed away. "It is. Methusal had access to it."

"So does everyone else in Rolban," Methusal snapped in frustration. "They're stored in plain sight."

"A bloody knife proves nothing, Liem." Erl's voice was gentle.

"It proves my son was murdered!"

"Maybe so. But it doesn't prove Methusal did it."

"The note proves she went to the bluff!"

"Methusal says she never received it. I believe her. An equally logical theory is that the true murderer planted the note in her room. That way she'd look guilty."

With gratitude, Methusal glanced at her father.

"Your theory is a day's run from reason," Liem bit out. "Face facts, Erl. Your daughter murdered my son. I want her in jail. Now!"

Erl sent Petr a look. The bigger man shuffled his feet and cleared his throat.

"Erl's right. We need more proof."

Liem's face flushed even darker.

Petr turned to Methusal. "The proof is piling up. This won't go away."

"I'm innocent, and I'll prove it."

With shaking hands, Liem gathered up the knife again. "I'll prove you murdered my son. This is not the end. I'll prove *that*." He strode from the room.

Methusal drew a shaky breath.

Deccia hugged her. "Are you all right?"

"No. It's only a matter of time before Petr throws me in jail."

"I'll help you find Renn's killer. Just tell me what I can do."

△ △ △ △ △

Two cauldrons of goop later, Methusal's arm ached from ladling. She carried her bowl of cold, pasty cereal to a table where Aali sat with Behran and Timaeus. Deccia hesitantly sat down too. After a quick glance at Timaeus, her lashes swept down against her cheeks.

"Are you all right?" Behran asked Methusal. His faint frown actually appeared concerned.

"I'll be fine, thanks," she mumbled. Actually, she was a complete mess, but she didn't want to say so. "After I talk to Kitran, I'll investigate the cliff. Maybe I'll find something else Petr missed."

One blond brow flicked up. "Really? I thought you were confined indoors."

Methusal ignored this technicality and turned to Timaeus. "Did you just get back from a trip? I don't think I've seen you for a few days." She asked this because her sister would not. She also knew that Deccia had been pining to see Timaeus during the entire week he'd been gone.

His white teeth flashed in a grin. "I went to Dehre and then Aestoff." Aestoff was a three day's run from Rolban.

"How are things in Dehre?" Behran wanted to know. "Any better?"

"No. They're starving, except for wild beast meat. The good news is, the beasts finally stopped raiding the town at night."

"Why?"

"They're hungry, but the Dehriens are hungrier." Timaeus offered a wry smile. "You know the Dehriens, Behran. They're fearless. Lately they've been pitting one man to a beast, just for sport. The beasts are wary now, so they circle outside the town at night, waiting for children to stray."

Deccia gasped softly. "How awful! Don't they have a wall, or any protection?"

"One wall is partway done. Word is, Tarst is giving them access to their pack beasts and their lower timberline. That's all in exchange for half the logs the Dehriens harvest, plus wild beast oil."

The oil glands of the wild beasts produced a pure, non-smoking flame for Rolban's lamps, too. The slow burning oil was highly prized, and difficult to obtain, because Rolbani hunters hated to hunt the dangerous wild beasts.

Methusal said, "Does Dehre already have an Alliance with Tarst?"

"If they do, it's informal. It's probably like the arrangement we have with Tarst now. But Dehre's main need is food. I think that's the reason why Mentàll is pushing so hard for the Alliance with Rolban. With Tarst, too."

Methusal wondered if Rolban had enough food to trade away to their potential allies. From her brief stop in the supply room two days ago, provisions looked low.

Deccia at last spoke quietly, "Mentàll Solboshn is their Chief?"

When Timaeus smiled at her, a faint blush crept up her cheeks. "Yes. He's coming here tomorrow. In fact," he glanced upward at the pale sunlight streaming through the ceiling cracks, "I need to ask Erl if he has another missive ready for Dehre. If I leave now, I can be back with Mentàll's response by tonight."

He stood, and Behran did, too. "I need to get to work," he explained. Both cleared their places at the table and with a word of farewell, left the girls.

Aali fluttered her eyelashes at Deccia. "Oh *my,*" she said in a breathy voice. "Timaeus can run all the way to Dehre and back in one *day!*" With a dramatic hand to her forehead, she pretended to swoon.

Deccia rolled her eyes. "Finish your breakfast. It's almost time for class."

"But he's so strong and *dashing,*" Aali gasped. "Don't you just want..."

"Aali!" Red colored Deccia's face, and she cast a furtive glance at the archway through which Timaeus had exited. "Stop it."

With a grin, Aali spooned up a glob of cereal. "You love him. You know you do." Her voice was smug, as only a thirteen-year-old's could be. Boys weren't anything to waste time on, as far as she was concerned.

Deccia didn't answer, but a frown pulled at her brows.

"He smiled at you," Methusal encouraged.

"Maybe he loves you," Aali suggested. Sing-song, she said, "Deccia and Timaeus, strolling down the hall…"

Deccia swatted her arm.

"Ouch!" Aali grinned, and slurped tagma juice.

"You know Father doesn't like it when you do that."

"Father isn't here." But she whipped an uncertain glance over her shoulder. Her next sip was quiet.

Deccia changed the subject. "Thusa, have you decided on your job yet?"

"No."

"Old Sims needs a new assistant."

Aalicaa pulled a gruesome face, doubtless remembering poor Renn.

"I know." A weight settled in Methusal's heart as she thought about Renn's death again. Not to mention the threat of prison and possible execution hanging over her own head. Even so, she would decide on a job today, even though she'd rather continue to put it off. Barak was becoming impatient, and she didn't want his volatile temper unleashed upon her. She could only handle so many problems at one time.

"Everyone else decided months ago. What's taking you so long?" Deccia asked gently.

"I've had a lot on my mind."

"You mean all you've cared about is making the Tri-level. Now you have your chance to beat Behran."

Unexpected tears stung Methusal's eyes. She blinked them back. "If I get to play."

"What do you mean?"

Apparently, Deccia hadn't heard the full story. Methusal explained Petr's threat to throw her out of the Kaavl Games.

"I'm so sorry." Deccia looked shocked.

"Father is so mean!"

"Thusa, that's horrible. I'll speak to him, and try to make him see reason."

"Thank you. But we both know Petr never changes his mind about anything."

"Even so. I'll talk to him later."

"Kitran is the only one who can ban me from the Tri-Level Game," Methusal said. "I'll talk to him after class. Maybe he'll choose to take my side."

"We have to find the real murderer," Aali spoke up. "Then Father will have to let you play."

"No, Aali. *We* won't do anything," Methusal said at once. "I don't want you involved. Someone's already killed Renn. I'm sure he'd kill again if he feels threatened."

"He wouldn't catch me."

"Is your kaavl that good?"

Aali flushed, as if embarrassed by a memory she didn't want to share. "Mostly. But sometimes I get too focused on one detail."

"Keep your focus moving all the time," Methusal advised. "Try to concentrate on something different every few seconds."

"Thusa!" Deccia hissed. "Stop. You know Father doesn't want you to teach Aali kaavl precepts."

Methusal couldn't help but roll her eyes. Right now, she couldn't care less what the close-minded Petr wanted. He was wrong about her part in Renn's death, and according to her father, he was wrong about the Alliance, too. Denying Aali permission to pursue kaavl was wrong, too. At least, it was in her opinion.

"Why?" she asked her sister. "Because kaavl is a weapon of war? We're not at war, in case Petr hasn't noticed."

"Thusa. Do you want to stay on his bad side? Especially now."

Methusal sighed. "I'm sorry. But it's so wrong! Petr loves kaavl. He's at the Bi-level, and he wants to advance. How can he deny Aali the right to pursue it, too?"

Aali scowled, and Methusal felt sorry for her. However, she didn't offer her cousin any more kaavl bits of wisdom.

"It seems to me," Deccia said thoughtfully, "that we need to focus on one thing right now. Clearing your name. How can we do it?"

Her twin's staunch support comforted her. "I want to try to break into the ore mine."

Deccia gasped. "*No.* You'll be arrested."

"I have to try. I think the thief left my necklace in there. The mine is somehow tied into Renn's death and the ore thefts. I need to figure out who has access to the mine. If I can't break in, probably no one can. That means only someone with authorized access could have left my necklace inside. Renn's murderer would be on that list."

A frown still worried Deccia's brow, but she said, "How can I help?"

Methusal leaned closer, "Do you know where the mine is?"

Aali leaned in, too. She whispered, "I do."

Both Methusal and Deccia stared at her. Methusal spoke first. "How?"

A smug smile curved her lips. "Practicing kaavl. It's easy to follow those guards. They're not careful at all. Plus, I know *all* the passageways in this old mountain."

"Can you show me where it is?"

"I could draw you a map. It'd be hard for two of us to get far without being noticed. Even though we could both easily get through the first door into the ore mine hall, after that, more passages branch off. Guards are posted at three different places in the halls."

"Oh. Behran said there was only one guard." Actually, he had said no such thing, Methusal realized. She'd misinterpreted his statement.

"One guards the door to the actual mine," Aali agreed. "You can't get past him."

A new thought entered her mind. "Who are the guards? Maybe I could ask them who has access to the ore deposits."

"Good idea. But I only know one, besides Renn. I sneaked past the middle one and didn't see his face."

Methusal waited. "Who's the one you saw?"

Aali cast a sly glance at Deccia. "Timaeus. He guards when he's not messengering."

"I never knew that." Deccia flushed. "I've seen him guard the entrance gate, but..."

In a sing-song voice, Aali lilted, "You looove him."

"Aali, will you give me a map later?"

"Sure. And a key to the first door. You'll need that. Luckily I know where my father keeps it."

"Is there a guard on the first door?"

"Not anymore. Barak asked for more workers a while back. They probably think they have enough guards inside the hall, so they don't guard the door with the lock."

The brightness of the sun through the roof portals told them it was time to go. The three cleared their places, and Aali scampered off to her class.

"You know, Thusa, you never did say why you haven't chosen a job yet. Is it because of kaavl?"

Methusal dumped her dirty dishes into the proper tub, now piled high with plates. "It seems silly now, especially since I may not be able to play at all."

Her sister waited, her green eyes concerned.

Methusal bit her lip. "I don't want a job to cut into my practice time. I've finally made the Tri-level, Deccia. I only have *one* chance to beat Behran. Is it selfish to want to focus on that? It probably is. It's just that I've practiced so hard, for so long... If I can't keep practicing hard, I'll lose. And I can't stand to think he'd win. I *know* that's selfish. But I'm sick of him looking down on me. I don't want it anymore."

"Why don't..."

"If I get an internship, I'd have to start work now. I want to wait until after the Game to start, that's all."

"Maybe they'd let you wait..."

"Sims needs help now. So does Barak. And look at you. You're already working for Verdnt."

"Part-time. Stop worrying. Just decide. I'm sure your supervisor will give you time to practice today and tomorrow."

Deccia's logic made sense. But even if her new supervisor did give her the time, she'd still have to practice inside, thanks to Petr. Practicing the hardest skills of integrating short and long distance kaavl while running would prove impossible.

Once out in the hall, they veered left and headed down the passageway where classes were held. When they slipped inside the classroom, Methusal noticed that Timaeus sat in the back of the class. Deccia noticed him, too, if her soft, indrawn breath was any indication. Erl had probably delayed the message to Dehre for an hour, so the runner could attend class. Timaeus, as well as all of the graduating students, was required to attend a general review class before graduation in two weeks. It was supposed to ensure that they hadn't forgotten any of the basic math, reading, and writing skills they had learned over the last ten years. Of course they hadn't, and usually little was accomplished in the class.

But this morning Methusal had a question for their teacher. It had been simmering in her brain ever since her parents' fight last night. "I've heard about the Alliance. Will you tell us more about it?" Her teacher, Maxmil Verdnt, was on the Council, as was every man over the age of thirty. Plus, of course, he was running for Chief. So he should know all of the details.

Verdnt's eyebrows shot up. Usually, the only time he could capture Methusal's attention was when they discussed kaavl.

"I'm glad you brought that up." He reached into the cubbyhole beneath the black slate writing board. "It's an important issue. And one that will soon affect all of our lives."

He paused, fingers scrabbling in the hollow beneath the smooth sheet of rock. His black brows wrenched together. "Where's my chalk?" Gray eyes pierced the class. "Has anyone seen it?"

No one answered.

"I'm sick of this! That's the fourth time it's disappeared." He stalked from the room.

"Why would someone steal chalk?" Deccia whispered to Methusal.

"Why steal skins or plates? Or ore?"

A faint snicker tickled Methusal's sensitive ears, and a glance over her shoulder spotted Pogul shoving a meaty fist into his pocket. The heavy-set young man was a well-known troublemaker.

Their tall teacher strode back in, clenching a stick of light colored, powdery rock in his fingers. "Now. Where were we?" His gaze focused on Methusal. "Ah, yes. The Alliance."

Dark head bent, he paced the front of the class room. His head snapped up. "How many settlements are within a day's run of Rolban?" He scanned the class. "Timaeus! You're a messenger. Answer the question."

Timaeus stood. "Three settlements, sir. Dehre and Tarst. Also Eerpor, to the east. They prefer no outside contact."

"What about within a two day run?" Verdnt shot back.

"Two more, sir."

"Three days?" Verdnt barked.

"Five more, sir. If you include Rolban, that equals a total of eleven settlements on our land mass of Koblan."

"Thank you, Timaeus." Verdnt's gaze raked the class. "Who can tell me what types of settlements they are?"

Methusal spoke before being called. "Four mountain settlements, including ours, two plains, and five coastal."

Verdnt's eyes narrowed. "Correct, Methusal. Now, who can tell me how an Alliance with Dehre and Tarst would benefit Rolban?"

"More women," Pogul leered. A few snickers erupted from the back of the room.

Verdnt sent him an icy glance. "A diversification of families could be a benefit, Pogul. But what else, class? Think."

"In an emergency, we could help each other," Deccia said quietly.

"Good, Deccia." Verdnt's face warmed into an approving smile. "What else?"

Methusal had no idea. Apparently, neither did anyone else.

Chalk snapped against the smooth black wall. "*Culture*, class. We would meet new people. And do activities together—like Inter-Community Kaavl Games."

Methusal sat up straighter. Kaavl Games with other settlements? Fantastic idea! Dehre and Tarst both produced great kaavl players. Behran and Verdnt were examples in point, since both had emigrated from Dehre.

If only she could win Rolban's upcoming Tri-level match. With pleasure, Methusal imagined beating Behran in the game. Then, in the Inter-Community Games, she could go up against the best—maybe she could even be Tri-level champ of the whole land...

A rude voice broke into her pleasant daydream. It was Pogul again. "My father says the Dehriens are lazy, shiftless good-for-nothings. All they'd do is mooch off of us—or *steal...*"

"Ignorance!" Verdnt's snapped. His ear tips flamed red. "A few of Rolban's best citizens have come from Dehre. Or perhaps you don't agree?"

Verdnt had emigrated from Dehre seven years ago, but he was such a respected member of the community that people tended to forget his origins—although he did go to Dehre at least once a month to visit old friends. That was why the Rolban's Council had allowed him to put in a bid to be Chief of Rolban in the upcoming elections.

A brief, uncomfortable silence elapsed. "I didn't mean you," Pogul muttered. His scalp, beneath his blond hair, reddened.

"I'm surprised you'd throw the first stone, Pogul." Verdnt's gray eyes looked as hard as a blade. "Seeing that you and your family are from Tarst." Pogul fidgeted.

Verdnt turned his frown upon each member of the class. "And let's not forget that Petr emigrated from Wyen thirty years ago. Don't be ignorant, class. You don't know what the Dehriens are really like. And you won't, until you meet them personally. And visit their settlements."

"I already know," Pogul insisted, but under his breath.

Another student thankfully changed the subject.

Methusal doodled on a dried white parchment leaf, using a sharpened stick of charcoal wrapped in a rolled leaf as her writing instrument. The Alliance sounded like a great idea to her. She didn't care too much about culture. But kaavl! Her eyes glazed as she slipped into another daydream. The games expanded, new competitors to beat....

The class ended a few short minutes later, and Verdnt called Deccia to his desk. The teacher pointed to a stack of papers, and the two dark heads bent together.

Timaeus sent the two a sidelong glance as he slowly gathered up his books.

Methusal waited for her sister in the hall. It didn't take long, and she soon fell into step beside her twin. "I've never asked—how do you like being Verdnt's apprentice?"

Deccia hesitated, and then moved out of earshot of the classroom. "It's okay, but..." she glanced back, and whispered, "I think Verdnt might be...interested in me."

Methusal could not be more shocked. "*Interested* in you? But he's ancient."

"Not that old," Deccia said, a bit defensively.

"He's *thirty-one*, and you're eighteen. What about Timaeus?"

Deccia gave an uncharacteristic toss to her head. "I don't *like* Verdnt, Thusa. It's just kind of flattering that a man might actually be interested in me."

And Timaeus had never shown interest. At least, nothing overt...so far. She felt compelled to advise, "Don't do anything you'll regret."

Deccia actually laughed. "Like you're one to lecture me."

As Deccia departed to attend the primary grade class she helped to teach—more time with Verdnt—Methusal mulled over her sister's small dilemma. She'd never considered Verdnt in a romantic context before, and it felt odd to do so now. He'd always been her teacher. But he wasn't married, and he was fairly good looking—tall, dark, and handsome. She supposed Deccia could do worse. Even so, it did seem a bit unsettling for a teacher to show interest in his apprentice.

However, she reminded herself that Deccia's opinion was the only one that mattered. And she seemed flattered that Verdnt might like her.

Even though Timaeus was her true love.

△ △ △ △ △

Methusal wanted to speak to Kitran next, but a glance into his office proved he was in the middle of instructing the Quatr-levelers. With a sigh of frustration, she decided to try again later.

A flash of movement next door caught her eye. Blond hair glimmered, and then Aali scuttled down the hall.

Methusal smiled. Apparently, her cousin had cut class in order to spy on Kitran's kaavl lessons. Petr would have a fit if he knew.

Since talking to Kitran would have to wait, Methusal decided to investigate the crop plateau. Liem had found the bloody knife there this morning. Maybe she could unearth another clue. Of course, going up there meant she'd also see Barak.

Tension knotted in her gut. She needed to choose a job today. What should she do?

Her stomach rumbled. She'd eaten little of her unappetizing cereal this morning, so now she slipped into the dining hall and grabbed a grain disc for a snack. Slowly, she headed for the supply passage, which also lead to the cropland and cliffs overhead. While she crunched off a bite of the grain disc, she again reviewed the pros and cons of each job.

The supply room attendant job could quickly become responsible. Sims Nalg was the manager, but he'd passed the age of productivity long ago, and since Renn had died, he desperately needed a sharp young replacement. If she became his apprentice, she'd probably advance soon to the position of supply room manager.

Sims kept inventory of supplies, and also calculated how much food Rolban would need during the long, cold winter. This included estimating crop sizes each year. Overall, it sounded like an interesting task.

One thing was for sure, Methusal thought as she forced the hard lump of grain down her throat. If she became supply room attendant, she'd make sure Rolban stored up a better variety of foods for the winter months. Eating the same few foods every day was intolerable.

If only she could become a kaavl instructor.

Unfortunately, the Council elders didn't think teaching kaavl was a productive activity. It didn't provide food or water, or do anything else constructive for Rolban—except give the entertainment of the annual Kaavl Games.

Only one full-time kaavl instructor was allowed, and that was Kitran Mehl. But he'd served first as a full-time messenger and part-time instructor for years.

Things had been different during the Great War. People gifted in kaavl were prized warriors back then. They'd attacked and retreated from the enemy virtually undetected. Now kaavl was solely a personal quest. It was still highly honored, but served no vital purpose in Rolban.

Regretfully, Methusal moved on. She would love to teach kaavl, but...

Her final vocational choice was crop tender. Barak Mehl was chief crop tender. He was also Kitran's brother. The idea of spending her days outside in the warmth of the sun strongly appealed. Of course, in the winter there were no crops, and she'd have to scour the plains and hillsides for edible nuts, fruits, and berries. It was cold in the winter. And she got cold easily.

Methusal realized that she'd reached the supply hall. Hanuh's garment room was empty at the moment, but next door, a frowning Sims wandered the supply room, muttering to himself. Methusal wondered what was wrong, but decided to ask him after investigating the cropland near the cliff. Now was her best chance to escape outside. She hadn't seen her uncle since breakfast.

Quickening her steps, Methusal hurried for the end of the hall where the passage turned right and led to roughly hewn stone steps. As she turned the corner, she almost barreled into Petr, who had descended from the stairs. With a gasp, she skidded to a stop.

CHAPTER SIX

PETR'S WHITE BROWS BRISTLED together. "Where are you going?"

"I need to talk to Barak," Methusal improvised. It was true, after all. "He wants to know my job decision." Petr didn't need to know that she also planned to search for clues that Liem or Petr might have overlooked.

"I forbade you to go outside. Remember?"

"You mean I can't go outside, even to talk about a job?" Could Petr be any more stiff-necked?

Petr's meaty hand gripped her shoulder. It hurt. He marched her back down the passageway. "Don't take that tone with me, girl! I told you, you can't go outside."

"But the job..."

"You can't *have* that job. I'll tell Barak myself." He released her when they reached the supply room door.

"But that's not fair! I haven't done anything wrong."

"You're under investigation. You will abide by my rules, or you will go to jail."

"I know I'm under investigation. But what about new clues? Have you found any of *those?*" Methusal's tone skated on insubordination, but she couldn't seem to help herself. Petr's accusations, not to mention him curtailing her freedom and manhandling her...it was all really too much.

His eyes narrowed. "Watch your mouth. If you want your freedom, tell me the truth. Who's your accomplice?"

"I don't have an accomplice!"

"So you did it alone?"

"I didn't do anything!" Methusal cried out. "I'm innocent. Why do you always think the worst of me?"

A thick fist grabbed the neck of her tunic. "One more shout, and I'll put you in jail."

She stayed silent, but tears burned her eyes.

"Good. I didn't think this day could come. Methusal quiet. Obedient."

"Let me go!"

Petr released her. "Show some gratitude. After all, I haven't put you in jail. Yet. But you're a selfish, willful girl— you'll never learn. Remember this: The penalty for murder is death. It may not be long before Liem forces my hand. Count your minutes of freedom, because they may not last much longer."

He left her. A sob caught in her throat, but she didn't let it out. He wouldn't hear how upset he'd made her. Jail time. *Death.* Her uncle had actually just threatened her.

Shaking, Methusal stood in the middle of the hall. She wrapped her arms around herself. Tears slid down her cheeks. She felt angry and helpless, but she'd been wrong to let her temper take over, yet again. As had happened too many times in her life, her undisciplined tongue had gotten the best of her. But Petr frustrated her. He wouldn't let her go outside to investigate Renn's death, and he wouldn't let her go out to practice kaavl, either. Soon, if not already, Petr would talk to Kitran. *She* had to talk to Kitran first.

"Thought I had more..." Sims' mutter from the adjacent cave interrupted her thoughts.

In the supply room, the tall, thin old man bent over a sack of dried meat. His gnarled hands shook as he tied the sack closed with twine.

He straightened slowly, his lips moving in a silent commentary to himself.

"Sims?" From the doorway, Methusal spoke softly. She didn't want to startle him.

Sims' shaggy white head swiveled, and his faded blue eyes smiled. "Methusal, my girl! To what do I owe the pleasure?"

"Is something wrong?"

"Heard me talking to myself, did you?" A snaggle-toothed grin flashed. He reached for the clipboard. "We're low on dried meat. Not sure how that happened. Last week I had eight sacks. Now I can only find five."

"Did you check downstairs, too?"

Rolban had two supply rooms—one on each level. The cold storeroom on the lower level served as a temporary holding area for meats before they were cured, and for grain or berries that had overflowed from upstairs. Most of the supplies were kept on the second level, however, for several reasons: because a flood would destroy the food on the first floor, and also because the food was closer to the dining room on the second level. In addition, if wild beasts ever broke in, the food was easily defended on the second floor, since the only way in was through the entry hall and up the Grand Staircase, or through several portals in the roof.

"No. I haven't had a chance."

"I could look, if you'd like." She probably still had a few minutes left before Kitran finished with the Quatr-levelers.

He sent her a keen glance. "This mean you're coming to work for me?"

Methusal hesitated—although she'd already made her decision, even before Petr barred her from going up on the croplands. "If you'll have me."

Joy lit Sims' face. He reached her in two steps, and his warm, gnarled hands wrapped tightly around her own. "Wonderful. How soon can you start?" His voice was eager and hopeful.

Methusal's spirits sank. Now her worst fear was coming true. Sims wanted her to come work right now. He obviously needed help right away. And while she did want to help him, what about kaavl practice?

"I can start now," she said quietly.

The old man sent her a keen glance, and then released her hands. "In the mornings, then, after class. I know the Kaavl Games are coming up quick, so you'll want to practice hard for the next few afternoons."

Methusal smiled with quick delight. "They're the day after tomorrow."

"Could you work a little this morning, then?" The old man sounded hopeful.

"Yes, but first I need to speak to Kitran." And later, maybe after lunch, she'd investigate the ore mine.

"Off you go, then." Sims waved her out the door. "I'll see you soon."

With a light heart, Methusal sped next to her kaavl instructor's office. The Quatr-levelers had vanished, but Kitran Mehl was not alone. Behran, her ever present nemesis, lounged in the doorway.

"And here she is." Behran tossed her a mocking smile.

What was that supposed to mean? Her happy mood faltered. Had they been talking about her?

No. Kitran would never discuss his students with other players. Behran just wanted to rile her, that was all. "Aren't you supposed to be working?"

His lips twisted into an annoying grin. "Motr gave me the morning off so I can prepare for the Tri-level."

Methusal's expression remained carefully neutral. "That's nice." She glanced at Kitran, who sat ensconced in the small, warmly lit cave. "I'll come back when you have more time."

The large, broad-shouldered man glanced from Methusal to Behran. A smile twitched under his bristling black mustache. He knew about the long simmering rivalry between the two.

"Won't be necessary. Behran was just leaving."

With a half-smile, Behran stepped away from the door. "True. I have a little practicing to do. See you later, Kitran." He strolled away.

A *little* practicing to do. Methusal managed to remain silent. She really must stop biting the bait every time Behran chose to provoke her.

"Come in, Methusal, and close the door."

She did as he asked, and then perched on a chair facing her instructor. His intense black eyes held hers as he locked his hands together, his elbows resting on the narrow wooden table between them. Something was clearly on his mind. Had Petr already talked to him? Anxiety tightened in her chest.

Methusal couldn't read Kitran's expression. As always, it disconcerted her. Kitran's only passion in life was kaavl. As a result, he was extremely self-controlled, and highly accomplished in the art of kaavl. He would participate in the Primary Level Game this week. Unfortunately, he had no competition among the Rolbanis. Verdnt and Petr were his closest opponents, but each had only achieved the Bi-level.

A thought flashed through her mind. Maybe Kitran favored the new Alliance. Then he could go up against true competitors.

As if hearing her thoughts, Kitran finally spoke. "Have you heard about the Alliance? And what that could mean for the Kaavl Games?"

"Yes." Relief eased her anxiety. Apparently, Petr hadn't spoken to Kitran yet. Good. She could plead her case first.

His opaque black eyes held hers. "I was in Dehre yesterday. Mentàll..." a note of awe crept into his voice, "...the Dehrien Chief, asked us to join in their Kaavl Games a week from Thirdday. Tarst invited us to their Games a few days later. Provided, of course, the Alliance is signed by then."

Kitran had traveled to Dehre several times in the last several months, at Petr Storst's request.

A question formed, but Kitran answered it with his next sentence. "Yes. I've been relaying messages between Petr and the Dehrien Chief about the Alliance. I know Mentàll from my early messenger days, so Petr asked me to work out a rough Alliance while he took care of responsibilities here."

His reelection, Methusal surmised. Petr was determined to be reelected. Liem and Verdnt's challenges for the title had only fueled his single-minded obsession.

"Anyway," Kitran's voice pulled her back to the present, "you'll have a chance to participate in those Games if you do well here. I'm authorized to send the two best competitors from each level."

Methusal's cheeks warmed from that bit of praise from her enigmatic instructor.

Kitran held up a cautionary finger. "You'll need to practice hard these next two days. I've written up a list of exercises." A pale leaf, etched with bold dark markings, fluttered across the table. "The Tri-level event starts at noon sharp. I expect you to be prepared."

Methusal heard the note of dismissal in his voice. Although she grasped the parchment, she did not stand. "I have a problem. Petr wants to disqualify me from the Tri-level."

With a heavy frown, Kitran leaned forward. "Why? That's under my authority."

"I know." Kitran's black stare made it difficult to marshal her thoughts. "Petr thinks he's found Renn's murderer. Me."

Kitran leaned back again. A faint smile tugged at his mouth. "You're serious?"

Did he believe she was innocent? Methusal quickly explained the whole story. "I'm not a thief, and I didn't push Renn off that cliff."

"Of course you didn't."

Relief flooded her. Finally, a small break. "Then you believe me?"

"Of course. But Petr can still prevent you from playing."

"How? If you won't disqualify me..."

"He can lock you in jail. Or keep you under community arrest. Either way, you wouldn't be able to participate."

"But that's not fair. I'm innocent. Can't you do something?" Kitran was her best hope, because Petr might actually listen to him. He wasn't her relative, and even better, he held a high position of authority on the Council.

Kitran fell silent, apparently thinking it over.

"Please?" she added in a small voice.

He nodded. "I'll try. Your kaavl talent is unusual. Of all my students, you have the most potential. It would be a loss to kaavl if you couldn't play."

Methusal stood. "Thank you, Kitran."

He nodded toward the parchment in her hand. "Modify those exercises, since you'll have to practice indoors. You still could win."

"Thank you. I intend to win, if I can."

He smiled. "Good luck."

△ △ △ △ △

After speaking to Kitran, Methusal returned to the supply room.

"I checked the supply room downstairs," Sims greeted her. "The meat wasn't there."

"Maybe Matron checked it out, and forgot to write it down." Or maybe the thief had stolen it. But Methusal didn't mention this possibility, for fear of unnecessarily upsetting Sims. Of course, he had probably thought of that himself.

"Maybe," he muttered. "I'll ask later. When the Kaavl Games are done, my girl, we'll do a full inventory of both supply rooms."

"Okay. What should I do today?"

With a rueful smile, Sims gestured toward the three large bags of seed grain. "One and a half bags will be planted soon. The remaining grain needs to be sorted, and any molding seeds thrown out. I don't want moldy seeds rotting in the bags, waiting for the next planting. I'd like you to sort two full bags now. After that, those two bags of wildberries."

"That should keep me busy."

"For a few days," Sims agreed. "I promise, things will improve after that, my girl."

"I'll hold you to it." She smiled.

Sorting out molding seeds was an easy, if mindless task. The peace and quiet was welcome. In fact, as Methusal sat and worked, the unhurried pace of Sims' quiet shuffling soothed her. Tension relaxed from her tight neck and shoulder muscles. It felt nice to have a moment's peace, especially since she intended to create more drama after lunch.

Methusal carefully plotted how to break into the ore mine. First, she'd get Aali's map and infiltrate the ore mine. Hopefully, she wouldn't get caught. Or maybe she should hope she would. Because that would cut all kaavl players and eighty percent of Rolbanis from the suspect list. Then she'd know only authorized people could access the ore.

△ △ △ △ △

Since she couldn't go outside to practice kaavl, Methusal decided to get as close as she could, and practice for a few minutes to warm up for her ore mine adventure. At the moment, she perched on a wooden recliner at the edge of the open gates. On the opposite side of the hall, a young guard leaned against the gate. He glanced at her, and then outside. Methusal chafed to go out, but didn't dare.

Breathing quietly, she concentrated into kaavl. It was still an effort. True masters of the art, like Kitran, remained in a constant state of kaavl, always intensely aware of everything happening around them. A few aspects of kaavl were becoming a part of her, too. Like unconsciously increasing her concentration to listen in on conversations—although as a rule, she tried not to dishonorably eavesdrop.

Kaavl had improved her physical coordination, too. Now she easily won games involving hand-eye coordination and balance.

But discipline was the true key. Discipline of mind, body and spirit. Learning to concentrate on the important and ignore distractions was still a struggle for her. Thankfully, the full complexities of those skills weren't necessary until the Bi and Primary levels.

Methusal sharpened each of her senses. The plateau, a minute run away, sharpened into focus. Every tiny detail became crisp and clear.

Her hearing fanned out like a net. The guard's breaths blasted as loud as the north wind into her ears, and overhead *swooshed* the precise, powerful strokes of flying beast wings. Other sounds infiltrated, too; the slither of a whip beast twenty lengths south, and to the east, tagma leaves rustled in the strengthening breeze.

It was difficult to track so many noises at one time. Methusal couldn't possibly keep track of them all. Her goal was to follow three systems at once. Two was a challenge, and three a stretch—but the skill was a needed advantage if she wanted to win the Tri-Level Game.

As usual, she found it easier to track noises originating equal distances away. Tracking near and far sounds at the same time seemed impossibly difficult. She focused, and tried again and again.

After long moments of concentration, she managed to hear the guard's breathing and follow the movements of an apte forty lengths west at the same time. Other sounds intruded, but she struggled to keep her concentration.

The guard wandered outside, and the apte scampered closer. Methusal struggled to pick up a third sound—a flying beast overhead. It seemed utterly impossible, but she tried harder, again and again. And then, for one split second, she did it. Unfortunately, the success faded before she could remember how she'd done it.

Her frustration grew the longer she sat on the chair. She needed to run. Not just for speed and endurance, but also to integrate her long and short distance kaavl skills. She'd need that edge to win the Tri-level. How could she possibly win against Behran otherwise?

She *had* to get outside.

Her kaavl concentration broke, and Methusal drew a calming breath. She needed to clear her name first. Time to find the ore mine.

When Methusal stood, the paper Kitran had given her crinkled in her pocket. Great. She'd forgotten to practice his suggestions. Tomorrow, she promised herself. Right now, she needed to find Aali.

△ △ △ △ △

Methusal examined the rough squiggles that Aali had drawn on the parchment, and clutched the worn key in her hand. Few keys were used in Rolban, since few locks had been made, so this would only be the third time in her life that she'd use a key. Apparently, she needed to go north and then east, past her living compartment, and then deeper into the mountain. She counted the forks in the halls to reach the ore passage, and then committed the directions to memory and pushed the paper into her pocket.

She'd explored all of the main passageways multiple times as a child, of course. But she'd never been down any of the locked passageways. Quick steps brought her to the door. She concentrated into kaavl, and listened for movement on the other side.

Nothing. The key inserted silently, and she pushed down the polished lever and slipped into the secret passageway. Ahead, the hall curved right.

Footsteps whispered thirty lengths down the hall. Her heart beat faster, but she pressed on. What should she say, if questioned? Why hadn't she thought of this earlier? And then she remembered Aali and the guards, and quickly came up with a thin explanation for being in the hall. In other words, a twisting of the truth. She hated lying, and felt sick at the thought of doing so now. But she had to get to the ore mine.

The twisting passageway grew narrower, and the footsteps louder.

A council member approached. His bald head gleamed in the light of the fire sconces. He blocked her path. "Why are you here, Methusal?"

"My father has a message. Have you seen Timaeus?"

"Can't say. You could ask Pogul, though." The man seemed satisfied with her response. "He's a little further on."

"Thank you." Sharpening her hearing, Methusal moved on, but she heard no one else. From the man's words, however, it appeared that Pogul was the first guard in the ore passageway. Pogul would know Timaeus wasn't there. And she guessed the unpleasant young man would take great delight in escorting her out of the area. On the other hand, he wasn't the brightest star in the sky. Could she fool him with a simple trick?

Pogul's whistling breaths assaulted her ears long before she reached him. Was he snoring? She heard a snort, and then a rustle of movement. No.

She paused.

Ahead, the passageway curved right, and she pinpointed Pogul's location by the sound of his heavy breaths, and an odd *whump*ing noise. He was two lengths ahead. She listened carefully for footsteps.

None.

She tiptoed to the curve and peered around the corner. Pogul sat slumped against the wall near the mouth of another passageway. The ore hall. Over and over again, he banged his head against the rock wall.

What was that about?

Boredom, most likely. He needed a little excitement, and Methusal was only too pleased to provide it. She scanned the passageway for loose pebbles. A few lay scattered here and there, and she gathered them up.

She flung one pebble after another down the hall, past Pogul. His head snapped right, tracking the tiny, clicking noises. His heavy brows knit in irritation, and he lumbered to his feet.

Methusal smothered a giggle. She lobbed another rock over his head. It skittered farther down the dimly lit passage. Pogul frowned harder. He looked left, then right, and strode after the suspicious sounds.

Methusal sprinted into the hall that Pogul had been guarding. Since she wasn't sure where the next guard was stationed, she sharpened her hearing and ran to gain the first curve in the hall. Pogul might glance down this ore hall, but he probably wouldn't investigate further.

There. She'd safely passed the first curve, and was out of Pogul's view. She paused. Where was the next guard?

The silence told her nothing.

Cautiously, Methusal continued on. She approached a stone stool. A plate with crumbs sat beside it, as well as an empty cup. The second guard's station, she deduced.

Warily, she continued on. Faint voices finally tickled her ears. Three men. She paused, and scanned the hallway for a place to hide, should it become necessary. No concealing crevices or dips in the wall were to be found. The voices grew louder, and her heart accelerated.

Great! Now what should she do? Retreat? Or continue? If she continued, would she find a doorway or a crevice in which she could hide?

Methusal elected to go on. Whether that was foolhardy or courageous, she wasn't sure. A few lengths ahead, the passageway cut sharply right. The voices grew louder. The men were just around the next bend.

Would she be caught so easily? Anxiously, Methusal crept closer to the corner. They'd catch her. How would she explain her presence in this restricted passageway?

And then she saw it. A shallow indentation in the rock, just before the turn in the hall. She slipped into the hollow. However, even scrunching flat against the wall, it barely sheltered her. Anyone coming from the south would see her, but the outcropping shielded her from the men approaching from the north.

A lone young man sauntered by, picking at his teeth. He was one of Behran's friends. She stood completely still, hoping he wouldn't look behind him. The voices to the north fell silent.

She listened for footsteps. They grew fainter. Were they retreating to the ore mine?

She couldn't stay here much longer. Once the guard sat down, he'd spot her.

Gathering her courage, she slithered around the outcropping and turned the next corner of the hall. Up ahead, the passage jogged left. Caution slowed her steps, and she scanned for crevices in which to hide, should the men return. There were none.

Silently, she crept to the next curve in the passage.

If only she could carry with vision. Then she wouldn't have to poke her head around the corner and risk being discovered. But since she had no idea how to perform that kaavl skill, she had no choice.

Methusal peeked around the corner, and then quickly withdrew. Her heart slammed in her chest. A lone man guarded a closed door. This was it! It had to lead to the ore mine.

The guard had looked grim. Wide awake, too. How in the world could she investigate the ore mine? And where had the second man gone?

Peering out again, she sized up the guard. He was probably Verdnt's age, and likely the senior guard. He was a big man, with dark hair and thick muscles. She'd seen him often in the dining hall, but it took a few seconds to recall his name—Vogl. He'd immigrated from Tarst a few years back.

Methusal flattened her back against the wall. Now what? Security was tight, but up until now, not too difficult to overcome. Getting inside the ore deposits, however, looked impossible. Only someone with authorized access could get past this guard, barring physical force. So the thief had to be one of a limited number of people.

Wasn't that what she'd wanted to know? Now she just needed to discover who those people were.

Retreating now seemed like the prudent plan.

Still, Methusal hesitated. She'd made it this far undiscovered, and now curiosity about the mysterious mine plagued her. If only she could catch a glimpse inside. To do that, though, she'd need to neutralize the guard. Not likely. If the heavy muscles in his neck and arms were any indication, he'd squash her like a bug.

Reluctantly, she decided to retreat. Before she could move, however, the mysterious door creaked open. She peered around the corner again, and then jerked back.

Behran. What was he doing here? He wasn't a guard, so he must be working on the water systems. Did they pass through the ore mine?

Now she really did need to escape. Methusal slipped back down the hall, heading for the concealing outcropping.

"Thanks," Behran said. "See you later." His moccasins whispered into the passage.

Methusal sprinted to gain the last protective crevice. But before reaching it, she glanced around the corner. The guard's eyes were shut. Good. She spun around the corner and into the protective alcove. Now, if only Behran wouldn't notice her, and the guard kept his eyes closed...

Her heart pounded. She felt vaguely sick.

Calm down. Take deep breaths. It'll be okay.

She'd taken two deep breaths when Behran turned the corner. Instinctively, she held her breath and froze. She squeezed her eyes shut, as if that would help matters.

A touch at her arm made her gasp. Behran's blue eyes gleamed at her. A firm grip pulled her from her hiding place. To her surprise, he marched her past the dozing guard. Once they'd rounded the next corner, though, he stopped and released her arm.

"Fancy meeting you here."

"I'm doing research."

"Research?" He moved closer. "On how to steal ore?"

She couldn't believe her ears. "I am not the thief!"

"Looks pretty suspicious to me."

"I'm investigating," she hissed.

"And what did you discover?"

She lifted her chin. "You're here. Maybe you're the thief."

He laughed quietly. "I have authorized access. Should I turn out my pockets to prove it?"

"Don't be ridiculous."

"Well, you accused me..."

"I want to get out of here."

He flashed a mocking grin. "I'm sure you do. But how? Do you have a plan?"

"Of course... Sort of." Unfortunately, she hadn't clearly thought out a retreat plan, although being careful seemed the prudent choice. Meeting Behran had only complicated matters.

"I'll need to report you to Pogul."

"Of course. You'd love for me to get in more trouble. That way you won't have to compete against me at the Tri-level. Afraid?"

He continued to smile. "Doesn't look like I have much to worry about."

Methusal heaved an angry breath. "This *isn't* the Kaavl Games."

"Real life is so much crueler, isn't it?"

"This isn't like the Kaavl Games at all!"

"Think what you want. Now come on."

Methusal had no choice. She walked abreast of him, refusing to follow him like a conquered beast. He loved this, of course. As usual, one step above her. "Why do you have to be such a whip?"

"You brought this on yourself. You didn't think through your plan. Now I'm stuck. If I don't report you, I'll get in trouble."

"No."

"No? I could let you creep out of the hall after me. But what if you're caught? Am I supposed to lie, and say I didn't see you? No one would believe that. I'd be accused of conspiracy."

Methusal hadn't thought about that. But she still didn't like her position—captured, as it were, by Behran. And now Pogul would report her illegal activities to Petr.

At that very moment, the stocky young man stepped into the hallway. Oh, goodie.

"Methusal!" His lips curled. "How did you get in that hall?"

"It wasn't hard."

Pogul grabbed her arm. "I'm turning you in." His fingers hurt.

Behran raised a hand. "Hold on." He turned to Methusal. "Haven't you been practicing kaavl?"

"Yes..."

"As you can see, she lost to me," Behran told Pogul. "Don't humiliate her further."

"She doesn't belong in there. I'm reporting her to Petr."

"Go ahead," Methusal agreed. "I'll tell him how easy it was. In fact, I'll say you left your post so I could walk right in. How would he like that?"

Ugly rage radiated from Pogul. "You little..." He worked his thick lips. "You'd better watch your back."

"Don't worry. I don't plan to be anywhere alone with you."

Behran gripped her arm and directed her down the main hall. "Thanks, Pogul. See you later."

Pogul didn't respond.

Behran hissed, "Think that was smart?"

"Yes. I had to scare him, or he'd report me to Petr."

"A little harsh, don't you think?"

"Maybe," Methusal admitted. "But I don't like him. He's always lewd and rude in class. By the way, thank you for helping me."

He smiled. "You owe me."

She eyed him warily. "I guess." Behran had convinced Pogul that she was practicing kaavl, rather than trying to break into the ore mine. Definitely a lesser offense, should Petr find out.

"Stay out of that passageway from now on."

"I will. I found out what I needed to know."

"I hope you did. That was pretty reckless."

"Your life isn't on the line. Mine is. I'll do whatever is necessary to clear my name."

He chuckled. "See you later."

∆ ∆ ∆ ∆ ∆

The Maahr family table was empty when Methusal turned away from the buffet table holding a plate filled with overcooked leftovers from lunch, and garnished with logne leaves. She'd noticed a few people eyeing her as she entered, and remembered this morning, when Liem had accused her of murder. How many people thought she was guilty? What did they really think of her? She was acquainted with everyone in Rolban, of course, although she wasn't close with many.

Now, as she stood at the end of the buffet line, she noticed a few more groups of people whispering together and sending frowns her way. That made her feel uncomfortable, and she tried to ignore them.

Deccia waved from the Storst table, and her sister's smile made her feel better. The people who loved her knew the truth. And she'd prove the truth to the others. Slowly, Methusal headed over to where her sister sat with her father, Verdnt, and D'Wit. Although she did want to eat with Deccia, listening to more of her uncle's threats wasn't an appetizing prospect. However, Petr seemed to be deep in conversation with D'Wit and Verdnt. Maybe she'd get lucky, and he'd ignore her.

Petr clapped Verdnt on the back and roared with laughter when Methusal sat beside her sister. "You'll make a good Chief someday, Verdnt. But not *too* soon." He laughed again.

"I know I won't win this election," Verdnt murmured, with a glance at Deccia. "Dehriens still aren't fully trusted. But next time…"

"Next time, you'll be my fiercest competitor." Petr turned to his trusted advisor. "Don't you agree, D'Wit?"

"I'm thinking you shouldn't give him too much advice," came the doctor's scratchy, disapproving voice.

"I'm not worried. This election's just a trial run for the boy. Isn't that right, Verdnt?"

A swift emotion glittered, and then vanished in the teacher's dark eyes. "If I had lived here for thirty years, as you have, Storst, the election's outcome wouldn't be so certain."

Petr laughed, instead of taking offense, which surprised Methusal. As did his apparently affectionate squeeze of the younger man's shoulder. "The balance of power tips to me now. But in the future," and he glanced at Deccia, "you may obtain everything your heart desires. I'm a friend you want to keep."

With a smile, Verdnt glanced at Deccia and then back to Petr. He lifted his cup. "To the future."

Petr smiled broadly and lifted his cup. "To strong alliances."

What was going on here? With a frown, Methusal glanced at her sister. A flush touched Deccia's cheeks, and she looked down at her plate.

The men clicked cups and drank while the hunched D'Wit looked on with a disapproving stare. For once, Methusal agreed with Petr's closest advisor. What exactly had Petr promised Verdnt? A future election, possibly. But worse, Petr appeared to have given Verdnt his seal of approval as a son-in-law. Clearly, he had not bothered to speak to Deccia about the matter, because Deccia loved Timaeus, not Verdnt.

Petr's callous highhandedness grated on Methusal's nerves, as usual. She hissed to Deccia, "Decc. Did Petr just..."

Her flush deepened. "Shh."

"Why won't you speak up for yourself?"

"I said, *shhh!*"

"What's wrong?" Petr's heavy frown targeted Methusal, surprise of surprises.

Although it was difficult, she managed to remain silent.

Deccia said, "Everything is fine, Father."

Petr *harrumphed*. With a glare at Methusal, he returned his attention to Verdnt.

Methusal, however, sent her sister a frown of concern.

"Don't," Deccia warned in a low voice.

"I care about you," she hissed. "I can't stand to see Petr walking all over you."

"I don't need to start that war today."

"Maybe not. But someday you'll need to speak up for yourself."

"I'll choose when. It's not today."

Out of the corner of her eye, Methusal spotted her parents in the buffet line. Behind them stood Liem. Renn's father caught her gaze, and his silver brows ratcheted together into a glare.

Heart thumping, and feeling slightly sick, she looked away. Always before, when she'd gone to visit Renn at his compartment, Liem had seemed like a kind, mild-mannered man. Apparently not any longer. He clearly wanted her executed; probably the sooner, the better. She wondered how many other people felt the same way.

All of a sudden, sitting at the Storst table with Petr, who also disliked her, felt too uncomfortable to bear. He'd already turned Methusal's life into a living hell, and apparently he planned to do the same to her sister. It really was too much. She wanted to sit with her parents who loved her, and who would support and defend her.

She stood. "I see my parents. I think I'll go sit at our table now."

Eyes troubled, Deccia nodded.

Methusal didn't want her sister to feel abandoned. She gently touched her shoulder. "I love you, Decc. I just can't stand..."

"I understand."

Methusal carried her plate to her family's table, which, for the moment, was still vacant. The stew from lunch had turned to mush, but at least the meat was easier to chew. Out of the corner of her eye she saw that Liem had retreated to his table, and he faced the far wall. Good. His eyes had felt like daggers in her back the whole time he'd been in line.

Behran sat down and placed a steaming bowl before him. His eyebrow lifted. "So, are you ready to beat me at the Tri-level?"

Behran's flippant attitude was a welcome distraction from Liem and Petr. And wasn't it just like him to rub it in that he'd caught her skulking through the restricted area? In his mind, obviously a kaavl win.

"Yes, thank you." She didn't bother to ask if he was ready. Clearly, he was convinced he would win. Fine. Maybe his ego would blind him. It might improve her chances of winning.

"Will Kitran let you play?"

"Yes, he will. He'll speak to Petr soon."

"Better hope he doesn't find out what you did today."

"I was trying to clear my name," she pointed out.

"Do you think Petr will see it that way?"

"He already believes the worst about me. And he won't find out unless you tell him."

"I won't. But Pogul might."

"Pogul's a troublemaker. Everyone knows that. And he won't want me to report that he was sleeping on the job, either. He'll keep quiet."

"So you're not worried?"

Her patience evaporated. "Thank you for pointing out that I should be."

"All I'm saying is that you should be careful, Thusa. Sneaking into restricted areas is not going to help win your case with Petr."

"What do you suggest, then? Should I sit quietly in a corner while Petr tries and convicts me?"

"No. But take more reasonable steps. Talk to the guards. See..."

"I am," she interrupted. "I will. But first, I had to see if someone could easily break into the mine. Don't you see? If I could break in, others could, too. That would increase the list of suspects. But now I know it has to be someone with authorized access. Don't you agree?"

Respect darkened his blue eyes. "You're right. I hadn't thought of that."

"See? I'm not entirely stupid."

"I never said you were."

"Didn't you?"

"I'm sorry. Sometimes I come off wrong, when I talk to you. I just don't want you to get in more trouble. Believe it or not, I'm looking forward to competing against you at the Tri-level."

Methusal relaxed a little. "Think you'll beat me?"

"Maybe. But don't think I hate you, because I don't."

His serious gaze met hers and for once, a mouthy comeback escaped her. Behran meant it, and she felt strangely touched. "Thank you."

He smiled. "But don't think I'll go easy on you. Because I won't."

She tossed a roll at him. Her parents and Behran's mother sat down. Hanuh sent Methusal an admonishing look, but said nothing.

The meal passed quietly. Erl frowned to himself the entire time. Hanuh and Poli murmured between themselves about garments they stitched for the community, and also about Verdnt, who had visited them today.

"He's such a nice young man," Poli enthused. "He's so serious about running for Chief, too. I can't believe he asked our opinions about how Rolban could be improved. I wish I'd thought of new ideas for him."

"Catching the thief who is stealing our pelts would be a good start," Hanuh said grimly.

"I heard that Liem spent the whole day outside looking clues," Poli said.

This was news to Methusal. "Did he find anything, besides the knife?"

Hanuh shook her head. "I'm sorry, Thusa."

So, she was still suspect number one. Fantastic. "Do you still think Liem will run for Chief? The election is only three weeks away."

Of course, she hoped he'd drop out of the race. If elected, Liam would probably hasten the trial process, and execute her as swiftly as possible. Unless, of course, he found evidence to exonerate her. A grim smile touched her lips. Why didn't she believe that would happen? Maybe because every clue found so far had diabolically pointed straight to her. Someone wanted her to take the blame for Renn's murder.

"I don't know," Hanuh answered. "But if Liem does plan to keep his bid for Chief, he'll be hard to beat. He has great ideas, and now he has a big sympathy factor, too. That will gain him votes."

Ben Amil, Behran's father, arrived carrying a bowl heaped with stew. He sat across from Methusal's father. "Don't feel bad, Erl. You gave it your best shot. If it makes you feel better, I talked with a lot of people who feel the same way you do. Liem is one."

Ben must be talking about the Alliance. With difficulty, Methusal turned her attention to the new topic of conversation. Had her father called that special Council meeting, like he'd threatened last night?

"Thanks, Ben." Erl sighed. "I'm glad Liem is on our side, but the Alliance vote will take place before he's elected Chief."

"So he's still running?" Methusal asked.

"Yes."

Great. Dread filled her. She'd better prove she was innocent fast.

Erl returned to his original train of thought. "At least I've had my say to the Council. I'm still afraid Petr will push the Alliance to a vote too fast. We haven't even seen the agreement yet, and the Dehrien Chief will bring it to sign tomorrow. That doesn't give us much time to look it over, or do any negotiating."

"We don't need to sign it tomorrow," Hanuh pointed out gently. "He'll drop the treaty off on his way to Tarst. Surely we'll have as much time as we need to discuss it."

Erl nodded. "You're probably right. But I want to make sure we consider all the facts first, before we sign."

Politics was not Methusal's favorite subject, but she found herself favoring the Alliance. It had a lot of good points. A few were the Inter-Community Kaavl Games, the benefit of neighbors helping neighbors, and putting to rest the distrust of the past two centuries. Relations had already improved with Dehre and Tarst. Why not become closer allies?

"What about you, Hanuh," Erl said abruptly. "Do you favor the Alliance? What do you sense about it now?"

A faint frown creased Hanuh's brow. "Logically, it could help us all. I've had an uneasy feeling for a while. But that is centered on Thusa. I haven't been focusing on the Alliance..." Her frown deepened, and her eyes seemed to shutter as she withdrew within herself.

Methusal's mother was able to read people, situations...and even the future sometimes. However, those impressions spontaneously slipped into Hanuh's mind. She did not seek them out. As a result, Methusal had never seen her mother consciously try to reach the other world...the future world...before.

A few moments passed, and then a spasm crossed Hanuh's face. Her hands fisted. Slowly, her eyes opened. They looked dark, lost, and troubled.

"Something bad will happen with this Alliance," she murmured. Her gaze fixed upon Methusal. "Everything...I don't know why...but it centers upon you, Thusa. The danger is pinpointed on you."

"Danger?"

"Yes. Something isn't right. It may be the Alliance, or something closely related to the Alliance. I can't tell. I just sense...something...amiss." Tears glistened, and her gaze rested upon Erl. She whispered, "We must stop it. The Alliance cannot be passed."

Chapter Seven

Dehre
Firstday evening

ALONE IN THE DARK, Hendra crept home from the orphanage tent. She'd delivered half of her food rations to the hungry children, as she always did. One of the adult helpers was home sick, so Hendra had stayed longer than usual to help feed the children and tuck them into bed.

Hendra never wandered Dehre alone in the dark, and felt scared to be out now. Since her fellow Dehriens were hungry and desperate, many men fed their bellies with racmun spirits, like her father had. It made them mean.

The thought of running into one of them terrified her.

Hendra crept through the dark, slipping by shacks and tents. Ryon had not risen yet, so only the stars and the few bonfires burning on the outskirts of town lit the night. The fires effectively repelled the marauding, nocturnal wild beasts.

Wood for fires was getting low, thanks to the drought this year, but the slow burning, fast growing tagma bushes helped protect the town. Their new supply of sturdy trees, traded from the Tarst in exchange for Dehrien wild beast oil, were used to build the new wall around Dehre. They were not spared for bonfires, for the logs took a great deal of time and labor to roll all the way to Dehre from the Tarst mountains. The southern wall was partially completed, but at the current rate of building, it would take years before the entire wall around Dehre was completed.

Because of the scarcity of trees near Dehre, fewer fires burned now than in the past. The tagma bushes helped, but only a little. Soon, none may burn at all—unless they burned the Tarst trees. Mentàll refused to allow that, however. He said using the trees for that temporary purpose would be short-sighted, especially as Dehre had other means to defend itself from the wild beasts. Building the wall would provide Dehre with a permanent defense against all predators.

If they ran out of fuel for the fires, night terrors could hold a new meaning. Then wild beasts could slink into the town, tear apart flimsy tents and shacks and eat the weakest Dehriens. She shivered at the thought. Dehrien hunters guarded the town, and thankfully they were adept at killing the nocturnal beasts. Lately, it appeared the wild beasts had developed a healthy fear for the hunters, for they did not sniff around the town as often as they had in the past.

If only the walls would go up faster.

To her left, Hendra heard a curse, and then a lurching stumble and thump as someone staggered into a wall.

"*Scienth!*" the man mumbled.

He was close.

Fear pumped through her. Her Quatr-level kaavl helped her detect how far away the man was. Two lengths. More footsteps scuffled toward her, but these were from a different direction.

She slipped between two shacks and almost stumbled into the back of her cousin's large tent. It loomed huge and white in the blackness. A faint light glowed within. But she still wasn't safe. She had to circle right, to her own tent. The shuffling footsteps padded closer.

"C'mere, sweetie," slurred the man. "Saw your shining hair. You an angel? Lemme see."

Sick fingers of panic gripped her. What if he caught her? What if she couldn't escape? What if...

The old horror froze her entire body. She felt like an apte about to be devoured by a whip beast.

No!" A tiny whimper escaped. No. It would not happen. Not...

"C'mere lovey," trilled the man, three steps away...now two.

Panicked, Hendra scrambled for Mentàll's tent. She plucked up the bottom edge of her cousin's tent and burrowed underneath, yanking her feet through before the man could see them. Shaking, Hendra sat up. She was in her cousin's closet. The sweet scent of cured leather filled her nose. Neatly folded, bleached leather clothing lay stacked on shelves on either side of her. She sat in the middle of Mentàll's moccasins.

Safe. Hendra quieted her gasping breaths. As she did so, new voices reached her ears. Her cousin was talking to someone—hopefully not his latest woman! She recoiled at the thought.

But then the other voice spoke. It wasn't a woman; rather, a man—an older man, if the faint quaver in the deep tone was any indication. Who was visiting Mentàll at this late hour?

Did the meeting have something to do with the fires she'd smelled burning at night? Or maybe the Alliance?

She peeked around the closet's hanging leather door. Mentàll's bed chamber was empty. The voices came from his sitting area.

Hendra hesitated. She shouldn't be in here at all. And the last thing she wanted to do was be caught in a man's— any man's—bed chamber. The very thought made her shudder with fear. Even if it was her cousin's bed chamber—a man who had never harmed her.

But what if Mentàll was talking about his secret activities right now? If she found out more, maybe she could stop him from doing something foolish.

If he listened to her.

Although spying on her cousin wasn't an honorable thing to do, she wanted to protect him; from himself, if necessary. He had saved her life, and as a result, she owed him a debt that could never be repaid. She would gladly lay down her life to save him, if she could.

Trembling a little with fear, she crept to the section of leather wall which was closest to the sitting room. Lying flat on the floor, she lifted the edge just the tiniest bit, and pressed her eye to the opening.

Fortunately, the two men sat across the room, so she could clearly see Mentàll's guest. Hendra had never seen him before. Tufts of white hair crowned his brown, wizened face. The man wore a patchwork, over-sized tunic. His gnarled feet were bare, and he held a walking stick in one skinny hand. His dark eyes flicked in Hendra's direction, and her heart jerked with fear.

But he returned his attention to her cousin. "As I told you once, Mentàll, I am the Prophet." Though the old man's voice was surprisingly deep, it quavered a little as he spoke. "I have come to warn you."

"The Prophet is dead." Her cousin's words sounded cold. As a child, Hendra had heard stories of a Prophet who wandered the land, speaking The One's word to those who needed to hear it. No one had seen him in years.

The old man chuckled. It sounded faintly breathy. "I have come to deliver a warning, Mentàll."

"Speak, then."

"Discard your deceitful plot."

A silent moment elapsed.

"I am pursuing an Alliance." Warning sounded in Mentàll's low voice.

"All who draw the sword will die by the sword."

Mentàll drew a harsh breath. "I seek only to save my people."

"You seek vengeance."

Her cousin stood abruptly. "You do not know what you are talking about."

"Already one is dead. More will die if you persist in this plan."

"I did not order his death!"

"Blood stains your hands. You are responsible for making an alliance with the traitor in Rolban."

"Why do you speak to me, Prophet, if that is who you are? The One did not hear my cries as a child. *I will not hear him now!*" Mentàll snarled.

A chill cut through Hendra's soul. Although she knew little about The One, defying him seemed dangerous and foolish.

The old man's hand whitened over his stick. He struggled to his feet. "You hear me not, young man. But you have been warned."

Her cousin stood, his shoulders rigid, and made no move to show the old man out. Rude, and no doubt doubled the wrath upon his head.

The old man paused in the tent doorway. "Young man, you may abandon The One. But he will never forget you." He slipped into the black night.

Hendra felt like she must do something. Mentàll had surely just invited judgment upon his head.

She slipped back into the closet. After a quick listen to make sure the drunk man was gone—or had passed out—she poked her head out. Ryon had edged up into the sky, and green moonlight bathed the blades of dry grass and the slanting, rickety shacks behind the Chief's tents.

Safe. Hendra slid out and ran around the tent, hoping to find the Prophet.

There! He was making his way toward the two bonfires that protected Dehre's eastern border. Hendra sprinted to catch up. Out of the blue, panic stabbed her.

Her footsteps faltered. What was she doing? She never spoke to men—let alone a stranger—unless absolutely necessary. They all terrified her—including her cousin, whom she trusted more than any man she knew.

But wasn't it for Mentàll that she was here? Didn't she want to help the one man who had helped her? Hendra forced herself to run after the Prophet.

When she drew abreast of him, the Prophet stopped. Dark, fathomless eyes peered at her. "Hendra."

In her bewilderment, she forgot to be afraid. "How do you know my name?"

"You want me to speak a good word for your cousin. To The One."

"Yes." This time, Hendra did ask not how he knew. She just stared at him in wonder. Her fear evaporated as she looked into his kind eyes.

"Your cousin is a stubborn man. He rushes to his destruction."

"Don't let him. Please." Surely, a man who spoke to The One could save her cousin.

"I cannot stop him. Can you?" The old man peered at her. "Will you?"

"What do you mean?"

"The One loves you, Hendra. Do not forget it." Once again, the Prophet shuffled for Dehre's eastern border.

"But what about Mentàll? How can I stop him?"

"Fear The One, Hendra. Not men." The note of finality in his voice seemed to indicate that the conversation was over.

Hendra stopped and stared after him. What did he mean? And how did he know about the fear that had ruled her since childhood? ...That ruled her even now.

"Wait!" she cried out. "You can't go out there! The wild beasts will attack you."

The old man smiled back at her, but said nothing. She watched him pass the fire line, and then he was gone.

Hendra headed for her tent and pondered his words. Fear The One, not men. How was she supposed to do that?

And what was she supposed to do about Mentàll? She didn't even know what he was planning. Nothing good, apparently. Likely something to do with metal—the Prophet had mentioned swords. But surely her cousin wasn't forging weapons! What's more, the Prophet had mentioned that Mentàll had allied himself with a traitor in Rolban. What traitor? And for what purpose?

Apparently, a man had already been killed. A shiver slid through her soul. She looked up at the clear night sky.

Could God be real? For the first time in years, she wondered. "If you *are* real," she whispered, "show me what to do. Help me stop Mentàll. Please don't let him die."

A horrifying thought came to mind. If Mentàll died, Jascr would become Chief, since he was the next best kaavl contender. Her life would become a living hell.

Never! She shuddered. Somehow she must protect her cousin. He deserved all of her loyalty. He had saved her life, and she would return the favor, if possible. But to do that, she must first discover what he was hiding in the hills.

△ △ △ △ △

*It is time to finish my report and ready it for our
faithful messenger. Matters are proceeding well.
Seeds of distrust and greed are sprouting, watered
by the spirit of vengeance. Even better, rich Rolban
will soon hunger for the Dehrien Alliance, just as
you desire. Rolban is desperate for strong leadership. This fact is pushing your plans forward on
several fronts. Our deepest spy will soon upset
matters in a different area. Our ally is convinced
Rolban is soft, and ripe for the plucking. Victory is
certain.*

Chapter Eight

ROLBAN
Secondday

ALL THE TALK in the dining hall the next morning was about the imminent arrival of Mentàll Solboshn, the Dehrien Chief. He had never visited Rolban before, and everyone was eager to meet him. He was supposed to arrive sometime that afternoon, and would leave the next morning before the Kaavl Games began. Normally, Methusal would pay little attention to any of this, but the Dehrien would be bringing the Alliance—a topic that now worried her, too. She was also curious to meet him because Kitran seemed so awed by him.

"What do you think, Thusa?" Deccia asked. She and Aali sat with Methusal while they finished up breakfast.

"About what?" She had been lost in her own thoughts, thinking about Hanuh's warning about the Alliance last night. It worried her. Frankly, putting her life in more peril wasn't at the top of her list right now.

"The Alliance, silly," her sister interrupted her thoughts again. "What everyone's talking about. What do you think about it?"

Methusal told the others about the impression Hanuh had received last night.

Deccia frowned. "That's odd. I wonder what kind of danger she meant."

"I don't know. But I don't want any part of it. My life is complicated enough right now."

"I agree." Deccia continued to frown. "On the surface, the Alliance sounds great. Our communities could help each other during hard times. And we could trade more freely. The Great War Peace Plan could be loosened, and we could allow traveling merchants within our walls. It could be wonderful. The Dehriens could provide us with more wild beast oil, and the Tarst make beautiful tapestries. I'm sure both communities have a lot to share."

"Who cares about the old Alliance, anyway?" Aalicaa muttered. "I say, scrap it. Father's only for it so he can look important, and be Chief again. All he cares about is getting his own way."

"Aalicaa!" Deccia said, in clear shock. "How can you speak about Father..."

"Bother Father! I'm tired of the way he orders us around. Do this, do that. Mother was never like that, was she? Why couldn't we have Mother instead of *Father?* He's mean, and I hate him!" Aalicaa burst into tears and fled from the table.

"What was that all about?"

Deccia sighed. "She's going through a rebellious stage. She keeps testing him."

"About what?"

"Kaavl. Father just found out she's been secretly practicing. He's forbidden her to learn it, but you know Aali. Father's furious. He's old fashioned, and doesn't think girls should learn kaavl, since it used to be a weapon of war. But she refuses to give it up."

Methusal remembered Aali listening in on the Quatr-level instruction. "And she shouldn't."

Deccia sighed, "Thusa..."

"Did you want to learn kaavl too, Deccia?"

"No! Not really. Please, Thusa, try to understand. Father is of the old school, and Aali needs to obey him. It's a power struggle, that's all. Aali's just testing him."

Methusal agreed it was a power struggle, but she didn't think Aali's desire to learn kaavl should be crushed just on Petr's say so. Especially if she was gifted. It would be a crime to suffocate kaavl talent. However, it was pointless to argue, because Petr was inflexible, as she knew all too well. He would never change his mind—not about her guilt, nor about anything else. But it was a shame about Aali.

Deccia changed the subject. "How is your investigation going? Have you found any clues?"

"No, and it's frustrating. The Kaavl Games are tomorrow, and I want more than anything to concentrate only on that. I talked to Kitran, and he believes I'm innocent. He said he'd talk to Petr about letting me play in the Tri-level. But I don't know if it will help."

"I'm sorry, Thusa. I forgot to tell you, but I spoke to Father about the charges against you. He wouldn't listen."

Methusal wasn't surprised. "Thanks, anyway."

"If I can do anything to help you clear your name, let me know. If you need to investigate outside...or anything," Deccia insisted.

"I'll let you know if I do."

"Were you able to investigate the ore mine?"

She told Deccia about her misadventures at the mine, and that Behran had unfortunately apprehended her. "At least I know now the thief has to be someone with authorized access. How many people, do you think, are on that list?"

"Ask Timaeus." Deccia blushed. "Remember, Aali said he's a guard for the mine sometimes. He must have access to the list."

"Good idea." Methusal's mind went to the recent thefts. "I don't understand why pelts, food, and pots have been stolen. No one in Rolban is hungry, and if they are, they can go to the kitchen and get a snack."

"Dehre needs food. But I heard they're trading with Tarst now—at least for lumber. Besides, no Dehriens come here, except for messengers. And I haven't seen any of them running off with big pots in their arms."

Methusal agreed. "It has to be a Rolbani. But do you know what's really bothering me? The ore. Why would someone steal ore? No one needs it. We're not short on hunting knives, or pots...well, we've lost a few of those, I guess."

"The Peace Plan banned ore melting."

"Right. Because people can make weapons with it." This fact sent an uneasy chill through her. Slowly, she said, "What if the food thefts are just a distraction? What if they're meant to divert attention from the ore thefts?"

"You think someone could be making weapons? But where, and how? It would have to be smelted. Someone would see the smoke, or smell it."

"You think it's a crazy idea."

"No. Maybe not."

"Timaeus might know," Methusal said. "He's a messenger to Tarst, Dehre, and Aestoff. I'll ask if he's seen any strange fires while he's been out."

"Good idea." Deccia flushed slightly, and looked down.

"Or *you* could ask him," Methusal slyly suggested.

"No. ...*No,*" Deccia said more firmly. "I don't want to come across as too...pushy. I already talked to him this morning. I don't want to chase him."

"You barely speak to him. You're not chasing him."

"Still. If he's interested in me, he should make an effort, too." Deccia abruptly changed the subject. "I love my teaching apprenticeship."

"What about Verdnt?"

"He's still behaving."

"Good. Thank goodness he's not taking advantage of Petr's marriage endorsement."

Deccia eyed her. "No need to be sarcastic."

"How do you stand it?" Methusal managed not to roll her eyes in complete frustration. "Okay. I'll stop. Tell me more about teaching."

"Verdnt is overworked, so he's giving me more of his teaching load. It does mean we're spending more time together. Besides teaching, he's been talking to people about the problems in Rolban. And, of course, he's campaigning to be Chief."

"Doesn't that bother you? I mean, he is running against your father."

"No. He's so excited about running for Chief that it's kind of fun to listen to him. He has a lot of good ideas. Like giving honors to people who work especially hard, and updating the school texts. Things like that."

"Hmm." Those things didn't sound terribly exciting, but she didn't say so. "What about Timaeus? You said you talked to him today?"

Deccia flushed. "We stood in line together this morning."

"Uh huh..." Methusal wiggled her eyebrows. "What did you say?"

Deccia smiled. "I said it looks like a sunny day, and he said he was looking forward to guarding the entrance this afternoon. That way he can be outside for a while."

Methusal squeezed her twin's arm. "That's wonderful, Decc."

Her sister looked quietly pleased.

Methusal was glad that her sister had made the effort to conquer her shyness and talk to Timaeus. In her opinion, Deccia should talk to him a little more. But maybe her twin had a point—if Timaeus was interested in her, he should definitely take more initiative, too.

Class would start soon. Methusal quickly finished the last of her cereal and hurried to the classroom with her sister.

A rash plan had begun to form the minute she'd learned Timaeus' schedule for this afternoon. First, she'd ask him about the ore mine authorization list, and about any suspicious fires he might have seen in other communities. Then she'd put her next plan into motion. She sketched out a few details in her mind as she slid into her seat, and then briefly slipped into daydreams about the Tri-Level Game tomorrow. Tomorrow! She hadn't heard from Kitran yet. Hopefully he'd convince Petr to let her play.

Fidgeting, she waited for Verdnt to finish speaking about the Great War, which ended 200 years ago. He was pointedly stressing that *both* Dehre and Tarst had invaded Rolban back then. Ancient history. Her mind wandered. After class she'd help Old Sims. After lunch, she'd visit Timaeus at the gate.

The details of her rebellious plan continued to take shape, too. Should she do it? Prudence said no, but Petr's unfair treatment rankled deep. She was innocent, after all.

Would this class never end?

Her fingers drummed softly on the desk. She had so many things to do.

Verdnt was discussing the Alliance again, but Methusal had heard enough about it. She blocked out the lecture and attempted to listen in on the class next door. First level math.

Boring.

She became vaguely aware that someone was calling her name.

"Methusal!"

Uh oh. She'd tuned out her present surroundings *too* completely. Her eyes focused upon her teacher's irate face. "Yes, sir. I'm right here."

Snorts of laughter erupted in the class.

Verdnt scowled. "I'd appreciate your complete attention."

"I'm sorry, sir."

He turned his back on her. "That will be all, class."

Next to her, Deccia whispered, "Be careful, Thusa. He could get you expelled from the Games."

"I know." Worry gripped her. What a fool she'd been. All she needed right now were both Verdnt and Petr allied against her. "Do you think he'll talk to Kitran?"

"No." Deccia scraped together a few parchment leaves. "I'll put in a good word for you. I don't think he'd report you this close to the Games, anyway."

Methusal spotted Timaeus over her sister's shoulder, and subtly elbowed her. "Look," she hissed. "It's Timaeus. Talk to him."

Deccia shot her a warning look. "No."

"Why not? Or maybe you're interested in Verdnt, after all?" Methusal only said this to try to provoke her sister into action. They slipped into the hallway together.

"Thusa!" Tears brightened Deccia's eyes, but her mouth settled into a straight line. "I don't like Verdnt. I'm just *sick* of wondering if Timaeus likes me. I wish he'd make an effort, if he does. I want to know how he feels."

"I'm sorry, Deccia. I didn't mean to upset you."

At that moment, Timaeus exited from the classroom and glanced at Deccia. The frown she shot his way made him stop in obvious surprise. Deccia turned and marched away.

Timaeus stared at Methusal. "What was that about?"

Maybe she was making another mistake, but the two clearly needed some help. Their relationship had crept forward at a slug monster's pace over the last several months. And now, with Verdnt in the running...

She chose her words with care. "Have you ever felt nervous about talking to someone?"

Timaeus' mouth drooped. "Sometimes I feel that way with Deccia."

Methusal smiled to herself. Easier than she'd thought. "Maybe you should talk to her. A little *more*, I mean."

Hope dawned in his dark brown eyes. "You think so?"

"It wouldn't hurt." She smiled.

He flashed a grin. "Thanks, Thusa." He swung away, his steps light.

"And what was *that* about?" Methusal turned to find Behran watching her with a quirked eyebrow. "Playing matchmaker?"

It was amazing how fast her warm feeling of accomplishment could turn into irritation. "Don't you have somewhere to be?"

"Temper, temper." Grinning, he sauntered down the hall.

He'd done it again. Biting her lip, Methusal slipped toward the supply room. When would she ever learn?

Today Sims wanted to do a detailed inventory of all the upstairs supplies. The ongoing job of sifting the two bags of seed grain would have to wait. Terrific. Methusal was thrilled to postpone that boring job.

"The grain for meals is kept in that corner," Sims pointed. "Be sure to count the seed grain in a separate column."

"All right. But I have a question—maybe it's dumb. What is the difference between seed grain and the grain we eat?"

"Not dumb at all, my girl. We sort through the seeds and choose the heartiest kernels for replanting. Those have strong, intact skins, with no blemishes or marks. Then we soak them in hot water for a time, which helps prevent certain diseases from infecting the crops. After treatment, we carefully and thoroughly dry the grain. Usually, those kernels provide the best crops."

"That's interesting. Did you say Barak will plant half of it soon? What about the other half?"

"Two crop cycles are planted. One will begin shortly, and the other will begin halfway through summer. That way, if one part of the summer is too hot, or if the insects are bad, we have another crop to count on. Of course, drought is never a problem, because we have the Rolbani River and Motr's irrigation system."

Behran helped Motr to engineer better water systems for the community and croplands. An important task, but Methusal had never fully realized how important until now. "I'm looking forward to the summer months for another reason," she said. "Fresh vegetables will be a nice change from grain and meat every day." The logne leaves were the first of the summer's leafy vegetables.

"I couldn't agree more. Seems we've been eating the same things for months."

Methusal silently agreed. Supplies of grain and meat were all well and good, but variety would be awfully nice, too.

She spent the next two hours counting supplies for Sims. She also swiftly learned the layout of the upstairs supply room. Sacks of regular grain and wildberries did seem low; especially since she knew how much grain was necessary to make breakfast for the entire community each day. Barely a two month supply remained.

After she'd handed Sims the parchment with her tallies of the food supplies, she said, "Do we have enough food to last until the new grain grows?"

"That, my girl, is the question." Sims slowly lowered himself onto a stool. He scanned her parchment. "Combined with the supplies downstairs, this should be enough, but just. I'll be glad when the first crops come in."

"Why is the grain so low? Is that normal for this time of year?"

"No. Last year the aptes multiplied faster than we could count. They ate a quarter of our crop. This year should be better. The aptes, just like everyone else, are suffering. And the crop tenders have created new traps. Those wily beasts won't get the best of us this year."

Although Methusal would rather save animals than kill them, she knew saving the grain crop was the priority. "We'll get more fresh meat. Pelts, too."

"That we will." Sims glanced at the three large sacks resting against the far wall. "Barak will need the grain soon. Tomorrow you'll finish sorting the seeds."

"Fun." Methusal grinned.

Sims smiled, too. "Off with you, then. You're done for today. I'm sure you've got lots to do, with the Games taking place tomorrow."

Yes, she did. And first up—right after she grabbed a grain disc for lunch—was to set her risky plan into motion.

CHAPTER NINE

AFTER A QUICK LUNCH, Methusal headed for the Grand Staircase. The plan that had been fermenting in her head all morning now seemed rash. Her steps slowed. The Tri-Level Game was tomorrow. Maybe she shouldn't take unnecessary chances. If Petr found out, he'd expel her, for sure.

"Methusal." Kitran's grave voice halted her steps. The flickering, reddish-orange lights of the hall silhouetted his large frame. His face was cast in shadow. "I need to talk to you."

Had he spoken to Petr? Had Verdnt reported her poor behavior in class? Her stomach sank with dread.

Methusal followed Kitran into his office. He curtly motioned for her to sit, and she perched nervously on the edge of the wooden chair. Thankfully, he didn't leave her waiting.

"I talked to Verdnt. He said your attitude in class this morning was poor, bordering on insolent."

Uh oh. Her stomach gave a queasy lurch.

"But I didn't mean..."

"It doesn't matter what you meant, Methusal. You *know* how important discipline is in kaavl."

"Yes, I know. But..."

"Don't worry. I won't expel you from the Tri-Level Game for Petr's allegations, and I won't for this, either."

Hope leaped. "You won't?"

"*If* you listen to me now."

"Of course. I understand." Methusal sat back and waited for the inevitable lecture. But she felt relieved.

"Verdnt didn't intend to expel you from the Games, either. It's simply become clear to both of us that you don't understand the importance of discipline."

Methusal nodded. "I'm sorry."

Kitran continued, "I've learned a new kaavl secret, and I'll share it with you now. Discipline and self-control are vital building blocks to achieve the Bi-level, and ultimately the Primary level. Only those tools will hone your skills and take you beyond the ordinary. Kaavl becomes a part of your very being."

"What do you mean?"

He hesitated, clearly searching for the right words. "This might seem like a leap, but listen carefully. The intensity with which you experience kaavl is directly related to how you discipline your emotions. Emotions can either help you, or hinder you. They can help, if you channel their energy along productive paths. But they can hinder if you allow them to overwhelm you, and make you act according to how you feel."

"So...," she groped to understand. "I can't act how I feel?"

He sighed. "You must *use* your emotions, Methusal. Focus that energy to concentrate more fully into kaavl."

"So I should use the energy of my emotions?"

"Yes. Channel them. Make your emotions work for you."

"What about *feeling* my emotions, then?"

"I know this is hard to understand now, but you will. Feeling emotions is not important. *Use* your emotions. Don't let *them* control *you*."

"So feeling emotions distracts me from what is really important. Instead, I should ignore how I feel, and give all of my energy to kaavl?"

Kitran's expressionless gaze flickered. "That's crude, but pretty close. To advance past the Tri-level, you'll need to prove you're capable of that kind of discipline. Your behavior this morning is a symptom, telling me you need work in this area.

"If you use the principles I've just told you about, I see no reason why you can't step up to the Bi-level within two years. You're extremely gifted. To be honest, I'd hate to see you get off track."

"I understand." And she did understand—a little. To become a competitor at the Bi-level, she must use—or channel—her emotions, and ignore all of her feelings. This was the first time she had ever heard about this, and it disturbed her. She rose to her feet.

Kitran eyed her for a moment, and then joined her at the door. "I hope you do understand. Remember, to advance to the Bi-level, you must come in first or second at the Tri-level this year and next year. Plus put in a year of practice."

Methusal hesitated. "Have you talked to Petr? Has he agreed to let me participate?" Even though Petr could not officially expel her from the Game, he could prevent her from competing simply by confining her indoors, or by throwing her in jail.

"I'll speak to him now. I'll do whatever I can to convince him—provided you agree to concentrate and work hard."

"I will. Thank you, Kitran."

Methusal slipped into the hall. With Kitran firmly on her side, she hoped Petr might see reason for once. The rest of her conversation with Kitran disturbed her, however. It was the first time she'd heard about using the energy of her emotions to advance in kaavl. How was that even possible? And he'd said he had just learned the precept. But how? And from whom? He was the only Primary level contender in Rolban.

She struggled to push the new precepts to the back of her mind. That was a worry for another day. Right now she needed to practice hard so she could beat Behran tomorrow. ...*If* she was truly allowed to play.

Her adversary crossed her path when she reached the Grand Staircase. Behran lifted one eyebrow and snapped her a mocking salute before he disappeared into the dining hall.

With an eye roll, Methusal trotted down the staircase. How was she supposed to control *all* of her emotions? It was hard enough to control her small flashes of temper. The whole thing seemed ridiculously impossible.

Behran's flippant salute had only served to stoke her burning desire to beat him. What she really needed to do was run outside, and simultaneously practice kaavl at all distances.

Those combined skills were obviously impossible to perform inside.

Nearing the open gate, she gazed longingly at the brown, bush dotted plain, blanketed by a deep blue sky. Before community arrest, she'd never fully appreciated her freedom.

"Hey, Thusa." Timaeus straightened from where he'd been leaning against the gate.

"Guard duty, huh?"

"Until supper."

"What is your job, exactly?" She daringly stepped closer to the entrance. Freedom beckoned, mere steps away.

"Keep out invaders and wild animals. And keep the kids in."

Had Petr actually ordered the guards to confine her inside? Yesterday she hadn't tried to find out.

"Doesn't sound too difficult," she agreed. "Anything else?"

He smiled, but his brown eyes mirrored his regretful tone, "Petr ordered me to keep you inside, too."

"I see." Disappointment, along with her better sense, finally kicked in. Maybe her rash plan wasn't the best idea anyway. If she got caught, she could lose her only chance to play in the Game. Worse, Timaeus could get in trouble, too. She didn't want that. With regret, she let the crazy idea go and turned her attention to the investigation. "You guard the ore mine too, don't you?"

He didn't appear surprised by her question. "I heard about your adventure yesterday."

Uncomfortably, Methusal wondered who else knew. Kitran hadn't mentioned it. Maybe only the guards had discussed it. "It's a long story."

"Rumor says Renn found your necklace in the ore deposits."

She nodded. "I'm still not sure how it got there. I found out yesterday it's impossible to break into the ore room. That last guard is impossible to get by."

He smiled. "Pretty much."

Timaeus seemed to know a great deal. "So, how do *you* think my necklace ended up in the ore mine?"

He considered the question. "Must have been left there by a guard. Or someone with authorized access."

"I need to find out who."

"Can I help?"

Methusal was pleased that Timaeus wanted to help her. Finally, something was going right. "Maybe. Do you know who has access to the ore room? Could you give me a list?"

Timaeus eyed her for a moment. "It's privileged information. Promise not to tell anyone."

"I won't."

Timaeus ticked off names on his fingers. "Guards first. Well, there's Pogul and me. Renn was one, plus about six other men. We have limited access. All the senior members of the Council have access, too. That includes Petr, your father, Kitran, Barak, Verdnt, old Sims, and a quite a few others. Plus Motr, Behran, and Goric, who engineer the water systems. Do you have a piece of paper? I could write them down."

Methusal fished a parchment from her pocket. It was the parchment on which Kitran had written kaavl instructions yesterday. Timaeus produced a bit of charcoal and scribbled names.

When he finished, she said, "That helps, thank you. But it's still quite a few people." There were over thirty in all. How could she narrow down that list to find the murderer?

"Yes." With a sympathetic glance, he handed her the list, which she pocketed again.

"Have you seen anything unusual at the mine lately? Anyone visiting more often than normal?"

Timaeus shook his head. "Most people go in about once a month. Nobody more than once a week."

"What do they do in there?"

He shrugged. "Old Sims inventories the ore. So does Barak. That's how they discovered ore was missing. The council members go because they check on each other. No one is trusted. It's pretty serious stuff."

"Thank you, Timaeus. I appreciate your help. " Unfortunately, the authorized access list was dauntingly long. Any one of them could have dropped her necklace inside. Even Behran. That thought made her snicker a little. She couldn't imagine Behran being so underhanded. If he wanted to trouble her, he'd do it face-to-face. In addition, she couldn't imagine him murdering Renn. And her father couldn't be guilty, either.

Frankly, she couldn't imagine anyone she knew murdering Renn. Except for maybe Pogul. However, in her opinion he wasn't smart enough to carry out a systematic plan of thefts, let alone kill anyone; although he *had* stolen the chalk from Verdnt yesterday morning. Pogul was definitely a troublemaker. He could be involved in the thefts. But he certainly wasn't the mastermind of the whole convoluted plot.

Methusal tried to remember the last question she wanted to ask Timaeus. "Oh...here's a strange question. When you've carried messages to other communities, have you noticed anything usual? Like fires that smell strange?"

"Strange...how?"

"I don't know. Like burning ore?"

His dark brows drew together. "You think someone is stealing ore, and using it to make weapons?"

"I don't know. Why else steal ore?"

"Good question. But no, I haven't seen or smelled anything strange lately."

"That's good, I guess." Although fires could be burned in areas where messengers never went, for example. "Thanks again for your help Timaeus."

"No problem."

With a sigh, Methusal cast a final, longing glance out at the plains. "I've always taken my freedom for granted. Now I'd give anything to practice outside."

"I'm sorry, Thusa."

"It's not your fault."

He hesitated. "I can't let you out. But if I don't *see* you go...."

Much as that had been her rash original plan, she shook her head. "No. I don't want you to get in trouble. Thanks, though, Timaeus."

"Will you practice on the chairs, then?"

"I guess so."

Methusal retreated to the recliner closest to the gate and sat down. Her spirit felt heavy. Timaeus had helped a lot by providing the mine access list. But how could she narrow it down?

And the Tri-level match—how could she ever win if she couldn't fully practice kaavl? After all, Behran had captured her in the ore deposit hall yesterday. And he'd successfully snuck up on her the other day, when she'd rescued that apte. Kitran was right. She did need to work on discipline and concentration. Would she lose to Behran, after all?

Stop it. She drew a steadying breath. Falling apart would solve nothing.

Methusal again pulled from her pocket the list of exercises that Kitran had given her. Before unfolding it, however, she concentrated and became aware of everything around her. Objects, people...

She sensed no one nearby. Surprised, she glanced left and right.

Timaeus was gone.

She glanced back at the Grand Staircase. No Timaeus. No one else was in sight, either. Had he left on purpose so she could escape outside?

Excitement made her heart pump faster. Should she take the opportunity Timaeus had just given her?

Chapter Ten

THE TEMPTATION TO RUN outside and practice kaavl nearly overwhelmed Methusal's better sense. She wanted so badly to beat Behran. One final practice outdoors might make all the difference in winning the Game.

She hesitated, and thought fast. Could she do it without being found out? One risk was being spotted by the crop tenders. Could she escape the notice of Barak and the others on the crop plateau? She listened hard, but only heard three men digging near the Rolban River, near the intersection of the crop plateau and the cliff. Even if others were near the bluff's edge, she might escape notice if she ran out on the plain and darted from bush to thick tagma bush to the kaavl plateau. The tallest of the bushes stretched one length high— a little taller than a large man.

Timaeus would be on duty for three more hours. She could practice for two hours, and be back before anyone was the wiser.

Finally, the cool voice of reason spoke. What if Petr found out? Or Kitran? She was already walking the fine line of expulsion from the Games.

But if she couldn't practice fully, why play the Tri-Level Game at all? Clearly, she needed more practice. Behran had already proven twice that he could beat her.

The desire to go out overwhelmed her, and she closed her mind to the voice of reason. Mind made up, she glanced once more into the Great Hall and then darted into the bright sunshine. No one stopped her. The sun felt warm and delicious on her face, and she ran like the wind to the first tagma bush and ducked behind it.

No shouts. No cries of alarm.

She glanced back at the entrance, and also at the plateau above it where Barak and his helpers worked. No one was in sight. Now was her chance. She sprinted from bush to bush until she reached the far plateau, and then slipped to the far, southern side.

Still, silence reigned. No one blew the warning horn. She had escaped!

Methusal sprinted to the short distance to the top of the narrow, lonely plateau. It was a hill with the top chopped off, plunked down in the middle of the plain. It was also the starting plateau for the Kaavl Games, and her personal, favorite place to practice kaavl.

Cool wind caressed her cheek as she took the final steps to the top. Not another soul was in sight, and a scraggly bush hid her from view from Rolban. Sprigs of hearty vegetation spread their thin, pointed leaves toward the sky, drinking in the sun's warm rays.

Her worn moccasins pressed lightly into the tan, gritty soil. A new hole was forming in one. She'd mended both moccasins so often that the soles now consisted of overlapping, worn patches. Soon she'd need a new pair, but hopefully these would last for a good while longer, since skins were in short supply, thanks to the thefts.

She crossed to the eastern side of the plateau and glanced down the steep, rocky face. Tomorrow the Kaavl Games would start—right here.

Her gaze lifted and swept across the network of tough, scraggly bushes that dotted the plain until it collided with the black bluffs to the east, which were a good twenty minutes away running time. This was the playing field, and within it rested her future.

She sat cross-legged on the uneven earth and made sure the scraggly plant hid her from the view of the Rolbani crop tenders. She opened the parchment Kitran had given her yesterday. He'd written two instructions. The first was: "Heighten sensory awareness." The key senses of kaavl were vision and hearing.

The second instruction read: "Heighten awareness of others in relation to yourself." "Others" referred not only to people, but to any tangible object. Awareness also included the ability to measure distances between herself and another object.

Methusal concentrated and gazed across the plain. Below, about ten lengths away, squatted a small apte beast. Its fur was short and dusty brown in color, and easily blended into its surroundings. Its arms and legs were mere stubs—barely longer than her little finger—and tiny striped ears bristled from its round, furry head.

It was time to practice her newest kaavl skill.

Concentrating still harder, Methusal *carried*—mentally calculated the distance to the apte, and then projected her hearing and fanned out in an area surrounding the apte. It was almost as if she stood in the very place the apte crouched, and heard everything the apte heard. She could not carry with vision, so she concentrated, hoping to break through on that front as well. Few people over the centuries had ever been able to carry with one—let alone both. Only the Old Kaavl Master, Mahre, had accomplished this.

Rustlings in the stubbly, straw-like vegetation to the east caught her attention, and her eyes strained to see what her ears recognized as coming. It was a low, fast wriggling whip beast.

The apte saw the whip beast the same instant Methusal did, and hopped rapidly, as if its short legs were made of springs, into a nearby bush and disappeared neatly from sight.

Silence.

The long, thick whip beast couldn't tell where the apte had gone, and neither could Methusal. A victim of a short attention span, the whip writhed away to search for fresh prey.

But where was the apte?

Suddenly she saw it, and Methusal almost lost her concentration by laughing out loud. The round little beast was perched high in the bush. Now, how had it climbed up there? Maybe it had hopped up and become stuck? No. Even as she watched, the small creature dropped to the desert floor and rapidly hopped away—in the opposite direction from the whip beast.

The sun sank lower in the sky as Methusal practiced. She also concentrated on the less important senses—smell and touch. Already her nose could discern smells and pinpoint their origin by taking into consideration three things: the direction and strength of the breeze, coupled with the intensity of the fragrance. That required a lot of concentration, however.

The sun hovered a finger's width above the far, western mountains when she finally felt ready for the last step of today's practice. Only an hour of daylight remained. She'd need to make the most of each minute. Right now she needed to exercise her body and four senses to the fullest, so she could win the upcoming game. And she'd practice close and long-range kaavl awareness at the same time.

Methusal scrambled lightly down the rocky hillside, concentrating fully on each footstep and becoming sharply aware of the placement and texture of each surface she trod. At the same time, she fanned out her hearing range, trying to capture sounds near and far simultaneously, and to determine their distances from her, too.

The moment her foot touched the plain, she began to run, breathing lightly, moving effortlessly, toward the distant bluffs. Tuning each of her senses keenly into her environment, she felt sharply aware of each twig or stone she stepped on, and the placement of every bush, rock and small boulder she approached and passed. Her ears strained, catching the movement of an apte beast sixty lengths away, and then hearing the whistle of the wind sighing through a cluster of bushes twenty lengths to her right. She worked hard at trying to assimilate stimuli from three different locations at once.

It strained her concentration to the limit, to constantly receive and decipher simultaneous sources of input. Capturing three different sources at once only happened twice on her run to the bluffs, and she felt pleased with that. As hard as she tried, though, she knew there were still a lot of things she missed. But she felt confident that she'd detected the most important details.

She approached the base of the far cliffs. The sound of rushing water filled her ears now. The Rolban River. Really, at this point, it was little more than a stream, because it was only a length across right here. High on the crop plateau, it watered Rolban's crops, and provided all the water for Rolban's needs. It began as a rushing waterfall high in the Rolban Mountains, and gathered into a deep blue lake a half day's hike from Rolban. The river flowed from the lake, following the contours of the Rolban Mountains until it flowed down next to the crop plateau, and then cascaded in a waterfall downhill, and then rushed out into this stream that followed the bluffs south.

Methusal scanned the stepping stones across the stream. Dry and safe. The water level was lower now than she'd ever seen it before. Hopefully next winter would bring more rain. She sprinted across, and then stopped and gazed up the cliff face. She took note of the dark shadow in the bluff above. It might provide her with the winning edge in the kaavl game. It was a cave—a unique one—and hopefully an advantage Behran knew nothing about. She retraced her steps and headed back. Her breathing was still even, steady, and silent—the result of long years of regular running. Panting would give away her position to her competitors in the Tri-Level Game.

Reaching the plateau again, Methusal glanced at the descending sun. Her best time yet. Soon it would be time to return home.

Her sharpened kaavl senses suddenly detected the "whoosh" of flying beast wings, and she turned north. Her heart accelerated. The dark flying beast was flying straight for her!

She stiffened. Flying beasts avoided humans...so why would this one attack her? It banked, and circled in low, lazy spirals over her head.

Could it be? With a smile, Methusal pursed her lips and emitted three high, sharp chirps

The flying beast continued to circle, but it flew lower now. Methusal drew in a breath to whistle again.

Three sharp chirps sounded from behind her. Startled, she spun. A tall, blond-haired giant of a man had gained her plateau, and now strode toward her. Uneasiness jolted through her. She carried no weapon. He was stranger—a rarity in Rolban—and he carried himself with sure confidence.

Either her concentration had slipped just now, or the man was very, very good at kaavl. Her unease deepened as he neared. Swiftly, she scanned the newcomer.

The man looked to be almost thirty, and he thankfully stopped two lengths away. He was powerfully built, with lean, sleek muscles, and he wore bleached leather clothing. The wind kicked up the edges of his short, white-blond hair, and his high, wide cheekbones emphasized the angular planes of his face. He was good looking, if one liked harsh, unusual features. His nose was straight, with a small hump in the upper quarter. Perhaps once broken and never properly reset. He exuded an overwhelming sense of power and purpose—far more than any man she'd ever met before.

His eyes...Methusal's appraisal stopped short, and for a second she froze.

She'd never seen such a pale blue before. They were the freezing, pale blue of a glacier. A shivered started, deep in her soul. A warning. She wasn't empathic like her mother and sister, but something told her this man would be a danger to her.

She struggled to ignore the illogical feeling. The stranger's face gave no clue to his thoughts. His disturbing eyes assessed her; as though she were being sized up, and perhaps assigned a threat level.

A rush of wings, low and close behind her, broke into her unsettled thoughts. The blue-black flying beast glided in and settled on the stranger's shoulder. Its bright eyes darted, and its feet shuffled, as if realizing it had come to the wrong person.

Feeling protective, Methusal chirped twice, sharp and fast. At once, the beast opened its wings wide—an impressive length from wing tip to wing tip—and swooped to Methusal's offered forearm. Sharp claws pierced her leather tunic. The beast felt heavy on her arm.

"A pet?" A harsh note grated through the stranger's words.

Was he sneering at her? Methusal couldn't tell. She couldn't read the stranger at all, and it made her feel uneasy.

"Beasts are happier free." She examined the wing with light, delicate fingers. The last chips of clay had worn off, and the wing appeared strong.

"It was injured." Strange, how he didn't ask it as a question. As if he was supremely confident in his powers of observation and deduction.

"Yes," she admitted. "But it's fine now." She stroked the beast's smooth, glossy head. It stared at her with unblinking black eyes, and lifted its beak to the wind.

"I found one as a boy." The stranger spoke in a curious, grating voice that smoothed out as he talked. "Its leg was broken."

"Did you help it?"

His light eyes narrowed, as if displeased by her question. "As much as I could. It was killed soon after."

"I'm sorry."

"It is the way of nature, for the weak to fall prey to the strong."

"But those with the greatest strength will show mercy," she returned.

"So you know the writings of the great Kaavl Master."

"Mahre came from Rolban. We know all of his ways. At least, all we can from his writings that remain." She didn't mention that she was his descendant.

He smiled, but it didn't reach his chilly blue eyes. "You refer to the elusive *Second Book of Kaavl.* Rolban, then, has not found it?"

"How could we? The Dehriens took it during the Great War."

"Ah, yes. My ancestors."

Methusal's curiosity sharpened, and so did her hearing, because she heard footsteps climbing the plateau now. "You're a Dehrien?"

His small smile seemed to mock her ignorance. "I am Mentàll Solboshn, Chief of Dehre."

She swallowed in surprise. "I see." Methusal took note of his small entourage of three that had just crested the plateau. "Then you'll want to see my uncle, Petr Storst."

"Yes." A small pause elapsed. "Doubtless I will see you again."

"Doubtless."

The pale eyes cooled to ice. Shadows cast by the swiftly setting sun cut his angular face into predatory planes, and Methusal felt another frisson of fear. Who was this Dehrien Chief? He'd been polite, but only just. Perhaps her parents were right not to trust the Dehriens. Maybe she'd be wise to give him wide berth. She watched him stride down the hill, in the direction of Rolban.

The sun was setting. Only a few minutes remained to practice kaavl. The Dehrien Chief might tell Petr that he'd seen her on the plateau. Although he didn't know her name, a description would provide Petr with her identity.

She'd better make the most of her opportunity to practice. She glanced at the sun. Thirty minutes remained before Timaeus left guard duty. If, by some chance she still had a hope of returning undetected, she should return within fifteen minutes.

△ △ △ △ △

The time passed all too quickly, and soon Methusal turned for the gates of Rolban. Hopefully no one had noticed her absence.

Unfortunately, the instant she arrived at the heavy gates, Pogul dashed out and grabbed her arm. Red flushed his florid face, and cruel glee danced in his black eyes.

"I saw you go outside. And guess what? Timaeus is in detention."

Methusal felt awful. Great. This was all her fault. She'd never wanted her friend to suffer.

"I made sure Petr knows." He licked his lips and grinned. "I'm supposed to personally deliver you to him."

Methusal twisted her arm free. "I'll see Petr on my own."

Pogul grabbed her elbow again. His fingers hurt. "I'm in charge. March."

Struggling to control her simmering temper, Methusal walked fast, leading the way. Pogul jerked on her arm. "Slow up," he huffed.

"Got to be prompt. Petr doesn't like laggards."

Pogul scowled.

Unfortunately, the fast pace meant they arrived at Petr's office all too soon. Maybe that hadn't been her smartest move.

Pogul knocked on Petr's office door and thrust her inside. "Methusal Maahr, sir."

Petr stood, and so did Mentàll Solboshn, the Dehrien Chief. Apparently, their arrival had interrupted a chiefly conversation.

"Thank you, Pogul. That will be all."

Pogul gave Methusal another baleful glare before he disappeared through the door.

"So, Methusal. You disobeyed me. Can't say I'm surprised."

Methusal remained silent, but met her uncle's gaze without flinching.

"No excuse?"

"What's the point? You accused me unfairly. Justice isn't your goal. If it was, I wouldn't need to explain."

Red boiled up her uncle's face and clashed with his white hairline. Apprehension licked through her. Although she knew he wouldn't harm her, she did regret her disrespectful words. When would she ever learn to control her mouth? She had to stop saying what she thought! Even if Petr was wrong, getting on his bad side was simply foolish.

"You are an impertinent girl." Petr turned to his guest. "If you will excuse me for a moment."

The Dehrien inclined his head, and Methusal followed her uncle through a doorway draped by a blue leather curtain. The thin door afforded little privacy, and she wondered why they'd left the room at all. Surely the Dehrien Chief would hear everything they said.

"You've gone too far, Methusal."

"I'm sorry. I needed to go outside to pract..."

"That is no *excuse!*" Petr roared.

Methusal bit her lip, and anger sparked again. "You've accused me without proof. It's unlawful for you to confine me inside."

"I will confine you, Methusal—to a jail cell!"

She gasped. "But I've done nothing wrong!"

"You've disobeyed the orders of the Chief of Rolban."

"You're my uncle. How can you punish me if there's no proof against me?"

"It's my job to uphold the law in this community. Just like your father did before me." He waved his finger under her nose. "And don't think you'll go crying to him for help."

"Someone will come."

"Kitran won't help you, either. I don't care how much he wants you in those Kaavl Games. Women have no place in them."

"In your opinion. Many women of the past have been great kaavl players."

"Kaavl is a weapon of war. War is not for women."

"So that's why you won't let Aali play. Even when it's what she wants most."

Petr's white brow lowered. "Don't speak to me about Aali. We're talking about you."

"Kitran won't expel me from the games." Methusal knew no such thing. "He'll help me."

Petr laughed. "Really? Do you think so? He just spoke to me about you. His argument that you're the best, and fastest advancing kaavl player he's ever seen means nothing to me. Do you hear? You are a brazen, disobedient young woman. Erl should have disciplined you when you were young. Now it's my job. You're going to jail!"

"Jail!" Methusal couldn't believe it. Her close-minded, stubborn uncle had taken a leap off the bluff of reason. "But I haven't been formally charged with a crime!"

"You have now. Come on." He grabbed her elbow and propelled her out of a wooden door and into a narrow hallway. Pushing her ahead of him, he forced her down the steps and into the jail ward. There he took a giant key off the wall, unlocked a cell, and thrust her inside. The solid door, flanked by floor to ceiling bars, clanged shut.

"My parents will worry if I don't come for dinner."

"Don't concern yourself. I'll tell them." Petr disappeared through the ward door and slammed it behind him.

Methusal sat down on the hard, narrow cot, which was the only furnishing in the cell. No other soul occupied the jail. She was alone. Unexpected tears slipped down her cheeks. It was so unfair. Yes, she'd disobeyed, but she'd broken no law. She was accused of a crime she hadn't committed, and now she was being punished for it.

For a long time, Methusal sat silently, wiping her cheeks. And what about Timaeus? What punishment would he face? Would his guard job be stripped away? It was a prestigious assignment. She felt sick that her actions hurt him, too. Why hadn't she listened to reason? And what would Kitran say? Would he expel her from the Game now?

Of course he would. Hadn't her actions proven yet again her complete lack of discipline and obedience? He'd warned her, and she hadn't listened. And now apparently she'd been formally charged with a crime. The threat of conviction—of execution—suddenly seemed more real and imminent. It scared her. She had been stupid. Focusing on clearing her name should have been her priority the entire time. Yes, she wanted to win the kaavl game. But her *life* was at stake here. What had she been thinking? She wiped away more hot tears.

Long minutes—perhaps hours—passed. The torch on the wall outside her cell gave off the only light, so she had no idea what time it was. Her stomach rumbled, though. Would someone bring her food? Would Petr tell anyone where she was? Would anyone come to visit her?

An eternity of minutes ticked by. She walked the perimeter of the cell, restless with misery.

How would a jury of Rolbanis judge her behavior? Not respectful of the Chief, certainly. Perhaps not respectful of the law at all. Maybe even a murderer...

Methusal sat and buried her head in her hands. "Oh, God," she whispered. "I'm sorry. Help me to do better."

Was The One listening? Was he real? She didn't know, even though she'd been taught to believe it. After her brief prayer, she felt a little better. A little calmer.

If she ever got out of here, she'd apologize to Petr, as hard as that would be.

Finally, she was honest with herself. She had no chance, after five years of hard work, to challenge Behran at the Tri-level. And it was all her own fault.

More time crawled by, and she wiped her cheeks dry. She felt subdued and a little older now. Priorities finally became clear. Somehow, she'd get out. Without freedom, she had nothing.

And she'd enlist help. She couldn't find the murderer by herself. Methusal felt better, having made these decisions.

She waited and waited. Her stomach rumbled every few minutes, and she began to fantasize about juicy meat and crisp vegetables. It felt like it was the middle of the night, but it was likely only late evening. Would anyone bring her food? Or was this part of her punishment?

She slipped into kaavl and focused on the hall outside the jail ward. Nothing...wait.

Faint footsteps.

She scrubbed the salty tear trails from her cheeks. She'd love to see anyone. Even Petr. Maybe especially Petr.

The metal ward door creaked open, and Methusal stared. This was last person she'd expected to see.

CHAPTER ELEVEN

"Methusal Maahr." Mentàll Solboshn shut the door behind his powerful frame.

Apprehension curled in the pit of her stomach. "Why are you here?"

"Curiosity."

"About me? Or our jail ward?"

Although a faint smile curved his lips, his gaze remained steady and calculating. "You are the best kaavl player in Rolban."

"No. Just the fastest to advance."

He inclined his head, as if waiting for her to elaborate.

"I reached the Tri-level in five years.'"

"Impressive." He scanned the jail cell. "And why are you here?"

"Petr thinks I pushed someone off a cliff." If she had wanted to startle the Dehrien, or crack his expressionless mask, she failed.

"Did you?"

"No! Of course not. I'd never kill anyone. Or steal..."

"Steal?" Swift as a whip beast, he pounced.

Methusal shut her mouth. The Dehrien didn't need to learn about Rolban's thefts. "Why are you talking to me? How could I possibly be of interest to a Dehrien Chief?"

"Kaavl is a passion of mine, as well."

If Kitran was in awe of him, then the Dehrien's kaavl abilities must be remarkable.

He slowly paced closer. The jail ward somehow seemed very small with him in it.

Subtle threat exuded from him and Methusal tensed. "I have nothing to say to you."

"You don't trust me."

"No."

"Because I am a Dehrien." He now was only three hand-breadths from the bars, but she refused to step back.

"Dehriens have been our enemies for over two hundred years."

He gave a thin smile. "No longer, Methusal."

She didn't like the sound of her name on his tongue. "Because of the Alliance? Is it signed already?"

"I will present it to Rolban in the morning."

"You think it will pass."

"It is in your best interest."

"And yours." Unexpected insight flashed. "The Alliance is a trap, isn't it?"

Those pale eyes froze to ice, and the friendly façade disappeared. She saw the predator again, and a flicker of barely bridled fury...and hatred.

She took an involuntary step backward, suddenly glad of the bars between them. "You won't win. I'll stop you."

His eyes glittered. "We will see how brave you are, Methusal. I am not a man you will easily cross."

He left as silently as he had come, but the clang of the door reverberated behind him.

Methusal felt shaken. Her words had been brave, but foolish. Again, her mouth had outrun her better sense.

She had just made an enemy. And, she suspected, a powerful one.

CHAPTER TWELVE

DEHRE
Thirdday

HENDRA SLIPPED OUTSIDE into the bright morning sunshine. Her spirits lifted, although she knew today the well water and the food supplies would be more meager than ever. A week ago, men had begun to carry barrels of water from the diverted Tarst River.

On mornings like this, anything seemed possible...especially today, for Mentàll was in Rolban. Perhaps the Alliance would be signed. Maybe they would not starve to death this summer.

Hendra breathed in great gulps of the fresh, cool air. The Rolbanis and Tarst just had to sign the Alliance. Then her community would only need to pray for rain to replenish their water supplies, and for new seed to plant crops.

Hendra glanced at her cousin's huge tent. The bleached leather rippled in the breeze. Since Mentàll was gone, today was her opportunity to investigate the fires in the hills.

Quickly, she formulated a plan. Her journey would be noticed, and most likely reported to Mentàll when he returned. So she had to make the journey look innocent. Perhaps she could take the orphaned children for a walk into the low hills, to the stream diverted from the Tarst River. They could carry buckets of water back to the orphanage, and find fresh tagma berries, as well.

Hendra was about to hurry to the orphanage when she remembered that another child had been admitted yesterday. She ducked back inside her tent and picked up the folded leaf she'd prepared, which was filled with food. The child's mother had died yesterday of fever. Her body had been too weak and undernourished to fight.

Depression touched Hendra's spirit, thinking of the little boy with the sad brown eyes. She tucked the leaf, filled with half of her own breakfast ration, into her pocket. How he must have suffered, watching his mother die. Fear and grief were emotions too hard for a child to bear alone. As Hendra imagined the misery the child must be feeling, pain ripped through her own soul.

And then the curse...or the blessing...of her life intruded again.

Like water down a drain hole, all of the painful emotions swirled away. Coldness swelled, filling the void.

"No," she whispered. Not today.

Why hadn't it come when Jascr had attacked her on Firstday? Why now, when she only wanted to feel empathy for someone?

Hendra bit her lip as the unstoppable coldness grew, killing every emotion. Sorrow, pain...every feeling inside her froze into nothingness. The joy of the morning shattered into broken, dead pieces. Every human emotion vanished. Only numbness remained.

In some far recess of her mind, terror ghosted through her, as it always did.

Logically, Hendra understood why the ice took over her soul. When she was younger, it had been the only way she could cope with her violent home life. But now, even though she lived in safety, the coldness still attacked her. It would not stop. She feared it never would.

Today, like so many others before it, she'd try to ignore it. It was the only way. She'd learned that if she acted like she cared, the children never knew the difference.

But inside, she knew something was terribly wrong with her. So many days she lived either terrorized by fear, or frozen emotionally. She hated both. Of course, sometimes—especially with the children—she did feel love and compassion. It was one of the reasons why she worked with them. Their smiles, and her own deliberate acts of kindness helped to melt the ice again.

If she witnessed too much misery at the orphanage, however, then the lurking coldness would creep back through her soul and protect her heart. Sometimes it only lasted a morning, and sometimes for days.

Hendra pushed aside her tent flap door. She would work with the children now. They needed her care, whether she felt loving and compassionate or not.

"Hendra." She tensed. Jascr stood a short distance away, just outside Mentàll's tent door.

The coldness was welcome now. It deadened her fear.

Ignoring her brother, she headed for the orphanage. Jascr deserved no courtesy. He was vile. And evidently he didn't know their cousin hadn't returned home yet. She wouldn't enlighten him, that much was for sure.

But why did Jascr want to speak to Mentàll? The two men hated each other. ...Unless Jascr meant to talk to him about Wortn's proposal. Dread slithered through her. Never. She'd never allow it. She would run away first. Or die trying.

Quick footsteps followed her. Tensing, she whirled and side-stepped seconds before Jascr grabbed for her arm. With cold satisfaction, she watched his hand claw empty air.

He staggered, and bared his teeth in a snarl. "You've won a reprieve, little sister. Know this: When your cousin returns, your life of ease will end."

Hendra stared at him without blinking, her features blank and expressionless. It was one of the few times when she was thankful that she felt nothing but cold emptiness.

He sneered, "Afraid to speak?"

Hendra did not respond, although unexpected light prickles of fear ran up her scalp. Refusing to let him sense it, she continued her frozen stare. "Are you finished? May I leave now?"

A smirk twisted his lips. He spat into the dirt. "Run while you can ..." A degrading name rolled off his tongue, and despite herself, Hendra recoiled. "Soon you'll be under my authority. And then Wortn's." With a hissing chuckle, he left her.

Fine shivers slid down her spine as she hurried for the orphanage. Jascr would speak to Mentàll when he returned. She couldn't stop that. But Mentàll hated her brother as much as she did—well, almost as much. Her cousin would not listen to Jascr.

Surely he wouldn't.

She had to find out what Mentàll was hiding in the hills. Time to suggest a long walk to the older orphanage children.

Chapter Thirteen

ROLBAN

ALL NIGHT LONG Methusal suffered through vivid nightmares. Crazy ones. She ran for her life across the hot, dry plains with Mentàll in hot pursuit. He gained on her, inch by inch, using extraordinary kaavl skills to hunt her down.

Fear leant wings to her feet. Suddenly she was trapped at the base of a sheer, black bluff.

The Dehrien Chief advanced on her. A tiny, pleased smile curled his lips.

"Peace, Methusal."

She pressed back against the smooth black rock. "Never," she spat. "You don't fool me. I will never trust you."

His smile edged higher. "Come walk a day in my moccasins."

Arms crossed, she huddled against the cold, unforgiving stone. He was too close. Too dangerous. Too powerful. Too...knowing. But what did he know? "Leave me alone."

His harsh chuckle shredded the silence of the plain. Dark clouds had gathered overhead, and she hadn't even noticed. An omen? Rain?

"You will never escape me, Methusal."

Terror whispered through her mind. Her throat felt parched. Rain. It would provide sweet relief. She gazed skyward and whispered, "Please."

A lightning bolt flashed, and rain poured down. Water cascaded down her face, soaking her skin, permeating her clothes. Mentàll's large body became indistinct, blurred by the downpour from heaven. Now was her chance!

She sidled left and ran, as fast as she could. Maybe she could escape him. Maybe she could make it home. The cleansing rain splattered down. Her thoughts and her mind washed crystal clear. Clearer than ever before in her life.

A voice from on high whispered, "Follow me."

Was it The One? Methusal had never tried to talk to The One before, but now it seemed perfectly natural. Obvious, even, and easy. "How?"

"I will show you when the time is right. Do not turn away."

"I won't." It seemed perfectly obvious that she would not. Why would she? "When?"

"It is for a future time. Do not forget. And do not be afraid."

And then the clarity in her mind faded, and all she saw again was the rain, mixed with blurred images. The blurred images were people, she realized in horror. Locked in mortal combat. Hundreds of them. Perhaps a thousand. They fought, and surged closer to her. She ran faster, but the cries of the wounded filled her ears, amplified by the thunder of the storm.

Terror choked her. She could not escape from them.

And yet they didn't seem to know she was there. Ahead, a sliver of light broke through, and she ran for it.

And then she heard Mentàll's harsh, mocking laugh again. "Accept your fate, Methusal."

"Never!" she gasped. Where was he? In front of her? Behind?

The bright spot widened. She was almost there!

"Accept."

"Never," she shouted over her shoulder. But she'd taken her eye off of the light, and when she looked forward again, it was gone. Nothing but gray, pouring rain. "No," she screamed.

She sensed him gaining on her. Ahead, the rain streamed down in long, silver strands. They looked like the silvery bars of a jail cell.

"No," she gasped again. Hairs prickled up on the back of her neck. "No!" She sprinted for the gray bars. Surely beyond them lay relief. Surely beyond them lived the light, and warm, safe sunshine.

"You will never escape, Methusal," hissed the Dehrien.

Thunder clapped overhead.

Gasping, and with tears running with the rain in rivulets down her face, she cried out, "Help! Help me!"

"Listen," whispered from on high.

She felt her enemy's presence close behind her. He was about to touch her shoulder.

"Accept."

"No!" she screamed again. With a final burst of speed, she slammed into the gray bars. It was over. This was the end. There was no way to go forward. And the past was about to catch her...

"No," she moaned aloud, and crumpled to her knees. With arms clutched protectively over her head, she pressed her forehead against the cold bars, praying for release. For an escape from the fate she had chosen for herself.

Methusal woke up gasping and clutching the cold metal bars of the jail cell. As in her dream, she knelt on the ground, forehead pressed against the cool bars. But only the cold sweat of terror chilled her skin. Her breath came in sharp pants, and a deep shiver worked through her soul.

"It was only a dream," she choked out. "A *dream*."

A nightmare unlike any before. And so real.

She'd slept-walked again.

Shaking, Methusal staggered to her feet and crumpled onto her cot.

She thought she'd outgrown sleepwalking. The last time had been when she was twelve. It had happened after she'd been locked outside Rolban's gates. She'd almost been locked out all night with the wild beasts. The terror of those moments, when she had screamed for someone to let her in—it had scrambled her dreams that night. She had felt gripped with savage, gut deep fear. Just like she'd felt tonight, locked up in jail. And the visit from the disturbing Dehrien Chief—he had played a far too prominent role in her dream.

He was a danger to her. Methusal felt this more clearly than ever before. What was his true purpose in Rolban?

The other voice from the dream whispered into her thoughts, too. *"Follow me."* The One? She'd never dreamed about God before. More perplexing, the past and the future had somehow melded into one in her dream—at least, it had seemed that way. And the outcome was disastrous if she chose the wrong path.

Methusal curled up in a ball on the cot, heart thumping hard against her ribs. Never had a dream upset her so deeply. And never had one seemed more real.

△ △ △ △ △

After many long hours, Methusal finally drifted into an exhausted doze. She awoke feeling stiff, cold, and hungry. Her tablet necklace had poked a sore spot into her jaw. Compared to her dream, that discomfort felt welcome.

This morning, with a clearer mind, her nightmare seemed absurd, and the prickles of terror irrational.

But the dream had been a warning.

How did she know this, deep in her bones?

Methusal sat up and struggled to close her mind to the nightmare. She'd spent far too many hours thinking about it already.

She yawned, hoping to clear her head still more. With sudden disbelief, she realized that Petr had left her in the cell all night. Would he come now? Or would he leave her here all day without food?

Her stomach felt hollow and empty, and she longed for a cup of water. Why hadn't her father come? Would *someone* come for her? And today were the Kaavl Games. Truthfully, they were the least of her concerns right now. Funny how facing a jail sentence changed her priorities.

The door handle to the jail ward rattled and Petr stepped in. He was alone. The big, white-haired man shut the door. "Well. How do you feel this morning?"

His judgmental tone scraped on her raw nerves. Methusal stood. "How do you think?"

"Hopefully wiser."

The words she'd rehearsed last night caught in her throat. Angry ones wanted to fly out, but she bit them back.

"Nothing to say? Shall I leave?" He turned to go.

"No. Wait."

He turned back. His heavy white brows bristled together.

"I'm sorry. I shouldn't have gone out. I was wrong to do it." She bit her lip.

"Do your really believe that?"

"Yes. I was angry, and I felt desperate because I wanted so much to beat Behran in the Kaavl Games." Her throat closed for an aching second. "I've been practicing for five years."

"Anything else?"

"Please don't punish Timaeus."

"Did he leave his post?"

Methusal wouldn't lie, but she didn't want Timaeus to get in trouble, either. "One minute he was inside the gate, and the next he wasn't. I don't know where he went. The point is, it's my fault. I took advantage and slipped out."

"Mmhm." He sounded skeptical.

"It is."

"I agree." He paced the outer room. "You are solely responsible for your actions."

"I know. And I'm sorry."

He returned to stand in front of her again. "Are you really? Will you obey my instructions from now on?"

"Yes." It was hard to say it, but she did mean it. After an endless night to think it over, she had at last realized she must follow the right path if she ever wanted to get her life back in order.

"You must to learn to listen, Methusal." He inserted the key into the lock.

Listen. The word resonated from her dream. The One had said she must listen, too. Had he meant now, or later, in the future...when a war happened?

Disturbed, she tried to dismiss the thought. It was only a dream. Right?

She blinked when the barred door swung wide. "You're letting me out?"

"You needed to learn respect. And humility. I hope it's a lesson you won't forget."

"I thought you'd formally charged me with a crime last night."

"I was angry. Evidence is still not strong enough. Not yet."

Relief overwhelmed her as she slipped out of the jail cell. She *had* learned more respect for her uncle, she realized. Her behavior had been atrocious. It didn't matter how wrong Petr was; she had to respect his authority. Kaavl demanded it. So did common decency.

"May I go to breakfast now?"

"Your parents are waiting for you."

"Thank you." She meant for letting her out, and he knew it.

He nodded. "You'll find your father is far from pleased with me."

She smiled. So, she hadn't been forgotten after all. Petr had been the dragon keeping her rescuers away. Maybe she had deserved a night in jail. It had certainly helped to readjust her priorities. She headed up the stairs.

"Methusal."

She glanced back at her uncle.

"Today are the Kaavl Games."

"I know. I understand I can't play."

Petr Storst regarded her for a long moment. "Erl thinks I've been too hard on you. I can see you've learned your lesson. Do you promise no more disobedience?"

"Yes."

"Then I give you permission to go outside. For today only."

Her mouth dropped open. "Really?" she screeched. "Thank you!" She flew at her uncle and hugged him— something she'd never in a million years thought she'd do.

"All right, then." Gruffly, he pushed her away. "But I'm not the one you should be thanking. I still have Renn's note as evidence against you. In my mind, you shouldn't be allowed to leave the gates at all. Liem will surely have my head for this."

Methusal's jubilation ceased. "Then why are you going to let me go outside?"

Petr frowned. "Pressure has been brought to bear. In the interest of diplomacy, I will allow you this one freedom. Do you understand?"

Methusal nodded, but the weight of the accusations against her returned. Petr still thought she was guilty. She hadn't been freed at all. "Did my father pressure you?"

"He was one. Now go on, before I change my mind. Kitran is waiting for you upstairs in my office."

Kitran. Any remaining joy fizzled. What would he say about her behavior? Searching for hope, she turned to Petr once more. "Did Kitran..."

"Not Kitran." Grimly, Petr indicated that she should move on.

Methusal obeyed, but her apprehension built with each step she took upstairs. Kitran hadn't spoken for her release. After Petr had agreed to let her play in the Kaavl Games, would Kitran expel her? Unease deepened in her heart. But she did wonder—if Kitran hadn't pressured Petr, then else who had?

Petr opened the door and ushered her inside. Kitran sat behind Petr's desk, looking stern, and Methusal's heart sank further.

Petr said, "Don't be long. We're presenting the Alliance soon."

"I'll be there," Kitran promised.

Petr closed the door, and Methusal was left alone with her kaavl instructor.

"I know what you're going to say," she said.

"Do you?"

"My behavior stinks, and I should be expelled."

A small smile lifted the corners of Kitran's mustache. "You pull no punches."

"Neither do you." She waited. Her heart's desire lay on the line. One word from Kitran, and all of her hopes would be crushed.

When the silence continued, she shifted uncomfortably. "Aren't you going to say anything?"

"Explain your behavior."

Methusal tried to read Kitran's expression. What should she say?

"The truth, Methusal."

"I wanted to go outside and practice kaavl. I disobeyed Petr. I was wrong to do it. Even worse, I got Timaeus in trouble, and I feel terrible about that."

Still silence.

Desperation licked through her. She felt like she was walking through a fog with no compass. "I was wrong, Kitran. I'm sorry. I apologized to Petr. I won't ever behave like that again. If you want to expel me, I'll understand."

"You'll understand."

"Yes." She had accepted her fate last night, and she still did. "It's okay. I understand. I broke the kaavl rules of respect." More silence elapsed. "Say something, please."

Kitran leaned forward. Frown lines scored his forehead. "You learned a hard lesson last night, didn't you?"

A lump formed in her throat. "Yes."

Long moments passed while Kitran contemplated her fate. She'd never seen Kitran look so serious, which was a feat for her sober, intense instructor. "All right. You can play. But no more disrespect, or I'll demote you to the Quint-level."

She gasped. "Thank you, Kitran! I won't disappoint you."

"See that you don't. I'll see you at noon."

With a grateful grin, Methusal let herself out and closed the door quietly behind her. Then she let out a squeak and ran-skipped to the dining hall. She'd play at the Tri-level! And best of all, she could eat! She was so hungry.

△ △ △ △ △

The dining hall was crowded. Usually breakfast was a quiet time, when people trickled in and out at will. Today, families sat clustered together at their tables, talking loudly to one another. The din was almost overwhelming, after the quiet of her jail cell. Apparently, everyone wanted to hear the Alliance presented. Methusal did, too.

She glanced at the platform at the far end of the dining hall, and recognized the tall figure of the Dehrien Chief. He stood with Petr and a cluster of council members. His head glinted blond in the early rays of sunlight. At this distance, he easily topped Petr's height, who was the tallest Rolbani up there. He smiled and laughed with the people clustered around him. Magnetic charm seemed to exude from his every pore.

Methusal's concern about the Alliance grew. What was the Dehrien's ulterior motive? She felt certain nothing he presented would be as simple as it appeared.

She approached the counter to get her breakfast. Timaeus stood there, ladling out the sticky cereal. He glanced at her and then away.

"Timaeus. I'm so sorry!" Words couldn't express how awful she felt.

He shrugged. "I let you escape. I deserve my punishment.'

That only made her feel worse. "Did Petr fire you from guard duty?"

"For a full pass of the moon. I get to serve breakfast instead."

"Timaeus! How awful. Could I help you? Maybe take a few of your days?"

"No." A small smiled tugged at his lips. "Haven't you learned that Petr likes his orders followed to the letter?"

"Yes. But I feel horrible. I want do something to help you."

"You can."

"Really? What?"

"Tell me...do I have a chance with Deccia?" He flushed.

Methusal smiled. "Talk to her. I can't tell you more, but...do it."

He nodded. "I'll be gone messengering to Tarst and Quasr for the next few days. Maybe when I get back."

"Good."

Petr banged the podium with a mallet, and Methusal slid into place at her family's table. Her mother was there, as were all three Amils, including Behran. A frown pulled at the tense lines of Hanuh's face. "Are you all right, Thusa?"

"I'm fine, don't worry. Where's Papa?"

Her mother gestured across the hall. Erl, Petr Storst, Liem, Verdnt, and several other important council members stood clustered at the other end of the speaking platform, arguing quietly among themselves.

"You just missed your father's speech. He called an open meeting to discuss his concerns about the Alliance." Worried lines etched Hanuh's mouth. "Petr might force a vote this morning, just to end the argument. He hates dissension."

"Are you still getting a bad feeling about the Alliance?" Methusal hoped something had changed. She didn't want more trouble heaped on her plate, that was for sure.

"Yes. But logically...I don't know. It sounds like a good idea. We need to carefully consider how the Alliance would affect our community."

Ben Amil nodded. "I agree."

Methusal also agreed that every detail should be scrutinized. But she didn't trust Mentàll Solboshn. And as much as she would love to participate in new Inter-Community Kaavl Games, she'd rather the Alliance fail, than be allied with the possibly dangerous Dehrien Chief.

She glanced at Behran. His face revealed none of his thoughts.

Erl Maahr now threaded his way toward their table. An angry scowl knit his brows. He sat down hard. "This is foolish! The second clause *gives away* our autonomy. Dehre and Tarst only need to agree together on any issue and we'll be forced to go along with it!"

"What do you mean?"

"Dehre and Tarst can join together. Pass any law they want. We'd have to abide by it, even if we disagreed. Petr says that would never happen." He growled, "*Arghhh!* I don't like this at all. Petr's too interested in reelection to think clearly. Signing this Alliance could cost Rolban everything!"

Surely Petr wouldn't agree to an Alliance that could hurt Rolban—no matter how much he wanted to be reelected. Methusal's uncomfortable stay in jail last night returned to mind. She'd learned first-hand that Petr would go to any lengths to achieve his goals...and to prove he was the boss. She touched her jaw, still sore from sleeping on her tablet necklace on the hard cot. All of a sudden, the necklace felt constricting. She took it off and placed it next to her plate, and turned around on the bench so she could see the front of the room better.

Kitran made his way to the speaking platform with the shell amplifier in hand. He motioned for silence.

"As we've heard, the Alliance is a contentious issue. Signing it means taking a step of trust and friendship toward our old enemies, the Dehriens and the Tarst. As most of you know, we already trade with the Tarst, and Erl and Petr have become good friends with their leader, Pan Patn. We trust them. Now Dehre has extended its hand of friendship to us, too. Years of mistrust and hatred can end now. We can begin to build friendships that will endure for centuries. For our children's children.

"Friendship or fear. Today we make that choice." Kitran shook Mentàll's hand.

People in the hall burst into chatter. The din reverberated in the stone room.

"Silence, please!" Petr bellowed through the shell amplifier. "This morning we have a special guest with us; the honorable Mentàll Solboshn from Dehre. Mentàll, we are pleased to have you here."

With a smile, the Dehrien Chief bowed slightly.

"Mentàll journeyed from Dehre to bring us the Alliance. We certainly appreciate your effort."

The Dehrien Chief inclined his head.

"This morning, we've heard Erl Maahr's concerns about the Alliance, and Kitran's argument in favor of peace and friendship. Now we will hear from Mentàll, himself. As co-author of this new Alliance, he has worked long and hard to design a treaty that will advance the best interests of Rolban, Dehre, and Tarst. He is a visionary, in my opinion.

"Fellow Rolbanis, please warmly welcome Mentàll Solboshn, Chief of Dehre!" Petr stepped back, and the Rolbani people clapped enthusiastically. New faces were a rare treat, and many people were probably eager to hear what a Dehrien Chief might have to say.

"Fellow Rolbanis!" With a smile, Mentàll Solboshn stepped forward. "I feel honored to finally meet you face to face. Kitran and Petr have told me a great deal about Rolban, but already your warm, generous welcome has far exceeded my hopes. Thank you. Someday soon, I hope to be able to return your kindness."

He glanced about the room, and a wide smile stretched his angular face. "I'd never visited Rolban before, but already I can see it is a fine community, with citizens who are forward looking and eager to embrace the future. These are qualities I applaud, and ones vitally important to this new age."

He paused, and his tone took a serious turn. "The Great War is behind us, and I believe it is time to forge on to the future. We must learn to trust each other, and form ties that will help not only ourselves, but each other. I firmly believe this Alliance will provide that stronger future." He paused again, and glanced slowly about the room, as if trying to meet each person's gaze.

"We must work together if we want to improve life in our communities. Each community possesses different skills and talents, and I believe we need to pool our resources. Work together. I believe this is the only way to strengthen us all.

"I desire a strong, secure future, and I trust you do, too. So I strongly urge you to sign this new Alliance. I am convinced it is in Rolban's best interests, just as it is Dehre and Tarst's. May we put the past behind us and reach *together* for the future—a future truly bright with hope and promise. Thank you."

Deafening applause broke out as he stepped down from the platform. Slowly, Methusal clapped, too. He was definitely a charismatic speaker. If she didn't thoroughly distrust him, she'd be inclined to favor the Alliance. In fact, even being suspicious of Mentàll Solboshn couldn't dislodge a small part of her that wished the Alliance could be for the good.

Petr held the amplifier now, and when the hubbub subsided he spoke, his voice strong and ringing with conviction.

"I hold in my hand the terms of the Alliance. The document has already been signed by Dehre, and the Tarst will sign it tomorrow. Pan Patn has assured me of this fact. It awaits only my signature for it to become law for our community, too." He paused, his gaze seeking and challenging each individual council member who sat in the dining hall.

"We have heard Erl's concerns, and they are legitimate concerns. But we've also heard Mentàll's call to the future. I believe it is a call we must heed. Now is the time to put away all doubts. We must join together, so we can all be strengthened." He paused. Echoes of his voice rang in the cavern.

His white head bent to the paper he held. "I will now read the document."

We, Rolban, Tarst, and Dehre do solemnly commit to uphold the statutes of this Alliance as written herein:

Number One: We do commit to freely trade among ourselves with no restrictions being placed on buyers or sellers of any community.

Number Two: We do commit to open dialogue and an exchange of ideas—no one community bearing the authority to strike down or resist any mandate or law passed by both the other two communities combined, and

Number Three: We do solemnly commit to the safety of all citizens traversing to and within our settlements, and do commit to help each other in times of distress."

Petr paused for a significant moment. "In my opinion, we must sign this treaty. This Alliance protects our future, and our children's future. This is our golden moment in history, and we cannot afford to pass it over in ignorance or fear. We must act now!" He gazed boldly about the room. "We will now take a vote. Raise your hand if you are with me, and for the future of this community!"

A wave of hands exploded into the air. Petr's jaw elevated in triumph. "All those opposed?"

An audible *whoosh* as hands fell. In their place rose a few scattered arms. Her mother and father, and Ben and Poli Amil were among them. Methusal glanced around to see who else opposed the treaty. Old Sims was one, and Liem...

"The motion is passed!" Petr dropped the white decision stone to the floor. The crash made Methusal jump. The remaining hands quickly lowered, so she wasn't able to see who else opposed it. She glanced behind her, at Behran. How had he voted?

Petr Storst strode down to a table and with bold marks signed his name to the Alliance. He raised the white parchment above his head, tightly clenched in his fist. "It is law! Long live the Alliance!"

Applause burst out, sounding and resounding throughout the hall, and the Dehrien Chief stepped down to shake Petr's hand.

Methusal's father looked bitterly discouraged. Foreboding grew in the pit of her stomach as she watched council members walk forward to shake Mentàll's hand. They clearly trusted him.

There he stood, smiling at everyone. A cold smile, in Methusal's opinion. A calculating one. He'd manipulated everyone to do his will. But what was his plan? Besides what her father had said, the Alliance appeared harmless. In fact, it could help each community in many ways. So what was his ulterior motive in forming it?

As Methusal ate her cold cereal the exultant, boisterous crowd gradually exited.

"I'm sorry, Erl. You gave it your best try." Hanuh gently squeezed his hand. Her eyes looked troubled. Methusal felt more than a little troubled, too. She hadn't forgotten her mother's prediction that the Alliance would put her in danger.

It wasn't hard to guess how. After clashing with Mentàll in the jail cell—not to mention suffering through her nightmare—her mother's premonition didn't seem so far-fetched. Foreboding settled in her spirit.

Erl sighed. "Let's wait and see what changes this will bring."

"It may turn out fine," Ben said hopefully. "We stand to gain a lot. What I wouldn't give for some racmun spirits! The plains people make it the best."

Erl nodded. His gray eyes blended with his tired, pale face. "You're probably right. Maybe I'm just a paranoid old fool."

Her parents and the Amils soon left, so Methusal finished her breakfast alone, and then deposited her plate and utensils into the sudsy water and headed for the Grand Staircase. Once out in the main passage, however, her hand flew to her neck. Her necklace! She couldn't lose it again. She hurried back to the table and snatched it up. As she turned, she almost bumped into someone.

"Oh! Sorry." Looking up, she froze. Mentàll Solboshn. The dream flooded back. And her terror.

His lips curled into a cold smile. "I see you are free."

"Petr released me."

His gaze fell to the necklace in her hand and narrowed for the briefest moment. He eyed the raised "M" and then, to her surprise, reached out and flipped the tablet over in her hand. One tanned finger lightly traced the large "M" scratched into the surface, and the small "r" in the far right, bottom corner. His presumptuous action startled her so much that she didn't react for a second, but then her fingers curled protectively around the necklace.

Those pale eyes focused on her again. "A family heirloom?"

"Yes," she said shortly. It took every ounce of her willpower not to back away. She refused to reveal her fear to this man.

"Guard it well, Methusal Maahr." The low words sounded like a threat. It reminded her of the nightmare. He bared his teeth in a small, hostile smile and brushed by her.

She struggled to forget the disturbing dream. It wasn't real.

Why was Mentàll so interested in her family's necklace? And why did he warn her to guard it? The necklace was old, but it wasn't valuable.

She decided to take the Dehrien Chief's warning seriously, however, because he struck her as one who chose his words with care.

Her feeling of disquiet persisted as she slipped into class, but she paid close attention to Verdnt's lecture.

Afterward, she went to the supply room to finish sorting the seed grain, but Old Sims said, "Not today. You'll be wanting to practice for the Tri-level. Go on with you, then."

"Sims! Thank you so much!" Methusal impulsively hugged the elderly man, and a faint flush crested his cheekbones.

"There now, girl," he said gruffly. "No need to go on about it. I just want you to do your best."

"I will..."

"You won't!" This snarl came from the doorway.

Methusal whirled. A scowl contorted Liem's features. Several prominent council members crowded around behind him. "You're coming with me."

Liem wielded no authority over her, and if he thought she'd meekly go with him, then he was sadly mistaken. She tried to keep her tone level and respectful, even though it was difficult. "What's wrong?"

"You will not play in the *Kaavl Games*," he spat the words. "You are going to jail."

The number of people in the hall tripled.

Methusal's tongue engaged before her brain could. "Do you—and your mob—plan to force me back to prison?"

Liem's face mottled purple and he lunged for her. Before she'd realized that he'd moved, Sims stood between Methusal and Renn's grieving father. She'd never known Sims could move so fast.

"Hold on, young man." Sim's voice quavered, betraying his true age. "I know you blame Methusal for Renn's murder. But she is innocent until proven guilty. And if you want my opinion, she's innocent. Your facts need checking, Liem."

"My *facts*," he glared, "point straight to her!"

"Circumstantial evidence." Methusal interjected. "And I tell you, I'm innocent! I'd never hurt Renn. I cared about him like a brother."

Liem's furious expression made it clear he did not believe her.

Time to remind Liem of the facts before it was too late. She would not let an angry, grieving man—or his mob—drag her back to prison. She never thought she would use her uncle's name in her defense, but she did so now.

"Petr released me from jail. He knows the evidence against me is weak. It cannot prove that I'm guilty. He's the Chief of Rolban. He told me I can play in the Kaavl Games, and that is what I'm going to do."

"Petr is incompetent!" Liem spat. "He'll lose this election. And as soon as I gain office, you'll go to jail. And you'll pay the ultimate price for killing my son!"

Methusal's tenuous hold on her temper snapped. "Then *you* will be guilty of murder!"

"Move aside," Petr rumbled. Erl and Petr shoved their way into the supply room.

"What is going on?" Erl demanded.

Sims retreated and took a shaky seat on his stool, apparently content to let Methusal's father defend her now.

"Liem wants to throw me back in prison," Methusal exclaimed. "And he's gathered a mob to drag me there now."

Erl turned a scowl upon Liem, who took a step backward. "Is that true?"

Liem jabbed a finger in the Rolbani Chief's direction. "Petr freed her. What message does that send to our children? That murderers can freely roam Rolban's halls and be rewarded with the Kaavl Games? I say *no!*" Behind him, the crowd murmured in agreement. "She needs to be locked up. No one is safe with that murderer running loose, and walking the same halls as our children!"

"Yes," murmured a few mothers in the tightly packed passageway.

"I am innocent," Methusal cried out. Fear made her chest feel tight. Clearly, Liem would go to any lengths to punish her for a crime she hadn't committed. "But you can't see reason. You just want to execute someone! Who cares if I'm innocent? What is *wrong* with you?" Now she was screaming, and Erl took her arm and pulled her backward.

Her heart pounded, and she struggled against her father. "I won't be executed for a crime I didn't commit!" Tears streamed down her cheeks.

"Silence!" Petr thundered. When Liem opened his mouth, Petr roared, "*Silence!*"

One could hear a whip slither in the utter quiet that followed.

"Good," Petr said. He straightened his burly frame to achieving his full, intimidating height. His white beard bristled with irritation. "Liem, I know you're grieving your son. But my decision stands. The evidence is not strong enough to convict Methusal. Yet."

People in the crowded hallway murmured. Methusal couldn't tell if they agreed with Petr or not. Her uncle frowned at Methusal, clearly not thrilled to have to defend her. By doing so, he may have hurt his reelection prospects. So why had he done it? Out of fairness? Or because of the unknown pressure brought to bear that he'd previously mentioned?

"The truth will come out, I promise you," Petr said. "And the real murderer will be punished."

"She'd better be!" someone in the passageway shouted. It sounded suspiciously like Pogul.

"As for you, Liem." Petr scowled. "Your emotions are driving your decisions. You are not thinking clearly. To become Chief, you must be able to think clearly in all situations, and most especially personal ones. Methusal is my niece, and yet she is first on my suspect list. In addition, she spent the night in jail. Liem, you must learn to separate your emotions from your actions, if you want to be a good Chief."

Petr's words reminded Methusal of Kitran's new kaavl training precepts. His next words seemed to confirm it.

"If it wasn't for kaavl training, I would be just like you, Liem. I'd let my emotions cloud my judgment. I would be a poor leader. But just like the successful leaders of Dehre and Tarst, I am one of the top kaavl contenders in our community. I continue to grow in kaavl wisdom and discipline." Petr clearly addressed the crowd now, and it sounded suspiciously like a rehearsed campaign speech—albeit one she had never heard before. "A man who possesses these qualities will make the best leader for Rolban."

Liem's face darkened. "Kaavl is not a part of leadership here, Petr. Anyone can become Chief."

Methusal knew that the position of Chief in both Dehre and Tarst could only be won by the very best kaavl contenders in their communities. On the other hand, the Rolbani elders had always upheld that kaavl could not be a deciding factor in any election. All men should be allowed a chance to become Chief.

Petr nodded. "As it should be, Liem. But I submit to all Rolbanis now: Consider, for the first time, the qualities required of Bi-level and Primary kaavl contenders. To reach those levels, one must prove that one is focused, disciplined, hardworking, highly observant, and smart. These are also the qualities required of the finest leaders.

"I have trained for years in each of these kaavl leadership qualities. Liem has not. I understand that you are grieving, Liem. But rash fits of anger and gathering a lynch mob is not the way to run a great community like Rolban. Consider my words. Besides Kitran, I am the highest level kaavl player in this community. And I will continue to grow in both kaavl and my responsibilities as Chief when I am reelected in three weeks."

The crowd was silent. And then Methusal heard the soft sounds of moccasins slipping down the hall. The spectacle was over.

Methusal was thankful for Petr's support. Amazed, too, at how he'd turned the entire incident around to extol his own superior qualities as Chief. And he'd entered kaavl into the election debate—unheard of in Rolban. Also a gutsy move for her uncle to make.

"This isn't over," Liem snapped. "I'll prove Methusal is guilty. And when I do, you'll go down, right along with her." With a hard twist of his stocky shoulders, he disappeared down the hall.

Methusal felt relieved, but a bit shaky, as if she'd been punched by invisible fists. She turned to her uncle. "Thank you."

Petr frowned. "Don't make me regret it." He lumbered into the hall.

"Are you okay?" Erl wrapped a tight, comforting arm around her shoulders.

"I'm fine, Papa." Tears stung her eyes at his uncharacteristic gesture. "Thanks to you. And Sims, too." She offered a wobbly smile to the supply room manager.

"Off with you, my girl. Time to practice your kaavl," Sims said bracingly.

Erl tightened his arm. "I'll be rooting for you. Remember, you're never alone."

"Thank you." She hugged him. But she couldn't deny it—she was scared. "Papa, what if Liem finds more evidence? Someone is trying hard to frame me. What if he plants so much evidence that I'm convicted of something I didn't do?"

"Shh," Erl said. "I won't let that happen."

"How? If Liem is elected Chief, he can do whatever he wants. He could order me executed!"

"The Council must agree."

"Papa. With evidence..."

"You will be fine, Methusal, I promise you."

"I would be fine if *you* were Chief." And that was the perfect solution to her problem. "It's not too late. You could put in a bid to become Chief again. You're more popular than both Petr and Liem put together. And Verdnt doesn't have much of a chance. What do you think?"

"Thusa, it's late in the game. And it's not fair. I was Chief for eight years..."

"And Petr has been Chief for four. He's had his turn."

Erl shook his head, but she could tell he was thinking about it. Her spirits rose. "You'll do it?"

"No." Her spirits dropped again. "But," he amended, "I *will* put my name in as an alternate, in the unlikely event two candidates drop out of the race."

That would never happen, of course, but Methusal kissed her father's cheek. "Thank you, Papa. I appreciate it."

Chapter Fourteen

THE NEWLY ORPHANED BOY ate little of Hendra's food. After nibbling a few bites, he retreated to a far corner of the orphan's tent. He did not want to be touched. In fact, he whimpered if anyone came near him. Hendra understood the feeling, so she left him alone.

The woman in charge of the orphanage had approved the idea of a long day walk, and had organized the older children to go with Hendra. The younger ones would stay behind. Hendra felt certain the walk would not be dangerous—not in the daytime. She didn't think anyone would be there during the day. And even if there were men working at their secret tasks, they probably wouldn't feel threatened by Hendra or the children. Still, she'd scout ahead to ensure the children's safety. And she'd make her own secret observations, too, before the men could hide their activities.

Hendra gathered her six charges, along with dried meat for a snack and several water skins and buckets for the return trip, and they started out. She and several of the older boys also carried kaavl sticks in case they encountered a whip beast. It was early morning now, and still cool. She estimated they would reach the hills before it became uncomfortably warm.

"Where are we going?" asked an older girl named Srata. Her stringy hair fell in clumps around her thin, dirty face. With the scarcity of water, full baths were impossible in

Dehre. Hendra used a cloth and a bucket of water to keep herself clean, but it wasn't enough. Today, she'd brought several bars of soap from the orphanage in case they found a private place to bathe.

"There." Hendra pointed in the direction in which she believed the fires burned at night.

The children did not question her decision. They walked silently beside her. Several found a few tagma berries along the way. Gobbling them up lifted their spirits. Soon they sang old battle chants, and Hendra joined in. It took several long hours to travel the long distance. As they drew closer to the hills, though, she fell silent. Sensing her mood, the children did too.

"What's wrong?" Srata asked.

"Let me look ahead. I think I saw something." In truth, Hendra had seen something—smoke—several nights ago. "Stay here until I call for you," she instructed.

"Why?" a boy objected. "We're not scared."

"Stay," Hendra repeated. "I'll be back in a minute."

The boy grumbled, but obeyed. Hendra sprinted up into the low hills. A few sparse, bent and withered trees grew there, anchored deep in the dry, pebbled earth. It had been a long time since she'd seen a live tree. She pressed on, moving quickly. She didn't want to leave her charges alone for long.

She crested the hill and a faint, acrid scent drifted to her nose. Her gaze swept the small valley. The new stream, recently diverted from the mighty Tarst River, flowed through a shallow gorge in the center. Grassy banks edged it, although only a few scraggly, dead looking plants dotted the upper reaches of the valley.

The rushing stream was about two lengths wide, and the shallow ravine it flowed through looked like it had been cut through the earth long ago. Perhaps the stream had naturally run through here long ago, even before the dam up north had diverted the water here. Hendra hadn't seen so much water in years, and she itched to run and soak her feet in it. But first she needed to make sure it was safe for the children.

Again, she scanned the area. Empty. No one was there, so it was safe. Plenty of fire pits edged the stream, but she saw nothing else. No tools. No ore. No weapons.

Whatever Mentàll's men had been doing, they had apparently completed their project and packed everything out.

Time to get the children. She quickly brought her charges up the hill.

"Look!" a girl cried out. "Water!"

"Be careful," Hendra called. Most of the children ran down to the stream to fill their buckets, but Srata dogged Hendra's steps. The girl seemed to need a friend. Hendra longed for a friend, too, and was happy to be Srata's. But she wished she had one her own age, too.

"What is this?" Strata wanted to know, kicking the blackened debris with her moccasin.

"I don't know." Hendra scanned the ground, searching for clues. It felt strange to walk through trampled green grass. She'd felt nothing but hard dirt beneath her feet for so long. Tiny green bushes sprouted along the water's edge. The valley would be the perfect place to plant crops. If they had seeds. ...Or maybe not. During a rainy year the stream might widen and flood this valley. That would destroy the crops planted on the riverbanks.

"Look!" Srata cried. She tugged an enormous metal hammer from the ground. She didn't lift it very far, however. "It's heavy."

The large, thick tool was fashioned of ore. When Hendra took it, it felt heavier than a four-year-old child. Only a strong man could wield a tool this monstrous.

"In the old days they used hammers like these to pound ore into shapes," Srata supplied helpfully. "My teacher showed me one, once. He said now metalworkers use them to fix hunting knives, or old pots."

"You're right." So what metal shapes were Mentàll's men fashioning with this huge hammer? Large pots?

Hendra snorted. Of course not. They were making the objects in secret for a reason. They probably needed high tensile strength. And the fruit of their labor was likely prohibited by the Great War Peace Plan 200 years ago. Otherwise, why work here in secret, in the dark?

Swords?

Was Mentàll breaking the Peace Plan? She didn't want to believe it, but...

The unease in her gut grew. What was Mentàll planning? The Alliance might be signed even now by Rolban, and Tarst was a given. What more could her cousin want?

The next few hours passed quickly, and Hendra found no other clues. She and the children bathed in the river, taking turns to ensure privacy, and then filled their water skins and buckets and headed home. Hendra didn't know what to do with the information she had discovered. Little enough as it was. Certainly no *proof* of illegal activity.

Should she confront Mentàll with it? Her cousin was smart...in fact, she suspected he was brilliant. He would quickly deduce that she'd gone spying on purpose. Would he be angry with her?

What would he do to her?

Fear squeezed her insides, but the logic of their long history together argued against it.

Mentàll would never hurt her. Hadn't he taken her into his tents four years ago? More than that, he'd protected her, whenever he could, for her entire life.

No, she was safe with him. He would certainly never raise a hand to her. In fact, she'd only seen him raise his hand to two people in her life. Both men. And both had bitterly deserved it. But she'd heard tales of others Mentàll had ruthlessly cut down to size in other ways. Had they all deserved it? Or had he done it to keep his grip on power?

Why was she so afraid? Hendra bit her lip until tears formed. He was her cousin. And she loved him, even if she may not fully understand the man he had become. She couldn't let him speed to his destruction. The Prophet had warned that those who wielded the sword would die by the sword.

Die.

She couldn't let him die. She *wouldn't* let him die.

Mentàll deserved her loyalty. She would speak to him when he returned. She had to stop him before he made a fatal mistake.

CHAPTER FIFTEEN

METHUSAL SLIPPED down the Grand Staircase, through the Great Hall, and into the bright sunshine. She'd managed to clear her mind, and was now ready for the Tri-Level Game. No morning haze lingered outside; just a crystal clear day with a brilliant blue sky. The black bluffs cut a crisp line across the distant eastern horizon.

The opening ceremonies were about to begin. She climbed Rolban's mountainous hillside and sat next to Behran and the other kaavl contenders. He grinned at her, and both turned to pay attention as Petr strode to the forefront, flanked by Kitran and a few elders. Time for the opening speeches. This was the boring part. She craned her neck, looking for her parents and friends. She saw them far above her, and Deccia sat below her, near the Dehrien Chief.

So, Mentàll Solboshn hadn't gone home yet. Her eyes narrowed. Was he sizing up the competition for the Inter-Community Kaavl Games? Probably. Since he was Dehre's Chief—and also because he'd been able to approach her, unheard, on the plateau yesterday—she knew he was a top kaavl contender. Probably at the Primary level.

The speeches took forever. Afterward, Kitran tied colorful Rolbani flags to poles, and with great ceremony inserted them into special holders at the four corners of the plateau.

Would the games never begin? Methusal shifted her position, waiting for the events to start. The Quint-levelers did not get to participate, as none had achieved any extraordinary kaavl abilities yet. As a result, the Quatr-Level Game was first, and then the Tri-level. Only one game was played for each level. This rule was patterned after an actual battle in a war. A warrior had only one chance to attack and victoriously retreat from the enemy. All the practicing Methusal had done this year came down to just one chance to beat Behran. Nerves made her feel on edge. She couldn't make any mistakes. She had to make the most of this opportunity. And she'd enjoy her freedom, too, while she still had it.

The four Kaavl Games events would last all afternoon, and would end with more speeches and a winner's march. Methusal longed to be a part of the winner's march. But first she had to win. And before that, the Quatr-levelers must play.

Currently, the Quatr-level contenders stood in a line at the top of the lonely plateau. Kaavl flags fluttered from their waists, and the players looked tense. A kaavl stick hung from each of their belts, although the weapon was not allowed to be used in the game. It was only carried in order that the participants could defend themselves against a real attack from a whip beast. Leather kaavl strips were the only capturing tool allowed in the games.

The kaavl disks clashed, signaling the start of the contest, and the players sprinted down the hill.

Soon she would run that course, too. Perspiration slicked her palms and she shifted restlessly. Soon she and Behran...

A collective gasp from the audience jolted her from the daydream. A wave of brown clad Quatr contenders scrambled down the cliff. But wait! Another figure had sprung up from behind a bush on the plain. A slight figure with long, pale gold hair darted into the competition.

"Who's that?" Behran said.

Pride and consternation made Methusal gasp. "Aali!"

"Aali? When did she learn kaavl?"

"I don't know. I've seen her listening in on the Quatr-level instruction, but..."

Fingers clenched, she rooted for her gutsy young cousin. Clearly, she had learned the rudiments of kaavl on her own, and now braved her father's wrath to compete in the Quatr-Level Game.

Petr. With apprehension, she glanced downhill to Petr and Deccia. The two could not look more different. Deccia leaned forward, her hands clasped, visibly rooting for her little sister, but Petr sat like a stone. A hard mask tightened his features. Aali would soon pay for her disobedience. But for now, she was in her glory.

The seven contenders ran for the distant bluff. Soon it was impossible to tell them apart. By the time the contenders reached the halfway mark at the bluff, four had been eliminated from play. Only three remained now, and they ran back for the plateau. Had Aali managed to escape capture?

Breath bated, Methusal watched the three figures become more distinct, and then a surge of relief and pride straightened her spine. Aali's long blond hair was unmistakable. Retra and Lina flanked her—two fifteen-year-olds that Methusal had competed against in the past.

The three now scrabbled up the cliff. Lina fell a little behind, but Aali and Retra still ran neck and neck. Methusal bit her tongue, wanting to scream, "Go, Aali! Go!" But cheering was strictly prohibited in the Kaavl Games.

In the end, it was Retra, a little older and with more reserves of strength, who surged ahead, toppling first over the edge of the plateau which served as the finishing line. Gamely, Aalicaa finished next, and then Lina.

Methusal leaped to her feet with the rest of the crowd, screaming and clapping as loud as she could. Aalicaa definitely had kaavl talent—that would show Petr! But she didn't look at him again, because she was afraid of what she'd see.

"Retra's scores," Kitran trumpeted through the shell. "Capturing, ten! Evading, ten!"

A perfect ten was the highest score a player could earn in a game. Retra had done well. He draped pendants about the necks of all three girls, and the cheering went on for a good while longer. Then the trio descended from the plateau and sprinted to join their families on the hillside. But Aali did not climb up. Instead, Petr stalked down, fury evident in every line of his stocky body. Deccia rushed after him and placed a pleading hand on his sleeve. Angrily, he brushed it off. Both disappeared from view.

At least Deccia would be there to help protect Aali from Petr's wrath. But the Tri-Level Game was next, and Methusal could only focus on that now.

△ △ △ △ △

Methusal stood at the top of the plateau. A brisk, warm wind blew her dark hair away from her face. Clad in the traditional earth brown leather tunic and breeches, and with a tan kaavl flag and kaavl stick tucked into her waistband, she felt completely relaxed, and kaavl. She'd slipped so easily into a kaavl state of mind after reaching the plateau—as if it was becoming a natural part of her. She'd never felt so confident before. Surely, this was a good sign. Her fingers tightened around the long, narrow kaavl strip looped across her palm. Two more strips waited in her pocket, just in case she needed them.

Facing the Tri-level contestants, Kitran put his lips to the large, cone-shaped shell of the rare, land bound slug monster. The inhabitant had long ago been boiled and removed as a delicacy—served only to the Chief.

"Are you ready?" His amplified voice rolled richly, carrying easily to the rows of spectators perched on the lower hillside of their nearby mountain.

Methusal nodded, and glanced down the line of participants at Behran. He was her true opponent in this game. Behran had already earned himself a place of outstanding at the Tri-level. Last year he had placed third—not good enough to move on to the Bi-level yet—but excellent for a first year Tri-level. This year it was his goal to win, or place second. Another win next year, and he'd be able to advance to the Bi-level. Methusal meant to do the same, if she could. To do that meant she had to either win or come in second today.

Behran caught her eye and shot her a cocky grin. Gaze narrowing a bit, Methusal looked away.

Kitran told the six contenders, "The winner will be the first person to reach the far bluffs and return here, to the starting point, without being captured. Just to be clear, if a contestant reaches the far bluffs, only the contenders who have also reached the far bluffs may capture him—or her—on the run back to the plateau. At the Tri-level, only two may cross the finish line. The other four must be captured first."

Each kaavl level was a little different. The Quatr-level allowed three contenders to cross the finish line, and the Tri-level allowed two. The Bi and Primary kaavl levels were the most stringent of all. Only one could cross the finish line. All others must be eliminated first.

His voice rose a notch. "Now, if you are all ready... Begin!"

The crash of the traditional kaavl disks released the six participants from their waiting stillness. Methusal and the others scrambled down the side of the plateau. Reaching the scrubby plain, each fanned out in a different direction. In an effort to camouflage his or her intended plan of attack, each person disappeared behind the thick tagma bushes or the lower lying scrub brush and occasional thick clumps of lynnte weed. The two main points of the game were to capture and to evade capture.

Ears sharpened to detect every sound, Methusal tracked each competitor as she swiftly followed her favorite path for the distant bluff. One adversary sprinted ahead and cut in front of her, looking for an early capture, but Methusal easily evaded her by darting behind a densely leaved bush and tossing rocks toward the east. When the unwary hunter stepped into full view, Methusal flicked out her kaavl strip and it wrapped tight around her opponent's knees. She fell with a startled screech.

Methusal's first capture. Only four competitors remained in the game.

"How...how...," Daltha spluttered, giving up her tan flag to Methusal. But Methusal just smiled, retrieved the kaavl strip, and swiftly tucked the flag into her waistband. When she sprinted on, she only heard three participants running in the game now.

The familiar black bluffs grew steadily closer. She ran silently, careful to take note of the tough root systems that tangled from time to time across the surface of the plain. Another system of movement fell silent, and Methusal knew

Behran was systematically stripping away the opposition. As a Tri-level spectator last year, she'd carefully studied Behran's capturing methods. He was a dangerous opponent.

Still another system of movement fell silent. Now it was just Methusal and Behran. Despite her confidence in her abilities, Methusal felt uneasy. Behran had eliminated the competition much too quickly this year.

Admiration grew for her rival, and she slowed down and searched for a concealing bush to hide behind.

The match now was for first place. The winner could either reach the finishing plateau first and allow the other competitor to come in second, or the winner could capture his opponent, and there would be no second place winner. She knew Behran wanted to capture her. Just like she burned to capture him. The rivalry between them demanded it.

The crack of a twig signaled that Behran was circling behind her, and to the right. Methusal intensified her concentration. She kicked a stone ahead of her, and stepped lightly behind a huge clump of dense lynnte weeds.

Behran darted into full view and froze. His gaze darted back and forth, and unease slid across his features. Methusal almost laughed—but that would have given away her position. Behran melted back into the bushes.

Everything was silent except for the rush of wings far overhead. But Methusal wasn't fooled. Behran was waiting for her to make a move.

She weighed her options. The bluffs were a four minute run away. Only there could she spring her best trap on Behran. But she had to figure out how to get there first, and this seemed like her perfect opportunity. She needed to fool him into thinking she was still here, when really she was on her way...

Behran could not see her now. She scanned the area, and planned an angle of escape blocked from his view. She smiled. Tagma bushes! A line of them stretched to her left and angled toward the bluff.

Satisfied her plan would work, and sure Behran still waited unsuspectingly, Methusal darted from one tough, prickly tagma bush to another. She heard no movement from her rival. Confidence buoyed, she sprinted for the towering black bluffs.

A small sound touched her ears. What had caused it?

Then it came again. The soft whisper of flying feet. Behran was almost upon her!

Aghast, Methusal whipped a glance over her shoulder. How had he tracked her so easily? Admiration surged, along with a spurt of fear. In ten steps, he would see her. She instinctively dove for a nearby tagma bush. Her body slid. Rough, gritty rocks scraped her palms as she fought to stop her forward momentum. When she finally stopped, her face was in the bush. Thorns pressed into her cheek. *Ow.* But she didn't dare move.

Methusal listened, hardly daring to breathe. He was closer now. He must have heard her slide across the ground. What should she do?

She couldn't see him, but she could hear him. That was her sole advantage. No one else could hear like she could. And she was fast realizing that if she wanted to escape from Behran, she'd need every advantage she could find.

She felt much too vulnerable, lying in the dirt. Stealthily, she went up on her knees and pulled her stinging face from the stickery bush.

Now she heard nothing. Where was he?

Perspiration slid toward her dusty, stinging palms. She didn't like feeling deaf and blind. Was he sneaking up behind her? She whipped a glance over her shoulder. Nothing. Only the flat plain, dotted by bushes, stretched west as far as her eyes could see.

Feeling even more uneasy, Methusal shot a glance at the bluff. She had to get there before Behran did. That way she could see him coming, instead of the other way around. And if everything went according to plan, she might even capture him. That hopeful thought brought a curve to her lips.

Keeping her breaths silent and shallow, Methusal mapped out another plan of escape. Bushes were becoming few and far between now, so she'd have to be fast. Finally deciding upon her course of action, she leaped up and darted on, ducking from cover to sparse cover, heading for the stream and the rocky jumble near the base of the bluffs.

She kept her ears keenly tuned into her environment. A warm, soft breeze caressed her skin as she sprinted for her destination. Soft wind sighed through the plains bushes. Then she heard another sound. The sound of human breathing.

Her heart rate accelerated. Where was he? For a moment, panic disrupted her concentration. She whipped her head right and left, trying to pinpoint his position. Then she saw him dart out of the plains behind her, and just to the north.

Pulse pounding in her ears, she sprinted for the cliff. Each of them must touch the black wall before they could return to the plateau. The terrain ahead was bare of vegetation. There was nowhere to hide.

She heard his swift footsteps.

Her brain rapidly assimilated the terrain ahead of her, memorizing and cataloguing each stray rock or twig. She couldn't trip now. She wouldn't. She wouldn't let Behran capture her.

She sprinted across the stones of the stream and scrambled up into the rocky pile at the base of the bluff. He was close. His panting breaths rasped in her ears.

Panicked, she lunged over the top of a small slope and suddenly one of the patches in her threadbare moccasins split. She slipped. Her feet flew out from under her and she fell hard on her bottom. She skidded down the pebbled hill and crashed into a huge boulder. It knocked the breath from her lungs.

She didn't have time to lie there, gasping. Lunging to her feet, Methusal staggered toward the bluff. Her moccasin flapped under her foot, and she forced her trembling legs to scramble over the huge boulders blocking her path. At least the rocks helped hide her path from Behran. But he was still close. Much too close.

At last she spotted her goal and gasped with relief. The crevice in the cliff. She'd often played there as a child. Again she prayed that Behran knew nothing about it, since he'd grown up in Dehre.

A step later, she bolted through the dark, narrow opening. The rough stones scraped her shoulders, and she lunged down into a crawl, scuffling rapidly along on her knees in the pitch dark.

She put out her right hand and felt along the wall. There!

Empty air. It was a short tunnel leading to a chimney, which shot straight up. She'd climbed it often as a child. Could she do it now?

After crawling inside, Methusal began to climb, using her stiffened legs and feet to grip the stone. Dim light shone from above. Two lengths later, she scrambled out into a small, sunlit cave.

She crawled to the nearby ledge. It provided an excellent view of the broad plain below. Her arms trembled badly. She had escaped from Behran. For the moment. Now it was time to turn the tables on him. First, though, she pulled off her torn moccasin. It had completely ripped across the bottom, and she was afraid it might catch on something, or fly off while she was running. And the hole in the other one had grown larger. It could rip apart at any moment, too. She stuffed them both into the back of her waistband. Her feet were tough. She could easily run barefoot. A thorn or two would be a small price to pay to beat Behran.

Methusal slid sideways onto her stomach, and angled herself behind a small bush. It partially obscured her view, but hopefully it would hide her head from Behran's sharp gaze. She scanned the rocky pile below for her opponent. A second later he stepped into view, frowning in puzzlement. He stood right below her. He looked left, and then right, obviously wondering where she had gone.

If only she could distract him. Or maybe divert his attention in order to make him believe she was somewhere she wasn't.

Lying motionless on the ledge, Methusal flicked a pebble off the outcropping. It skipped down the boulders a length to her right.

Behran's head whipped up. He seemed to look right at her!

Pulse skittering, Methusal ducked back down. The warm, rough rock scraped against her cheek. Her ploy hadn't worked. Chances were he *had* seen her. The scrabble of feet on the cliff rang clearly in her ears.

Hastily, she gave up her plan to capture Behran. She was fast beginning to feel like the hunted, rather than the hunter, and didn't like the feeling. She needed to escape. Evading capture was equally as important as capturing, after all.

After giving him time to climb halfway up the cliff, Methusal quickly scooted back down the rock chimney. Then, feeling fully exposed, she took off across the rocky jumble, hopped across the stream, and slipped into the cover of the plains. Behind her, Behran noisily descended the cliff and headed west into the plains, hard on her heels.

Methusal increased her pace and intensified her kaavl concentration. Every pebble on the ground felt as tangible to her as the warmth of the sun toasting her skin. Her feet flew, avoiding roots, branches and rocks. Unfortunately, a few thorns pierced her bare feet, but she ignored the pain.

Behran was gaining on her. She couldn't outrun him to the finishing plateau. If she wanted to capture him, she'd better form a plan. An idea glimmered. Feet moving as swift as thought, she plunged left, at a sharp angle south, away from the finishing plateau.

She heard Behran follow for a few steps, and then he changed the direction of his footsteps. He'd taken the bait! He wouldn't chase her. Instead, he would make a direct dash west for the finishing plateau.

Methusal immediately cut back toward the finish line. Behran was ahead of her, but now she ran on a path parallel to him, but a dozen lengths south.

Behran suddenly cut left, toward of her, and slowed down.

He was setting a trap. Changing her direction slightly, she continued on, keeping a sharp eye out for anything unusual.

She spotted the kaavl line snare twenty lengths away, and at the same time her extra-sensitized hearing pinpointed her opponent's location. She ducked out of his line of vision and sprung the trap with a well flung, broken branch.

Behran charged around his bush, but pulled up short when he saw his empty trap. Methusal bit her lip to keep from giggling. Looking perplexed and uneasy, her rival quickly strode for the finishing plateau.

Methusal trailed behind him, keeping well out of sight. Twice, she heard him stop and then resume his pace. He seemed determined to capture her. Good. It slowed him down. More opportunity for her to win. She made a great point of skirting around each of his potential traps, and sped on.

The finishing plateau was close now, and Methusal increased her pace to a fast sprint and cut ahead of Behran like a silent, invisible ghost.

A few lengths away from the base of the finishing plateau, another system of movement touched her ears. It was close. *Too close.*

One length away, a thin young man entered her peripheral vision. Hadn't all her opponents been captured?

Suddenly she felt a tug at her ankles, and she fell hard onto the dirt. Behran's panting breaths approached. He stared at her, shocked, as he sprinted by. Methusal rolled over and pushed up into a sitting position as Behran raced the other young man to the top of the plateau.

Captured. She had been captured! Methusal couldn't believe it. How had she missed the other player? When had he touched the far bluffs? How had he passed her, undetected?

Her palms burned from hitting the ground so hard. Her thorn pierced feet didn't feel so terrific, either. Other scrapes, earned earlier in the game, stung now, too. Slowly, she gained her feet and climbed the plateau.

"The winner! Behran Amil!" Kitran boomed to the audience. He announced his perfect scores, and then placed the chain, and wooden pendant in the shape of a soaring flying beast, around his neck.

A wild cheer swelled from the mountainside. Spectators rose to their feet, stomping and clapping their hands,

Still feeling a bit stunned, Methusal shook Behran's hand, and offered a handshake to the slightly built man who had come in second place. Goric was his name, she remembered. He'd moved here from Aestoff three years ago. His smile looked exultant, but his gaze didn't meet hers.

After Behran shook Goric's hand, he turned to Methusal. His deep blue eyes looked puzzled when he muttered, "Where did he come from?"

"I don't know. I thought you'd captured him."

"And I thought you had."

Methusal was suddenly near tears. Not only had she lost to Behran, but she'd come in *third*. Even worse, it wasn't a good enough placement to travel to the Inter-Community Kaavl Games.

"Congratulations," she managed to tell Behran. "You did a great job."

"You almost had me. How did you do it?"

"Do what? Lose?" Methusal climbed down from the plateau. Behran followed her.

On the plain, Behran caught at her shoulder. "Slow up. That's not what I meant, and you know it."

Methusal struggled to hold back her ridiculous tears. "You won, Behran, fair and square. Congratulations."

"How did you do it?" he insisted.

"How did I do what? Evade you?" Anger finally bubbled up. "I'm good at kaavl, Behran! You never thought I'd cut it, did you? Well, now you know. If it hadn't been for Goric..."

"I never said you'd fail at kaavl."

"No, but you've always made it clear what you think of me. All these years...all your condescending put downs... You've *never* thought I had what it takes. Apparently, you're right. I don't."

"Methusal...'

"Leave me alone. For five years, I've put up with your smirks, and put downs, and your cocky attitude. I can't stand it anymore. It's petty, and it's rude, and I don't have time for it. In fact, until you decide to treat me with respect, I don't have time for *you* anymore!"

Behran's jaw dropped. Chagrin dawned in his gaze. "I never meant..."

But Methusal turned her back on him and strode away.

Chapter Sixteen

Back inside Rolban, in her family's compartment, Methusal cleaned up her feet and pulled on an old pair of too small, patched up moccasins. She'd definitely need to re-patch her current ones, or else get a new pair from her mother soon.

She tried not to think about the debacle that had been the Tri-Level Game. She had lost to Behran. While this was hard to swallow, she could accept it. After all, he had a lot more kaavl experience than she did. Goric, however, was another matter. *How* had he won? How had she missed seeing him tag the far bluff? Was he that incredibly fast? He must be.

Unless he had cheated.

No. Methusal pushed that uncharitable thought from her mind. No one ever cheated in the Kaavl Games. Honor, discipline, and integrity were such important precepts of kaavl that they were ingrained into everyone who learned it. Even though Goric had been trained in Aestoff, and had moved to Rolban a few years ago, she felt certain that Aestoff's kaavl contenders valued the same principles.

However, no judges checked to make sure contestants reached the far bluffs. ...And it was too far away for Kitran, on the plateau, to have seen.

"*Stop it,*" she told herself. "Stop being such a poor loser."

Clearly, Goric was an excellent player. She had concentrated on Behran, when she should have learned more about her other competitors. Behran had never mentioned how skilled Goric was before.

The feast for the kaavl winners would begin soon. It was time to join the festivities. If she concentrated on controlling her emotions—maybe channeling them into constructive paths, like Kitran taught—maybe she could survive the evening without bursting into tears.

Feeling alone, and more than a little depressed, Methusal made her way to the noisy dining hall. She turned the corner, and nearly bumped into Pogul.

"Watch it!" His eyes narrowed. "Loser."

Methusal rolled her eyes. As if she cared what he, of all people, thought.

Timaeus appeared. "See ya, Pogul. Bye, Thusa."

"Where are you going?" she asked.

Pogul burped in her face and sidestepped to intersect the path of a dark-haired man. The stranger carried a bow and arrows on his back like a runner.

Timaeus scowled at Pogul, and returned his attention to Methusal. "Tarst. I'm traveling with Mentàll and his group. We'll reach the mountains before sundown. We'll be safe."

Out of the corner of her eye, she saw Pogul furtively pass something into the other runner's hand. Whistling, he then sauntered for the dining hall. Her investigation flew to mind.

"Who is that?" she hissed to Timaeus. "That runner. He looks familiar, but I can't place him."

Timaeus grunted. "That's Kilum. He's from Tarst. He keeps to himself."

"Is he going to Tarst, too?"

"No. Aestoff." Timaeus glanced over her shoulder and nodded to someone behind her. "Here comes Mentàll. I'm off. Say 'bye to Deccia for me?" He offered a shy smile. "I'll be back in a few days."

"Of course." She smiled back. "Have a safe trip." Although she didn't see the Dehrien Chief approaching from behind, an involuntary shiver slid down her spine, telling her that he was near.

"Timaeus," the Dehrien said curtly, coming into her view. Those pale eyes, like chips from a glacier, froze into Methusal like frostbite. His mouth curled in contempt as he passed by. And then both he, Timaeus, and the Dehrien's entourage disappeared down the Grand Staircase.

Kilum caught her eye as he turned toward the staircase. Although the contact lasted only a second, his dark brown eyes held her rooted to the spot for a moment. His were the deadest pair of eyes she had ever seen. A shiver of another sort worked through her.

Unnerved, she watched the Tarst runner disappear down the Grand Staircase. Two possibly dangerous men, one after the other, were leaving Rolban.

Pogul appeared again, now on his way out of the dining hall. She stepped in front of him. "So," she said. "Passing contraband to the Tarst?"

"What?"

"What did you give Kilum? Something Petr should know about?"

"You're an idiot," he snorted. "I gave him a note. For my family. Remember, I'm from Tarst?"

"Kilum is going to Aestoff. Not Tarst."

"Get outta my *way*," Pogul shoved her hard. His elbow rammed into her side. It hurt.

"Whip," she snapped. "I'll be watching you."

As a guard, Pogul had the means to steal ore. And by pilfering Verdnt's chalk, it proved Pogul wasn't morally averse to stealing. Still, that didn't mean she should let him know he was her prime suspect. Maybe she should watch her tongue a little more carefully.

△ △ △ △ △

Roasted wild beast was the main course for the Kaavl Games feast. Although it was tough and stringy, it was a welcome change from porridge, and the occasional apte or gamey whip beast.

Methusal ate the meat and the salted logne leaves, although she'd have preferred not to eat the wild beast at all. It brought back ugly memories of Renn's death, the thefts, and everything that went with it.

Nothing had been stolen recently. Maybe with both Liem and Petr after him, the thief had decided to lay low for a while. She hoped that wasn't true. If he went into hiding, it would be harder to catch him.

"Thusa." Behran sat down across from her.

"Behran." Methusal managed to affix a semi-pleasant expression upon her face. "Nice award."

The Kaavl Game award necklace dangled from his chest. Bits of gold and silver dusted the wings of the flying beast image, and a red stone marked its eye.

"Thanks." Deep blue eyes searched her own. His gaze looked troubled. "Maybe next year it will be yours."

"We'll see."

Aali suddenly plopped down beside her. "Father is shooting knives at me with his eyes. It's only a matter of time before he banishes me to my room."

"He won't. Or he'd have done it already."

"No. People keep congratulating me, and he doesn't want to look like a slug. He'll punish me later, you'll see." Aali's bright eyes looked defiant, and a little hard.

"You did a great job at the Quatr-level. I'm proud of you."

"Congrats," Behran agreed.

"Thank you." Aali grinned. Her expression grew more serious. "Okay, Thusa, time to talk about important things. You have to catch that thieving murderer, and fast. I want to help, and I have a plan."

"What is it?"

"We have to catch the thief in the act, right? It'll prove for sure he's guilty."

Behran raised his eyebrow. It looked a bit patronizing. "How do you plan to do that?" *This* was what had irritated Methusal so much over the last few years—how he'd looked down on her kaavl abilities. Now he was looking down at Aali.

"I'll watch and spy for the thief. I know all the hidden passages in Rolban, and no one ever pays attention to me. I'll catch him, fast as a whip!" She snapped her fingers.

"It would be dangerous. I don't..."

"I'm doing it," she stated. "And you can't stop me. So let's work together."

Methusal put in, "The garment room, kitchen, and supply rooms all need to be watched. All the time."

"Maybe Petr will post a few guards," Behran suggested, forking up the last of his logne leaves.

"Are you volunteering?" Methusal asked sweetly.

Behran's gaze held Methusal's. After a moment, he said, "If you need me to."

Methusal smiled. "Fantastic. Your superior kaavl skills can at last be put to good use."

His face darkened, and he looked down.

Aali looked from one to the other. "Would you ask Father for more guards, Thusa? He won't listen to me. I'm not on his approved list right now."

Methusal snorted. "And I am?"

Behran looked up again. "I'll ask him," he said quietly.

Any other sarcastic remarks died in Methusal's mouth. Behran meant it. He wanted to help. Now she felt bad about her previous comments. "I'm sorry, Behran. Thank you. That would be great. Let's do it now."

Aali whipped a glance toward her own table. Petr glowered across the room at her. "If it's all the same to you," she said in a cheery tone, "I'll stay here."

Behran and Methusal made their way across the room to Petr Storst. Behran explained the plan to trap the thief, and requested extra guards for the key rooms that had been targeted before.

To his credit, Petr did listen, but his white head was shaking long before Behran finished. "Sorry, Behran. Impossible. I don't have enough guards."

"We could help out," Methusal offered.

"No." Petr sent her a quelling glance. "You're to stay out of this investigation."

"But my life is on the line. I need..."

"*Out*," he thundered. "Do you understand?"

"But..."

"I've put my neck on the line for you. You will obey me, or you'll go back to jail." He nodded to the adjacent table. "Liem wants you there now."

Renn's father must have heard his name, because he glanced up. A scowl contorted his features when he saw Methusal.

"Go," Petr commanded. "And keep your place, if you know what's good for you."

Fury, like a white hot flame, shot through her, but before she could open her mouth Behran grabbed her arm and pulled her toward the Maahr table.

"Let me *go,*" she snapped, wrenching her arm free. "How dare you push me around?"

"Shut it," he said kindly. "I'm doing you a favor. Unless, of course, you want to spend the night in jail."

Maybe Behran did know her a little too well. That didn't mean he could manhandle her.

"Thanks," she muttered. "Now step off."

"I will," he said in a harder tone. "Later." He strode out of the dining hall.

Hanuh looked up when Methusal sat down. It was the first time she had seen her mother since the Games. Hanuh's gaze was sympathetic. "I'm sorry, Thusa. I know what the Tri-level meant to you. But you did a great job. I know you'll win next year."

"Thanks, Mama." Her small, uncomfortably tight moccasins thankfully distracted her thoughts. "My moccasins are in pretty bad shape. I'm wearing old ones now. I could re-patch them, but I was wondering—do you have a new pair available?"

Hanuh smiled. "Come with me after dinner, and I'll find the best pair for you."

Her mother's smile finally soothed the deep hurt in Methusal's soul. She smiled back. "Thank you."

△ △ △ △ △

After the feast, Methusal and her mother stepped into the dark garment room. The familiar sweet, dusky scent of cured leather filled Methusal's senses.

Hanuh touched a firestick to the lamp mounted by the door, and the medium-sized cave sprang to life. As usual, leather lay in heaps about the room, in various stages of garment completion. A new wild beast skin was stretched on the wall to dry, as were several smaller apte pelts, near the door.

Hanuh noticed the direction of her gaze. "That's the pelt of the beast that killed the hunter. It's a good one. It'll help out with our shortage, since we've had a few pelts stolen."

"But at such a terrible cost."

"I know," Hanuh murmured. "At least no more skins have gone missing. Otherwise, no one would get new moccasins." She scanned the scant line of moccasins in the dim light, and selected a pair. "Try these, Thusa. And let me see your old ones."

The new moccasins felt wonderfully soft, were the right size, and formed perfectly to her feet. "I love them!" Methusal exclaimed with pleasure.

With a practiced eye, Hanuh examined her old, small moccasins. "I think these have stepped their last. Bring your other ones by later, too. Maybe I can use them for scraps."

"I will."

Her mother smiled. "Enjoy your new ones."

"Thank you!" Methusal hugged her. She hadn't had a new pair of moccasins in three years. With all of the bad things that had been happening in her life, this was one small luxury she would enjoy for a long time.

Hanuh carried her old moccasins to the scrap bin, and then moved to a table strewn with very thinly cut ribbons of leather, each about a length long. Kaavl strips, Methusal saw with surprise. And a few of them were bound on the ends with Methusal's favorite, blue dyed thread. Hanuh had bound the thread around the strips in her signature band and cross hatch pattern.

Hanuh smiled over her shoulder. "I meant to give these to you before the Game. But then you went to jail, and the Alliance was signed..." She held out ten long strips. "Would you still like them? You mentioned a while back that you'd run out of your favorites."

"Of course I'd like them!" Methusal reverently touched the soft leather strips. The ones she'd carried during the game weren't nearly as good as these. The leather for these had been worked to be smooth and supple, with just the right amount of snap, so if flicked out, it would wind tightly around an opponent, a bush, or whatever it needed to adhere to. Her mother made the very best kaavl strips in Rolban, and she always saved her best work for Methusal.

She hugged her mother again. "Thank you so much. I don't know what to say."

Hanuh released her. To Methusal's surprise, tears glimmered in her eyes. "Just promise you'll be careful."

"What do you mean? Have you sensed something else? Is it about the Alliance?"

Hanuh nodded. "You're still in danger. I still feel that. More strongly every day. I don't know why." Her mother bit her lip. Methusal had never seen her so upset before, and frankly, it scared her.

"What should I do?" She tried to sound calm and levelheaded. Honestly, she wanted to calm both her mother's fears and her own, too. She wanted to believe that everything would be all right.

"I don't know, Thusa. I get the feeling there's not much you can do. Except be careful. And...listen."

"Listen?" Her strange nightmare returned to mind.

"Listen to good advice."

"I'll try."

Hanuh headed for the door and blew out the light. "Your father and I are playing whaal tonight. Would you like to join us?"

They stepped into the hall. The passageway seemed dimmer than it should be. A torch must have burnt dry.

Methusal drew the door shut, but a movement down the hall, glimpsed over her mother's shoulder, caught her eye. She caught the impression of height and broad shoulders before the person vanished around the darkened corner, heading for the stairway up to the plateau.

The door to the supply room was ajar.

Had someone gone inside? The evening meal had finished, so who would have a reason to enter the room now? Unless Old Sims had come by to check on something...

Methusal stared down the hall.

"Well?" Her mother waited.

"Umm...no, thank you. I'm tired."

"Goodnight, then." Hanuh's mind already seemed far away, and a faint frown pulled at her brows.

"Goodnight, Mama. See you tomorrow." She tried to dismiss her uneasy feeling about the supply room. It was nothing. Just Sims. Sims was tall.

But he was also stoop shouldered and thin. The man she'd seen wasn't.

On impulse, as Hanuh disappeared down the hall toward the gathering chamber, Methusal swung open the supply room door. Faint light from the hall lamp shone into the dark room. Shadowed humps of grain bags lay on the stone floor. Although the darkness of the room prevented her from counting the individual bags of grain, everything looked pretty much as it had earlier today.

With a frown, Methusal closed the door. Who had been in the room? If it wasn't Sims... Surely she hadn't seen the thief—or Renn's murderer. Had she?

Her heart beat a little faster. Why would anyone want to go up to the plateau in the middle of the night?

It did seem suspicious. She glanced down the hall, and wondered if she should follow him. But if he was the murderer, he could be dangerous. What if he tried to push her off the cliff, too?

On the other hand, if she didn't find the real killer, she could be executed for murder.

Methusal slipped down the hall and stopped at the roughhewn steps. She looked up. The trapdoor was open. Someone had definitely gone outside. Her palms broke out in a light sweat.

She crept up the stone steps, and reached the trapdoor all too quickly. A chilly breeze kicked across the plateau, reminding her of the late hour, and her thin tunic.

Gathering her courage, she peered outside. Her eyes darted right, to the east. Nothing. Just the rows of mounded earth that Barak and his helpers had tilled, preparing to plant half of the summer grain. Beyond that field, she heard the rush of the Rolban River, which hugged the towering Rolban Mountains. To her left, the bluffs ended in nothingness. That was where Renn had fallen to his death.

Methusal crept up the stairs into the dark, starlit night. Ryon wasn't up yet, although its faint green glow illuminated the tops of the eastern, Rolban Mountains.

Nothing. She saw no one. Though she did smell a foul, rotting odor.

A shadow moved to the east. It grew larger. He was coming closer!

Retreat inside, or hide and investigate further?

The person would be able to see her soon. Methusal ducked down and hurried to hide behind the wooden trap door she'd just come out. She rounded the corner...and stepped into nothingness.

Chapter Seventeen

Methusal gasped, and clutched at the earth sliding by. She landed on her knees in a soft, squishy mess. Too late, she remembered the pit of rotting, stinky compost Barak had pointed out a week ago, when he'd given her a tour of the farmland. Decomposing vegetables, plants, and leaves now slimed her arms to her elbows, and coated most of her legs. The smell made her gag.

A thump caught her attention. The trapdoor had closed. She'd missed her opportunity to identify the man.

She climbed out, dripping sludge. Great. How would she explain her filthy clothes to her mother? And her new moccasins! Slime squished between her toes. Had she ruined them? Methusal wanted to cry. She'd waited three years for a new pair, and now this!

She bit her lip, but her throat ached with frustration. Well, too late now. She'd clean them up as best she could. But first, she'd scout out the area where the man had come from.

Walking more carefully this time, Methusal attempted to retrace the man's steps. In this area the bluff curved, and on the northern side a sheer ravine cut into part of the farmland. Boulders had been mortared into a waist high wall in this location to prevent people from falling over the edge. Methusal was glad for it. One accident tonight was enough.

She was sure the man had come from this direction. But why would he stand at the chasm? It was too dark to see down into it. Methusal scouted the area further, but saw nothing to explain why the man had come over here. Unless he'd dropped something into the ravine. Stolen goods? Ore? But why? Who would pick them up?

Tomorrow she'd return in the daylight and investigate the ravine more carefully.

But for now, she needed to go in and deal with her filthy, stinky clothes. First, though, she grabbed handfuls of wild grass and wiped the worst of the slimy sludge off. Once inside, she would grab a change of clothes and head for the wash room. And she'd launder her own clothes, even though it wasn't her family's wash day. The wash room should be empty now.

△ △ △ △ △

Clean again, and thankful that she hadn't encountered anyone in the wash room, since the other Rolbanis were either at home or playing whaal, Methusal hurried to her family's compartment carrying her clean, dripping clothes and scrubbed moccasins. She passed the garment and supply room hallway—all quiet now—and continued on, hoping to avoid family and friends, and also uncomfortable questions about her soggy clothes.

Where the passageway forked she turned right, down a narrow wing which led to her family's living quarters. She slipped inside the door, and closed it again softly behind her. Thankfully, no one was home except for Chup Chup.

She chirruped to him and patted his head before she slipped onto the ledge balcony and into the soft green night. She hung her clothes over the clothes line, and put her moccasins in a protected corner of the ledge. They'd be stiff in the morning. Maybe stained, too.

She glanced up the steep cliff. The plateau she'd just come from lay up there. Somewhere nearby was the mysterious ravine. Tomorrow she'd try to explore the plain below it. If Petr let her.

$$\triangle \; \triangle \; \triangle \; \triangle \; \triangle$$

Fourthday

THE NEXT MORNING, Methusal awoke early. She hoped no one had seen her clothes out on the ledge yet, because she'd rather not answer a bunch of difficult questions. If possible, she'd bring them into her room now so they could finish drying.

Unfortunately, her mother sat in the living room holding her morning mug of tea cupped in her hands. Her delicate brow rose.

"Methusal. Why are your clothes hanging on the line? Your new moccasins are damp, too."

Methusal sighed and hurried to inspect her new footwear. "Are they okay?" She still felt sick about sliming her new moccasins. And within the first hour she'd owned them, too.

"I brushed them out. They'll be fine." But Hanuh gave her a sharp look. "Care to tell me where you were last night?"

Hanuh wouldn't approve of her sneaking out to the plateau to follow a potential killer. "I fell into a mess. I cleaned them up as best I could."

"They'll stink for a while. Barak's compost heap is a little ripe."

Methusal lowered her eyes. "Yes." Her clothes were still damp, so she left them on the line. She pulled the damp moccasins onto her feet. They should dry in a few hours.

Hanuh said, "You won't say what you were doing, will you?"

"Unfortunately, there's nothing to tell. I'm trying to clear my name, but I keep running into dead ends." She glanced down at her moccasins. "Or slime pits."

A smile touched her mouth. "I'm sorry, Thusa. Something will turn around soon. I'm praying for that."

"Thank you." Methusal was glad her mother had chosen not to press further, and that she wouldn't reprimand her for going out on the plateau against Petr's orders, either.

"You're an adult now. But please be careful. Petr could make life very uncomfortable for you."

"I know. Believe me."

Her mother viewed her as an adult now. It was a new, strangely liberating feeling. She smiled and stood a little straighter. "I'm off to breakfast. Could I bring you something?"

Hanuh shook her head. "Just be careful. Please."

△ △ △ △ △

"*He?*" Deccia asked. "How do you know it was a he?"

"I saw a big man leave the supply room last night. I followed him to the plateau." Methusal told about her adventure, complete with falling into Barak's slimy compost pit. A smile tugged at Deccia's lips. "Don't tell anyone," she warned.

"I won't. Except Aali, if that's okay. She's probably going stir crazy right about now."

Petr had banished Aali to her room for the entire day. Apparently, he'd forbidden Deccia to bring her any food, either. Methusal would not let her mind go to the place where she'd like to assign Petr.

"Of course you can tell Aali. Will Petr let you see her?"

"Only to bring water at lunch and dinner." Deccia frowned, but returned her attention to Methusal's dilemma. "I want to help. What can I do?"

"I don't know. Timaeus gave me a list of the people who have access to the ore. It's well over thirty people. I don't know how to narrow it down." She shook her head. "Aali has the best idea. We need to catch the thief in the act. But that means more guards, and Petr won't post them. I have to think of something soon, though, before Liem finds more 'evidence.' It always seems to point straight to me."

"You're being framed," Deccia agreed. "The question is, why you?"

Methusal wished she knew.

△ △ △ △ △

When Methusal reported to the supply room for work, she found Old Sims wandering the large cave, muttering to himself.

"Er uld i'be?"

"What's the matter, Sims?"

He stared at her. A heavy frown creased his leathery, wrinkled face. "I can't find it!"

"Find what?"

"One of the bags of seed grain is missing. Barak needs one and a half bags right now. I was going to pour half into another bag, but..." his empty palms gestured toward the back of the cave. "It's gone. And Barak will be here soon to pick them up."

Methusal glanced at the back of the cave, where the three bags had been. Only two remained. A closer inspection revealed no clues. The sack of grain had disappeared without a trace. Worse, it appeared to be the bag she'd already sifted.

"Maybe Barak took it already," she suggested, although a sinking feeling in the pit of her stomach told her he hadn't. The man she'd seen last night must have done it. She hoped she was wrong. Before telling Sims, however, she decided it would be best to do a thorough search for the bag. She didn't want to upset him further, if there was no reason to do so.

Doubt wrinkled Sims' brow. "I only left the room once this morning. I don't think he came in then."

"Do you think the grain was gone before you arrived here this morning?"

"I just don't know. I didn't pay attention." The elderly man shuffled over to inspect the list posted near the door. Everything taken from the supply room had to be signed out, as that was the only way Sims could keep his inventory list current.

Now he shook his head. "No. Barak didn't sign it out." His troubled, confused gaze rested on Methusal. That grain was going to help provide food for all of next winter.

Why would someone take a bag of seed grain? No food rationing had been ordered—yet. Food was always available in the kitchen, so a theft from the supply room made no sense. But then again, none of the recent thefts in Rolban made sense.

Methusal thought quickly. "I could ask Barak about it, just to be sure."

"Did I hear my name?" The large, heavily muscled man charged in. Although his hair was dark and wild, like his brother Kitran's, there the resemblance ended. Whereas Kitran was quiet and well controlled, Barak was boisterous, given equally to fits of temper or shouts of laughter. One always knew where one stood with Barak, because he didn't hold anything back.

A quick glance at the two of them made his eyes narrow.

"What's wrong?" he boomed.

"One bag of grain is missing."

Barak scowled and strode for the far corner. He counted with quick jabs of his finger. "Two." He glared, as if they had intentionally hidden the bag from him. "Well? Where's the third one?"

"We don't know," Methusal answered. "Did someone already carry it to the plateau?"

Barak grumbled and shook his shaggy head. "No. I didn't order it." Several seconds elapsed as he considered the facts. "I'll ask my men," he said finally. "I'll let you know if it turns up."

He tossed one of the bags over his shoulder and stalked out. A scowl knotted his thick brows. He didn't take kindly to people usurping his authority, and Methusal pitied the person who'd feel the lash of his angry tongue. *If* someone had carried the grain to the plateau without authorization.

"I hope he finds it," Sims fretted.

"I hope so, too."

But the missing bag did not turn up on the crop plateau. One of the crop tenders came down to help Sims and Methusal look for it, although they had already thoroughly searched both supply rooms and the kitchen. Apparently Barak had questioned each of his workers, but no one had collected it.

Where *was* it, anyway? The sack was too huge to be misplaced for long. And if it had been stolen, it would be difficult to hide. Methusal's mind returned to the man on the bluff last night. He must have stolen the grain. But what had he done with it? It clearly wasn't on the crop plateau now. She had to tell Sims what she'd seen.

The loss of the seed grain displeased Barak exceedingly, and he soon returned to the supply room, his face flushed with temper.

"Give me a bag of regular grain, Sims. We're short on seeds, so I'll have to chance it. Either that, or we'll starve to death this winter!" He strode over to the bags of uncured grain and tossed one bag onto his shoulder. He glowered at Methusal as he lumbered out again. "Probably rot in the soil!" The door slammed.

Now their grain supply for meals had just shrunk to a dangerously low level. Sims had previously estimated that they had enough to last until the first crops came in, but now they were one bag short. What would they do?

She mentioned her concern to Sims, and he shook his head. "I don't know, my girl. We have to find that missing bag, or we'll go hungry."

Sims stiffly lowered himself onto the stool beside the inventory list. With a deep frown, he scanned it again. "I don't understand what could have happened to it."

It was time to tell Sims about what she'd seen last night.

Methusal kept her tone level, not wanting to upset Sims further, and explained what she had witnessed. She finished, "I couldn't tell if he was carrying a bag of grain. And I don't know what he could have done with it on the plateau. I was hoping I was wrong, but it seems like the grain has been stolen. And I'm worried about something else, too. I know we just did inventory, and everything seemed to be fine. But maybe the thief stole more than just seed grain last night."

Sims, if possible, looked even more upset now. He peered at the list still grasped in his shaking hand. "I'm thinking we should do another inventory count. This time you'll check the downstairs supply room. See if your count matches mine and Renn's. Renn had a sharp eye, and he was always on top of the inventory. If something was stolen, your count will tell."

△ △ △ △ △

Methusal struck a short piece of firestick against the rock wall and pushed open the heavy wooden door to the supply room. A touch of the stick to the lamp inside sprang the small room to shadowed life. It was sparsely filled, compared to the room upstairs. Sims was right. It wouldn't take long to inventory.

She pulled the inventory list from the peg on the wall and slowly walked about the room comparing, item by item, the actual supplies with the list. The knowledge that Renn had been here, doing this very same job a few days ago crept into her mind. And gnawed at it.

Why had he died? Because he'd found evidence pointing to the thief's identity?

And now the thief had stolen a bag of seed grain. Why?

As she finished counting food in the supply room, Methusal realized again that the theft may mean Rolbanis would go hungry this coming winter. Had it been an act of sabotage? But by whom? Dehriens? Why would Mentàll sign a peace alliance with her community if he wanted to destroy them? Nothing made sense.

And nothing was missing from this storeroom. Methusal did a quick re-check to confirm, but her conclusion was the same. Blowing out the lamp, she trotted back upstairs, where she found Sims frowning over his list again.

"What's the matter?" She peered around his thin shoulder.

"Hmph! Somebody signed out two sacks of dried meat two days ago, but I didn't authorize it. And I can't read the initials."

Her gaze followed the line of his misshapen finger. "2 d. mt." The signature was indecipherable.

"Maybe it was someone from lunch duty," she suggested. "We've eaten dried meat and grain discs every day for months."

"No. That's all accounted for. Matron Olgith is the only one who signs out supplies for breakfast and lunch."

Methusal hadn't known Matron Olgith was in charge of lunch, too—maybe that explained the lack of imagination in both meals.

Old Sims sighed and put away the well-handled list. "Nothing else seems to be missing. I'm not sure what else to do."

"I wish we could put a lock on the door." Unfortunately, Rolban only had a few built-in metal locks, and they were used for sealing off the passageways with safety hazards and the ore mine hallway, and also the front gate. Metal workers had made several dozen detachable locks before the Great War, but most had fallen prey to rust, and never repaired.

Although her words made Sims frown, he rose shakily to his feet. "We can. And maybe we should. Until this stealing thing is straightened out, at least." He bent to rummage through a bin. An angry mutter reached Methusal's ears. "Next time Verdnt comes around, I'll have something to tell him 'bout improving Rolban!"

At last he emerged, triumphantly brandishing a huge, old fashioned lock. A long, spiked key was tied across the face.

"Sims! Where did you get that?"

He fingered it lovingly. "My grandfather gave this to me, and his grandfather before him. Came from the time when metal ore was there for the taking. Used to be great metal smiths in those days. Even in Quasr, where I'm from."

Methusal had learned in her history class that long ago, before the Great War, the inhabitants of Rolban had been the greatest metal workers of all. They had fashioned huge, wonderful things out of the ore, as well as instruments of war. Little wonder, since most of the continent's ore deposits resided in their own mountain. The metal gates downstairs were a standing relic from those days, and still worked perfectly, despite the long passage of time.

The ore ran out during the Great War—or so the story said, although clearly that was not true—and with it went metal working. The Great War Peace Plan had ordered that all of the weapons of war be refashioned into planting tools, and hunting and kitchen supplies. It forbade further metal working, except to mend broken tools. The ore deposits were closed.

In any case, intricate metal working was now a forgotten art, and written about only in dusty history texts. Rolban had learned to live without new metal objects. Wood or clay served every day purposes just as well.

The round, silvery object looked heavy in Sims' palm. "Let's try it out." He freed the key and practiced snapping the circular lock open and closed a few times. Pride gleamed in his eyes. "Works good as new. Wish I had one for downstairs, too. But we don't have much in there at this time of the year. We could move it all up here, I guess. I'll think on that." He glanced around the room. "Guess we can leave now. Lunch will be ready soon."

In the hall, Methusal watched Sims deftly thread the lock through matching holes in the door and door jamb. Smoothly, it clicked shut. No one could get in now—unless they broke down the door. That would attract a lot of attention.

"I'll report the missing supplies to Petr." Sims slipped the key into his pocket and smiled at Methusal. "Thank you for your help, my girl. I'll see you tomorrow."

Delicious smells drifted from the dining hall. Methusal hurried to join the long line of people stretched out the dining room door.

Fresh stew, complete with vegetables and thickened with ground grain, was the main course. Fresh loaves of bread cooled on the counter. Maybe Matron Olgith had taken a day off from lunch duty. Alone at her table, Methusal tucked in.

The bread was delicious. Disappointingly, the stew didn't taste as good as it smelled. The wild beast meat was tough and stringy, and the flavorless broth was clogged with lumps of grain too quickly added to the pot. But it was nourishing, so she choked it down.

She definitely needed to talk to Sims soon about variety in the meals.

"Hello, Methusal." Her mother slipped onto the bench. Hanuh Maahr caught sight of her husband, and her face blossomed into a radiant smile. "Erl, dear! How is your day going?"

He kissed her with affection, and sat beside her. "Fine, thank you. What about you, Thusa? Has Old Sims been working your fingers to the bone?"

"No, Papa." Methusal smiled. She felt reluctant to tell him about the grain theft. Both of her parents had seemed troubled lately, and she was afraid her news would disturb them even more. All the same, they would learn about it soon enough.

"What's wrong?" her mother asked with a gentle frown.

"A bag of seed grain is missing." At her parents' deepening frowns, she told the story of the missing grain, and that Sims had put a lock on the door.

Grooves of tension now replaced Hanuh's happy smile. Her knuckles whitened around her spoon. "What will we eat this winter, Erl?"

"I don't know." He frowned and blew on a spoonful of hot soup. "You say Sims is reporting this to Petr?"

At Methusal's nod, he muttered, "Things are getting worse. People thought the Alliance would stop the thefts."

Methusal said slowly, "It is strange. The Alliance is supposed to bring our communities peace. But the thefts are creating suspicion and distrust."

Erl's frown deepened. "You're right. I hadn't thought of it that way. It does seems like someone might want to stir up trouble between our communities."

"But why?" Hanuh wanted to know. "The Dehriens clearly want peace. So do the Tarst."

Erl shook his head, his eyes troubled. "I don't know. But what worries me more is the missing grain. It has to be here somewhere. No one from Dehre or any other community has been here since yesterday afternoon." He would know. As the chief messenger, Erl was in charge of coordinating the incoming and outgoing messages to the other communities.

So he was right. The grain must still be in Rolban, somewhere.

Methusal said, "I might have seen the thief last night." Before her parents could react, she quickly explained what she had seen.

"So that's why you fell in Barak's compost heap," Hanuh said.

Erl frowned again. "That was a foolish thing to do, Thusa. What if he had caught you? He might have killed you, too!"

"I know, Papa. But I was careful."

A little while later her parents bid her farewell, and Methusal sat alone at the table, thinking more about the man she'd seen last night on the plateau. If he *had* been thief, he must have hidden the grain on the plateau last night, because when he'd climbed back down into Rolban, he had not been carrying a bag of seed grain. Where had he left the grain, then? Not anywhere obvious, or Barak would have found it.

Again, she remembered that the man had returned from the direction of the ravine. Had he dropped the grain *into* the ravine? Would someone come collect it later? Was it still there now?

Excitement grew. Maybe it was still there! She could go look.

Methusal cast a quick look at the Storst table, and noted that Petr was still eating lunch with his cronies. She didn't see Deccia. Maybe she was bringing Aali her nourishing cup of water.

Now was the perfect opportunity to check out that ravine on the crop plateau. Better yet, she could sneak out the front gate, circle around to the back of the Rolban, and check it out at ground level.

Methusal headed for the Grand Staircase. If a guard was at the gate... Well, she'd find a way around him.

△ △ △ △ △

"Hold up!" Liem's hard, belligerent shout slowed Methusal's steps halfway down the Grand Staircase.

She ignored him, and continued her downward flight. Renn's father was becoming an annoying, dangerous thorn in her side.

"Methusal!"

Reluctantly, she stopped at the bottom of the stairs and waited, arms crossed. "What?" she said shortly.

Liem's silver hair looked greasy, and his clothes wrinkled and creased, as if he'd worn the same clothes for days. Bags underscored his dark eyes, and weariness and a flush of anger mottled his skin tone. It was clear from his livid expression that he wanted to call her every name under the sun, but he controlled himself with visible effort.

He snapped, "I saw your clothes flapping in the breeze. It's not your family's wash day."

Methusal felt a sinking sensation in the pit of her stomach.

"I spoke to your mother," Liem pressed. "She admitted you fell in the slime pit last night."

Methusal didn't know what to say. She was sick to death of this man watching her, accusing her, and generally making her life a living misery.

"Explain yourself!" Liem shouted.

Her own temper flared. "Why? You clearly have all the answers."

"*Why* were you outside against orders?"

Although it surely did not help her cause, she said nothing. The man clearly could not hear reason. Why waste her breath?

"You deserve to be locked up!" Liem roared.

Footsteps scuffled down the staircase. Petr appeared. "What is going on? We can hear you in the dining hall, Liem."

"That girl," he pointed, "is a murdering, thieving criminal! She won't follow orders. She deserves to be locked up. Now!"

Petr's heavy frown turned on Methusal. "What have you done now?"

"I saw the thief last night. Well, the back of him. I couldn't tell who it was."

"What?" Both men fell satisfactorily silent.

"Yes," she snapped. "I saw the real thief climb to the crop plateau last night. I followed him."

"You mean you helped him steal the grain!" Liem shouted.

Methusal didn't dignify that accusation with a response, and addressed her next statement to Petr. "I think he threw the grain into the ravine. Maybe it's still there. I want to go check."

Petr's face turned an alarming shade of red. "I *told* you to quit investigating!"

"Right. So I should roll over and play dead while someone frames me for murder? I don't think so. I'm going to investigate until the real murderer is caught." Finally, she addressed Liem. "For the last time, I did *not* kill your son. But I won't rest until I find out who did."

"Go to your compartment." Petr's voice shook with fury. "Go *now*."

Petr's anger took her aback. It seemed out of proportion to the circumstances. However, she held her ground. "Who's going to check the ravine, then? If we don't find that grain, we'll go hungry this winter."

"You're grasping for the wind," Petr growled. "Go to your compartment!"

Methusal turned to Liem. "Will you go?"

His complexion didn't look any less mottled or furious, but he nodded. "I'll check. And I'll see if it proves you a liar...again."

"Liem..." But Petr's voice trailed away when Renn's father strode for the cave entrance. He scowled at Methusal. "You have your orders."

Without a word, she retreated up the stairs. She did go to her compartment, and she paced the floor for a long time. She wasn't sure how long she was banished to her room, but a few hours seemed like a good guess. After all, she didn't want to provoke her uncle further and end up in jail.

But Petr could not cage her thoughts, and she struggled to make sense of everything she'd learned so far. First of all, she couldn't help but think the theft could have been prevented. If Petr had posted a guard last night, like they'd requested, the grain would still safely be in the supply room.

As for the scene in the Great Hall—why had Petr been so upset when he'd learned that she'd followed the thief last night? And it seemed like he didn't want anyone to investigate the ravine. Even more suspicious, why did it seem like Liem was doing more investigating on this case than Petr? Even if all the evidence pointed to her, clearly Liem was trying to find answers. Was Petr?

△ △ △ △ △

Honorable Presidente,

Your brilliant plans are bearing fruit. The extra letter of agreement has been accepted, and payment made. Even better, the fool thinks the whole plan was his idea. Convincing him was easy, for kaavl is a sacred word here. It conveys power, and every Chief wants more. I continue to be amazed by the trusting stupidity of the Rolbanis. They are fools to allow immigrants within their borders. But I should not be surprised. They are weak, and have grown soft in their comfortable, safe dwelling. Our ally was pleased to find this true for himself, and a plan is set for the final harvest. I need only find the 2nd Book of Kaavl before judgment is executed upon Rolban. It cannot come too soon. Methusal Maahr and Liem are both threats. I will take all steps necessary to prevent them from uncovering the truth. No one suspects me, and your deepest spy remains undetected as well, although he has upset matters, too. You can be proud of him. Peace will soon end with the sword. I cannot wait to secure Rolban's treasures for Zindedi.

△ △ △ △ △

DEHRE

MENTÀLL HAD RETURNED from Tarst with the signed Alliance that evening. Dehriens had lined the dirt lanes and cheered.

Maybe now they could trade vats of wild beast oil for food from Rolban and Tarst, Hendra thought as she lay awake in bed later that night. Surely, she had been wrong about the Alliance, and her suspicions about Mentàll, too. Surely, everything would be all right.

Night crept by. Still, she couldn't sleep. But her body did urge a visit to the relief chamber outside. It was late, and the few people who might be up would be drunken men and hunters. Hendra sped across the Chief's compound to the relief hut. Ryon's green rays shone down, lighting the empty walkways. No one was out. But she did notice a lamp burning in Mentàll's tent. Voices murmured. Curiosity and suspicion reared their ugly heads again.

Hendra made use of the relief hut facilities, and told herself to go back to bed. Unfortunately, her feet took her straight to Mentàll's tent. She stood in the shadows and listened.

She recognized the voice of Ludst Lst, a particularly unpleasant runner and also a fellow Quatr-level kaavl contender. He said, "I retrieved it last night. It's a fine gift."

"Yes. Willingly, Rolban pays this first price. But it is only the beginning of the debt they must pay." Mentàll sounded grimly pleased. The skin prickled up on Hendra's arms. His tone changed. "So, the fool agreed to the plan."

"Appears so. Here's the note that came with it."

Silence elapsed while Mentàll presumably read the note. Harshly, he said, "Even better. Lust for power consumes him. He's not suspicious of our mutual friend's motives."

"Why not?"

"He believes it's all for kaavl. His ego blinds him to his vulnerabilities. Good work, Lst."

"Thank you, sir."

The tent flap rustled, and Hendra pressed back into the shadows, her fingers covering her mouth as Ludst exited and strolled toward his own home. Her breath felt choked in her lungs.

What was going on? What gift had Mentàll received, and who in Rolban had sent it? What debt did Rolban owe?

She knew Mentàll hated Rolban, as did most Dehriens. Rolban's protected croplands and community inspired envy in most starving Dehriens. However, Mentàll's hatred for Rolban had simmered for years, and she didn't understand the basis for it. Envy didn't motivate him. If she knew her cousin at all, it had to do with injustice, or a wrong done by Rolban. And yet Hendra knew of no wrong Rolban had ever done. Even during the Great War, two hundred years ago, Rolban had been the victim and Dehre and Tarst the aggressors.

So why had Mentàll hated Rolban for as long as she'd known him, and why did he think they owed Dehre a debt? Hadn't Rolban signed the Alliance? What more could he possibly want?

Chapter Eighteen

ROLBAN
Fifthday

LIEM CONFRONTED METHUSAL at breakfast the next morning. Deccia and Aali—who was glad to escape solitary confinement—sat with her. Aali didn't seem too troubled by the confinement. She had accomplished her goal, and Methusal had no doubt she'd continue to learn kaavl in the same impetuous, secretive way.

Without preamble, Liem said, "I checked the ravine."

Methusal felt a spark of hope. "Did you find the grain?"

"No." His gaze looked condemning.

Of course not. The news would be all over Rolban if he had. "Did you find anything at all? Any clues the grain was there?"

"I saw grain scattered on the ground." Liem's slow words indicated his reluctance to admit the information.

"So the grain *was* there!" Aali exclaimed.

"Was," Liem agreed. His dark eyes bored into Methusal. "Where is it now?"

He still didn't believe her. He *still* thought she was guilty. Discouragement felt like a dead weight around her neck. And yet why had she expected anything different?

With a tired sigh, she said, "I don't know. Your guess is as good as mine."

To her surprise, he left without accusing her of additional crimes. It didn't mean anything constructive, of course. He was biding his time and collecting more evidence against her. Once she was punished for Renn's murder he'd feel peace.

"You were right, Thusa," Deccia said. "The thief threw the grain down in the ravine."

"I'm surprised the bag didn't split open," Aali said.

"I've seen those sacks when I fetch grain for Matron Olgith," Deccia said. "They're tough."

"But who would steal the grain? And who took it from the ravine?" Methusal wanted to know. "The last runner left the day before yesterday—*before* the grain was stolen. No one from Dehre or Tarst has been here since."

"How do you know?" Aali said. "Maybe they secretly ran here, stole the grain, and slunk home before we could catch them."

"It's possible," Deccia agreed. "It's only a four hour trip to Dehre. Tarst is five hours. The grain must have disappeared sometime between the night you saw the thief, Thusa, and lunch time yesterday, when Liem searched the ravine. If a runner left Dehre at first light from either place, he could arrive here by midmorning."

"But Barak or the other crop tenders would have seen him," Methusal pointed out. "They were planting grain on the plateau yesterday morning. If Barak had seen something suspicious, everyone would know."

"So the runner—or thief—came in the night," Aali deduced. "A Rolbani traitor obviously threw it down into the ravine. And another thief took it home."

"What about the wild beasts?" Methusal said. "Do you really think someone would risk their lives to fetch a sack of grain in the middle of the night?"

Slowly, Deccia said, "A Dehrien might. They're almost starving, according to Timaeus. And I don't think they're as scared of the wild beasts as we are. They fight them off from Dehre all the time."

"We just signed an Alliance with them. Why steal from us?"

"It doesn't make sense," Deccia agreed. "None of it does."

"My father thinks someone is trying to stir up trouble between our communities."

"Why?"

"Maybe it's someone who is against the Alliance."

"But the Alliance is signed," Deccia said. "It's too late now."

As Deccia had said, none of this made any sense whatsoever.

"At least school is almost over," Aali said, gulping tagma juice.

School would officially end next week. Methusal was glad. It would signal the end of her childhood and the beginning of adulthood. Although truthfully, she felt like she'd grown up more in the last week than she had in the last seven years.

As if picking up on her thoughts, which her twin often did, Deccia said, "What happened at the Kaavl Games? Goric came in second? How did that happen?"

"I don't know." Methusal closed her eyes for a second, fighting the depression that continued to lap at her spirit whenever she thought about it. "I'm trying to forget about it. I have so many other things to worry about."

"Did you talk to Behran? Maybe he saw something you missed."

"Behran and I aren't really speaking." As Methusal remembered, the last time they'd spoken she'd told him to step off.

Deccia touched her arm. Compassion warmed her eyes. "Everything's a mess for you right now, isn't it, Thusa?"

Hot tears pooled in her eyes. Kindness just might be her undoing. For the last few days she'd been trying so hard to hold her life together and stay out of prison...but so many crazy things kept happening. She felt like she had lost control of her life, and it scared her.

"It's okay." Deccia hugged her. "We love you. We believe in you. It will all work out."

"It will," Aali piped up. "We'll make sure of it."

∆ ∆ ∆ ∆ ∆

In class that morning, Methusal tried hard to pay attention to Verdnt's lecture. She failed miserably. Kaavl, and her regrets and unanswered questions about the game, circled through her brain. So did Kitran's new kaavl precepts.

Currently Verdnt paced the front of the classroom, droning on about math equations that she'd memorized long ago. She stared at her parchment and doodled in the margins. In class yesterday she had tried to focus her emotional energy like Kitran had instructed her, but it had not helped her kaavl at all. Not only had it been impossible to block out her feelings and channel only the energy of her emotions toward kaavl, but she'd hated the way it made her feel. Cold, like a frigid, rushing stream. Full of energy, but dead to experiencing the world. She'd felt detached from her classmates—like one clinically studying bugs from a great height.

It had felt terribly wrong. Maybe she had been doing it wrong, but she felt more troubled than ever by the whole subject. As a result, she hadn't practiced kaavl since. In fact, that had been her only practice session since the Tri-Level Game. In five years, it this was the first time she'd slacked off in practicing kaavl. She felt guilty about it, but not enough to want to practice today, either.

And, much as she wanted to forget it, the loss to Goric ate at her soul. The Inter-Community Kaavl Games would start in five days, but she wouldn't be able to go. Until she'd lost, Methusal hadn't realized how much she wanted to participate in the new games. The first set of games would be at Dehre, and the second set would begin two days later, in Tarst. Kitran, Verdnt, Behran, Goric, and two Quatr-level contenders would compete—needless to say, Aalicaa would not be one of these. Methusal wished with all of her heart that she could go. She'd never visited another community in her life.

Her mind returned to the Tri-Level Game. How had Goric reached the bluff and run back, completely undetected by both Behran and herself? Darker thoughts crowded in. Had he cheated? Had he hidden on the plains at the start of the race and then popped back out when she and Behran returned?

She remembered that a system of movement had vanished about the time she'd captured Daltha. She'd thought

Behran had captured that person, but had Goric slunk into hiding then? She could ask Behran what he remembered. But maybe when the rift between them felt a little less raw.

Maybe she was only suspicious of Goric because she was a poor sport. That possibility kept Methusal silent. She wouldn't accuse Goric without proof.

△ △ △ △ △

In other news, Verdnt was again creating a problem in Deccia's life.

Methusal sat with her twin at lunch, munching on a hunk of bread topped with tough bits of boiled wild beast. "Verdnt did *what?*" Methusal said, chewing the same lump of meat for more interminable seconds. She hated gristle. If it wouldn't be horrible manners, she'd spit it onto her plate.

"He asked if I'd grade papers in his compartment tomorrow night." Deccia looked troubled. "I know it's just to work. But I also know we'd talk about the election. That's all he talks about now, and it's starting to bother me. He apologizes, because I'm in the middle, since Father's running against him, but he keeps talking about it anyway. And I don't think it's a good idea to go to his compartment. It might give him the wrong idea."

"It might," Methusal agreed dryly. Taking a large sip of tagma juice, she gulped down the glob of meat.

"What should I do?"

"Don't go."

"But he's my mentor. How can I refuse to work?"

"Easy. Say you can't. Offer to do the work some other time. Or do it in the dining hall. Somewhere public."

"I don't know." A frown worried her brows. "I don't want him to think I'm rejecting him..."

"Aren't you?"

"Well...yes, but I don't want to upset him. He could drop me as an apprentice. What would I do then?"

"He won't, Deccia. Just be tactful but firm—he won't even realize you've rejected him."

"I hope you're right."

"Does Verdnt really think he has a chance to win the election?"

"He talks like he does. But most people I've talked to plan to vote for Liem."

For Methusal, at least, this was bad news. "I think Petr might still have a chance. At least, I hope so."

"*You* hope so? Why? ...Oh." Deccia quickly understood. "Why do you think he still has a chance?"

"Remember when Liem and the mob tried to drag me to prison the other day? Petr gave a whole speech about how kaavl will make him a better leader than Liem. He says Liem is driven by his emotions—which is true. Petr said that he's growing in kaavl, and all the best leaders from Dehre and Tarst are all high level kaavl players."

"Interesting. I heard him say something similar when Mentàll Solboshn visited."

Methusal hadn't told her twin that she had made an enemy of the Dehrien Chief. But she was curious about her empathic twin's impression of the man. So far, the Alliance seemed to be working out fine. Dehre had promised to send several heavy vases of oil soon, in return for five large sacks of logne leaves from Rolban's high mountains. Could she have misinterpreted everything? Was she wrong about the Dehrien Chief's motivation for the Alliance?

"What did you think about Mentàll?"

Deccia shot her an odd look. "Why do you ask?"

"I didn't like him. But now I wonder if I got the wrong impression. What did you think?"

"He was charismatic." Deccia hesitated.

"You didn't like him, either?"

"No. I couldn't get a good read on him, but... He *seemed* charming enough. He said all the right things, but the *way* he said them..."

"What do you mean?"

"The way he spoke—especially during the speech—was almost...condescending. Like every word was calculated to have a certain effect. No, I didn't like him, but Father thinks he's the sun and moon combined, and I think Kitran feels the same way. I overheard them all talking one night, before I went to bed."

"Interesting. He visited me in jail." At Deccia's raised eyebrow, she explained what had happened. "He doesn't like me, that's for sure. I told him I thought the Alliance was a trap. Whether that's true or not, I don't know. But I do need to watch what I say. He probably dislikes me because I rubbed him the wrong way, like I do other people."

"Thusa, you don't."

"Sure I do. I speak when I shouldn't, and make enemies right and left."

"Like who?"

"Behran. Petr. Pogul. Liem. Even Verdnt, in class. The list goes on and on. Who's the common denominator? Me."

"Sometimes you speak without thinking," Deccia agreed. "But everyone who knows you best, loves you. You have a soft heart, and a lot of spirit. You mean well, Thusa. You'd never intentionally hurt anyone. Don't be so hard on your-self."

"Thanks, Decc."

"But going back to Mentàll... The conversation I over-heard that night was pretty interesting."

"What do you mean?"

Deccia swallowed more juice, and looked uncertain about whether she should continue with the topic or not. "You know how Kitran thinks only people with kaavl abilities should hold important jobs, like Chief? He thinks their minds are sharper so they can lead better."

Methusal nodded. "He hasn't talked about it in a while. But the elders don't agree, and won't consider if it might be true. Making it into a law won't happen, even if Petr and Kitran both want it."

"Right. And I agree with them. It's not fair." Deccia bit her lip. "That night I found out that Father and the Dehrien Chief think the same way as Kitran."

"That's not so surprising, is it?"

"Well," Deccia paused. "I don't know why, but the whole thing really *bothered* me that night. Like..." She hesitated again. "Like something *wrong* was going on. I don't know what, but Father was really excited about it. He said straight out that he wished kaavl was a part of leadership. Maybe he thinks he could stay in power forever then, since Kitran isn't interested in becoming Chief."

"What about Verdnt? He's on the Bi-level too, just like Petr."

"Well, Father apparently plans to keep growing in kaavl. He probably hopes he'll reach the Primary level before Verdnt does. And he seemed pretty much in awe of Mentàll. He basically said the Dehrien is a visionary, and brilliant in kaavl."

Methusal remembered how the Dehrien had managed to approach her, undetected, on the plateau. He *was* extraordinarily good at kaavl. "Did you hear anything else?"

"No. They noticed I was listening, and Father sent me to my room. They talked in low voices afterwards. I only heard a few words. But if I didn't know better, I'd say they were talking about a second agreement—something to go along with the Alliance. How something like that would be in Rolban's best interest."

Methusal frowned. "That *is* strange."

△ △ △ △ △

After lunch, Methusal entered the supply room.

"Methusal!" Sims always seemed happy to see her. "Are you ready for something different? The seeds can wait for now."

Her first real smile of the day emerged, and she crossed her arms. "What now?" she asked with a mock sigh.

Sims smiled, and pointed to a stout stick in the corner. Lynnte weeds were tied securely to one end. "Spring cleaning. You'll sweep the floors and I'll clean off the ledges. How about that?"

It sounded like a lot more fun than sorting seeds. With vigor, she swept the open floor space. Then the supplies covering the remaining floor needed to be moved so she could sweep beneath them, too. The two worked in companionable silence.

Humming softly, she swept up after Sims, who dusted the shelves with a soft piece of old leather. A folded parchment leaf fell to the ground, but Sims didn't notice. Methusal picked it up. The writing consisted of tall letters, with sharp, angular points.

1 plate
2 skins
3 knives
2 skins
1 plate
2 pots
1/2 bag of dried meat
10 forks
6 spoons

She frowned. What a strange list. It reminded her of something, but since she couldn't think what it was right then, she tucked it in her pocket. She would ask Sims about it later.

Soon the stone floor shone a dull gray, and Methusal moved everything back to its proper location. Then they tackled the store room downstairs. Because of the thefts, Sims decided to move all of the supplies upstairs, where they could be protected by lock and key. In the end, her arms and back ached.

"Go on to supper, Methusal," Sims said. "We've done more today than I thought we would. Whatever did I do before you came along?"

"You had another apprentice?" Methusal meant it to be a joke, but her own smile faltered and Sims' wrinkled face drooped.

"Yes. He was a good helper, too—always working hard, making lists of what should be stored, and so on." Sims sighed as he shakily lowered himself to his stool.

Lists. Methusal pulled the folded parchment from her pocket and showed it to him. "Do you recognize this? It fell from a ledge."

"Let me see." Sims peered at it. "Aah. It looks like one of young Renn's lists. Yes, that's what it is." He handed it back. "Doesn't mean much, I don't suppose. Only he knew what half of them were for."

"Thank you, Sims. I guess I'll see you tomorrow."

"I guess you will, young lady."

Methusal stared at the paper for a second. Renn's list. Something about it bothered her. Like there was something she was supposed to notice. With a frown, she tucked it into her pocket and hoped the answer would jog to the surface soon.

CHAPTER NINETEEN

DEHRE

HENDRA HAD NO MORE EXCUSES. She had to speak to Mentàll today about what she'd seen in the hills. And she had to question him about his conversation with Ludst last night.

She'd do it soon. After she'd helped with the orphans.

Dread built in her heart as the morning crawled by. Over and over again, she rehearsed what she would say to her cousin. As the time drew closer, fear licked like a whip through her. Mentàll would not be pleased. If that was the worst of it, she would be lucky.

After lunch, Hendra gathered her courage and approached his tent. The bleached leather rippled in the warm, gentle breeze. It felt calm and serene outdoors. Nothing like the storm she would unleash inside.

With a trembling hand, Hendra rapped on the wooden knocker beside the entry flap.

"Come."

Taking a deep breath to steady her nerves, Hendra lifted the flap and entered the dim interior. Mentàll had company, she saw at once. His chief scribe.

A snarl contorted Mentàll's lips. "Copy it *exactly,* as I told you."

The bony man with the thinning hair scowled. He was at least twice her cousin's age, and probably didn't like being reprimanded by one younger than himself. "I thought a change in wording would make it read more smoothly..." His voice was high and nasally.

"I employ you to follow orders."

"Of course." The man offered a brief, obsequious bow and headed for the exit. His dark eyes flashed as he passed Hendra, and his jaw was clenched.

The coldness of Mentàll's gaze impaled Hendra, and then softened slightly. "Hendra. What do you need?"

She licked her lips. Now wasn't the best time to accuse him of underhanded activities. Clearly, he was not in the best mood. "I'm glad you returned safely. And we're all glad that Rolban and Tarst signed the Alliance."

Her cousin relaxed a little. "Rolban has accepted the invitation to our Kaavl Games."

"They have? That's wonderful."

"Behran won the Tri-level. He will come."

Hendra's heart leaped. "He will?" Behran was an old friend. Long ago, he'd helped her begin to learn kaavl. Of course, he'd quickly advanced far beyond her. But his quiet patience and friendship had meant the world to her. And now he would return.

Her cousin watched her, his expression cool and distant. "Do you require something else? I have work to do."

Hendra swallowed. She clenched her fingers and struggled to remain calm. "A few days ago I took the children for a walk in the hills."

Although her cousin regarded her without any noticeable shift in expression, a barely detectible hostility prickled. As if he guessed what she meant to say before she said it.

Struggling for courage, she said, "We found the fire pits. Remember, I asked you about them?"

"I asked you to leave it." Mentàll had never used that low, freezing tone with her before. "It is none of your concern."

Fear dripped icy rivulets through her heart. "Yes, but...we found them anyway." She moistened her lips. "And a hammer, too. It's used for metal working. And it was large, so it had to be used..."

"Leave it!" he snarled, and in one fluid, predatory movement, uncoiled to his great height.

Hendra involuntarily stepped backward. Her heart battered inside her ribs like a flying beast trying to beat its way out. But she had to finish.

"I only looked because I was worried about you," she whispered. "I don't want... I don't want you to die. If you're planning...what I think you might be."

He came no closer, but rage stiffened his features, and fury contracted every sinew in his body. Never before had he seemed so large, overpowering...and frightening. For the first time, Hendra saw why no one dared to oppose him any longer. She already knew no one dared to challenge him. Not after defeating all competitors at the Primary level at age eighteen. Not after becoming Chief at twenty-four. Both unheard of. Both extraordinary.

And not after making examples of every man who had proven himself disloyal. He'd exiled them from Dehre forever. Under threat of death, they could never return. Those had been warnings to each and every Dehrien, including herself, that he was not a man to cross.

Tears sprang to her eyes, but Hendra refused to cry. Instead, she matched her cousin's freezing stare with an unwavering one of her own. He could not know how she quailed inside...how she longed to flee and forget all about the fires, and all they meant. And yet she could not let it rest.

Boldly, she said, "You're not planning to attack Rolban—are you?"

Fury flashed, cracking through the familiar, icy mask. He hated Rolban. That was clear, and he was planning something. *He was.* But what was it?

"Rolban deserves the fate they have willingly embraced. Do not worry, little cousin. I have everything under control."

Hendra felt sick inside. Did he plan start a new war? If so, it made no sense. What about the Alliance?

"But what about the innocents?" she whispered. "What about the children?"

Mentàll looked away. And in that second, Hendra knew that a little of her dear, familiar cousin still lived inside this glacier of a man. He was still—at least a little—the man who had rescued and helped heal a helpless flying beast when he was sixteen... Hendra flinched at the memory of her father, and the end of that flying beast.

Mentàll did not speak for several long, excruciating moments. She suspected he was struggling to bind his emotions under that icy control he always possessed.

"Hendra." At last the cold, harsh word came. "Who is Chief?"

"You. But..."

"Do you trust me?"

She scanned his features. Familiar, and yet foreign. The protector she'd known since childhood had turned into this cold, distant man. A little warmth did still live in him—but only deep down inside. And perhaps that would not survive much longer, for fury and hatred must be killing it. Both were unexplained, unless rooted in the terror of their childhood home. But he'd left at sixteen—twelve long years ago. It could not be so simple. It must have something to do with Rolban, but how, and why?

"I...I want to." Her voice trembled, and she swallowed, willing it to stop. Gripping her courage, she dared to say, "Mentàll, rage lives in you. Has it eaten up the man I used to know?"

The tension unexpectedly eased from his body. "I am still the man you have always known, Hendra."

She wanted to believe that. Desperately. "Then you're not..."

"You must trust me. My intent is only to do what is best for Dehre."

Hendra believed him. Her cousin did want what was best for Dehre. But deeper waters stirred beneath his opaque words. What wasn't he saying?

Perhaps she could get him to tell her if she pushed a little harder. "The Alliance was a good idea. Soon it will help us. Oil should be sent today. Logne leaves should arrive soon."

He turned to pour a cup of water. Tension again stiffened his shoulders. Unease unfurled within her, although her statement appeared harmless enough on the surface. Without expression, he said, "It is not enough."

Dread inched higher. So he *would* tell her. Maybe.

Questioning her own boldness, she pressed, "Why not? We already have new garments from Tarst..."

"It is not enough!" he snapped. "We need food, not garments."

"But surely soon..."

"Leave me." The freezing mask had returned. "Do not question me again, cousin. Do you understand?" That pale blue gaze felt like shards of ice lacerating her soul.

"Please... Don't take unnecessary risks." Quickly, she exited.

Outside, the afternoon sunlight failed to warm her. She felt afraid. The Prophet was right. Mentàll was up to no good. Equally clear, her cousin had set his path, and he would walk it. The Prophet had not swayed him. She had been foolish to think he would listen to her.

What should she do?

CHAPTER TWENTY

ROLBAN

METHUSAL SAT ALONE at the dining table and dug into her meal, feeling too hungry to wait for the others to arrive. The last rays of shadowed sunlight touched the stone dining table, giving it a dull, opaque sheen. A movement sent her glance darting upward. Behran. He sat down and placed a steaming bowl before him. Blue eyes clashed with hers for a long moment, and then he lowered his gaze and fell silently to his meal.

Methusal chewed on a crust of bread, trying to ignore him. But somehow the food had lost its flavor. She hated the uncomfortable silence between them, but she didn't know what to say.

"Hi," she said.

"Hey." Behran fell silent. Apparently, he wasn't too thrilled to speak to her, either. Fine.

She pulled the list from her pocket and studied it.

"What's that, Methusal?" Her mother slid in beside her. Her troubled frown—now a constant part of her expression—subsided briefly as she glanced at the smudged parchment.

"An old list of Renn's."

"Oh," Hanuh did not appear to be very interested.

Methusal, however, continued to stare at the list, suddenly gripped by the peculiar feeling that something was about to come clear.

Then she saw the common thread. *Every item matched something stolen over the last few months!* Her heart thumped faster.

Why had Renn compiled a list of the stolen goods? Had he been investigating the robberies?

An unexpected shiver chilled her. Maybe the thief had found out, and killed him.

She'd run her new theory by Deccia. Maybe her intuitive twin would come up with more ideas.

△ △ △ △ △

Sixthday

Methusal wasn't able to corner Deccia until breakfast the next day.

"Look." She explained about the note and her hunch to her twin and Aalicaa.

"It *does* look like a list of the thefts," Deccia agreed, eyeing it thoughtfully. "I wonder why he made it."

"Maybe he was searching for the robber!" Aalicaa popped in enthusiastically. "Only the thief murdered Renn before he could reveal his identity!"

"That's what I've been thinking." Maybe Renn's murder had nothing to do with her necklace at all. "But I wonder how the thief found out."

"We'll never know," Deccia said. "But why steal in the first place? For example, why steal a pot? Does he want to cook his own food?"

"That doesn't make sense," Methusal agreed. "We've figured out the thief must be giving the stolen goods to a runner, but who? And from where?"

"Dehre makes the most sense—for the grain, at least. They don't need pots or pelts."

"If they're starving, they might trade the pots and pelts for food from a different community," Methusal pointed out. "Let's find out when the Dehrien runner will arrive. While he's here, we should post guards in the garment room and kitchen." Although where would they find guards? Earlier, Petr had refused to help.

"Good idea," Deccia said. "But I think we'd better guard the rooms the day before the runner comes, and the next day, too. Remember, the grain disappeared *after* the runner left." She shook her head. "But which Rolbani would steal grain and give it to Dehre?"

"A Rolbani would never steal and give to another community," Aali said.

"Maybe not," Deccia agreed. "But we do have a lot of immigrants. Mostly from Dehre and Tarst. And of course, Father is from Wyen."

"How many immigrants do you think we have? Twenty? Thirty?"

"I could ask Father."

"If we're right about the thief being an immigrant, we can narrow down the suspect list." Hope lifted Methusal's spirits. "Remember, we figured out the thief must have authorized access to the ore mine. So we'll need to find out which immigrants are guards for the ore, and which ones are on the Council."

"That would probably cut down the list to about fifteen people," Deccia said. "But I can't believe any member of the Council would turn traitor. Or murder someone! To be on the Council means they've lived here for at least five years."

"If we're right, and stolen items are going to Dehre, then the traitor might be from Dehre. That would cut down the list even more," Methusal said.

"We can't assume anything. Just because Dehre is hungry doesn't mean they're thieves," Deccia cautioned.

True. A wild idea flew to mind. "Do you think someone moved here with that plan? To infiltrate Rolban and commit treason?"

"That would be pretty cold-blooded."

"Someone pushed Renn off the cliff. That's cold-blooded."

"Whoever he is, he's a whip beast and deserves to be flayed!" Aali exclaimed.

"The sentence for treason is death," Deccia said.

"Same for murder. As your father and Liem remind me every day."

"Father would never convict you with only that one note for proof."

"Liem thinks the knife ties me to the murder, too. Unless I find the real killer, I'm their number one suspect." The mention of the note sparked another tantalizing memory, but it quickly slid away again.

"We can't let Father murder Thusa, Deccia! We have to help her."

"He *won't*."

"I'm going to help you. I don't care what Deccia says."

Deccia glared at her little sister. "We need to be careful. The thief could murder *us*, if he suspects what we're doing."

"I don't care! I'm smarter than any dumb old thief."

"I want to help Thusa too, but it's not smart to rush in. We could stir up a lot of trouble."

"Father would get mad," Aalicaa scorned. "Bother that, Deccia. We have a mystery on our hands. It's our *duty* to see justice done."

Deccia frowned. "I'm not afraid of Father. I just want to be careful."

Aali scowled.

"Who's on the Council that we know, and who's an immigrant, too?" Methusal couldn't let that investigative lead go.

"Poli and Ben Amil are from Dehre, and Pogul's parents are from Tarst. And what about Kitran and Barak—didn't they move here from Quasr years ago? And Verdnt, of course, is from Dehre. Even Old Sims. I don't remember where he's from, but he moved here more than thirty years ago. And that's probably only half," Deccia said.

Methusal couldn't imagine any of those people being a murderer. But she chewed over one interesting detail. "Pogul is a guard, too," she said thoughtfully. "And Vogl, the guard at the ore mine door, is from Tarst. Timaeus said the water engineers have access to the mine, too. Both Behran and Goric are immigrants."

And both had beaten her at the Tri-level. An interesting coincidence? Or maybe she was being overly suspicious. She definitely couldn't imagine Behran murdering Renn.

"We'd better keep this to ourselves. We don't want to create suspicion toward innocent people."

"Or let the murderer know we're searching for him," Deccia agreed.

"And I'm pretty sure it's a man. Remember how I saw the back of him the night the grain was stolen?"

"Do you think he'll steal again?"

"We can watch and spy," Aali supplied instantly. "I could do it. I'm good at it."

"You certainly are," Deccia said dryly. "Did you know, Thusa, that's how she learned kaavl? Listening in on Kitran's lessons to the Quatr-levelers."

"I know." Methusal smiled.

Deccia cast a censorious, but mostly humorous glance at her little sister. "Aali knows all kinds of ways to hide and sneak through this mountain."

"If Father won't post guards, then I'll be a guard. No one will catch me."

"Catch you doing what, little one?" Timaeus appeared with a grin. He looked weary, and his clothes were dusty from the plains, but his smile, now directed at Deccia, lit up the room.

Deccia's cheeks pinkened. "You're home."

"And I have news. Behran is calling for Petr and the others. They'll be here in a minute."

Erl, Petr, Liem, and Behran soon joined them at the table. A frown knotted Petr's brow. "What is going on? What's your report?"

Timaeus said, "I just got back from Tarst, sir. While I was there, I saw two Rolbani pots on the serving tables."

Erl frowned. "Are you sure?"

"Rolban's triangular pattern was stamped under the top lip of each pot."

An incredulous silence fell. Methusal knew from first-hand experience that each of Rolban's pots was stamped with a distinctive triangular pattern. Timaeus had also served kitchen duty, so he knew it, too. And yet she couldn't believe it. Her suspicions had centered upon the Dehriens. So why had Rolban's pots turned up in Tarst?

Erl finally spoke. "There must be an explanation. I've known Pan for over forty years. He's an honest man. He'd never steal from Rolban."

"Maybe Tarst traded for those pots," Deccia suggested. "What if Dehre stole them, and Tarst bought them?"

"I thought of that," Timaeus agreed. "I asked Pan's wife, who's in charge of Tarst's kitchen. Aenill said they haven't traded with anyone recently—except for Dehre's oil in exchange for Tarst's trees. That's it. She didn't know when the pots arrived in Tarst, and she didn't know the pots were Rolban's. And she was very upset when she learned they were. She insisted on sending one back with me. Another runner—Dastn, or Kilum—will bring the other one home on their next trip."

"At least we'll get the pots back," Liem's frowning gaze rested upon Methusal.

Methusal turned to Petr. "Do you see now that I can't be involved? I've never been to Tarst! How could I possibly be the thief?" She turned to Liem. "Or Renn's murderer?"

"*Someone* in Rolban is the thief," Petr thundered. "And that someone is secretly sending stolen goods to Tarst. Maybe Tarst is behind the thefts. Maybe not. It's too soon to tell. But you, Methusal, are tied to both Renn's death and the thefts. Your necklace was found on his body. An incriminating note was found in your room. You had access to the bloody kitchen knife, which was the murder weapon. And you also work in the supply room, where the seed grain was stored. What am I supposed to think right now?"

Methusal gasped. Now she was guilty of stealing the seed grain? "I didn't steal the grain! For one, I could never lift it. But I saw who did."

Petr flushed, and cleared his throat. "You *say* you saw him."

Methusal's temper soared. "I *did* see him—his back, anyway. And it was a man. A big one."

"Why should I believe you? If you're guilty, you'd lie about this, just like you'd lie about everything else."

"Petr," Erl warned.

Methusal jumped to her feet. "*Please* think logically! Yes, the thief must be a Rolbani. But it's not me, and if you want to find out who it is, you'd better open up your mind and look at *all* of the facts!"

"Methusal," Petr roared. "Sit down!"

Methusal ignored him, determined to have her say for once. "Runners from Dehre or Tarst must be carrying away the stolen goods. Papa, who are the main runners from those communities?"

"Ludst Lst, from Dehre. And Dastn and Kilum from Tarst."

Methusal turned to Timaeus. "You know those runners. What are they like?"

"Ludst is a whip. Dastn is a great person."

"And Kilum?" she pressed.

Timaeus hesitated. "He keeps to himself. Not real friendly. He's always been decent to me, though."

Methusal remembered her impression of Kilum the other day. "I've seen him, too. And maybe I shouldn't say this, but there's something about him I don't trust. Pogul handed him something to take to Tarst. It was too small to be any of the stolen items, though."

"Do you have a point to this...this insubordinate diatribe?" Petr demanded, his face still flushed with anger.

"Yes. I think you're forgetting the most important question here. *Why?* Why are these thefts happening? We just signed an Alliance. There is no need to steal. We can trade! Look at the bigger picture, please. The thefts will destroy the Alliance. I think that is the thief's ultimate goal."

Silence elapsed while the others thought through Methusal's words.

Erl finally spoke. "You've made some good points, Thusa. But please speak with respect to your elders."

"My elders," she glared at Petr and Liem, "want to kill me. If I don't stand up for myself, who will? If I don't investigate, who will?"

"I'm investigating," Liem growled. "And I've found no proof of your innocence."

"Or my guilt." She turned to Petr. "Are you investigating?"

"Thusa," Erl said sharply.

"It's a legitimate question, Papa. Liem has found several clues. So have I. Petr hasn't. In fact, when Behran and I asked him to post extra guards on the supply room and kitchen, he refused. And that was the night the grain was stolen. Why didn't he post any guards?"

Petr's face was a frightening, bilious purple now. He slammed his hand on the table. "You are a belligerent, mouthy young woman. I have a good mind to throw you back in jail right now!"

"*Thusa!*" Deccia muttered.

"I'm sorry," Methusal told Petr. "I truly am. But I'm scared! I don't want to die. I didn't do anything wrong, and I just want my life back. Don't you understand?"

Petr didn't answer. He looked away.

Methusal made one last attempt. "Papa, when will the next runner arrive?"

"Ludst is coming tomorrow. Dastn will come the next day."

"I still think we need to post extra guards," Methusal said, but no one commented.

Timaeus said, "I'll run to Tarst tomorrow and come back with Dastn. On the trip, I'll ask if he's seen anything suspicious."

"Thank you," Methusal said quietly. She felt spent. She'd been insubordinate, belligerent—everything Petr had accused her of being. Her outburst had probably made things worse for herself.

Deccia patted Methusal's arm as she stood. Compassion warmed her eyes. "I hate to break this up, but I need to see Verdnt."

The teachers usually used the last two days of the week to catch up on lesson plans, since there was no school on those days.

Methusal remembered that Verdnt had asked Deccia to work in his compartment today. "I thought you'd told him..." she glanced at Petr, "you couldn't."

Timaeus' gaze sharpened.

"I'm just picking up the lesson plans." She explained, "I'll teach the lower grades when Verdnt goes to the Inter-Community Games."

"Do you think that will solve the problem?" Methusal murmured, not wanting to create another drama, but concerned for her twin. "He'll want to *discuss* the plans, too."

Deccia flushed. "I'll be quite clear about what I will and will not do."

Timaeus unexpectedly spoke up. "Can I walk you there?"

Deccia's mouth fell open. Her eyes brightened and her cheeks pinkened still more. "Well... Thank you. I'd like that."

"Great." Palms on the table, Timaeus pushed himself to his feet. Deccia cast a backward glance at Methusal as they left the dining room together. Her wide, delighted eyes said, *can you believe this?*

Methusal smiled, happy for her twin. Deccia deserved this. Timaeus was such a nice person, and she was glad her sister might finally have a chance with the man she'd liked for so long.

A glance at Petr, however, revealed the opposite reaction. He scowled after the two. Well, Petr couldn't dictate true love. And Methusal felt happy that for once, her uncle would not get his own way.

△ △ △ △ △

Goric intercepted Methusal on the way to the supply room. "Methusal. Wait up."

Seeing the slight, medium height young man brought a sick feeling to the pit of her stomach. Was she really such a sore loser? She should congratulate him, instead of feeling sorry for herself for losing the Tri-level.

Although she couldn't quite force a smile to her lips, she did manage to say, "Congratulations on the Tri-level."

"Yes. Thanks." His pale hair fell in thin spikes down his forehead, and his eyes didn't meet her own. "Kitran wants to speak to you."

"Okay. Thanks." She wondered what Kitran wanted. When Goric made to turn away, she blurted, "I'll bet you're excited about the Inter-Community Games."

"Yes. Of course. Why wouldn't I be?" His eyes shifted away.

"Too bad the games won't take place in Aestoff. Isn't that where you're from?" For the first time, Methusal wondered why Goric had moved to Rolban three years ago. He didn't seem to fit in, and he didn't seem to want to try. In fact, she'd never really noticed him much before now. His only contribution to the community was working with Motr and Behran on the water systems. Otherwise, he kept to himself.

Opaque gray eyes bored into hers. "Yes. You know I'm from Aestoff."

"How did you do it?"

"Do what?"

"Come in second at the Tri-level."

"I'm good. Better than you, apparently." He gave a small, nasty laugh.

Methusal swallowed back a smart remark. "Did you plan your strategy beforehand?"

"Of course. Who doesn't?"

"What was it? Obviously, I need pointers."

His lips curled. "Simple. I ran straight to the bluffs and back. I didn't stop to capture. And I beat both of you."

"That's imp..." She stopped. She wouldn't tip Goric off to her unusual hearing abilities. "I guess capturing isn't one of your strengths."

"I captured you." With a smirk, he left her.

It was probably irritation made her feel more convinced than ever that Goric had cheated. She'd bet anything that he'd hidden on the plains and run nowhere. And then he'd sprinted for the finish line at the last minute. But how could she possibly prove it?

△ △ △ △ △

A few minutes later, Kitran curtly motioned Methusal into his office.

"Goric said you wanted to see me?"

His penetrating gaze bored into her. "Have you been practicing?"

"No," she admitted.

"Not since the games?"

"No. Well, not really." That short time in class couldn't really count.

"You lost. But your kaavl is good, and it could be great. Quit moping."

"I..."

"I know you wanted to beat Behran. Get over it."

"I'm trying. It's Goric. I can't believe he got by me."

"Why do you say that?"

"He says he ran straight to the bluffs and back. But I didn't see him. Neither did Behran."

"Are you accusing him of cheating?" Warning deepened Kitran's voice. Slander was a serious charge, and she'd need proof.

She swallowed. "Of course not."

"Sulk. Or get back to work. Your choice."

"I'll practice today." Methusal felt ashamed as she left his office. Was she really that pitiful? Whining, on the verge of slandering Goric...

But Kitran was right. The world hadn't ended because she'd lost the Tri-level. She needed to pull herself together and work even harder. Next year, she'd win. Next year, she'd make sure a judge was stationed on the far bluffs, too.

△ △ △ △ △

Methusal and Liem are becoming more dangerous. They are fools, and fools do not enjoy a long life span. It's laughable that Methusal does not realize the key to the 2nd Book of Kaavl hangs around her neck. A fool, like all Rolbanis. My ally wishes to see the necklace, but I fear he must languish with disappointment. I have the information I need. Now only to find the book, and unravel the peace between Rolban and her "allies," once and for all. I will take care of my own enemies swiftly, for the glory of Zindedi.

△ △ △ △ △

The remainder of the day passed in relative peace. Aali had compiled a list of immigrants who were either guards or served on the Council, and had given her findings to Methusal that afternoon.

Fourteen men remained on the list. Narrowing it down still further would be difficult.

Catching the thief in the act was obviously the best solution. Even though the pots were found in Tarst, Dehre still could be involved in the thefts. And their runner would come tomorrow. That meant if Dehre was in allegiance with the Rolbani thief, items might be stolen tonight or tomorrow night, and tossed down into the ravine for pick up. Petr continued to refuse to post guards, so she would have to take matters into her own hands.

First, though, she'd practice kaavl, and then she'd stake out the garment room. A hunch told her it would be the thief's next target.

Methusal sat cross-legged on the pallet in her room, quieted her mind, and then concentrated fully into kaavl. Today she'd study an excerpt from the ancient *First Book of Kaavl*, written by the Old Kaavl Master, Mahre. It was the only text they had which detailed how to learn kaavl.

If only they had the *Second Book of Kaavl*. Unfortunately, it had disappeared from Rolban during the Great War. Legend said a Dehrien had stolen it, but no one knew for sure. The man and his cohorts had died at the end of the war. Most people believed the book had been destroyed then, too. After the Great War, Rolban had sent search parties to every corner of the continent to find the book, but no trace had ever been found.

The *First Book of Kaavl* had been copied many times, but the Maahr family, as direct descendants of Mahre, owned the original copy. Methusal opened the brown, brittle cover, and traced the inscription inside the first page.

By Mahre. For all succeeding generations.

A few more words were scratched onto the first page:

Love The One
with all your heart
and with all your soul
 and with all your mind,
...and love your neighbor as yourself.

She'd known these scriptures all of her life, but how did you love a God you didn't know? Who was he, and what was he like? Rolban was not a particularly devout community. Sometimes, on the seventh day of the week, someone would read a few words from the thin, tattered *Word of The One,* but usually not.

As she'd done many times over the last few days, Methusal thought about the dream she'd had in jail. It still made no sense to her. Why had she dreamed about The One at all? She never thought about him during the daytime.

Not true. Lately, she had been—because of Renn. His death made her wonder what lay beyond that final door. If The One was real, then what did he expect from her now?

Methusal turned the next page of the ancient book. The *First Book of Kaavl* outlined how to reach the Quatr, Tri and Bi-levels of kaavl. It contained a few tips about the Primary level, too. Complete control of body, mind, and emotions were the goals. One interesting paragraph caught Methusal's attention. The ancient Master of the art, unparalleled since his death three hundred years ago, had written:

Kaavl is not a religion, and cannot provide moral rules to guide one's life. Rather, it is a method by which one can more truly experience life by mastering control over one's self and senses. Self-control provides one tool by which one can practice what is right and true.

Self-control helped a person do the right thing. But did complete self-control include milking all of her emotions dry? Did it mean she should channel that emotional energy to intensify her kaavl?

Had the Old Kaavl Master used emotional energy? She had never read about that concept in the *First Book of Kaavl*. But surely Kitran knew what he was talking about.

Soon she would have to choose—to continue on to the Bi-level or not. But the idea of climbing to the second level now felt like stepping into a cave with no way out. Only grays and blacks and shadows... No colors with which to experience life.

But the paragraph had said that kaavl was one way a person could truly experience life.

It made no sense. Frustrated, she wondered what the *Second Book of Kaavl* said about the matter. According to legend, it resolved all conflicts and clearly explained how to reach the Ultimate level—which only Mahre had achieved, late in life. If only she could read that book!

The endless questions weren't helping her to concentrate. After all, she didn't have to decide now. But her reluctance to continue up the kaavl ladder made her feel scared, and a little empty. What could she pursue instead of kaavl? Was kaavl the only thing that gave meaning to her life?

Stop it! Time to practice.

Methusal squeezed her eyes shut and concentrated. Gradually, her worries melted away as she focused on her hearing.

Tonight, for the first time, she would try to carry into the gathering room down the hall. No one was playing whaal tonight. Instead, she soon heard a few council members in the room discussing the upcoming visit of a group of Dehrien merchants. They would arrive on Sixthday; one week from today. The delegation would be twenty in number, and would stay in Rolban for two days. Rolban had never hosted such a large group from another community before, and the council members—especially Petr—seemed eager to make sure that all went well.

Methusal heard the low tones of her father, and concentrated harder. He would be the focal point for her carry.

"Where would they stay, then?"

The carry was difficult, and her nails bit into her palms as she concentrated. This was the first time she'd ever tried to carry through twenty lengths of solid rock, without the aid of her eyes to pinpoint the location of her carryee. In her struggle to accomplish the near impossible, she missed the reply, and instead focused upon her father's voice, who spoke again.

"Whose compartments, then? And where will our people stay?" At last! Methusal pinpointed her father's location, and mentally completed the carry her hearing had already made. It was almost as if she sat in the very place her father sat, and heard everything he heard. Only she was blind, and could not see the others in the room. She could only tell them apart by their voices.

She couldn't relax her concentration for an instant, or she'd lose the carry.

"We'll double up," said Barak, to her father's right. "Let's see a show of hands. Who's willing to give up their compartment for a few days?"

To her frustration, Methusal heard only a whoosh of hands.

"Good!" Directly across from Erl, Petr sounded pleased. "One problem solved. Sims! Do we have enough food?"

Old Sims' voice came from Erl's left. "We're running low, since the grain was stolen. Fresh meat would help."

"Noted." Petr did not sound concerned. "Now..."

Suddenly exhausted, Methusal relaxed. The carry had drained all of her energy, and her stomach gave a protesting gurgle. A snack before staking out the garment room sounded appealing.

She blew out the lamp above her pallet and slipped from the compartment. It was late, and the passageway deserted. Methusal glanced into the gathering chamber as she passed by, and was pleased to note Sims, Petr, Barak and her father all in the exact positions she had pinpointed during her carry exercise.

A single lamp burned just inside the entrance to the dining hall, leaving most of the large room and the kitchen shrouded in shadows. Moving too quickly, she bumped into the buffet rock outcropping. She bit back a cry of pain and cautiously advanced forward again, hands stretched ahead like feelers.

In the kitchen the light filtered weakly through the serving window, making the counters appear gray, but the floor remained black, looking like a deep pit. Carefully, she moved to the far wall. Her fingers patted up, over the rocky ledge and touched the earthenware bowl filled with leftover dried meat. At last. Greedily, she grasped two roughly textured meat strips and ripped off a bite.

"Looks like I've caught the mysterious food burglar." Behran's voice, a shade of its old mocking tone, sent her spinning around. She almost choked on the food sliding down her throat. For a moment, she didn't know what to say. They had barely spoken for several days. And his first words were annoying, as usual.

"I'm getting a snack. What are you doing here, Behran?" Defend and attack. Not much had changed. Strangely, though, she was glad they were speaking again.

He shrugged. "I'm hungry."

Methusal approached the ledge that separated them. "Have a meat strip."

"Thanks." Accepting it, his gaze returned to her. His face was partly in the shadows, and his eyes were dark and unreadable. Silent seconds ticked by.

Feeling uncomfortable, Methusal crossed her arms. "Well?"

"Well, what?" The dancing shadows revealed a quirked brow.

"You're staring at me. Why?"

He bit off a corner of the meat strip. "You okay now?"

"With what?"

"Losing to me and Goric."

"I can accept losing to you. You're really good." It was the truth. Behran deserved her respect. "But I don't understand how Goric got by us both. I never saw him reach the bluff."

"Neither did I."

"Where did you capture your two people?"

"The first one was halfway to the bluffs, and the second was a little further on."

Three systems of movement had remained after Methusal had caught Daltha at the start of the course. "He hid on the plains, right in the beginning." She gritted her teeth.

"Can you prove it?"

"Of course not."

"Why do you think he hid?"

Although Methusal didn't want to tell Behran about her unusual kaavl abilities, she could say a little. "I was tracking sounds of movement. Two sound systems stopped when I captured Daltha. Daltha was one. Goric must have been the other. After that, three remained—you, and the two people you captured later on."

"Maybe you missed him."

"You, too?"

"It is pretty suspicious," he agreed. "Goric's been at the Tri-level for all of the three years he's lived here. He's okay, but he's not terrific."

Tentatively, she asked, "Do you think he cheated?"

"It's possible."

"Would you go to Kitran with me and tell him the facts we do know?"

"Yes. If you'll forgive all the rude comments I've given you over the last five years."

Methusal went very still. She met his steady blue gaze. "I will. But only if you'll forgive me, too."

"Done."

She smiled. "Truce, then."

"Teasing isn't the same as being rude, you know."

"So that's what you call it now?"

He grinned, but did not reply. After a moment he said, "If Goric is expelled, you'd go to the Inter-Community Games."

"If Petr let me."

"I'm surprised he hasn't found another suspect yet."

"I don't think he's looking for one. He has that note and the bloody knife, and apparently that's all the proof he needs."

"Pretty cynical. Have you found any new clues?"

"Yesterday I found a list Renn wrote..." Methusal stopped. All of a sudden, the tantalizing facts that kept slipping out of reach snapped into place. She breathed, "Renn didn't write that note!"

"The note Petr found in your compartment?" Behran guessed.

"Yes." Methusal couldn't believe she'd missed the truth staring her in the face this whole time. "He couldn't have written the note Petr found in my compartment. I'm surprised I didn't notice it sooner." She returned to the first topic. "Anyway, like I said, yesterday I found a list Renn wrote. Sims verified that it is Renn's writing. But here's what's strange. The zero in the date on the note is completely different than the zero on the list!"

"Is that important?"

"Renn always wrote his zeroes with a slash through them. The note didn't have a slash through the zero. And the note's writing...it's just not right. It's smaller and cramped, like someone was trying to copy Renn's handwriting. Renn's handwriting is taller and more angular."

"Show Petr. See what he says."

"I'll take Sims with me." Methusal wanted a witness, and also someone to corroborate her facts. Excitement swelled within her. And better yet, hope.

"If Petr agrees you're innocent, and if Goric is disqualified, then you can go to the Kaavl Games!"

Methusal shook her head. "I'm afraid to believe it. I'm afraid to hope."

"Do you feel like you're ready for it, if you can go?"

"I'll need more practice. But I think so. What about you?"

Behran nodded. "I wish we knew more about the competition."

"They're at the Tri-level," she pointed out. "If they were much better, they'd compete at the Bi-level, according to the *First Book of Kaavl*." Mahre had laid out strict guidelines regarding the placement of contenders. A student was judged according to his or her abilities. No one was allowed to compete at an inappropriate skill level.

"True."

Talking about the Bi-level reminded Methusal of Kitran's new kaavl ideas. Cautiously, she said, "Do you plan to advance to the second level? You're almost qualified now."

An unexpected pause followed her query, as if Behran was giving serious thought to her question. Finally, he said, "I don't know."

Surprised, she said, "Why not?"

"I don't know if I have what it takes."

"What do you mean?"

He shrugged, and his face turned slightly, so the faint light revealed the troubled look in his eyes. "I've seen the future. And I'm not sure I like it."

"How so?"

He leaned forward, so his elbows rested on the counter between them. Quietly, he said, "By the future, I mean Kitran. I could never be like him."

Finally, Methusal understood. She and Behran were having the same doubts about climbing the kaavl ladder.

Time to be candid. "I can't control my emotions like that, either. And I don't want to."

Behran's brows flew up. "Then you know what I'm talking about?"

"Yes. But I don't understand one thing—the *Book of Kaavl* doesn't tell us to use emotional energy to improve in kaavl."

"The *first* book doesn't."

"That's the only book we have."

"I know, but Kitran thinks he knows how to make that final jump to the Ultimate level—by using the power of emotion. He thinks it's a key factor to quickly reach the second and first levels, too."

"How do you know all of this?"

"He told me. He's trying to achieve the Ultimate level right now." Behran inclined closer. "And he's discussed it with kaavl leaders in the other communities. They all agree with him."

Methusal knew that Kitran stayed in close contact with other kaavl instructors—he had once been a messenger, and now kept up old friendships. He'd also become acquainted with Mentàll during that time. But she did wonder how Behran had learned all of this information. "Why did he tell you this?"

"I told him my doubts about advancing."

Methusal's mouth fell open. "Really? You mean you told him to his *face* you don't want to be like him?"

A grin flashed in the shadowy light. "Not exactly. I used tact. That's when he told me his philosophy."

"So it's only a theory?" Relief flooded her.

Behran nodded.

Could it be true, though? Was Kitran right about how to reach the fabled Ultimate level? Complete self-control, using every scrap of emotion to focus into kaavl, not to mention feeling no emotion...

Behran straightened. "I don't think he wants this to become general knowledge yet. He wants to prove it first."

Methusal wondered how Kitran could ever prove it. If the *Second Book of Kaavl* was destroyed, how could they ever know if it was the true path to the Ultimate level? But if it *wasn't* destroyed... What a gift to kaavl that would be. And, she realized, what a source of power it could be for those communities which chose leaders based on kaavl abilities. With that book, someone could conceivably stay in power forever.

"I won't say anything," she promised. But it seemed clear that she wouldn't be able to climb to higher kaavl levels unless she focused her emotional energy like Kitran taught. He believed his theory was the only way to advance, so he wouldn't allow anyone to pass who didn't practice it.

Behran interrupted her troubled thoughts. "I'm supposed to blow out the lights downstairs. Want to help?"

"Sure." Methusal was more than happy to move on to a new subject. Her favorite occupation was creating a problem in her otherwise focused life. And that was the crux of her dilemma. Because for the last five years, kaavl had been her only focus in life.

"Let's start with the lamps nearest the gate," Behran suggested a few moments later, when they reached the Great Hall.

That made sense. By extinguishing the lights in order—farthest away to nearest—they wouldn't have to retreat from the hall in total darkness.

"I'll do the left side," she offered.

A strong, cool night breeze swept through the cave. It swirled and eddied, and caused the flames to flicker against the rough stone walls. Ahead the shining, crisscrossed bars of the gates were etched in silver against the black night. The huge ceremonial sword had been thrust sideways through the center—a warning to past and present enemies. Methusal imagined the wild beasts roaming beyond, and a shiver slipped down her spine.

The faint moan of the wind grew louder as she drew closer to the gates. Quickly, she blew out the first lamp. The noise was eerie, and sounded exactly like someone whimpering in pain.

Turning, Methusal bumped her way behind the dark recliners to the next lamp, but an unexpected obstruction in her path made her trip. She clutched at the wall but that didn't help, and she sprawled with an undignified "Ooof!" just beyond the huddled person. And a person it was, hunched over and knees drawn to their chin, and apparently the source of the whimpering. The person did not look up, even after that rude jostling.

"Are you okay?" Behran had already finished dousing the lights on his side of the cave.

"Someone's here! Hurt, I think." Methusal paid no attention to her bruised elbows and knees and sat up, peering at the unknown soul, who was shrouded in shadows. In a heartbeat, Behran knelt by her side.

"Who is it?"

Methusal touched the person's shoulder. "Are you okay?"

The sobs grew louder.

"Should we call a doctor?" Behran sounded worried.

"No!" the figure choked out.

Methusal knew that voice. "Deccia?"

The sobs came even harder.

"Deccia, what's wrong?"

"Oh, Thusa!" her sister wailed. Methusal hugged her tight.

"What happened?"

Deccia's sobs slowly quieted and she pulled away, visibly trying to collect herself. "I'm okay," she gulped.

"What happened?" Behran said.

Deccia turned to Methusal, and whispered, "Father won't let me see Timaeus again!"

"What?" Methusal was confused. "Did something happen? Did Timaeus ask you out?"

"Not...not officially." Deccia sniffed, and wiped her eyes. "But he's going to Tarst tomorrow. Remember?"

"Yes."

"Well, he asked if I would spend the afternoon with him when he gets back. We were going to hi....hike!" Fresh tears erupted. "But Father found out. I don't know how."

Instant indignation bubbled. "He *forbade* you to see Timaeus?"

"No. That was later."

This wasn't making much sense. "So what exactly happened?"

Deccia pushed a shaky hand across her eyes. "This didn't start off about Timaeus at all. It's about the thief, and what we were talking about earlier—about Renn's list of stolen things. I saw..."

"Wait!" Behran interrupted. "What list? And what about Renn?"

Methusal explained, "He wrote a list of every item that's been stolen in Rolban. He might have been investigating the thefts before he was murdered.

"Really." This idea seemed to take him by surprise, for he fell silent.

"Go on," Methusal urged her twin. "What happened tonight? Did you see something suspicious?"

"Yes. But Father found Aali and me hiding in the garment room and demanded to know what we were doing. I said we were trying to catch the thief."

Methusal was surprised. She'd been planning on staking out the garment room tonight. Deccia and Aali had beaten her to it. "I'm sure he loved that."

"Oh yes," Deccia murmured bitterly. "But I couldn't lie."

"I know. What happened then?"

"Before or after Father caught us?" An uncharacteristic edge bit through her voice.

"Before. Did you see the thief?"

"Almost. Aali convinced me that if the thief planned to steal again, it would be from the garment room. That hall is deserted at night. No one would see him stealing, like they would if he tried to sneak out of the kitchen."

"And it couldn't be the supply room, since that has a lock now," Methusal agreed. "Too bad we don't have another lock for the garment room."

"Right." Deccia drew a deep breath. "And I had a strange hunch that something would happen tonight. So Aali and I hid in the garment room, and *someone came in!*"

"Who?" Behran said.

"We couldn't tell. It was too dark—we think he blew out several lights in the hall. We saw his dark silhouette, and then he slipped into the room. He left the door open a crack so he could see—and it was a man, like you said, Thusa, because he was big—but we couldn't make out his face at all. Then we heard footsteps in the hall, and the man ran and hid in one of the dressing chambers. That's when Father came in—maybe he saw the door ajar and wondered about it. He lit the lamp and that's when he saw us, hidden behind the garment bins." For a second, Deccia's tone sounded dryly morose.

"He stared at us like he couldn't believe his eyes. Then, without saying a word, he dragged us out and marched us back to our compartment. I tried to tell him what we'd seen, but he wouldn't listen. He shouted that I'm supposed to be a role model..." gulping sobs came again, "and how I can't see Timaeus again until I prove I can act like an adult."

"That man!" Methusal wanted to grind her teeth in frustration. "Doesn't he care about catching the thief? Or Renn's murderer?"

Deccia continued to weep, and didn't seem to hear.

Methusal and Behran soon escorted Deccia home, and then Behran walked Methusal to her door.

"So, Renn was investigating the thefts."

Methusal's hand pressed lightly on the latch to her compartment. "Maybe he found something incriminating. Maybe that's why he was killed. And maybe it's about more than thefts. The thief could be hiding a bigger secret." What, though, she could not guess.

"A bigger secret..." Behran fell silent, apparently contemplating that idea.

"I'd better go."

"Oh...yes."

They stared at each other for a moment. For the first time ever, she realized they were actually on the same side about something. The feeling was unfamiliar, but not unpleasant.

"Goodnight, Behran."

"Goodnight, Thusa." His voice was soft, and it followed her as she stepped inside. "Remember, I'll help out when you talk to Kitran tomorrow."

"Thanks, Behran."

Chapter Twenty-One

Seventhday

METHUSAL SLEPT IN LATER than she'd planned the next morning. When she entered the corridor, throngs of people wandered toward the dining hall, ready for breakfast. Usually she got up early to beat the rush, but she'd stayed awake late into the night, thinking. Finally, she had figured out how to best use Renn's list to persuade Petr of her innocence. Hopefully it would work, and she'd regain her freedom. After breakfast, she'd talk to Sims and convince him to help her.

The crowd thickened as she approached the dining entrance. People clustered together, standing in line for food. Methusal edged her way to the right, and stepped down the stairs of the Grand Staircase, trying to find the end of the line.

A hard elbow jabbed into her back and shoved her forward. With a gasp, she wobbled, teetering on the step.

Horror stabbed her. *She was going to fall.*

She screamed.

A rough hand grabbed her arm and yanked her to a stop. "Whoa, there." Barak's strong, meaty hand gripped Methusal's arm so hard that bruises would probably show up later. But she was grateful. So grateful.

"Thank you!" she gasped. Tears burned her eyes. Her heart thundered. "I was about to... Someone pushed me..."

Barak's heavy brows knit together. "Someone pushed you?"

"It was an accident... I'm sure." Shaking, she scanned the wall of people above her. All of them were people she'd known her entire life. Surely none of them had pushed her. Aali's immigrant list sprang to mind. Was anyone on that list nearby?

No. But a short distance away she did glimpse a few... Petr, Verdnt, Pogul, Goric, Behran, and even Liem, who was not an immigrant. But none of them were near enough to have pushed her. Surely it had been an accident.

Her pounding heart gradually quieted. Still trembling, though, she made sure her feet were firmly planted on the stairs before gently tugging her arm free. Barak's bruising grip released her at once.

"Thanks, Barak," she said again. Her voice wavered a little. "I'm so glad you were here."

He nodded, but his frown remained. "Be careful."

She felt safe, and glad Barak stood behind her as she waited for breakfast. Surely no one had tried to push her down the stairs. But if they had, they wouldn't try again with Barak close by.

By the time she'd scooped breakfast onto her plate, Methusal felt considerably better, and had convinced herself that the shove had been accidental. Probably someone had pushed his way into line. Rude, but not malicious.

Behran sat at the Maahr table, and she greeted him cautiously. Their newfound truce still felt awkward and unfamiliar.

He shoveled a sticky clump of cereal into his mouth and glanced over at the Storst table. Swallowing hard, he muttered, "I don't see her."

Methusal glanced at the Storst table, too. Anger kindled in her heart when she saw Petr laughing with a neighbor and swigging back a mug of tagma juice. Aalicaa sat beside him, hunched over her plate. A quick survey proved her sister was not in the dining room, and Methusal glanced back at the Storst table. Aalicaa now sat alone, poking at her food.

"I'll be back." She jumped up and zigzagged over.

"Hi, Aali." She sat beside her.

"Mmph." Tears glistened in her eyes.

"Where's Deccia?"

The child sniffled loudly. "At home. Father's making her stay home all day." Her wide eyes beseeched Methusal. "But what happened was all *my* fault!"

"Of course it wasn't!" Methusal gave her a quick, comforting hug. She tried to control a flare of anger. Petr was too much! Couldn't he see that his daughters were only trying to help Rolban? She was surprised he hadn't banished Aali to her room, too. But maybe Deccia's punishment made Aali feel guilty, which was punishment enough.

"Father said he looked in the garment room later, just to prove we were wrong to spy. Nothing was stolen!" Aalicaa blurted. "So why did that man sneak in?"

"You probably scared him off."

"That's what Deccia thinks, too."

"Do you think I could talk to her?"

Aalicaa glanced at her father, who now strode out of the dining hall. "*He* would be mad. She's not supposed to have visitors."

"Just one minute."

"Okay." Aalicaa defiantly tossed her head and snatched up her bowl. "It's safest if we go now. *He's* going to inspect the fields."

Methusal followed her cousin down the passageways to the Storst compartment.

"I'll check inside to make sure it's safe." Aalicaa disappeared for a moment, and then reappeared, waving her hand urgently. "Be quick," she hissed, peering down the hall.

Methusal found Deccia sitting on the bed pallet in her room, knees drawn up to her chin. A writing utensil listlessly drooped from her fingers. A page of half-completed lesson plans lay in the middle of the floor, as if tossed there in a fit of frustration.

"What am I going to do, Thusa?" Her voice sounded dull. "Father says I can't see Timaeus again. Not until he says so."

Methusal rolled her eyes. "He's being ridiculous, as usual. Are you really going to listen to him?"

"I have to. He's my father. I have to respect and obey him, no matter how much I might disagree with him."

Methusal remembered her night in jail. "I understand. But it's still not fair. He wants you with Verdnt, not Timaeus.

This is his excuse to keep you and Timaeus apart. How can you stand it? Doesn't it make you mad, for goodness sakes?"

"Of course!" Finally, a bit of anger broke through.

"I don't know how you do it."

Deccia closed her eyes. "It's simple. I want Father to respect me, and I want to be a good role model for Aali. Who knows how she'd behave if she thought she could act any way she pleased. And I want to be a teacher, and eventually go out with Timaeus—with Father's approval. The only way to do all of those things is to obey Father now."

"I'm sorry, Decc, but I just don't get it. Can't you see that he wants to control you? He won't let you think for yourself. And he punishes you if you don't think and behave exactly like he wants. Look at poor Aali. He won't let her practice kaavl. In fact, he won't let either of you be your own person!"

Deccia remained silent. A frown pulled at her brows.

"You know I'm right. I agree that you should respect him, but he has to give a little, too, and listen to you. We're adults now—we're eighteen! You have to stand up for yourself."

"Hurry!" Aalicaa hissed from the doorway.

Methusal loved her sister, but sometimes she frustrated her a little. "See you tomorrow." Deccia did not respond. Methusal slipped quietly into the hall. "Thanks, Aali."

A cold bowl of cereal greeted her in the dining room. Behran had vanished. She ate alone, and tried but failed to understand Petr Storst's cold, narrow-minded ways, and why Deccia was afraid to speak her mind to her father.

Right now, though, she had plenty of problems of her own. Hopefully Sims would help her solve one of them this morning.

△ △ △ △ △

"Good morning, Sims," Methusal let herself into the supply room. Across the room, Old Sims stacked blank parchment sheets into a pile.

"Good, you're here," he smiled. "Today I want you to copy the inventory list onto clean parchment. My old eyes can hardly read the old one anymore. It's been marked out and changed too often."

"I'd be happy to do that," she agreed. But first things first. "Sims, remember the list I found yesterday? The one Renn wrote?"

Sims scrunched his eyes, and then his expression cleared. "Oh yes, of course."

"I need to show Renn's handwriting to Petr. Would you come with me this morning, and tell him the list is in Renn's writing?"

"Let me see it again." Methusal took it from her pocket and Sims examined it. "Surely it is Renn's writing," he said at last. "And you say this is important?"

She nodded. "It could help catch Renn's murderer."

"All right, then. Let's go now. The inventory can wait for a few minutes."

"Thank you, Sims!"

Δ Δ Δ Δ Δ

Nerves attacked Methusal as soon as she and Sims stepped into Petr's office. In her heart, she was afraid Petr wouldn't listen to reason, no matter what she said.

"Sit down, Sims. Methusal." Petr shot her a disgruntled look. He wasn't pleased to see her, that was for sure.

Sims spoke. "Young Methusal found some evidence. It might help catch Renn's killer."

"Oh?" Petr's brows rose. "And what evidence might that be?" Clearly, he was already preparing to doubt whatever she might say.

Frustration simmered, but she tried to ignore it. Better yet, maybe she should use that emotional intensity to clearly lay out her case. Kitran would be proud.

"I found a list Renn wrote. Sims verifies that it is Renn's handwriting."

"Why is that important?"

"The handwriting on the list and the writing on that note you found in my room are different. The notes were written by two different people."

"Can you prove it?"

"I'll show you the list. Compare the writing of each one, side by side."

"All right." Petr rose to his feet with the air of someone embarking on a fool's journey. He fetched the note, and Methusal lay the list beside it on the desk. To her relief, the difference between the two samples was just as different as she remembered. The writing was small and cramped in the note, and tall and angular in the list.

Sims leaned forward and peered at them, too. He traced the letters on one parchment, and then the other. "No question. The writing on the note isn't Renn's. He always put a slash through his zeroes, too."

Methusal was glad Sims had mentioned the zeroes.

Petr frowned. Then he leaned back in his chair, his face impassive. "Writing samples prove nothing. We all write differently when we're happy, sad..." he looked at Methusal. "Fearful. Small writing doesn't prove anything."

Her worst suspicions were coming true. Petr would not listen. Struggling to tamp down her rising frustration, Methusal took a different tack. "Have you checked Renn's room? Surely he wrote other notes. Do any of them match the small writing in that note?"

Petr's brow lowered. "Are you trying to tell me how to run my investigation?"

"I'm trying to clear my name!" she snapped.

"You're walking the cliff's edge, Methusal. *I* will decide whether this information will help the investigation—or just help you. Thank you for coming, Sims. Methusal, you are dismissed."

Fury scalded her. Would Petr never listen to reason? Or was he being deliberately obtuse?

"Do you *want* to find the real murderer?" she challenged. "Or is it just easier to accuse me?"

"Methusal Maahr!" His voice rose in warning. Ignoring it, she turned her back and followed Sims out the door. She slammed it behind her for good measure.

"Methusal. My girl," Sims said. "Was that wise?"

"Nothing I do matters. Petr has already made up his mind. I'm guilty. Period."

Sims led the way back to the supply room. His faded blue eyes regarded her. "I'm sorry Petr and Liem think you killed Renn."

"I didn't!"

"I believe you. You wouldn't harm a hair of an apte, would you, girl?"

"I try to help them."

"I thought as much." His gnarled hand rested on her shoulder for a moment. "It'll all work out, don't you worry."

"How do you know?" Methusal felt despondent.

"Have faith in The One who sees all. Justice will be served."

"I wish I could believe that."

"Mahre did. Haven't you read the first lines in the *Book of Kaavl*?"

"Yes. ...I didn't know you knew kaavl."

He smiled. "I know a great deal, and I've seen more places and people than you've ever dreamed, Methusal. Perhaps one day you will, too." He turned and said, as if to himself, "And I've seen the Prophet."

"The Prophet?" As a child, Methusal had heard talk of the Prophet. "You've met him?"

Sims smiled. "Oh, but surely. The One sends him to all true seekers."

"Is he alive now?"

"I don't know. I haven't heard of him in years. But he could be. He's about my age."

Methusal had never known anyone who'd spoken to the Prophet before. The very idea intrigued her. She'd love to meet a real Prophet; someone who talked to The One. Could the Prophet answer her questions about life and death? About where Renn was right now? And could he tell her if her disturbing dream might be prophetic?

Her mind returned to something else Sims had said. "Who is a true seeker?"

"The ancient writings say those who seek The One will find him. If they seek him with all their heart, and with all their soul. The Prophet helped me along that path." Sims smiled. "Now, if I've answered all of your questions, it's time for work."

△ △ △ △ △

After lunch Methusal found Behran, and together they headed for Kitran's office to speak to him about Goric. After her confrontation with Petr that morning, Methusal felt apprehensive about the meeting with Kitran. After all, she planned to accuse Goric of cheating, and she had no solid proof. Would Kitran judge it to be slander? Would he demote her back to the Quint-level?

If so, right now the risk seemed worth it.

"Yes?" Kitran looked up when Behran rapped on his open door. His eyelids flickered when he took in the two of them, standing together. "Well." He leaned back in his chair and linked his hands behind his neck. "To what do I owe this pleasure? The adversaries have joined forces?"

Methusal glanced at Behran. "I want to talk about the Tri-Level Game. Behran wants to report what he saw, too."

"It's about Goric." Kitran guessed, his black gaze unreadable. "Go on, then. Behran, you first."

Behran, as usual, cut straight to the point. "I saw Goric two times on the course; at the beginning, and at the end. Both times were near the finishing plateau. I didn't hear or see him anywhere else on the course. And I didn't see him reach the far bluffs."

"That's a serious charge." Kitran's brow lowered. "I hope you have proof, or you'll both be disciplined for slander."

"Behran hasn't slandered," Methusal said. "He just reported what he saw and what he didn't see."

"All right. What did you see, Methusal?" Warning darkened his tone.

Methusal heaved a breath. Carefully, she explained how she had tracked systems of movement during the game. By that proof, Goric had hidden at the beginning of the race. "Also, like Behran, I only saw him at the beginning and end of the race. I never saw him reach the bluffs. I'd like to know if anyone saw that."

"You're telling me that you can track five systems of movement simultaneously."

"Not exactly." Methusal wasn't sure why, but she still didn't want anyone to know about her unusual kaavl skills—

that she could hear clearly at all distances, and carry with hearing, too. For one thing, Behran was still a potential competitor. For another, Kitran might be one day, too. "I can track three systems at a time—sometimes. And I can track from one to another pretty fast." She didn't mention that she could have heard Goric reach the far bluff even if she'd still remained at the beginning of the course.

Kitran's eyes narrowed. Did he suspect her unusual abilities? Had she let too much slip?

"So you're saying there's no chance he slipped by you, and ran out of range while you captured Daltha?"

She could say "none," but that would sound arrogant, and it would feed Kitran's suspicions. Instead, she said, "Unlikely. Especially since Behran didn't see or hear him, either. And Behran was further along the course at that time."

Kitran's frown deepened. "I don't like this. I don't like unfounded accusations, and I don't like questioning the final ruling of the game."

"Maybe in the future we should station a judge at the far bluffs. Each person might need to grab a halfway kaavl strip, too. Then we'll be sure this never happens again."

"You haven't established that it *has* happened!" Kitran exploded. "You've brought me no proof—just conjecture. Behran, I'd like to speak to Methusal alone."

"Thank you, Behran." Methusal watched him exit.

Kitran had visibly reigned in his temper during the small amount of time it took for Behran to close the door. Anger still simmered in his dark eyes, however, and Methusal felt uneasy.

"Methusal, you walk the edge too often. You're accused of thefts and murder, you daydream in class, disobey Petr, and get thrown into prison. Again and again I've stood up for you. And now you're accusing another player of cheating. Why should I side with you again?"

Put that way, she did sound pretty awful. "I'm sorry I've been such a problem," she said in a small voice. "I was wrong to daydream, and disobey Petr. I've told you that before. But I didn't kill Renn. Surely you know that."

"I believe it, for good or bad. Maybe that's the problem, Methusal, I believe too much in your kaavl abilities, and I'm blind to your lack of discipline."

"Then why did you let me play in the Games?"

"I thought you'd learned your lesson. Now I'm not so sure."

Despair pricked at her. "Is it wrong to stand up for myself? Is it wrong to want justice? Petr has already convicted me in his mind. So has Liem. And I'm convinced Goric won unfairly. I won't take it lying down. I've learned that if I don't stand up for myself, no one else will."

Amusement flickered. "And there's the fire." He shook his head. "Of course it's not wrong to stand up for yourself. As far as kaavl, you could be great, Methusal. If only you'd learn how to harness your emotions and your talent. One day, your kaavl could far outshine almost anyone on the planet."

Astonished, she said, "You really believe that?"

"I'm not the only one. Who do you think convinced Petr to release you from prison, just so he could watch you in the Kaavl Games?"

"Who?"

"Mentàll Solboshn."

"*No.*" Disbelief gripped her.

"Yes. While he was here, I told him all about your kaavl abilities—at least the skills you've told me about." Kitran smiled a little, and Methusal knew then that he suspected her hidden kaavl talents. "He wanted to see for himself if it was true."

"Why?"

"Maybe to see his future competition? Or maybe because he was curious."

Methusal believed the curiosity part. She didn't think the Dehrien Chief would ever condescend to consider her an equal threat on any playing field.

"So that's the pressure Petr meant." It disturbed her to know that the Dehrien had been instrumental in both her release from jail and her participation in the Tri-level. She didn't believe he'd helped her out of the kindness of his heart. No. She didn't trust the Dehrien one handbreadth.

From the little she knew about him, she guessed his every move was calculated. Calculated to benefit only himself.

"I'm sorry I didn't meet your expectations," she told Kitran.

"You performed well."

Boldly, she asked, "Did you see Goric run the course, or reach the far bluffs?"

He frowned. "No. I thought he'd been captured at the beginning. Then, when I saw him sprinting for the finish, I realized he must have slipped through the course under cover of the bushes."

"I want the truth to come out," Methusal said. "If Goric beat me, then fine. But if he didn't, I want the second place spot. I want to go to the Inter-Community Games, and I want to be able to advance to the Bi-level next year if I progress well."

"I know you do." Kitran pressed his fingertips together. He fell silent for a while. "All right, Methusal. One last time, I'll take your side. You and Goric will face off against each other tomorrow afternoon. Same conditions. Winner earns the right to second place, and a trip to the Inter-Community Games."

"Kitran!" She leaped for joy. "Thank you so much!"

"Keep it quiet to prevent gossip. Behran will help judge. I'll station him at the bluffs."

"Okay."

"Noon sharp, during lunch," he ordered. "And I'll okay it with Petr."

Methusal couldn't believe her good luck. A match-off with Goric! What could be better? She'd tell Behran later that evening.

△ △ △ △ △

Methusal sailed through the rest of the day in a sunny mood. Now, if only she could beat Goric. And if only she could convince Petr that she was innocent. She had a plan for tonight that just might accomplish that goal.

Her good mood only faltered when she entered the dining room that evening and saw Matron Olgith in the kitchen. Doing triple duty today. The evening supervisor must be sick.

As she feared, the meal displayed the characteristic lack of imagination that was Matron Olgith's hallmark. Meat baked until all the juices ran dry, and a thick, porridge-like side dish that was mixed with cut up logne leaves. It looked tough and tasteless, and quickly lived up to the expectation.

"Ugh!" Methusal wrinkled her nose after tasting the porridge. She wished Matron Olgith wasn't Petr's aunt. Otherwise, she'd have lost the important kitchen supervisor job long ago.

Erl sat beside his daughter. "Be grateful, Methusal. At least we have food to eat."

She could argue that usually it was edible. But she held her tongue and ate quietly, listening with half an ear to her parents' low conversation. Erl seemed to be trying to placate Hanuh, who looked quietly troubled.

"I know, Erl. I just feel on edge, like something dreadful is about to happen."

Hanuh's words made Methusal remember being poked in the back this morning, and almost falling down the stairs. Surely it had been an accident. And yet her mother had had the premonition that she would be in danger. Was it coming true now? Was someone trying to kill her?

"Maybe you should go to bed early tonight," Erl told Hanuh. "Get some rest."

Behran slid in across from Methusal. "I forgot to ask you. Did you talk to Deccia?" His voice was low. "How is she doing?"

"Okay. Petr's punishing her as an example to Aali."

Behran shook his head. "Poor kid."

Methusal's eyes narrowed at the "kid" reference, since she was Deccia's exact age, but chose to ignore the remark. Instead, she told him about her rematch with Goric. "Kitran wants you to help judge. Noon sharp."

"So you convinced him to help you." Behran looked amused.

"Why are you smirking?"

"You have him wrapped around your little finger."

"Excuse me?" She raised an eyebrow. "Are you suggesting Kitran has inappropriate feelings for me?"

"No. I'm suggesting you're his favorite student, and you can get away with murder. Not literally," he added hastily, when she glared.

Methusal swallowed back a retort. Kitran was right. She definitely needed to work on discipline and controlling her temper.

After chewing on gristly meat for a few moments, she told him, "I think Deccia and Aali were on the right track last night. Do you know if the Dehrien runner, Ludst Lst, came today?"

"I saw him. He left about noon."

And he might hang around outside until later tonight, waiting for the thief to drop more stolen items into the ravine.

She smiled. "Good."

Eyes narrowed, Behran leaned toward her. "What are you plotting?"

Her grin widened. Finally, she might get her life back and catch Renn's murderer at the same time. "The thief might strike again tonight."

"Okay. And that's important because..." Behran continued to eye her suspiciously.

Another person would be a definite help. She leaned forward and whispered, "I'll tell you after supper. Downstairs, in the Great Hall."

"All right." He had to be satisfied with that.

They fell silent, quickly stuffing the tasteless porridge into their mouths, but Methusal continued to try to work out the finer points of her plan.

Her parents left a little later. Both were frowning now.

"Look!" Behran signaled for her attention.

Methusal glanced over and spotted Deccia sitting at the Storst table with Aalicaa and Petr. So, she wasn't banished to her room any longer. That was good news, at least. A few tables over, Sims caught her attention. He was sitting at a table all by himself.

Surely he didn't always eat alone. The idea disturbed her. Why hadn't she noticed before? Maybe she should invite him to eat at their table.

Δ Δ Δ Δ Δ

Perched on the edge of a wooden recliner downstairs, Methusal waited impatiently for Behran to arrive. The sooner they set her plan in motion, the better. Maybe tonight they'd catch the thief.

Where could Behran be? Feeling fidgety, she leaped to her feet and paced the length of the long, deserted hall.

"Thusa!" The hiss came from behind her.

By now she was so agitated that she grabbed Behran by the sleeve and pulled him into the middle of the hall. No one would overhear them there—if indeed someone was hiding nearby. Although that was unlikely, it seemed foolish to take chances.

"What is it?" Behran sounded impatient. His tone both surprised and irritated her. "Hurry up, Thusa. I don't have time for childish pranks."

Childish pranks! Her cheeks flamed. "Maybe I don't need your help after all!" Why did he always act like such a whip? Just when she'd thought they were getting along. And he had made her lose her temper again.

"All right!" he said, hastily catching her arm before she spun on her heel. "Tell me. I'm listening."

She frowned. "I hope you're serious, because this is not a game."

"Okay."

"Here's my plan. I think the thief will steal something tonight—especially since he wasn't able to last night."

"Maybe."

"So," she went on, ignoring his dampening tone, "we need to lay a trap like Deccia and Aali did last night. Only we'll split up and cover more ground than they did. I'll hide in the garment room, and you can cover the kitchen."

"How will you see the thief? He might blow out the lights in the hall again. And the garment room will be dark."

"I don't know. I'll work that out."

"What if the thief catches you? Remember, he's probably the murderer, too. If he's cornered, he might kill you. And besides that, how long are we supposed to keep watch? I have to go to work in the morning."

Methusal felt a swell of irritation at his nitpicking. "*I'll* wait all night if I have to. Why did you come down here, if all you want to do is criticize?"

A short silence elapsed. "I'm worried, Thusa. Maybe Petr's right. This is dangerous. You could get hurt."

His concern mollified her. "My life is already in danger. I could be executed, remember. Please, Behran will you help? I need to find Renn's killer."

"Promise to be careful. Hanuh must have a knife in the garment room. Grab one for protection."

"You do the same."

They decided that Behran would position himself in the dining room after lights out, but Methusal would go hide now, since the garment room was already closed for the evening.

"Good luck," Behran said at the top of the stairs. "And be careful," he muttered softly. Concern darkened his eyes.

"I will." She smiled. "Good luck to you, too."

The back halls were deserted, so Methusal was able to slip unnoticed into the dark garment room. Carefully, she made her way to the far back corner, where bits of leather dangled over several tables, ready to be sewn together in the morning. The thief wouldn't steal these long, narrow pieces, she reasoned. Instead, he'd probably steal the freshly cured apte pelts hanging to dry on the wall near the door. They were small and easily hidden, but provided a lot of leather.

She found a knife on the work table and crouched in the corner under the largest table, partly shielded by strips of dangling leather. Even if the lamp was lit, the thief probably wouldn't spot her.

And she waited. Her legs grew cramped, so she stretched them out and pressed her aching back to the wall. She had no idea how much time had gone by, but knew the minutes were passing very slowly. It gave her plenty of time to think about her strategy. How could she be sure she saw the thief's face?

Should she try to strike a firestick, or try to capture him? No. Either would be foolish. She frowned in the dark.

Grain, skins, metal pots, and pans. Her necklace. The list of thefts scrolled through her mind. Why were those items stolen? After all, most were available upon request, although maybe not in large quantities. She shifted into a cross-legged position, trying to find a more comfortable way to sit on the hard floor.

Her eyelids were drooping when a soft scratching sound came from the door. Instantly, she straightened and peered through a gap in the leather. The strips tickled the side of her nose. A slit of dim light appeared. The slit widened, revealing the large, dark outline of a man. It must be the thief. He'd blown out most of the lights in the hall again. Her heart beat faster, and she sat very still.

The dim light from the hall revealed only dark hair as the figure sidled inside. Softly, the door closed to almost a crack, and she saw shadowy movements as the man groped his way over to the apte skins. Just as she had thought!

She heard a short, tearing sound and then some soft, muffled movements. He was stuffing them inside his tunic, Methusal guessed, struggling to see. She needed more light to identify him.

The man opened the door a bit wider, again revealing dark hair. Then he darted out and swiftly pulled the door shut. Methusal leaped out of her hiding place.

But her legs were numb from sitting for so long, and she half-stumbled, half-hopped to the entry and flung it wide open. She staggered into the hall. But all she saw, as she had on the night the grain had vanished, was a tall, broad back darting around the corner. Only this time he had headed toward the main hall, and not the plateau.

Legs stinging with pins and needles, she limped on as fast as she could to the end of the passageway. But by the time she reached the main passage, it was deserted. Frustrated, she bent to massage her prickling, painful legs. So close, and yet so far.

The moment she was sufficiently recovered, she sped to the dining room. A hoarse whisper summoned her spying partner and rival from the gloomy depths.

He raised an eyebrow. "Well?"

"No one's come in here, have they?"

"No. Did you see something?"

"Yes! Just like I thought, the thief came and stole some skins."

"Did you see him?"

"I tried. But it was too dark, and I couldn't think of a way to shine a light on him without being seen."

Behran exhaled sharply.

"I know. Think how I feel. But it was definitely a man, and he's tall, with dark hair." Methusal felt awful, like she had failed her mission, but Behran caught her tone and unexpectedly touched her shoulder.

"It's okay, Thusa. Better he didn't see you, and that you're safe. At least we have more information. Who do we know who has dark hair?"

"Practically everyone!" Methusal laughed shortly, blinking back tears of frustration.

"Not Petr, and not your father, or mine—they all have white or gray hair."

"But it could be anyone else! Kitran, Verdnt, Barak, Timaeus...they're all tall with dark hair. And they all have access to the ore, too. I can't remember what Pogul's father looks like, or who else on the Council has dark hair."

"Pogul has blond hair, but his father's is dark."

"I need to ask Papa which council members meet all the criteria I've found. And which guards, too."

"Good idea."

"I don't know, Behran." Methusal felt stupid, and like she'd failed, because she'd let the thief escape again. "I don't think we've learned much."

"Yes, we have. We're narrowing down the list. And Petr needs to know what just happened. We might as well tell him now."

The evening was growing worse by the moment. Methusal slowly followed Behran to the Storst compartment. There, she let Behran do all of the talking.

"Is this true?" Petr turned a heavy, condemning frown upon her. "I can't believe you'd follow the foolish notions of a thirteen-year-old child!"

Methusal just stared at him. "Did you hear Behran? Someone stole skins tonight!"

Petr's gaze narrowed. "Don't speak to me like that, girl! Do you understand? Now, I'll give you the benefit of the doubt and take a look at the garment room. But if you're wasting my time..." The threat hung heavily in the air.

He retreated to another room and Methusal spotted Aali peering around the doorway of her room. Her eyes looked bright and excited. Petr returned in a moment and slammed the compartment door shut behind them. "I'll ask your mother to come with us. Then you'll show me what you saw."

They roused Hanuh Maahr from her early slumber, and after pulling on some comfortable clothes, she followed them down the hall to the garment room. Worry pinched her features. She lit a lamp, which softly illuminated the room, and then she turned automatically to the skins on the wall.

A distressed cry was all the proof they needed.

With a frown, Petr moved in to take a closer look. "How many skins are missing, Hanuh?"

"All three! We had just finished them....All that work!" Her face crumpled.

Petr roughly patted her back. "Now, now, don't cry. We'll straighten it all out. Go get some rest. If I have more questions, I'll ask you in the morning."

When Methusal made a movement to go with her, Petr crooked a preemptory finger at her. "Not you, young lady. I have a few more questions."

Hanuh hugged her tight. "It's okay, Thusa. I'll be fine. At least you saw something that might help us catch this thief." Despite her brave words, her shoulders sagged as she left.

Petr drew the garment room door closed, and then Behran and Methusal followed his silent footsteps to his office. Lamp lit, and that door shut, he motioned for them to sit. They obeyed, and gazed up at his towering height. Methusal was glad when he finally sat, because she was getting a crick in her neck.

Petr drummed his fingers on the desk. "I don't approve of what you've done. I want you to know that. But seeing it can't be changed, I'll have to ask you if, during this escapade, you were able to determine the identity of the thief."

This was as close as the Chief would come to admitting their plan might have produced information of merit.

"I saw the outline of a man—a tall one—with dark hair," Methusal said.

"That's all you saw." A statement, as if he found her testimony wanting.

"Yes, sir."

"And you saw nothing, is that correct, Behran?"

"Yes, sir. But Deccia and Aali saw a man yesterday, too."

"I see." Several long moments crept by, and Methusal suspected he was trying to intimidate them still further. But when he looked up, it was clear he had come to a decision. "Behran, you are dismissed."

Behran glanced at Methusal. "I'll wait in the hall."

She nodded. After the door closed Petr remained silent for a moment, frowning.

"I did see the thief, and it's a man," Methusal told him.

"So you say."

"I *did*. When will you believe me? And when will you believe that Renn never wrote that note, and I never went to the bluffs? I didn't leave my necklace in the ore deposits, either!"

"Why did Renn have your necklace in his pocket? And why did someone leave your necklace in the ore cave? Hmm? Tell me that."

"I don't know!" Methusal felt incredibly frustrated. Would Petr never see reason? "Maybe he planted it on Renn. To point blame toward me."

"And why would someone want to blame you?"

"Because...because Renn had been investigating the thefts. Maybe the thief knew that. Maybe Renn had found something incriminating. The thief knew he'd have to eliminate Renn, so he left my necklace on Renn to direct the blame away from himself. A false lead."

"Sounds like you're grasping for the wind, Methusal. Why would someone target you, specifically, of all the people in Rolban?"

"I don't know. I've been trying to figure that out. Maybe it all happened by chance. I lost my necklace. I'm always taking it off, because it gets heavy. I probably left it somewhere and the thief found it. Maybe he realized he could use it to his advantage."

Petr shook his head. But his gaze looked conflicted. For the first time, Methusal felt a little hope.

She said, "All I know is I've never been to the ore deposits. I didn't leave my necklace there, so someone else did."

"You've never been to the deposits?" Petr's white brows ratcheted together. "Is that so? Lies will only dig you in deeper, Methusal."

Hope drained away again, like water through a drain. "What do you mean?" she said wearily.

"Pogul saw you and Behran in the ore passageway last week. Behran has authorization. You don't. Why were you there?" Petr's fist slammed the table. "To steal more ore?"

"No!" she cried out. Frustration churned. "If you must know, I went there to get information. I used kaavl to get by Pogul, because I wanted to see the ore deposits. I wanted to see how easy it would be for someone to sneak into the ore mine. Basically, I wanted to get information to clear my name! I'd never been there before."

"Uh huh." Petr leaned back in his chair. "You expect me to believe that?"

"We have proof the thief is a man. It's not me."

Petr drummed his fingers on the table. "Maybe." After a moment, he continued, "But I will continue this investigation. And it is *my* investigation, so stay out of it."

"I can't. You've trapped me inside this community, and taken away my freedom. I'm charged with a crime I didn't commit. If I'm convicted, I will be executed. Added to that, if I beat Goric tomorrow I know you won't let me participate in the Inter-Community Kaavl Games. I'll continue to search for the thief until my name is cleared and I'm free to go."

"Go, then."

"What?"

"Go to the Games. If you win tomorrow. I won't stop you." Petr turned away to thumb through some parchments.

"*What?* Why have you suddenly changed your mind?" Methusal couldn't believe the sudden turn in events.

"I haven't changed my mind about your guilt or innocence. But I'll let you go on one condition."

"What's that?"

"You stop investigating these crimes. It's my job, and if you continue, you're going to get yourself, Deccia, or Aali killed. Do you understand?"

"I understand, but..."

Petr stood. A clear dismissal. "Agreed?"

"I agree not to involve the others. But I still need to clear my name so you'll believe me. I won't go to jail now—or in the future—for a crime I didn't commit."

Petr threw his arms into the air. "You are a belligerent, obstinate girl! Do I have to spell it out for you?"

Methusal also stood, and took a step away from her unpredictable uncle. "What do you mean?"

"If I tell you something, will you keep your lips sealed?"

She frowned. "Yes."

"You're no longer my primary suspect in this crime."

She gasped. "What? But..."

"If the murderer thinks you're my primary target, he'll relax. Maybe he'll make a mistake."

"You think I'm innocent?"

"I'm not sure. But the handwriting and this latest evidence both prove someone else is involved. And he is probably the murderer. *But,*" he cautioned, "I'm still not sure about your involvement."

So, she wasn't completely exonerated. But it was a step in the right direction. "What about Liem?"

"Let me worry about Liem. But I have another condition, if you want to go to the Games. If you win against Goric, of course."

"What's that?"

"Act like you're still my number one suspect. Make everyone believe it. You can go, if you agree."

It appeared that Petr really was investigating, although she'd seen little proof of it until this minute. Either that, or he wanted her to quit investigating so much that he'd let her go to the IC Games, just to get her out of Rolban. She wasn't sure what to believe right now. But his offer, on the surface, at least, was too good to refuse.

"So I should keep ranting about how unfair you are?"

"The usual tirade should work." He smiled a little. "Agreed?"

"Agreed." She reached for the door handle. "Thank you."

Behran waited for her in the hall. "Well?"

"He'll let me go to the Kaavl Games!" Methusal let out a small screech. She grabbed his hands and danced in a circle.

"Okay, Thusa. Remember, you have to win, first." With a smile, Behran freed himself. "Are you free and clear now?"

"Not exactly." Methusal didn't like keeping information from Behran, since he'd gone out of his way to help her. "But it's a step in the right direction, right?"

Behran lifted an eyebrow. "It's not like you to stick your head in a hole, Thusa. You still don't have solid proof you're innocent. And what about Renn? Do you really think Petr will find his killer? As far as we know, your leads and Liem's are the only ones he has."

It was true. If it hadn't been for their investigation, she'd still be Petr's number one suspect. How hard *was* Petr investigating? "He wants to be re-elected. He'll do all he can to find the killer."

"So, you trust him now?"

"No. Not entirely. I just feel so happy..." she trailed off, feeling a little irritated. "Why can't I have this one happy moment, Behran? Why do you have to be such a thick fog?"

"Just trying to keep your eyes open."

"I can do that on my own, thanks."

"I'm not the enemy," Behran said softly. "I just don't want to see you get hurt."

Surprised, Methusal searched his eyes. He meant it. "Thank you, Behran. Good night."

He returned her smile, and she slipped down the halls to her compartment. Behran was right. Until the murderer was arrested, she'd never truly be free. But for now, she'd concentrate on beating Goric tomorrow. If she won, she could go to the Inter-Community Games. Maybe in Dehre and Tarst she could continue her investigation. She still believed that an immigrant, maybe from one of those communities, was involved in the thefts. And maybe a messenger, too.

△ △ △ △ △

I was almost caught tonight! Methusal Maahr escaped with her life this morning, but matters will not be so pleasant for her from now on. She has stirred up enough trouble. Liem is also an increasing threat. I must terminate these problems before the plan unravels prematurely. I will write a note and warn my ally, should Methusal still be a problem at the time of the IC Games. If so, he will be prepared to eliminate the threat she poses. My tracks will remain covered, and our plans safe. It is laughable how easily my ally can be manipulated; he is a fool. Rest assured, Presidente, I will terminate my opposition, and it will be done immediately. Victory is within reach.

CHAPTER TWENTY-TWO

DEHRE
Firstday

HENDRA HAD FOUND NO EVIDENCE of swords in Dehre. She'd looked in storerooms, and even asked a few friends if they'd seen anything unusual lately. None had. Maybe she should search Mentàll's tent, too, but she couldn't bring herself to violate his privacy. Anyway, she'd been in his clothes room last week, and had seen no evidence of swords in there. So where were they? Was she wrong about everything?

Or had her cousin ordered all of the weapons to be stashed somewhere secret?

Another development—one that troubled Hendra even more—had arisen, too. Mentàll had ordered a delegation of twenty "merchants" to visit Rolban this coming Sixthday. A peace mission, supposedly, but Jascr was to go, as well.

Why would Mentàll send a man he hated and distrusted to Rolban?

Why send a man of violence on a mission of peace?

△ △ △ △ △

ROLBAN

METHUSAL AWOKE EARLY, feeling more relaxed than she'd felt in a long time. Petr seemed to have doubts about her guilt, which was great news.

She hoped she could beat Goric, because she wanted to attend the Inter-Community games on Thirdday. She'd love to visit Dehre and Tarst. She'd never been to either community before, and had always longed to visit new, exciting places.

She wondered how Behran was feeling about returning to his home village of Dehre. Would it be bittersweet? Would the Dehriens still see him as one of their own, or as a defector, and now a Rolbani?

She strode swiftly down the hall, her ponytail swishing the back of her neck. A change in hairstyle seemed to fit her change of mood that morning. Too bad she had kitchen duty. It was the only unpleasant task on the horizon.

Petr exited from the dining room just as she arrived. Maybe he'd been visiting his aunt, because breakfast wouldn't start for another hour.

When he saw her, his white brows knotted into a scowl. "Remember what I told you last night. No investigating...*at all.*"

Methusal blinked, taken aback by the ferocity of his tone. "I..."

"Or else," he growled, and disappeared toward his office.

With a frown, she joined Deccia and Matron Olgith in the kitchen. The sticky gruel was again on the breakfast menu. She stirred and then served until it was her turn to eat breakfast.

Deccia and Aalicaa sat alone at the Storst table. Since Petr had long ago eaten breakfast and left, Methusal joined them with her bowl of steaming gruel.

"We heard what you did last night!" Aalicaa gazed at her with something akin to worship. "Did you see the thief? What did you learn?"

"Not much. Except the thief is a man, like we thought," Methusal said. "Petr doesn't want us to investigate anymore." Not that she'd listen, of course—not if she found another clue to follow, anyway. But for now, she'd toe the line. "So that's it, then."

"You can't give up! You know Father needs help."

"I know. But he asked us to stop, so we'd better. At least for now."

Aalicaa scowled. "Why does Father always ruin every-thing? Just when we were starting to win!"

"Aali..." But the girl up leaped and ran into the hall.

The older girls silently ate their porridge. After a while, Methusal said, "When will Timaeus get back from Tarst?"

"Tomorrow."

"Will you speak to him?"

"I don't know. Father may not let me." Deccia didn't look happy.

Methusal sighed. "Stand up to him, Decc. Choose what makes *you* happy."

"We'll see." A few minutes later, Deccia said, "Well, I'm off to class." Her voice was calm, and her gaze serene. Methusal marveled at that. If Petr was her father, she didn't know what she'd do.

Although Methusal was sorry her sister and Timaeus couldn't see each other, at least Deccia had someone inter-ested in her. She felt a pang of jealousy when she considered her sister's ability to draw male attention. Timaeus, Verdnt....Why were so many men interested in her, and none in Methusal? They were both pretty—they were identical, for goodness' sake. But Deccia's personality was gentle and kind, whereas Methusal was prone to emotional outbursts, and only focused on one thing in life—kaavl. Evidently, those weren't appealing characteristics to men.

She drew a quick breath. Why was she thinking about this? And what did she care, anyway? Her life was full enough now. Certainly, she didn't need any man to compli-cate things even more.

△ △ △ △ △

Class was boring, as usual, but for the sake of staying on Verdnt's good side, Methusal paid close attention. It was hard. Especially since after lunch she would get to challenge Goric. Excitement made her heart flutter. She slipped into kaavl, and carefully focused on Verdnt's voice and several other sounds at the same time. Several times she was able to follow three isolated sounds at once. Her spirits lifted. She couldn't wait to challenge Goric.

At the end of class Verdnt announced, "Tomorrow will be the last day of school for this class. You will receive your certificates of graduation at that time."

Methusal added her cheers to the whoops of the class.

"What about the other class levels?" Daltha asked. "Is tomorrow their last day, too?"

"No. They'll go to the end of the week. Deccia will finish up for me." Verdnt directed a smile at Methusal's sister, who offered a nervous looking one in return.

Several classmates turned to Deccia with smiles and congratulations. The experience would mean she'd get to teach her own class next year. Probably just the youngest children, but a real step forward for her. Methusal was happy for her. For her sister's sake, however, she hoped Verdnt wouldn't try to finagle any more time alone with her.

After class, she burst into the supply room with a smile. "Good morning, Sims!"

"Good morning, my girl." His leathery face creased into a smile.

"I'll finish copying this list right away," Methusal promised, pulling the inventory sheets from the wall.

"Good, good," Sims nodded. "I'm going to inspect the crops in a little while. Would you like to come with me?"

The prospect of bright, warm sunshine and a clear, cloudless blue sky beckoned almost overwhelmingly. Oh, to get out of this cave! She hadn't been outside in almost a week. And since Petr was loosening his restrictions, he probably wouldn't mind if she went outside with Sims now. Another thought came to mind. She could investigate that ravine. Maybe the thief had thrown the pelts into it last night.

"Yes. I'd like that." She bent her head to the list. The sooner it was finished, the sooner she could go outside. And at noon she'd play Goric for the Tri-level.

An hour later, list completed, she headed down the hall after Sims and then up the narrow stone staircase, which led to the tableland on top of the mountain.

The plateau was rich in nutrients, and crop tenders tilled it to provide food for the community. Waste plant material from the summer's crop was plowed under in the fall, and provided an even richer soil for the next spring. Each year one of the four fields was left fallow, allowing it to rest for one growing season.

Methusal stepped onto the flat tableland. She smelled Barak's compost pit behind her, but tried to ignore it. She'd rather focus on the beautiful scenery.

The wide plateau stretched to the west for a short distance before it ended abruptly in a sheer cliff. The plateau stretched for a longer distance to the east, and provided room for three of the four fields. It ended just before the stream, and before the landscape erupted into the tall, rocky cliffs of the Rolban Mountains. The Rolban River rushed in a narrow stream between the plateau and the cliffs, and then cascaded in a waterfall to the floor of the plain. From there, the stream continued on and followed the bluffs south. It was the same stream that she would cross this afternoon for the kaavl game rematch.

The tall Rolbani mountain range partly encircled the valley to the south, and ended in the black bluffs, which were the halfway point for the Kaavl Games. To the north stretched another valley, which ended a good distance away in the Tarst Mountain Range.

This year the field to the west lay fallow. To the east, Barak's team of crop tenders dotted the plateau, carefully irrigating the mounded rows of dirt by using water piped from the stream. Last year Behran and the other engineers had finished this system. Several people were needed at strategic spots throughout the fields to turn the water flow on and off, but that was a small chore compared to the task of carrying water, pail by pail, from the stream.

Several men unplugged pipes now, and water spurted from the tough, hollow wooden rods, which were elevated from the ground by intermittent wooden stands. The stands prevented the wood from rotting too quickly. That way the system would last longer, according to Behran. A few workers carefully adjusted the rods, making sure the crops received maximum water.

Barak strode their way, his face gleaming with sweat. He rubbed a dirty palm across his forehead, streaking it black.

"Sims!" he roared. "Good to see you. Come take a look at the fields. Those two will be planted with grain and that one with berries," he thundered, pointing to the rich, freshly plowed earth. "We should have a great season this year—if that uncured grain sprouts." His thick black brow knotted in a frown.

Barak forged ahead, towering a half head taller than the crew under his command. Methusal and Sims followed, meekly observing each feature Barak indicated.

As they headed east, toward the mountain, Methusal quickly spotted the waist high wall bordering the ravine. Quietly she wandered north, away from Barak and Sims, but was careful to stick to the path so she wouldn't trample the newly planted seeds. She glanced over her shoulder. Barak and Sims crouched near a thin, spindly plant. They wouldn't miss her for a minute.

At the gorge, she leaned over the edge and examined the ravine, was was cut into the black rock of the plateau. At the far edge of the bluff the crevasse was two lengths wide, but it narrowed to a point where Methusal stood. Where had that man stood when he'd thrown the grain over edge?

About here, in the middle? She peered over the rock wall. It was a sheer, twelve length drop before it ended in a cluster of black boulders far below. And to her left, to the north, stretched the flat plain. To her right, toward the narrow end of the chasm, the cliff cut down at a sharp angle—almost like a steep slide—and ended with the boulders. Maybe the thief had rolled the grain down that incline.

Were the stolen pelts down there right now? She struggled to see, but black shadows darkened the bottom of the gorge.

"Methusal," Sims called. "We're heading to the other field."

"Coming." She concentrated into kaavl. One particular dark lump looked a shade lighter than the other rocks. Unfortunately, she couldn't tell if it was a roll of tied up pelts. Maybe she could ask Deccia to check. Her sister had said several times that she'd like to help with the investigation, and this seemed like the perfect opportunity. Especially since Methusal didn't know when she'd have time to investigate the ravine at ground level, since the rematch with Goric was coming up so quickly. If the pelts were there, the quicker they were retrieved, the better. She'd send a message to Deccia as soon as she returned inside.

"What're you looking at?" Barak bellowed. The amusement in his eyes reminded her of his brother, Kitran.

"It's steep," she commented.

"Cliffs are. Be careful." The dry comment reminded her of almost falling down the stairs yesterday. And how Barak had saved her from a nasty accident.

Barak lumbered on, pointing out details of the crop plateau. Methusal had trouble keeping track of it all. She supposed that as she learned more about the job, Barak's statistics would mean more to her.

By the end, they'd circled the entire plateau.

Methusal paused in the place where she knew Renn had fallen, and her gaze dropped to the rocky jumble below. A long way to fall. A shiver slid down her spine.

"Methusal?" Sims' voice wavered from the staircase door.

Glad to be pulled from her gruesome thoughts, Methusal hurried to catch up. It was almost time for lunch. But she grimaced when she thought about it. Lunch didn't vary much; tastelessness was its consistent quality. Maybe she should talk to Sims about that varied diet...

She followed Sims as he carefully climbed down to the second level. "Sims, could we preserve more varieties of foods for the winter? It's boring eating the same things every day."

Old Sims unfastened the circular lock to the supply room and motioned Methusal inside before answering her question.

"Grain, berries, nuts, and dried meats can be preserved," he lectured kindly. "Luckily, logne leaves can be picked half of the year, but the other foods we eat, such as tubers and certain green vegetables, can only be harvested in the summer. We can preserve some of those, too, but most food needs to be eaten fresh."

"So we can't change anything?" It was a depressing thought to have to accept the tasteless boredom of the winter foods. Or maybe it was just Matron Olgith's cooking that needed improvement.

Sympathy flickered across the old man's face. "Believe me, I wish we could spice up our meals, too. Long ago, I lived in Quasr, to the north. We had a nice variety of foods there. It's a coastal village, as you know."

Methusal nodded.

"The climate is mild. Tubers and all sorts of plants and flowers grow there year round."

"Maybe we could trade with them."

"Yes. Maybe." He fell silent.

"Why were you in Quasr, Sims?"

"Oh." He started. His smile looked sad. "I grew up there. Met the love of my life, a spunky girl." He chuckled and his smile softened. "Yes. The love of my life. She gave me a son, but I didn't know about him until much later."

"Why not?"

"Her father banished me. I wasn't good enough for her. Apparently, she felt the same. So I left."

"How awful!" Methusal touched his shoulder. "I didn't know you had a family."

"I don't. She married another, and my son is dead these many years. Almost thirty years gone, now."

"What happened?"

"My M'tilde did not tell him about me, his true father, until he was a man. He sought me out. But it wasn't enough time. Not enough time at all."

"Did he come here, to Rolban?"

"Yes. For a short while. And then he left. He was a wanderer, much like me. He died soon after in a wild beast attack."

"How horrible." And what heartbreak for poor Sims! The woman he loved had married someone else. His son was dead. He was alone in the world. She remembered seeing him eating alone last night. "You may not have a son anymore, but you could still have a family, if you'd like. An adopted one."

A twinkle glimmered in his eyes. "What do you mean, my girl?"

Maybe she should ask her parents first, but she didn't think they'd mind. "I just mean...maybe you'd like to sit with us sometimes. Our family is small, and I don't have any grandparents. What I mean is..."

Sims smiled, and to Methusal's surprise, his lips trembled a little. "I'd be honored. It would be a pleasure to sit with you from time to time."

"Terrific!" She grinned. "I'll tell my parents. I know they'll be thrilled."

△ △ △ △ △

Kitran, Goric, and Methusal stood on the plateau. A warm wind slid through Methusal's long hair. She saw Behran in the distance. He'd almost reached the bluffs.

Kitran said, "Do each of you understand the rules? The person who reaches the bluff and returns here first is the winner."

"Does the winner need to capture the other person?" Methusal asked.

"Absolutely."

Goric rolled his shoulders. Kitran lifted his hand and both contenders crouched, with one foot on the edge of the plateau.

"Ready? Begin!"

Methusal and Goric shot down the steep hill, slipping and sliding on dirt and stray pebbles. Once they reached the plains, Goric took off at a sprint. He was wiry and fast. He also made a lot of noise. Methusal realized she'd never match his speed, but keeping track of him would be easy.

It soon became obvious that Goric intended to run straight to the bluffs. Maybe he planned to capture her on the return trip, after she'd tagged the bluffs. He'd silently lie in wait on the plain like he had last time, and capture her then. She couldn't afford to let him get too far ahead.

Methusal pulled out one of the blue-banded, leather kaavl strips her mother had specially made for her. She wrapped one end around her hand, so she'd be ready when she needed it. She ran effortlessly, her breaths even and silent. In contrast, Goric, even though he steadily increased his lead, wheezed, and his moccasins scattered stones everywhere. Methusal had never heard such a noisy kaavl contender before. His racket convinced her even more that Goric hadn't run at all during the Tri-level. Everyone would have heard him crashing across the plain!

Goric was two minutes ahead of her when he reached the far bluffs. Splashes told her he'd reached the stream. After he touched the bluff face he stopped for a minute, bent over, trying to catch his breath. Finally he headed back, toward her. She put on a burst of speed, skirted around him, and tagged the bluffs, too. Behran sat on a high boulder. She offered him a jaunty wave, and turned and sped back.

Now was her chance. She had to capture Goric before he escaped further into the plains and found a hiding spot. He'd already proven that he could hide in virtual silence, which would make him a worthy foe.

Goric's footsteps stopped thirty lengths ahead.

Staying hidden behind scattered plains bushes, she cautiously slipped within visual range. He stood between two tagma bushes. His gaze darted about as he set up a trap with quick, jerky movements. He was nervous. Good.

Methusal cut directly ahead of him and swiftly flicked out her kaavl strip. It snapped around a nearby branch. She crouched, waiting, behind another thick bush.

Goric approached, and then paused. He'd seen her trap. He sprinted south, which was off course. She'd conserve her energy and head straight for the finish line.

A few minutes later, Goric swerved back on course. He passed her to the west.

Goric continued to run, and she loped in pursuit. She'd bet he planned to lie in wait near the finishing plateau again. Yes. Long minutes later, Goric's racket stopped twenty lengths from the plateau. Methusal smiled to herself. Simple, then. She'd head south like he had, and then swoop in directly behind him. He'd expect her from the east.

Methusal slowed to a walk when she was ten lengths south of Goric. She fanned out her hearing, listening for the sound of Goric's breaths. He was quiet now, and she struggled to pinpoint his location. Overhead, flying beast wings whispered, and ahead a small beast skittered into its hole.

Finally, she heard Goric's soft breaths, seven lengths ahead. She carried, and mentally took the leap to the source of the sound. He whispered, "Hurry up. Spring my trap, stupid girl."

Stupid girl? The gall of him—the *cheater!*—to call her names. Oh, she'd get him. No traps. Just personal, one on one combat. Adrenaline pumped through her. Caution, too. Her impulsive plan was dangerous. She could lose everything if he sensed her coming. But the satisfaction of the win—of walking right up and capturing Goric without him suspecting she was even there... It was the ultimate humiliation for any kaavl player.

Holding a new kaavl strip at the ready, Methusal silently glided closer to her quarry. Pebbles lay scattered over the plain here, so it wasn't easy to be quiet. Her concentration sharpened until her whole being was kaavl. Every nuance of input guided her path. The next stone was there...the breeze strengthened from the south... Leaves rustled.

Methusal swiftly and silently moved to within a length of him, and then hid behind a thick tagma bush. Goric peered east, and the breeze picked up.

It was now or never. Methusal circled west and crept up behind Goric. Half a length, one quarter of a length... She flicked out her kaavl strip, and the end curled around his torso. Before he could react, she'd flipped the long strip around him once, twice, then thrice.

"Hey!" Arms pinned to his sides, Goric struggled to his feet. "Where did you come from? You cheated!"

Kitran appeared. "She won, fair and square. Go to the plateau, Methusal. It's clear who should have won second place at the Tri-Level Game."

"No!" Goric protested. "I'm faster—didn't you see? I outran her last time, and I did this time, too. I won the first game, fair and square!"

"You ran nowhere at the Tri-level," Kitran voice sounded hard. "You run like a child. Crashing over rocks, tripping over pebbles. A Quatr-leveler knows more than you do. And a Quatr-leveler could have easily tracked your progress today. If you'd truly run the course last time, Behran or Methusal—most likely both—would have heard you, and captured you long before the finish line. Goric, you lose your second position. And I'm expelling you from kaavl entirely, for cheating."

Goric's face tightened into a mask of hatred. "You'll regret it."

"Really? Who'll make me regret it?" Kitran towered over the other man by at least two handbreadths. "I'll report your behavior to Petr. Any further dishonorable conduct will be disciplined. Maybe Motr will demote you to water irrigator."

"Kaavl is a stupid game, anyway," Goric spat. "Endlessly practicing for what? A stupid necklace? It's a waste of time." He ripped off Methusal's kaavl strip and snarled at her, "I will not forget!" and stalked for Rolban.

Another enemy. Great. How many had she gained in the last week? Pogul, the Dehrien Chief, and now Goric. But none of them were nice men, were they? Someone had to have the guts to stand up to them.

Feeling a little better, Methusal ran for the finish line at the top of the kaavl plateau. She'd won! She'd earned second place for the Tri-level, and she'd go to Dehre and Tarst the day after tomorrow. Her spirit soared, and she felt like dancing. But with Kitran and Behran approaching, she decided against it. They might laugh at her.

△ △ △ △ △

Although Petr had told her to stop investigating, Methusal found herself sliding a glance at the Storst table when she sat down to supper that night. A little earlier, Deccia had reported that she'd investigated the ravine at ground level. Unfortunately, the skins weren't there. Another dead end. What about Petr? Had he followed up on the lead she had provided?

A glance through the dining hall did not locate Liem. Was he still investigating? Although she wanted to find the true murderer, part of her hoped he'd quit, because all of the "clues" he'd found only seemed to point to her guilt.

At the Storst table, Deccia ate quietly and Aali scowled down into her food. Probably Petr had just lectured her about something.

"Hi." Behran's voice sent her gaze bouncing upwards, and he quirked an eyebrow. "Doing detective work?"

"I don't know what you mean." She spooned up mashed logne leaf.

"Weren't you just spying on the Storsts?"

"Don't be silly. I *was* wondering if Petr's found any new clues, but I doubt it."

"What are you going to do about it?"

She smiled. "Wouldn't you like to know? Besides, he ordered us to stop investigating, or don't you remember?"

"Oh, I know. Just wondering if you'd listen."

"Yes. For now."

"What discipline. Kitran would be proud of you."

Was that mockery in voice? If so, she tried to ignore it. "What about you, Behran? Are you ready for the games?"

With a slow grin, he said, "I'm ready to take *you* on. You'd better practice hard tomorrow, because you'll need all the help you can get."

She managed not to roll her eyes. Behran, *Behran*. Pitiful, really, reverting to his old, annoying tricks. If he thought she'd lose her temper, he could think again.

She smiled as sweetly as she knew how. "If that's the case, then maybe you'll give me a few pointers."

And that left him satisfactorily silent for a while.

Her parents arrived a bit later. Her mother sat down, but her father did not. He gently touched Hanuh's back.

"Would you like tea for your headache?"

"Thank you." Hanuh closed her eyes and rubbed at the frown between her brows. Erl strode for the drinks counter.

"What's wrong?"

"Oh, Thusa. I can't explain it. I just feel...awful."

The color on Hanuh's face ebbed as Methusal watched. Within moments, she looked as pale as a ghost. She asked, "Is it a headache, or are you sensing something bad?" Sometimes her mother's empathic abilities manifested in blinding headaches.

As if her words were a trigger, her mother gasped and she pressed her fingers harder into her temples. Her skin turned white.

"It's something evil...someone evil." She drew a slow breath. "Something awful is about to happen...Ah!" Her features contorted. "Or...it *is* happening. *Now*. I...*I just don't know*."

She gasped again. Tears slid down her cheeks. "Thusa...it's *awful!*"

Methusal quickly wrapped her arms tightly around her mother. "Mama, what is it?" she whispered. "Who is it?"

"I don't know." Her mother choked on a sob. "I hate this...*gift*. I can't help anyone!"

"Of course you're helping." She held her tighter, and wished she knew how to help. She'd never seen her mother so upset before. The closest she'd seen to this amount of distress had been the night someone had killed Renn. Heart in her throat, she said, "Mama...is it like...when Renn died?"

"It's *worse!*" her mother gasped. "Much worse. I feel like I know this person very well... Thusa!" Terrified eyes turned to Methusal. "Don't be alone, not for one minute, tonight. Do you hear me?"

"Y..."

"Do you *hear me?*" Hanuh's voice rose to a hysterical pitch.

Tears stung her eyes and Methusal pressed her forehead against her mother's "I hear you, Mama. I'll do what you say. I promise."

"Good." Hanuh's shoulders shuddered, and she dissolved into deep, quiet sobs.

Erl hurried up and murmured, "Do you want to lie down, love?"

Hanuh clutched Methusal's arm. "Promise me!"

"I promise, Mama."

"I'll walk her home," Behran said quietly.

"Good!" Her mother seemed relieved by Behran's words. Clutching Erl's shoulder, she slowly stood and the two shuffled out of the dining room. Others watched her go, concern written on their faces. Deccia jumped up and ran after them. Her sister's face looked pale, and Methusal wondered if she was feeling the same empathic premonition as their mother.

"I heard what she said," Behran murmured. "Someone's going to die."

"Oh Behran!" Methusal stared at him with tears in her own eyes. "Who could it be?"

Chapter Twenty-Three

Secondday

NO ONE HAD TURNED UP DEAD YET.

Hanuh had not arisen yet that morning, so Methusal wasn't sure how her mother felt today.

Methusal, however, felt nervous. She looked over her shoulder when she hurried the short distance to the dining hall that morning.

What if *she* was the killer's next target? She couldn't help but remember the shove she'd received on the stairs the other day. Maybe it hadn't been an accident, after all.

Logically, she was probably at the top of the murderer's kill list. After all, she was investigating. A nervous killer probably made for a dangerous man. Look at Renn. He'd been investigating the thefts, too.

After plopping a lump of gluey porridge into her bowl, she slipped over to the Storsts' table. Deccia and Aali sat alone. Deccia looked better than she had last night, and Methusal sat across from her.

"Good morning."

Deccia returned the greeting, but Aali sat unusually silent a short distance away, frowning to herself.

"My father said everything still seems fine," Methusal said. She tried to inject an upbeat note into her voice. "So far, so good, right?"

"I hope so." A frown settled between Deccia's brows. "I still feel...off. But I feel sad now, more than scared, like I did last night."

"Maybe the danger is over."

"Maybe."

"Timaeus is coming home today, right?"

"Yes." A wistful smile tugged at Deccia's lips.

"Will you talk to him?"

"If Father lets me." She sounded cautiously optimistic.

A "bother Father" whispered down the table.

"What's wrong with Aali?"

"I don't know." Deccia rolled her eyes. "She keeps picking fights with Father about everything—kaavl, the killer. I don't know what she's trying to prove." The two gazed at the younger girl, as much like a sister to Methusal as to Deccia, but Aali scowled.

Methusal's mind circled back to the killer. Much as she'd like to think about something else, fear kept knotting up her stomach. "Has Petr found more clues about Renn's murder?"

"Of course not!" Aali snorted from down the table.

Deccia sent her a warning glance. "He doesn't discuss it with us."

"All Father cares about is winning the election," Aali muttered.

"I promised him I'd stop investigating," Methusal said. "But after my mother's bad feeling last night, I think that would be stupid. She thinks I'm in danger. She could be right. The killer might see me as a threat, since I've spent so much time investigating. And after getting shoved down the stairs..."

"*What?*" Now she not only had Deccia's full attention, but Aali's, as well.

"I guess I forgot to tell you." She recapped the story of the elbow in her back, and how Barak had saved her from a nasty fall. "I thought it was an accident then. But now I'm not so sure."

Deccia's eyebrows had climbed her forehead. "Sounds suspicious to me."

Aali scooted closer. Her eyes gleamed. "We have to set a trap!"

"I wish we could, but how? I keep coming back to that ore mine authorization list. A big, dark haired man. An immigrant."

"He may not be an immigrant," Deccia reminded her. "We have to be fair. And we can't overlook other possible suspects."

"You're right," Methusal agreed, but she wasn't happy to admit it. She wanted to narrow down the list, but without the immigrant qualifier, it remained too long. "Let's list the immigrants first. Who meet the requirements?"

"Barak, Kitran, Verdnt...and one of the guards. Vogl," Deccia remembered. "Didn't you say he was the guard at the ore mine door, Thusa?"

"Yes."

"Any others?"

"Two council members. Iric, who's Lina's father, and Pogul's father," Aali put in. "Pogul is a beast. His father probably is, too."

"So, at least six men," Deccia said.

"If we include native Rolbanis, the list would probably triple."

Deccia shook her head. "It still doesn't make sense. Why steal? Why kill Renn?"

"Renn probably figured out the thief's identity."

"Still, why would that be a motive for murder? Even if Renn had turned him in, the punishment for theft is six months in jail! Murder seems so extreme."

"Don't forget the Alliance." Aali shoved her bowl aside. She'd barely touched her gray clump of porridge. "Why did Tarst steal our pots? I thought we were friends."

"We are," Methusal said. "I still think someone is stirring up trouble on purpose. Either to destroy the Alliance, or for some other reason."

"Should I give our suspect list to Father? He might see something we don't," Deccia said.

Methusal nodded, but she didn't think Petr would do anything with it. As far as she'd seen, her uncle had done precious little investigating on the case.

Aali was right. *They* needed to do something—maybe set a trap—but how, where, and when? Tomorrow she'd leave for the Inter-Community Games in Dehre. "Maybe I'll find clues in Dehre or Tarst. Runners must be a part of the scheme."

"What will you do? Interrogate them?"

"I don't know. I'll look for stolen items, at least." And if she found them...then what?

Aali jumped up. "Time for class."

"Our last class ever," Methusal grinned.

"Lucky! We still have to go for the rest of the week."

As they picked up their breakfast dishes, Deccia said, "Are you excited about the IC Games?" She dumped her dishes in the bin.

"Yes. I can't wait to see Dehre and Tarst. And I can't wait to compete with Behran again." Methusal's dishes fell with a loud clatter into the bin.

"I thought you two were getting along now."

"We are, for the most part. But last night he went all obnoxious again. He said I'd have to work hard to beat him."

Deccia smiled. "He wants to keep you on edge. Maybe he's trying to keep the competition exciting."

"Probably. He certainly wins at being annoying."

Verdnt took Deccia aside as they stepped into the classroom, so Methusal made her way to her desk alone. The last day of class! She could hardly believe it.

What would Verdnt talk about today? The elections? According to Deccia, he was brimming with ideas, and itching to discuss them in class. The very idea made her eyes glaze, and a yawn worked at the corner of her mouth.

"What did he want?" she asked when Deccia finally broke free.

A tiny frown puckered her brow. "He wants me to put in extra work time this morning, since he'll be leaving for the Games tomorrow. He wants to discuss the lesson plans for the younger classes."

"Remember, meet in a public place. Don't go to his compartment."

"Honestly, I'm not worried about that right now. It's the idea of teaching all by myself that scares me. I'm not sure I'm ready for this."

"You'll do fine."

But Deccia didn't look so sure.

To Methusal's relief, the last class was mercifully short. Verdnt called each graduating student up to the head of the class, said a few positive words over him or her, and handed over a graduation parchment. He had plenty of glowing things to say about Deccia, but only one for Methusal.

"You're one of the smartest students I've ever taught. Try to apply those smarts to real life."

Methusal shot him a sideways glance. That was a backhanded compliment, if ever she'd heard one. He regarded her steadily. Subtle dislike lurked in his unsmiling gaze.

He didn't like her. For some strange reason, that hurt her feelings. Well, maybe she hadn't always paid close attention in class, but she had tried. And she'd always completed her homework on time. She felt judged, and unfairly, too.

She accepted the white parchment. Her name was written in black ink script, and so was "Congratulations on your graduation!" Verdnt's name and Petr's name were scrawled across the bottom. She sent Verdnt a look that mirrored his own. "Thanks."

Something black flashed in his eyes, and Methusal quickly returned to her seat. What was wrong with her? Did she really want to gain another enemy? Maybe she'd better listen to Verdnt and brush up on her "real life" smarts.

△ △ △ △ △

That afternoon Sims released Methusal from supply room duty early so she could practice for the Inter-Community Games.

It felt wonderful to be outside again. Methusal climbed to her favorite kaavl plateau and shut all distractions from her mind. Excitement licked through her. Tomorrow their Rolbani team would travel to Dehre. They would participate in Kaavl Games that afternoon, and then travel to Tarst the next day.

Her stomach lurched with excitement. Soon her sheltered world would expand.

But one thing was for certain: Methusal was not looking forward to seeing the Dehrien Chief again. A shiver slid through her when she remembered the last time she'd seen him, in the dining room. And worse, the dream.

Methusal forced her thoughts away from the dangerous Chief and reviewed what little she knew about Dehre and Tarst. After the Great War, each community had retreated to its own, mutually agreed upon territory, and had left the others strictly alone. The Peace Plan had worked. Not wanting to tamper with success, the villagers had decided to remain isolated, except for sending runners to relay messages to one another. Relations had relaxed with Tarst, however, since Erl and Tarst's Chief, Pan Patn, had become friends forty years ago, during their messenger days. Gradual trust had built over the years. She wondered what would happen now, since Rolban's stolen pots had been found in Tarst.

Even though the villages chose to remain isolated from their neighbors, immigrants were accepted from time to time. Each was carefully screened before being accepted as a permanent resident.

That was why the Alliance was so significant—as was the twenty member merchant delegation arriving from Dehre on Sixthday. Methusal wouldn't be present for their arrival, since she'd be in Tarst. Apparently, the delegation would bring vases of wild beast oil to trade. Soon Rolbani gatherers would harvest logne leaves to trade.

A *screech* and the flapping of wings overhead jolted her into the present. Time to begin.

She closed her eyes, concentrating on her hearing and the gentle caress of the breeze rippling over her face. The light wind blew from the north. By automatically calculating these facts, combined with her sensory input, she could determine exactly where each sound originated. Relaxing, she concentrated more fully.

Wings rushed fifty lengths overhead. A whip beast slithered over the plains twenty-three lengths south. Behind her, a scrabble of rocks tumbled down the plateau. A grown man, climbing rapidly.

Eyes open, she turned to face the intruder.

Kitran's head popped over the ledge.

"Methusal!" He hesitated. Surprise flickered across his unsmiling face. Then his shoulders and the remainder of his large body slowly stepped into view. "I didn't know you were up here."

"I'm practicing." But Kitran could see that. Why else would she be on the plateau?

"I'd planned to do the same." His black gaze swept by her to scan the plain below. "Maybe I'll run first." His gaze returned to her. "Are you ready for the games?"

"I think so."

"Good." His dark eyes bored into her, and seemed to search into her very soul. "Have you given more thought to rising to the second level?"

Kitran's new kaavl theories and her conversation with Behran in the dark kitchen several nights ago returned to mind. She'd have to make a decision soon. Follow Kitran's teachings? Or abandon kaavl altogether?

Or remain at the Tri-level? It might be better to retire completely.

But Kitran was waiting, and her gaze fell before his. "I haven't decided. Not yet."

His black brow raised, but conveyed no discernable emotion. "It's up to you, Methusal, but I want you to decide soon. I'm starting a new, introductory Bi-level class in two weeks. I've decided you and Behran can sit in on it."

That was an honor, since she hadn't achieved the Bi-level yet. She nodded, and Kitran moved to the edge of the plateau. "See you tomorrow then, at sunup in the dining room."

"Okay." Her instructor vanished and then reappeared, sprinting west across the plain. Watching him, Methusal felt sure Kitran would win the Primary levels in both Dehre and Tarst. As he should. He'd dedicated his entire life to kaavl.

She resumed practice, but felt troubled now, because she wasn't sure if it would be any easier to decide about the Bi-level in two weeks.

After practicing on the plateau for a while, Methusal's senses felt sharpened enough to take her run. Although she could certainly run west as Kitran had, she decided to sprint south for a change of pace. She wanted to enjoy her last solitary run before the games tomorrow.

She ran down the hill and took off, running easily, breathing lightly. The breeze felt fresh and cool. Flying beasts circled and cawed overhead. Several whips slithered several lengths to the southeast. The scent of tagma leaves gave way to another smell...of blood. Of death.

Methusal slowed down. The smell was strong. If it was a small animal, she should almost be upon it. But she saw nothing. It must be a larger animal then, and further away. If it was a wild beast, other animals might be feasting on its remains right now. She should be careful.

She listened carefully. Snarling slurps reached her ears. Wolmites; ahead twenty lengths.

Heart pounding, she slowed down still more. Should she head back? Wolmites usually didn't attack humans, but if their food was threatened...

Something made Methusal continue on. She moved silently, staying downwind of the beasts.

She saw the wolmites, two of them, nuzzling something that lay sprawled against a prickly tagma bush. It was large, but not big enough to be a full grown wild beast. An adolescent, then. Methusal scanned for the wild beast's claws, trying to determine the dead beast's age. But she saw no claws. Instead she saw a bloody moccasin, attached to a human leg.

She screamed.

△ △ △ △ △

"Methusal!"

She opened her eyes. Kitran stood over her. Timaeus and another runner also stared down at her. She lay on the ground.

She'd fallen. She had bumped her head, too...

The memory came back. She moaned and covered her eyes. Welling tears slid down her cheeks. "Did you see?" she whispered.

"We saw," Kitran said grimly. He gripped her arm and pulled her into a sitting position.

Methusal couldn't help it—her eyes went back to the mangled human form. The wolmites were gone. A whip slithered closer, but Timaeus pivoted and hurled his hunting knife. The whip twitched and lay still. He swiftly retrieved the knife.

Wiping the bloody knife on a leaf, Timaeus pointed to the other runner. "That's Dastn."

The dark-haired runner nodded to her. After the cursory greeting, he pulled a bow and arrow from the quiver on his back, and held it at the ready, waiting for another animal to slink closer to the corpse. The Tarst runner looked to be the same age and height as Timaeus, but he was more thickly muscled in the chest and arms.

Methusal's gaze slid again to the bloody mess that had been a man. Kitran knelt by him, examining something at his neck. Bile rose in her throat. She staggered to her feet and vomited in a nearby bush.

"It's Liem," Kitran said.

Liem!

"How do you know?" she choked out.

He fingered a bloodied, looped strand. "This is his family's marriage necklace. He's worn it since his wife died."

Methusal crossed her arms and hugged herself. She could not look at the dead man—Liem—again. Tears ran in a rivers down her cheeks. "Mama was right," she whispered. Something awful *had* happened. Liem was dead. Murdered. Who would *do* such an awful thing?

"His wrists are tied to the bush." Timaeus said.

"I know." Kitran sounded grim.

Methusal gasped. "You mean...someone tied him there, and...and let the wild beasts...eat him?" A horrible, gasping wail left her throat. She pressed a hand to her mouth. "Who would *do* such a thing?"

"Look, Methusal."

"No. I *can't!*" Looking was the last thing she wanted to do.

"He's tied up with kaavl strips. The ends are wrapped in blue. Just like yours."

"*What?*" She couldn't help but look where Kitran was pointing.

Sure enough, blood and skeletal wrist bones were tied to the bush by blue-banded kaavl strips. Her kaavl strips.

"They're not mine!" she cried. "I would never... I could *never...*"

"I know. Timaeus, get Petr and Erl. Fast," Kitran said. "Leave your knife."

"Yes, sir!" Timaeus and Dastn took off for Rolban at a dead sprint.

Methusal sank down on the ground again, facing away from Liem. She could not believe this had happened. Liem was dead. And the killer had framed her again.

△ △ △ △ △

Erl and Petr soon arrived, along with two grave diggers. Timaeus came with them, but Dastn had had to continue on his run in order to reach Dehre before nightfall.

In the meantime, Kitran had searched the perimeter for footprints, but he said he'd found it hard to distinguish the killer's footprints from their own, as they'd all come from the same direction.

Methusal stood, arms crossed, shivering in the late afternoon's gentle breeze. She felt numb inside. "I didn't do it."

"We know, Thusa. Here." Her father pressed a cloth into her hand. She hadn't realized she was still crying.

"I *didn't!*" She pressed the cloth against her mouth, and tried to suppress her throat aching sobs. Tears streamed from her eyes.

"I know." Petr's quiet rumble surprised and comforted her. "I know you didn't do it."

She turned swollen eyes to him. "*How* do you know?" Her voice trembled. "Those kaavl strips might be mine. Every single clue points right at me!"

Gently, her father said, "We know because you're not that kind of a person, Thusa."

More matter-of-factly, Petr said, "And Liem would not have allowed you to lure him out here. He'd have been on his guard with you. He was a tough fighter, too. You could never have overpowered him. And if someone dragged or carried him out here—you couldn't have done that, either. The evidence is a little too convenient. Combined with the other clues you've found, I'm convinced you're innocent."

Thank goodness for that.

"But unless I miss my guess," Petr continued, "you're in danger. Liem was investigating, and now he's dead."

"Renn investigated," Methusal whispered. "He's dead."

"And you're investigating. I can lock you up, if you'd like," her uncle offered. "If he thinks you're out of the way, you might be safe."

"No!" She turned to her father. "I don't want to be alone in that jail cell. Anything could happen to me there."

"I agree," Erl said. "The safest thing may be to get you out of Rolban. Thank goodness the IC Games are tomorrow. You should be safer in Dehre."

She hoped. Methusal couldn't look at Liem again. "What will happen to him?"

"We'll bury him tonight," Petr said. Then, to the grave diggers, "Wrap him up. We'll have his service before supper."

△ △ △ △ △

Liem's service was short and sweet. Hanuh wept on Erl's shoulder. Methusal had never known it before, but Liem had been her mother's first love, when she'd been a teenager. While they had gone their separate ways as adults, she still cared for him very much. Maybe that was why she'd felt the premonition of his death so strongly last night

Liem's compartment was also searched. There were signs of a struggle, and a pool of blood found on the floor. It appeared that he had been killed there, and carried onto the plains last night. While the front gates were locked all night long, there was a steep path down from the crop plateau to the plains. It was located near the waterfall. The killer must have carried Liem's body out that way. At least Liem had been dead before the wild beasts ate him. A huge mercy. Still, someone had brutally murdered him.

Petr announced at the service that he would require every man with access to the ore mines to come in for questioning. He'd speak to Kitran and Verdnt tonight, since they would leave tomorrow for the IC Games.

At last, her uncle was clearly taking steps to find Renn and Liem's killer. Methusal couldn't help but wonder why it had taken so long. ...Unless he'd been investigating all along, and she just hadn't seen it.

A subdued group of people reentered Rolban for dinner. Fear was a noticeable undercurrent, as well.

Methusal was afraid she was next on the killer's list.

Although she wasn't very hungry, she joined her family at the table. The dining hall was quiet. Liem's spot was noticeably empty. When Methusal spotted Sims sitting alone, she rose to her feet and went to him.

"Sit with us," she urged. "Please," she added with a small smile. No one should be alone tonight.

Sims offered a small smile in return and walked slowly with her to the Maahr table.

Erl stood as they approached, and shook Sims' hand. "Sims. We're honored you can join us. Please sit."

Methusal had never had a chance to speak to her parents about asking Sims to join their family's meals, but her father seemed pleased by the idea, all on his own.

With an answering smile Sims sat down, and Hanuh and Poli immediately engaged him in conversation. The old man began to relax and enjoy himself.

Behran arrived a few minutes later. Then, to Methusal's surprised delight, Deccia and Aalicaa arrived, too. They wanted to eat dinner with Methusal tonight, since she'd leave tomorrow.

"Sorry I have to rush, though," Deccia said. "Verdnt wants me to put in a few more hours of work." A faint frown worried her brow, and the movements of her spoon were jerky.

"What's wrong?"

Aali glanced at her big sister. Her bad temper, which had been simmering over the last few days, had mysteriously vanished. "Yes, Deccia, what is it? You've splashed my arm twice with your soup!"

"It's nothing. Don't worry." But her gentle smile looked pinched, and eyes troubled.

"Her heart is breaking for Timaeus," Aali said, but not unkindly.

Deccia remained silent. Hurriedly, she finished her soup and rose to her feet. "I have to go. Good luck, Thusa. I know you'll do great. Remember, we're all pulling for you... And you too, Behran," she added with a faint flush, perhaps afraid that she had slighted him somehow. He smiled quickly to dispel her embarrassment. "See you when you get back!" Then she was gone.

"Verdnt must be turning into a slave driver," Methusal commented, untidily draining the last, surprisingly delicious drops of soup by tipping the bowl into her mouth. "I thought he was supposed to finish instructing her this morning."

"He's probably been distracted by preparing for the IC Games," Behran said, ignoring her bad manners.

"Methusal!" Hanuh frowned. "Please don't eat like that in Dehre or Tarst. They'll think we're uncivilized."

With a sheepish smile, Methusal put down the bowl. She wiped her mouth with the blot of lynnte weed distributed to each table for such emergencies.

"So, do you two think you're ready?" Erl asked with a faint twinkle in his eyes. Since Aali and the others had arrived, the mood at the table had lightened a little.

"I'm ready," Behran stated. One of his brows shot up in an arrogant manner when he glanced at Methusal.

"So am I." Calmly, she met his gaze.

"Good." Erl's mouth twitched. "Then let's have a toast to Behran and Methusal. Sims, you start it off."

"May you both bravely meet the challenges before you..."

"And put forth your best effort..."

"Remembering your code of ethics as Rolbanis..."

"Treating others with courtesy..."

"And above all...win!" This last impertinent bit was from Aalicaa, and they all laughed.

"One of us will win," Behran agreed.

Methusal only rolled her eyes and smiled.

△ △ △ △ △

Honorable Presidente,

Liem is dead, but Methusal still roams free. I could not prevent it. Logic and justice are not words Rolbanis understand. Again and again, they prove they are weak and stupid. Methusal, however, is far more of a threat than I originally believed. Not only does her investigation endanger our plans, but her kaavl is extraordinary, according to Kitran. She is a true threat, should we go to war. She cannot be allowed to live. Our Zindedi messenger has been warned of all issues. He will monitor the situation from afar. Should something happen to me, he will send you a letter detailing Rolban's last stand. However, I am not worried. Victory is certain.

CHAPTER TWENTY-FOUR

DEHRE
Thirdday

HENDRA STEPPED OUTSIDE into the clear, crisp morning. To-day the Rolbani team would arrive for the Kaavl Games. So would Behran—one of the few men in her life whom she'd granted a sliver of trust.

It had been five years since she'd last seen him. Lately she had been remembering how she'd been able to talk to him about almost anything. Would it be the same now?

Dared she tell him about her suspicions concerning Mentàll?

Again, worry conflicted with her lifelong respect and loyalty to her cousin. Had he ordered illegal swords made, or not? Was his secret plan a threat to Rolban? She didn't want Rolbanis hurt. Especially not Behran. But if she confessed her worries to him, would she be betraying Mentàll?

Of course she would. Behran may have been born a Dehrien, but now he was a Rolbani.

So what should she do?

If she could get Mentàll to tell her the root of the problem, maybe then she could try to steer him back on the right path.

Uneasiness settled in her soul. The Prophet had asked how she'd stop Mentàll. Well, she'd wait, and she'd watch, and when the time came, she would do what she absolutely must.

△ △ △ △ △

ROLBAN

PALE FINGERS OF SUNLIGHT slid beneath the curtain to her room as Methusal silently moved about, collecting together essentials for the trip. Extra clothes, a comb, and a few other items were all folded neatly into her coverlet, which was in turn folded and threaded securely with leather straps. Those hooked through her arms so she could carry the coverlet like a pack.

She slipped the pack strap over her shoulder. Time to go.

Sunlight streamed into the main chamber of the Maahr's compartment. Her mother paced the chamber with a cup of tea in her hands. Chup Chup sat on a chair, and his alert eyes followed Hanuh's movements with interest. Probably wondering when she'd feed him.

"Morning." Methusal gave the apte a quick pat on his soft, furry head.

Hanuh turned. A gentle smile touched her lips. "Thusa." She crossed the room and swiftly pulled her daughter into a quick hug.

When Methusal stepped back, she saw the worry that her mother tried to hide. "What is it?" Unease gripped her. "Is more trouble coming?"

Hanuh shook her head. "I don't want to burden you. I want you to enjoy your trip."

"Please tell me what's wrong."

"I could be mistaken."

Methusal remembered Liem. "I doubt it." In fact, she'd never known her mother to be wrong. She waited patiently.

Hanuh placed her cup on the table and crossed to the balcony ledge. She gazed out at the silvery pink dawn. "It's not over. The worst is yet to come."

"For whom?"

"You. Rolban." Her mother turned back. Tears glimmered in her eyes. "I'm glad you're leaving. It's dangerous here, Thusa. And..." she took a deep breath, "it's dangerous where you're going. Please be careful."

"I will. I promise."

"I know your father hopes Petr will find the killer before you return home. So do I."

"Me, too." Methusal didn't state the obvious—that the killer may have associates in Tarst, and possibly Dehre, too. She'd need to stay on her guard, which meant trying to stay in kaavl, aware of every nuance of her surroundings, at all times—if she could. Staying focused into kaavl was difficult for her. She had a lot to learn before she could reach the Bi-level.

"I'll be careful," she promised. "And I'll be back before you know it."

"Sixthday?"

"Sixthday."

"Go with The One." It was an odd blessing, and one her mother had never used before. Hanuh smiled, and Methusal quietly let herself out of her family's compartment.

She slipped down the hall to the dining room, where the other kaavl contenders and Matron Olgith stood waiting. When Matron saw her, her finger jabbed impatiently at a pile of grain wafers and dried meat and berries. Apparently those were Methusal's rations for the coming four days. Dehre and Tarst would probably feed their guests, but the custom had not yet been established. On the chance they would not, the Rolbani contenders would not go hungry. She scooped the food into a pouch created by the folding of her coverlet, and strapped the parcel to her shoulders.

Kitran stepped forward. "Thank you, Matron Olgith, for preparing our meals for the journey."

The fat, hard face of the matron dimpled for the handsome Kitran. Clearly, the work had not been a chore, if done for him.

Kitran's black eyes scanned the faces before him. Retra and Lina, the two Quatr-level contenders, stopped giggling.

Methusal and Behran were the contenders for the Tri-level, and only Verdnt represented Rolban's Bi-level. Actually, Petr had won the Bi-level competition last week, but he had decided to stay behind and welcome the Dehrien delegation. And Kitran was the only Primary level competitor.

His black eyes finished their piercing inspection, and Kitran pointed to the Grand Staircase. "Time to go."

Obediently, the five followed on his heels.

The silver rays of dawn had given way to a soft rose and orange tinted sky. The air was a crisp mixture of both warm and cool on Methusal's face as she stepped beyond the gates. Perfect walking weather.

Kitran halted. "It will take three hours to reach Dehre. I expect each of you to keep quiet and practice kaavl during that time. Your Dehrien competitors will be hard to beat."

Kitran set a brisk pace. Retra and Lina had to run from time to time to keep up with his long strides. Methusal was used to walking fast, so the pace didn't bother her.

She didn't mind Kitran's order of silence, either. Who would she talk to, anyway? Maybe Behran, but he'd probably be annoying. She eyed Verdnt, just ahead of her, and wondered if Deccia finally felt ready to teach the younger students' class.

As the sun rose, Methusal practiced hard, determined to become acutely aware of her environment in every way possible. She memorized the terrain ahead before her foot touched each stone, root, or twig. She also paid close attention to the sounds Kitran and Verdnt's footsteps made. Grass, dirt, sticks, and stones each made distinctive noises as they trod on them. And their gait and body movements signaled where the terrain rose and fell.

She filtered out and compartmentalized the noises her fellow travelers made before focusing on outlying sounds. A whip beast slithered through the dry plain ten lengths to her right. Leaves rustled in the light breeze sweeping the plain... And a few odd, light, and quick sounds came behind the kaavl team. After a while she ignored them. Probably a pack of curious aptes following them.

Time passed quickly. Retra and Lina quit practicing and whispered together. Kitran didn't hear them, but it became increasingly annoying to Methusal, who was still trying to concentrate. Fortunately, the trip was almost over. The gray wooden shacks and tents of Dehre sprawled in the distance. It looked open and defenseless, except for one partial wall built on the southern side.

How did Dehriens defend themselves from the wild beasts? And how much protection did the thin shelters provide against the winter's stinging rain and icy snow? She'd always taken the safety and security of her home within the mountain for granted, but not any longer.

The village grew quickly larger. It soon became clear that the tents were ringed by a protective row of wooden shacks. Deep fire pits alternated with the line of outlying buildings. Maybe the light and heat of the fires drove away the wild beasts at night. The plain surrounding the town grew steadily barer as they drew closer—probably from fueling all of those fires every night.

Behran's steps quickened as they neared the line of outbuildings. He must be looking forward to seeing old friends again. It seemed odd to think he had a life she knew nothing about.

"Kitran!" A loud shout drew their attention, and Methusal recognized the lean, blond-haired giant of a man striding up to join them. Mentàll Solboshn. The Dehrien Chief. Apprehension slid through her. Remembering his unhealthy interest in her tablet necklace, she swiftly tucked it inside her tunic.

He hadn't seen her yet, but the chill in her soul intensified when she again noticed his freezing, pale blue eyes. A wide smile stretched the man's otherwise expressionless face, and he turned his full attention to Kitran.

"Mentàll!" Kitran firmly shook the large hand of the other man. Mentàll towered over Kitran by a good handbreadth. "It's good to see you again. I was sorry we didn't have more time to talk while you were in Rolban."

"We will have to remedy that here," Mentàll agreed in his low, harsh voice. His pale eyes surveyed the little group clustered beside Kitran. "These are your kaavl contenders." His gaze settled on Methusal, and a faint smile bared his teeth. "Ah. The lovely Methusal."

With guarded caution, Methusal outstretched her hand in the customary, courteous gesture. What game was the Dehrien Chief playing? He certainly didn't think she was beautiful. He couldn't stand her.

Mentàll's hand gripped hers a little harder than strictly polite. "How nice to see you again." The words were low, maybe meaning to sound sincere, but instead they sounded threatening.

Methusal snatched her fingers free and offered a chilling glare in response.

A predatory light flashed in his eyes, and Methusal's heart rate accelerated. His gaze held a hint of cruel amusement. Clearly, he had just warned her, yet again, not to cross him.

She struggled not to let her emotions show. People like Mentàll probably thrived on power and fear. He'd wield neither over her. Methusal gritted her teeth and stared back.

The Dehrien Chief's freezing gaze moved to Verdnt, on her left. "Verdnt. How are you enjoying life in Rolban?" The icy eyes were unreadable.

"Fine, thank you." Verdnt's smile looked a bit nervous.

Mentàll speared Behran next with his gaze. "Behran. How is your family?" His lips stretched into a smile, but his eyes fleetingly glittered with contempt.

"Fine, sir." Behran met the older man's gaze, but his shoulders looked stiff. He only relaxed when Mentàll moved down the line to the Quatr contenders.

"Mentàll is the Chief of Dehre," Kitran announced to his students, as if they didn't already know. "And my chief contender at the Primary level."

"You honor me." Mentàll's tone was modest, but it also seemed clear to Methusal that he took the praise as his due. He turned smoothly. "This way to your quarters."

The little group strode to a nearby outbuilding, which had two doors; one at each end of the structure. "You may leave your packs here, if you'd like. I will take you to the dining table next." The Dehrien Chief flicked an expressionless glance over them. "Men in one cabin, and women in the other, of course."

A prickling sensation down her back told her the Chief's gaze followed her as she stepped up the two uneven stones and peered into the murky interior of the shack. An involuntary shudder rippled down her spine. Just a few days ago, she'd envied Deccia's ability to draw male attention. Well, she certainly had the Dehrien Chief's attention, but it wasn't for a good purpose. Instinct told her that he'd concocted some sort of a wild beast versus apte game, and she was the apte.

The unexpected stench of the room made Methusal gag as she stepped inside and crossed to a cot shoved against the far wall. She pulled the pack from her shoulders. The wall at the head of her bed abutted the room next door. She heard Behran's low voice speaking to Kitran. Letting the bundle slide through her fingers onto the narrow cot, she glanced around, while attempting to hold her breath.

The room was small, dirty, and bare, except for the three cots. A narrow gash in the wall above provided the only light in the room, and there were no lamps, no coverlets, and no source of heat. Luckily the day was warm, and she had brought her own coverlet for the chilly night.

"Ew!" Lina wrinkled her nose. "It stinks."

"It sure does." Methusal pinched her nose. It smelled like old sweat and rotting boards, and a certain other noxious fragrance. Maybe a whip beast lay rotting beneath the floorboards.

"Don't they ever *clean?*" Retra sniffed, scuffing her foot across the dirt encrusted floor. Maybe that was a source of part of the foul odor.

"Let's get out of here." The overpowering stench made Methusal's stomach churn. Her cabin mates were close on her heels when she left the building. She gulped in great gusts of fresh, crisp plains air. The men were already out, so Mentàll strode with Kitran toward the center of the community.

Methusal fell in to walk beside Behran. "Does your room stink?" she whispered.

"Yes." He offered a thin smile. "Welcome to Dehre. Water is scarce, so cleaning is almost impossible."

Other sights met her eyes as they hiked through the small town. Children were dirty and unkempt, and women stared at the Rolbanis with hostile expressions. Few of the men looked like they'd washed within the last month. Compared with the rest of his fellow citizens, Mentàll looked positively clean, suave, and sophisticated.

The whole camp had the smell of the cabin, and Methusal found her nose wrinkling more with every step. No wonder the Amils had moved to Rolban.

The only tents that looked fairly clean were arranged in a cluster to the northwest. One was much larger than the rest. All were made of white, sun bleached leather. Behran quietly told her that the seven tents were part of the Chief's compound. They were where he lived and worked.

"Here we are," Mentàll indicated two tables which were drawn up end to end together, and flanked by weather-beaten benches. A whole roast wild beast lay stretched out on the tables, with a baked apte clenched in its mouth. The large, furry beast was trimmed with decorative logne leaves and green wildberries.

Methusal had never seen anything so revolting in her life! Were they supposed to hack through the fur to get the meat? No plates were in sight—only knives and glasses of water. Were they supposed to eat directly off of the wild beast?

Dismayed, her steps faltered.

"Have a seat!" Mentàll waved them to the benches. "Helga will provide plates, and then feel free to start eating."

Plates! At least there were those. Methusal slipped onto the bench next to Behran. He could give her points of etiquette—if any existed. Helga placed a shallow platter before her.

"Welcome to Dehre." Mentàll was speaking again. "We are honored to have you here. If you need anything, just ask, and I will see it is provided."

Dehriens slipped onto benches across from the Rolbanis, and Methusal guessed they would be their kaavl competitors. She surveyed up and down the long table, wondering whom she would be competing against. Each man looked stony-faced, and her tentative smile went unreturned.

"Eat!" Mentàll's voice roared behind her, making her jump. Hot, unpleasant smelling breath drifted down to her nostrils. "Let me help you."

She froze as he leaned closer. Long fingers slid the knife out of her clenched hand. "This is how it is done." Quickly, with two long, swift slashes, a slab of meat miraculously appeared on her plate.

Her stiff lips muttered, "Thank you."

"You are welcome, Methusal," he said in a low voice, near her ear.

Appalled, she was only able to breathe easily again when Mentàll returned to the head of the table. What was he doing? Frightening her. And clearly on purpose. Feeling jittery, she stabbed into the brown, juicy meat.

"Looks like you've found an admirer." Behran's tone sounded mocking as he sawed off a piece of meat for himself.

Methusal glared at him. How could he be so insensitive? Behran seemed totally unaware of how uncomfortable she felt.

She took a deep breath and tried to look at the encounter objectively. The Dehrien hated her. Equally clear, he had not made any sort of advance on her. Rather, it had been another deliberate attempt to threaten her. Again, she wished she'd held her tongue instead of making an enemy of the Dehrien Chief.

Methusal attacked the meat and chewed it fiercely. Wrapped in a logne leaf, it wasn't half bad—apparently the Dehriens had one saving grace—they could cook. She had only chewed one bite when a soft voice spoke behind them. "Behran."

Methusal looked over her shoulder as Behran leaped to his feet. "Hendra!"

With surprise, Methusal watched him reach for a tall, slim, blond-haired young woman. The girl flushed and stumbled backward to avoid the embrace.

"Sorry," Behran said softly. He dropped his arms and extended his hand, instead. With a deeper flush, the girl briefly accepted this contact and then withdrew her hand to her side.

Clearly, whoever this Hendra was, she did not like to be touched. Methusal examined the Dehrien girl more closely. The young woman was probably a little older than herself. Maybe twenty. Her white-blond hair fell long and straight, halfway down her back, and her face was fine-featured, with unusual, dark brown eyes. She was beautiful.

Methusal quickly glanced at Behran. Who was she, and how did Behran know her?

Behran turned to her. "Thusa, this is Hendra. Hendra, this is Methusal Maahr."

Hendra's smile lit her eyes. "I'm pleased to meet you." Something fragile and vulnerable shimmered just beneath her smile. Methusal wondered about that. Hendra reminded her of a cautious, friendly apte, trying to detect friends from enemies.

"Sit with us," Behran said. He sat down and scooted closer to Methusal, so Hendra could sit on his right. "It's great to see you. What have you been up to all of these years?"

"Practicing kaavl, like you. I just reached the Quatr-level."

"Congratulations. You've worked hard for it."

"Twelve years. Better late than never, right?" Her soft laugh sounded like a clear bell.

"Thusa just reached the Tri-level."

Hendra smiled at Methusal. "Congratulations."

Methusal returned the smile. "You, too." She wasn't sure why she felt unsettled by Hendra's presence. Maybe because she didn't fully understand Behran's relationship with her. But why should she care? She and Behran were only friends—barely that, if the truth were told.

"Hendra and I learned kaavl together," Behran explained.

"I'm not the quickest learner. Behran was kind enough to help me through a few hard places."

"It is difficult," Methusal agreed. She forked up another bite of meat. "This meal is delicious."

"I'm glad you think so." Hendra's laugh sounded dry. "Usually we eat in our own homes, not outside and together like this."

"Do you live near here?" Methusal felt herself beginning to warm to the other girl. She seemed genuinely nice.

"In that tent." Hendra pointed to a small tent adjacent to the Dehrien Chief's large tent.

Methusal did a double take. Obviously, the small tent was part of the Chief's compound. Was Hendra one of his women? The thought horrified her.

"Thusa. Wipe the shock off your face," Behran grinned. "Hendra is Mentàll's cousin."

"Cousin?" Methusal repeated. If anything, she felt even more flabbergasted. "But you're nothing like him," she blurted. Except they did share the same white-blond hair.

Hendra's smile faltered. "He's been good to me all of my life. Especially since my parents died."

"I see." Methusal did not see. But then, she guessed even unpredictable wild animals took care of their own.

"Things seem worse in Dehre than when we left five years ago," Behran said.

"We've had two droughts, and the wild beasts trampled and ate most of our crops. So did the aptes. The well water is almost dry. But Mentàll recently ordered men to divert part of the Tarst River south, into the northern hills. Now we have access to more water."

"That was a smart idea." Behran nodded. "Water isn't a problem for us. But we haven't had much luck hunting lately."

"Neither have we. It's been hard."

So that explained the filth and hostile attitudes of the people of Dehre. They survived on the edge of starvation. Methusal felt bad. These people needed the Alliance to improve their quality of life. If only she didn't distrust their Chief, she'd think the Alliance was a good idea. As it was, she felt wary. And it didn't help that most of the Dehriens seemed to hate the Rolbani kaavl team.

"I'm sorry," Behran said.

"We had an unusual visitor recently," Hendra said, obviously wanting to change the subject.

"Who?"

"Have you heard of the Prophet?"

"Of course," Behran said.

"He visited last week."

"Really?" Methusal said, surprised. She'd just been speaking to Sims about the Prophet a few days ago. Now he'd just shown up in Dehre. "Why did he come here?"

"He wanted to speak to Mentàll, but he didn't stay long."

"What did he want with Mentàll?" Behran asked.

Hendra hesitated, and glanced down at her fingers. "I don't know the whole story. But my cousin didn't look happy afterward."

"Maybe the Prophet can see into a person's soul," Methusal muttered. If he could, he had probably seen blackness where the Dehrien's heart should be.

Hendra glanced at the angle of the sun. "The games will begin in an hour. Perhaps you should rest. I'll see you later."

"Nice to meet you," Methusal said, and the other girl smiled. Hendra headed toward the white tents.

CHAPTER TWENTY-FIVE

AFTER LUNCH, the Rolbani team retired to their quarters to pass the remaining hour until the games. The Quatr-Level Game would be held first, and all the Rolbanis would be present to support their teammates.

Earlier, Methusal had felt concerned that the Rolbanis wouldn't be as well rested as the Dehriens for the Games. Then she'd realized that trekking to Dehre and participating in the Kaavl Games all on the same day gave her team an advantage. They were warmed up—both physically and in kaavl. Methusal felt ready to take on the Dehriens.

Unable to bear the stench of the cabin, Methusal waited outside on the steps with her kaavl flag attached to her waistband. Although she was trying to relax, she felt keenly aware of her Dehrien surroundings. It was so different from home.

The little town lay tranquil as the inhabitants rested, and a few bleached leather tent flaps rippled in the growing breeze. A small boy wandered toward her, scuffing his feet in the dust. Maybe he wanted to get a closer look at the stranger from the mountains. He was all brown—clothes, skin, hair, and eyes. Caked on dust and dirt covered his feet.

Methusal smiled as he drew abreast of her, but she remained silent. Maybe this child wouldn't be as unfriendly as the other Dehriens. Frankly, their hostility set her nerves on edge. Why had the Rolbanis been invited to play in their Kaavl Games when they so obviously hated them? Another thought occurred to her. What kind of an attitude would the Dehrien delegation traveling to Rolban have?

The boy stood only half a length away now, feet firmly planted on the cracked earth. His expression shocked her. His eyes were slitted with hatred, and his teeth bared in a snarl.

"You Rolbanis think you're better than us, but you're not! You'll see. We'll drag you down and stomp on you. You'll be dead, but we'll live. Just wait and see!" Venom thickened the childish voice, and Methusal stared back, her mouth agape.

His little foot violently shoveled dusty pebbles at her.

"Go. Now!" The two harsh words cracked through the still air.

Behran stood on the stone stair of his compartment, his face stern.

"Traitor!" The boy spat, but sped away and ducked into a tent.

"Why do they hate us? Was it like this when you lived here?"

"No." He slowly stepped down. "We never hated the Rolbanis—though we *did* envy their gates and croplands." He shook his head. "No. This is new, and it bothers me."

"He seems to think they'll rout us in the games."

"Not if I can help it." His eyes flashed. "Dehre has good players, but we'll beat them. At least, you and I will, at the Tri-level. I'm not so sure about the others."

"Don't you think Kitran will beat Mentàll at the Primary?" she said, astonished.

With a frown, Behran glanced toward the Dehrien Chief's great tent. "Five years ago, it might have been a draw, but now... I don't know. Mentàll's become awfully powerful in such a short period of time. And here, that means his kaavl is much better than anyone else's."

"Dehriens elect their Chief according to their kaavl abilities."

"Yes. Just like Tarst. The best kaavl player becomes Chief. Chiefs can be challenged every three years."

"Really." This was what Petr was pushing for in Rolban. And since Kitran had never expressed the desire to become

Chief, that meant if kaavl ruled the election process, Petr would stay Chief until someone beat him. What a perfect way to hold onto power for years.

Behran said, "Kaavl is the most respected ability here. Unfortunately, the people who aren't gifted have to do all the hard chores, such as food gathering and cooking. But the people who are gifted practice it all the time—until they peak, and their final level determines what work they'll have to do from then on. The higher the level, the more important the position."

"I wonder if Mentàll has reached his final stage."

"Probably not. Otherwise, he wouldn't be Chief—at least, not for long. Someone else would eventually beat him. Being Chief is a strong incentive for people to keep honing their kaavl skills."

Dehrien culture was totally different from Rolban's. Methusal was glad she lived in Rolban.

Behran noticed her concerned look. "Kitran will do great, I'm sure, Thusa."

"It's not that. It's thinking that Mentàll might win. I can't stand him."

Rattling pebbles and a short, muffled cry cut Behran's response short. He frowned. "What was that?"

The sound had come from behind their building. The two ran to investigate.

At first they saw nothing but a short, ragged bush, but then Methusal spied a brown moccasin sprawled to one side, attached to a wiggling leg. Another step revealed its owner.

"Aali!"

Her cousin looked up and rubbed her leg sheepishly.

"Hi."

"What are you *doing* here?"

An irrepressible grin lit her face. "I want to join the games."

"Does Petr know you're here?"

"Of course not!" She scowled. "He wouldn't let me come, Thusa. You know that. So I had to sneak."

"Aali!" Behran's tone was stern, but Aali didn't seem to notice. She bounced to her feet, dusted off her dirty knees, and grabbed her small pack from the ground.

"See!" She showed it proudly to Methusal. "I planned it all out. I even brought extra food and water. Kitran can't send me home now!"

Aghast, Methusal just stared at her. "Your father is going to be furious. You shouldn't have come. And you certainly can't play in the games!"

Aalicaa's lower lip trembled. "Why aren't you on my side? You know Father is totally unreasonable. *I* should be the one competing, not Lina! Remember? I beat her!"

"It doesn't matter." Feeling helpless, Methusal stared at her cousin. For the first time, she realized the weight of responsibility Deccia carried, trying to provide direction for Aali. "Kitran has already promised Lina the spot. Besides, he wouldn't let you compete anyway. He knows how Petr feels about it."

"Bother!" Angry tears shone in her eyes. "Now you're just as mean as he is! Why did I have to make a noise so you'd find me?"

"So you planned to jump into the game, just like you did in Rolban," Behran interjected, arms folded.

"So?" Defiant tears trickled down her cheeks.

"Aali." Methusal put a conciliatory hand on her shoulder, but the younger girl shoved it off.

"Leave me *alone,*" she snapped. "I can't trust you anymore!"

Methusal's temper flared, mostly because she was forced to take Petr's side—a position she'd never thought to find herself.

"Don't speak to me that way, Aalicaa! You know you were wrong to come here. What did you think would happen? Did you think you'd sneak in and win the Quatrlevel? What if you did? What would that earn you? I'll tell you. Disrespect. Discipline is key in kaavl training. Kitran won't let anyone compete if he's not disciplined—it's a mark of immaturity, and you'll never be great in kaavl until you learn it."

Aali pressed her hands to her eyes and burst into tears. Methusal pulled her into a gentle hug. "I understand that you want to compete. But you have to go about it the right way."

"But Father will never let me! It's not fair," she sobbed. Methusal said nothing, because she knew it was true.

The deep trumpet of the slug monster shell resonated throughout the little village.

"Come on." Behran touched Aali's shoulder. "You can't play, but you can watch, so come on. The games are about to start."

Wiping her eyes, Aali slowly followed them around the side of the building. Methusal glanced at Behran, finally remembering they were still rivals.

He smiled and his eyes glinted, as if he had read her mind. "Best of luck, Methusal."

"And to you."

Kitran, Verdnt, Retra, and Lina emerged from the stinky cabins and gawked in one accord when they saw Aalicaa.

Kitran was much sterner than Methusal or Behran had been. "We'll have a long talk later, young lady," he promised. Aali, if possible, looked smaller and more miserable than ever.

Methusal and Aali trailed behind as Behran and Kitran led the way to the kaavl starting point on the far, western side of town. Dehriens straggled ahead of them and behind them.

Methusal had just been wondering how the spectators would get a good view of the playing field, since there were no hills or plateaus nearby that could be used as a vantage point, when a great structure came into view behind the large Chief's tent and the wooden shacks on the western side of town. She gasped in surprise.

It was erected a five minute walk beyond the town's last row of shacks, and stretched at least three lengths into the air. The contraption resembled rows of wide steps climbing to the sky, and a wide landing and railings composed the uppermost level. Mentàll stood up there, along with a few others.

Dehrien townspeople squatted on the rows of steps, and the higher seats filled rapidly. In the middle, a strip of uninhabited stairs stretched from the top to the bottom of the structure, providing easy passage up and down. Methusal had never seen such a contraption before. Even Aali's dull eyes brightened, and she looked about with reawakened interest.

Methusal's steps slowed down when she drew abreast of Kitran and the others.

"They can build this, but they can't wash!" Lina commented.

It seemed clear where Dehrien priorities lay. Kaavl. And power.

Mentàll stood on the top level, and beckoned them upward. Methusal followed Kitran up the roughly hewn steps. Maybe the Dehriens had traded with the Tarst for the lumber. A lot of time and effort had been put into making the structure.

Mentàll's cold eyes welcomed them. "Take the seat of highest honor—the top row." His eyelids didn't even flicker when he saw Aalicaa. He turned away, ignoring her.

"Beast!" Aalicaa snorted under her breath. Nothing like a challenge to get her back to sorts.

Methusal couldn't agree more. She followed the others to the topmost row of steps, which were located one step down from the Dehrien Chief's viewing platform. When they were seated, the top platform was behind them, separated only by a two board railing. At one point, Methusal sensed Mentàll's presence directly behind her. A shiver crept down her spine. The man was beginning to unnerve her.

The Dehrien Chief spoke through the shell amplifier to the crowd below, but Methusal blocked him out, focusing instead on a large white boulder rearing up from the parched brown playing field—it was probably the halfway point of the games. The Dehrien course looked like it was about a third of the length of the kaavl course at home.

Methusal would love to score a Tri-level win for Rolban. She'd also love to beat Behran, of course. But defeating the Dehriens came first. And she hoped Kitran would win the Primary match. That victory might knock Mentàll's arrogance down a notch or two.

Loud foot stomping signaled the end of his speech, and Retra, Lina, Hendra, and the other Quatr-level contenders climbed to the top platform. Aalicaa looked on, fidgeting enviously. There were six in all.

The shell trumpeted, and the boisterous crowd quieted. Latecomers shuffled quickly to the few remaining seats. Except for the scuffle of feet, the only sound now was the sigh of the strengthening wind sweeping through the open spaces of the tall structure.

Retra and Lina stood on the top stair, side by side, looking tense. Hendra looked fairly relaxed. Next to her stood her Dehrien counterparts. One was a runner Methusal had seen in Rolban before. His face was closed and hard, as were the faces of the other three men.

Retra or Lina had to win. Suddenly Methusal realized just how much that win meant to her. It was home versus the hostile Dehriens. It was about the best team winning—and Methusal desperately wanted that to be the Rolbani team. She was developing a dislike for the insolent Dehriens. Except for Hendra, of course. And she was beginning to understand why her father, with all of his years of experience dealing with the Dehriens, still distrusted them.

She glanced at Behran's unreadable face. Was he wholeheartedly Rolbani now? Or did a part of him still root for the Dehriens?

Mentàll's voice cracked like a whip through the hushed stand. "If the Quatr-level contenders are ready....Begin!"

The traditional kaavl disks crashed, and the competitors sprinted down the stairs. Methusal leaned forward, her gaze glued to the contestants. The Rolbanis reached the floor of the plain last, and then they were off, darting through the underbrush.

The crowd erupted into foot stomping cheers. Screams filled the air as people rooted for their favorite to win. A far cry from Rolban's silent, respectful audience.

Aalicaa screamed exuberantly, too. "There's Retra! See, Methusal? ...Uh oh!" A tall Dehrien male closed in fast behind her. It was the Dehrien runner, Ludst Lst. He had visited near the time of the seed grain theft. One swift tackle, and Retra sprawled on the ground. The Dehrien kicked her viciously, snatched her flag, and sprinted on.

Methusal sprang to her feet. Her cry of outrage was lost in the approving roar of the crowd. Kicking an opponent was against the rules! The Dehrien should be pulled from the game.

Lina was faring a little better, and had just rounded the far white rock. Now the other Dehriens couldn't touch her until they, too, had reached the rock.

Three players remained on the field. Hendra was one, but as she watched, Ludst nipped in, shoved her down and sped on. At the Quatr-level, the top three were allowed to cross the finish line. All three would receive awards. But now the tall Dehrien quickly closed in on the gritty Lina. She sidestepped, but he grabbed her arm and spun her to the ground, shoving her down hard when she struggled to sit up. He snatched the flag, and with another kick, dashed on.

At her side, Aali shouted with indignation, but Methusal had fallen silent, incensed. What kind of competition was this? This wasn't a test of kaavl—it was a test of strength and brutality!

The perspiring Dehrien sprinted up the stairs and stopped, chest heaving, at the top platform.

"The winner!" Mentàll trumpeted. "Ludst Lst!" He grasped the young man's arm and pumped it into the air. "Capturing, ten, and evading, ten!"

The highest points possible. No deductions had been made for poor sportsmanship.

"Kitran!" Her mentor's narrowed black eyes focused on her outraged bleat. "That's not fair!"

He nodded slightly, to let her know he had heard. He muttered, "Verdnt warned me the Dehrien games could be vicious. I'll tell Mentàll that kind behavior is not acceptable for Inter-Community Kaavl Games."

Mentàll presented Ludst with his medal, and the crowd slowly quieted. The dirty and bruised Quatr-level Rolbanis slid into their seats. Retra was crying openly, but Lina looked mad enough to spit.

Kitran briefly touched their shoulders when he stepped by to gain the top platform. There Methusal watched him engage Mentàll in a low-toned, vehement discussion. Kitran would straighten this whole thing out. He must.

An agreement had clearly been struck when the two stepped apart a few moments later. Kitran returned to his seat, his expression unreadable.

"The Tri-level contenders will now come forward," Mentàll commanded.

Behran and Methusal rose and joined their five Dehrien competitors on the platform.

Mentàll approached them. "Are you aware of the new rules? No pushing, shoving, or kicking in order to gain a flag. Only one clean tackle to capture. Understood?" His pale blue eyes traveled the line of contestants.

Methusal met his gaze steadily, unable to hide her contempt. He must know the Dehrien's acts of brutality were in direct violation of basic kaavl rules and ethics. But equally clear, Ludst would not be punished or stripped of the Quatr-level award for his actions.

"Get ready to begin."

The seven faced the stairs and the plain below, and Methusal charted a course to the right that curved to eventually meet the rock. With the Dehriens behaving barbarically, winning wouldn't be easy. Evading capture would be her best bet. Tension knotted in her stomach as she waited.

The shell blared once, signaling quiet.

"The Tri-level contenders are ready... Begin!" The disks clashed, releasing the seven, and the wooden steps thundered as the pack flew down. Methusal trailed behind on purpose, and upon reaching the plain, struck off to the right.

Forcing her mind to be composed, she slipped into kaavl. The roar of the crowd was difficult to filter out, but after ten long, agonizing steps, she felt tuned into her environment and the noises made by her competitors. One Dehrien had seen her cut to the right, and she heard him speed diagonally in her direction, looking to intercept her a few lengths ahead. She instantly adjusted her course to the left, while at the same time keeping careful tabs on the locations of her next nearest foes.

She flew silently over the plain as her keen eyes observed the path ahead and memorized the location of each stray leaf or twig. Perfect balance and precise foot placements enabled her to stay clear of those noisy position indicators.

The competitor who had been intent on cutting her off realized he had been tricked, and now charged back in the direction of the rock. But he had lost time, and Methusal was easily out of his range. In addition to this person and herself, three competitors remained, and all would arrive at the rock almost simultaneously—a dangerous situation.

She elected to cut slightly to the right again, circle the rock from behind, and then come around again on the other side. She would be adding distance to her trek, but also a margin of safety.

Rounding the rock, it quickly became clear that only two competitors now remained besides herself. Just as she had thought. The rock had served as a trap for two of the contenders.

The roar of the crowd intensified abruptly, breaking her concentration. She was running blind, with no idea where her competitors were.

Too late, she heard the fast rush of footsteps behind her, and then jarring pain as a muscular arm seized her by the knees. She fell hard on the ground, smacking her head against a large rock. A tug came at her waist, and then the person was gone. She hadn't even seen who it was—although it had the distinct smell of a Dehrien.

Head throbbing, she pushed herself up on one elbow. Bright flashes of light danced before her eyes and she squinted, trying to focus.

Gradually the dry, brittle vegetation stood still. She took several deep breaths and slowly rolled onto her knees, and then into a standing position. She clutched at a prickly tagma bush for support when her head swam. After a few steady breaths, she felt a little more stable, and cautiously stepped forward, using bushes for support, as needed.

By the time she reached the stands, her equilibrium had returned, but her head throbbed mercilessly. Kitran met her at the bottom of the stairs. A hint of concern warmed his expressionless black eyes.

"What happened out there?"

"I hit my head on a rock." Her voice wavered dangerously, but she swallowed back the self-pitying lump filling her throat.

"Let me see." With surprisingly gentle fingers, he examined her left temple, where a tender welt swelled. His fingers came away bloody. He stared into her eyes—maybe to see if they were dilated.

"You'll be all right. Wash off the blood and compress it with a coltac leaf. Did you bring some?"

"Yes." She always carried coltac leaves.

"Good. Go back to your compartment and rest. I'll send someone to get you when it's time for supper."

"But who won?" Illogically, that was all that mattered to her.

"Behran." Kitran gave a rare smile.

Methusal was glad her arch rival had won. Far better him than the brutal Dehriens. She wished her instructor luck in his event, and shuffled back through the deserted town to her shack.

Back at the cabin, she cleaned her wound as best she could and dribbled thick, healing coltac juice over it. Her head throbbed, but she didn't lie down.

Now was the perfect opportunity to investigate Dehre for clues about the Rolbani thefts. Everyone was watching the kaavl games. Including the Chief. What better time to search for missing pelts and the grain, too—if it hadn't been eaten already.

Looking left and right, and seeing no one, Methusal slipped outside and headed for the Dehrien Chief's massive, bleached leather tent.

△ △ △ △ △

A search of Mentàll's tent revealed nothing, except that he liked to wear bleached leather clothing, and he liked things neat. Every item had its place, except for his desk, which was a little messy. Either he had domestic help, or he had an orderly mind. But she found no Rolbani pelts lying around, and certainly no bag of grain. Methusal slipped back outside.

The slug monster shell trumpeted. The Primary level was about to begin. She'd been counting the ceremonial blasts. Still plenty of time before the Dehriens returned to town.

Methusal quickly searched each of Mentàll's other tents, but again came up empty. Only one tent remained when the shell sounded for the last time. Hendra's. Surely the Dehrien girl had nothing to hide.

But in the interest of being thorough, she should check.

"Hello?" Methusal said to the closed tent flap. Only a few minutes remained, so she'd need to be fast. She heard nothing, so she peeked in and saw a circular interior, which included an eating area to the left, and sleeping area to the right. Hendra appeared from behind a partition.

"Oh, sorry," Methusal gasped.

Hendra smiled and pulled aside the tent door. "It's all right. I'll show you around, if you'd like. Dehre must seem so different from Rolban. You live in caves?"

"Yes. Large ones. But they're all linked together inside the mountain."

"Interesting. That's where I spend most of my time." Hendra pointed to the eating area, which included a fire pit and a table with two chairs. A pitcher steamed on the table. "Are the caves natural, or did your ancestors dig them out?"

"Natural. The rock is really hard. It's difficult to carve out much. All of our passageways and caverns are naturally formed."

"You must feel so secure there." Hendra circled the short distance to the other side of the tent, and opened a curtained area which contained a wooden stand. Extra clothes were stacked on it—twice as many clothes as Methusal owned— and an extra pair of moccasins. A pallet with soft fur coverings lay adjacent to it.

"Our gate keeps out the wild beasts, if that's what you mean," Methusal said. "But other dangers live in our walls."

Giving her a quizzical look, the other girl led the short way back to the eating area. "Man or beast? Or disease?"

"All three at times, but lately, it's a man. Someone murdered an old friend of mine last week. And I think the same person killed Renn's father yesterday." Methusal watched Hendra carefully for any sort of reaction.

Hendra's hand flew to her throat. "Oh! *Oh no!* I'm so sorry."

"A thief has been stealing supplies in Rolban. Our Chief thinks Liem and Renn discovered his identity." A distressed frown flitted across Hendra's face. "Do you know anything about the thefts?"

"No!" Methusal believed her, but she also got the impression Hendra was hiding something. Hendra said, "Has your Chief found the murderer?"

"He thought so. Me."

Shock widened her eyes. "No. Certainly not."

"No. But I've seen the thief, and it's a man. So Petr can't hold me any longer."

"You were in jail?"

"For a night." Methusal didn't know why, but she wanted to trust Hendra, even though she was Mentàll's cousin, and even though she was clearly hiding something. Behran knew and liked her—maybe that was why.

Quietly, Hendra said, "You think Dehre is involved."

"Yes."

"And Mentàll?" Hendra turned to pour a cup of tea. She handed it to Methusal, and indicated a chair next to the table to sit on.

"I don't know." A diplomatic answer for his cousin. "I do know he doesn't like me."

Hendra's eyes clouded. "I've noticed. And I'm sorry. I'll admit I don't understand my cousin anymore."

Methusal sipped the sweet, fragrant tea. "Does your whole family live in these tents?"

"No. My father died four years ago, just after Mentàll was elected Chief for the first time. He hated Mentàll's election." Something dark shadowed the words. "My mother died six years ago. So after my father died, I had nowhere to go. My oldest brother got the house, but he wouldn't let me stay. My other two brothers wouldn't allow me in their homes, either. Mentàll offered this place to me. And a woman to cook and clean for me."

"So you're close to your cousin."

"No. No one is close to Mentàll."

"Why does he care for you, when your own brothers won't?" Although Methusal knew it was none of her business, she wanted to learn all she could about the Dehrien Chief.

"I don't know." Hendra paused. "He came to live with my family when his mother died. He was five, and I wasn't even born yet. All I know is my father always hated him, and so did my brothers. I was the youngest, and didn't understand any of it. We both loved kaavl, but Mentàll was much better than I was. It was the only link between us."

"So he cares for you."

"Materially. He provides for me like a brother, and I'm grateful to him. But does he care for *me*?" Hendra paused, and bit her lip. "I believe so. But he's very...closed."

Cold, you mean, Methusal thought. And as Chief, loaning a tent to a misplaced relative would be easy. As she finished her tea, she asked one final, bold question. "Have any unusual pelts or metal items shown up here lately? Or grain?"

Hendra went very still.

"I know you're loyal to Dehre. But until we find the murderer, everyone in Rolban is in danger. We need your help."

A quick, troubled frown pinched her brows together. "Behran is in danger, too?"

Methusal felt uncomfortable, but couldn't pinpoint why. "Yes."

"I haven't seen the things you mentioned. But if I do, I'll tell you...or Behran."

"Thank you." Methusal believed her. She heard voices outside, and footsteps trudged past. "Is it time to eat already?"

"Yes. I'll see you and Behran there."

Methusal slipped into the gathering dusk. An unsettled feeling poked her when she thought about Behran and Hendra. But that was silly. They were old friends. And what did she care, anyway?

Chapter Twenty-Six

Hendra sat still after Methusal left. She felt cold inside. Metal items were missing from Rolban. She had been wondering where Mentàll had found the extra metal to make swords—if that is what he'd ordered made.

It must be. Dread gathered in a heavy lump in her heart as all the facts came together in her mind.

The Prophet had spoken of a traitor in Rolban. Mentàll knew him, the Prophet had said. The traitor must be the metal thief. And metal, of course, was the most important requirement for a weapon making camp. A camp where men worked only at night, in secret, in the dark. The same metal thief must have killed Methusal's friends.

Hendra felt sick. Even though she didn't believe that Mentàll had ordered the deaths of Methusal's friends, wasn't he indirectly responsible, if he was receiving stolen goods from the thief? Had he planted the traitor in Rolban?

No. The Prophet's words replayed, word for word through her mind—it was one of the small kaavl talents she did possess. He had said Mentàll had made an alliance *with the traitor in Rolban*. So a traitor must have lived there before her cousin made his plan.

But why would a traitor live in Rolban? And why make himself known to her cousin?

What *was* Mentàll planning? And how many more people would die before his plan was accomplished?

Trembling now, Hendra hugged herself.

Did she know her cousin anymore? What had happened to the man who had defended her honor five years ago? That man would never treat a woman how Mentàll was now treating Methusal. She'd seen him intimidate many others before...*men* who had crossed him, yes. But never a woman.

Why Methusal?

Hendra thought back over lunch, trying to remember some nuance...something to explain her cousin's dislike for Methusal. First impressions of their new visitors flashed; Aali's mischievous smile, Methusal's sincerity...and, of course, Behran's steady, true friendship. She had liked them all. She instinctively trusted them all.

But Mentàll did not like Methusal. Hendra had never felt such intense dislike from her emotionless cousin before. He hated Rolban, of course, but his hatred for this Rolbani girl was over the top. Something must have happened in Rolban when he'd gone there to sign the Alliance.

Methusal must threaten him somehow. Hendra's deep, instinctive "knowing" that had kept her alive through the worst of her childhood, told her so. It seemed strange that she had sensed this, since she understood little else about her cousin. Maybe she'd been able to read it because his emotions had risen closer to the surface this afternoon than they had in years.

Did Mentàll know that Methusal was investigating the two murders, and the Rolbani thefts? That she suspected Dehre—and therefore Mentàll—was involved in it all? Of course he did. Her cousin was nothing if not sharp, with razor-honed survival skills. Methusal was a threat to his plans—whatever they were.

Was Mentàll now a danger to Methusal? To everyone who stood in his path?

Hendra's throat ached. She had heard Mentàll renounce The One with her own ears. Had her cousin lost his soul to the dark side? Was it too late to save him, and convince him to stop his plan, whatever it might be?

Clearly something was not right. Equally obvious, only she could prevent more bloodshed. A sob worked into a tiny cry in her throat.

She wouldn't allow another person to die. As a consequence, only two choices remained.

She must confront him and make him see reason, once and for all.

And if he didn't listen?

She must betray him.

△ △ △ △ △

Aali, Lina, and Retra met Methusal on the way to the dining table with the news that both Verdnt and Kitran had lost their events. Verdnt, to a man named Jascr, and Kitran to Mentàll. Even though Behran had predicted this outcome, Methusal still felt shocked that Kitran had lost to the Dehrien Chief. Mentàll must be extraordinary in kaavl—and a far more dangerous opponent than she had feared.

Methusal listened with half an ear to the other girls' chatter as they walked to the waiting meal. Her head throbbed. The three other girls seemed to have become the best of friends over the last few hours. Apparently Aali was over her bitterness at being unable to compete—probably because she hadn't had to suffer through the Quatr-Level Game, like the other two had.

"It was so exciting, Methusal!" Retra exclaimed. "It took Kitran and Mentàll *forever* to reach the white rock and come back. They kept circling each other and setting up traps and evading capture. Not like our game!" She gave a small, bitter smile.

The table lay unchanged since lunch. Evidently, cold wild beast was the order of the evening. The very thought made Methusal's stomach lurch. She sat reluctantly and contemplated the cold, fat congealed meat.

Aali elbowed her when she sat down. With a subtle head tilt, she indicated a prematurely balding, stocky, sandy-haired man across the table. In a loud whisper, she said, "Wortn came in second at the Tri-level. He's the one who tackled you."

"Really." Methusal frowned. The man, who obviously heard Aali's comment, briefly scowled across the table, but then returned his attention to his companions. Apparently causing a Rolbani injury did not concern him too much.

Methusal itched to say something to him, but curbed her tongue. For once, she would follow the higher path. It was difficult, though. She had to look away from him.

"Methusal!" Behind her, the familiar, harsh voice made her tense. The Dehrien Chief. Joy upon joy. A large hand gripped her shoulder, and she froze when he leaned in closer. "It is unfortunate that you were injured." His low voice electrified the hairs inside her ear. "If you require medical attention, I will be happy to arrange for the best that Dehre can offer."

A breathless panic choked her. She couldn't seem to move. "Go away," she whispered.

"If you do not want further attention, Methusal, keep your place." His fingers briefly tightened in a clear threat.

She forced out, "You don't scare me."

"Only the weak lie." Contempt sliced through the words.

"Why threaten me, if you have nothing to hide?"

A silent breath elapsed. "Only fools challenge me, Methusal."

She swallowed.

"Heed my warning. Or you will know the consequence." At last, the intimidating presence released her, and he silently strode away.

Methusal sucked in a deep, shuddering breath. The Dehrien had just warned her off. Clearly, he had something to hide—otherwise, why waste attention on a lowly Rolbani girl? Panic thumped in her heart. What would he do to her if he discovered that she'd searched his tents? Not a comfortable thought.

But *why* did he feel so threatened by her? It was as if he knew she was searching for evidence against him. But how could he know that?

The traitor in Rolban knew she was investigating. Had he told Mentàll? If so, that would confirm that the Dehrien Chief was tied into the thefts in Rolban.

One thing was for certain. His threats would not stop her investigation. In fact, she should feel encouraged by them. It must mean she was getting close to the truth about the Alliance, the thefts, and Renn and Liem's murders.

Beside her, Hendra spoke quietly. "I'm sorry for my cousin's behavior."

She had arrived sometime during Mentàll's subtle attack.

Methusal wondered what part the blond girl played in the whole mystery. "It's not your fault."

Hendra said softly, "I've seen him threaten many men. But never a woman."

"He's a beast!" Aali exclaimed indignantly. "You should punch him in the stomach next time!"

Methusal didn't think that would be a good idea. She turned back to the Dehrien girl. "So you heard what he said to me?"

"Yes." Hendra looked deeply troubled.

"What is he hiding?"

Conflict warred in her eyes. Relief replaced it when Behran slipped onto the bench across from them.

Hendra knew something. However, Methusal felt certain the Dehrien girl would not confide in her. Maybe she would tell Behran. She offered her rival a faint smile. "Congratulations on winning."

"Thank you." But his ready smile faded when he eyed her left temple. "Are you okay?"

She nodded, but directed a frown toward Dehre's Chief. "I'll feel better when we leave this horrible place."

Behran followed her gaze. "Mentàll's coming with us. Their best kaavl contenders are going to Tarst, and we'll compete against them again there."

"What?" She felt aghast. "Isn't he going to Rolban on Sixthday with the delegation?"

"He'll arrive late—traveling with us."

The dull ache in her head sharpened. Three more days of Mentàll! The trip she'd so looked forward to was not living up to her expectations at all. Not with Mentàll's threats, the hostile Dehriens, a whack to the head, losing the Tri-Level Game.... She glanced at the wild beast and sighed. Cold meat to eat.

Helga had a surprise that evening, and unobtrusively distributed bowls of a steaming substance to each person at the table. It was growing dark, and Methusal dipped into it cautiously. She wasn't sure what revolting new dish the Dehriens might consider a delicacy.

Across from her, the Dehriens fell greedily to their bowls, so she touched a bit to her lips. She licked them experimentally. But it was only porridge. She'd thought Dehre's grain crop had been small last summer. Was she mistaken? Or maybe this was the last of it. Whatever the case, Matron Olgith's tiresome gruel seemed to have followed her all the way to Dehre.

Reluctantly, she pushed a spoonful into her mouth. At least it was hot. And the Dehriens certainly seemed to find it a treat. Night fell as she ate.

After the meal, a light show was put on for the Rolbanis' entertainment. Probably thanks to their three wins that afternoon, the Dehriens had become almost friendly to their Rolbani neighbors. Now they clapped rapidly and rhythmically as three entertainers circled a giant orange bonfire near the great table.

The three men were bare to the waist, and held a lighted torch in each hand. The largest man extended his left arm in the air. Clearly this was a signal of some kind, for the rhythmic clapping slowed, but did not stop.

The large man slowly began to dance to the beat of the hands. The two other entertainers joined in, one by one, and then the first man tossed the lighted torch in his left hand over the fire to the entertainer on his right. This throw set both other men in motion, and lighted torch sticks flew end over end in the night sky, expertly caught and thrown again. Torches in their right hands spun off in the opposite direction.

Methusal watched, mesmerized. How beautiful!

The crowd's clapping increased in pace, and the entertainers' dancing and torch flinging sped up, too. Soon the torches flew faster than she could keep track, but still the dance went on.

Finally, the clapping slowed and burst into applause, and the three men flung their torches into the air. As the sticks rained down into the giant bonfire, their faces beamed, glistening with heat and perspiration.

Methusal clapped hard. She'd never seen anything so spectacular before!

Behran turned a grin on her. "I wanted to be a torch wielder when I was young."

"Really? Can you throw torches like they do?"

"No." He chuckled. "I gave it up when I realized I could barely catch the sticks one by one, let alone catch the right end."

Methusal laughed. Catching the flaming end would be a drawback.

When Mentàll stood to make a speech, Methusal whispered to Behran, "I'm going to rest for the night." At his nod, she whispered goodnight to Aali and Hendra, and then slipped from the table. She was tired, and all that clapping had begun to make her head throb even more.

The bonfires on the edge of the community guided her steps to the Rolbani cabin. The stinky room was pitch dark, and she tripped over a pack one of her roommates had left lying in the middle of the floor. A quick hop saved her from falling flat on her face. Reaching her bed, she sat down carefully, and then blindly unpacked the carry coverlet. She had to rely upon memory to remember how each piece was packed. Garments out, she carefully lay her food rations on top and put them at the end of her bed.

Drawing the cool leather coverlet up to her nose, she lay down, but it was a long while before she fell asleep, because something about the evening niggled at her brain. Just before she slipped into sleep she remembered. The grain! Where *had* the Dehriens got the grain for the porridge? Rolban certainly hadn't given it to them. But her head hurt too much to think about it any longer.

△ △ △ △ △

The party broke up a little after the fire dancers finished. Hendra said goodnight to the others and retired to her tent. She was glad to be home. Seeing Behran and Methusal reminded her all over again that her cousin might be a danger to them. Her stomach felt knotted, and it made her feel sick. Hopefully she would be able to sleep tonight. She headed for her bed chamber.

A knock sounded on the wooden board outside her door. Startled, she hesitated, and then returned to the main living area. Who could that be, at this hour of the night?

"Yes?" she said warily.

"Hendra. May I come in?" Mentàll's harsh voice surprised her. He had never asked to enter her tent at night before.

Apprehension clawed at her heart. What did he want? Had he guessed that she was thinking about betraying him? But that was crazy. How could he possibly know?

She refused to put a name to her other, unspoken fears. Mentàll had provided for her basic needs for four years. He had never harmed her. With trembling hands, she pulled open the door and stared up at her tall cousin. As soon as she saw him, her fears quieted. Her cousin would never harm her. Not on purpose, at least. "Of course. Please come in."

Maybe it was for the best that he was here. She needed to confront him about his plans for Rolban.

Mentàll took one step inside. He let the tent flap fall closed behind him.

Before he could speak, Hendra said, "I'm glad you came. I need to ask you something."

A faint frown creased his brow. "Speak."

"I talked to Methusal this afternoon. She said Rolban has suffered thefts, and two murders."

"*Two* murders?" That fact clearly took him by surprise. "Kitran told me about one, but not the other." Although the information was clearly new to him, the dark, icy wall that perpetually shielded him like armor appeared to thicken.

"Methusal said that pots, and other items made of ore, have been stolen."

His expression cooled by several swift degrees. "What does that have to do with me? And why did you speak to Methusal? She is not worthy of your attention. She is trouble."

"For whom?" Hendra said softly. "For you?"

Anger tightened his large frame. Silkily, he said, "Do not question me, little cousin."

It was too late to turn back now. Tonight she would get her answers. "You treat her horribly, Mentàll. Why?"

"It is none of your concern! Stay out of my affairs, Hendra." He had never used that hard, cutting tone with her before, and Hendra trembled inside, wanting nothing more than to abandon the discussion and return to her peaceful relationship with her cousin. But if Mentàll planned war, she must speak.

"Why do you hate her so much, Mentàll? Because she's a Rolbani?"

Hatred cracked the cool ice of his gaze. "She is the epitome of Rolbani arrogance. Everything I hate, and have contempt for about Rolban has been bred into that girl."

"She thinks you're up to no good. But you know that, don't you? Is that why you hate her—because she's a threat to you?"

Mentàll did not answer, but she sensed his rage building, just beneath the surface. Her courage wavered, but she made herself push on. "You must stop what you're planning. Before innocent people die. We have the Alliance. What more could you want for Dehre?"

His fists tightened, but he did not answer.

Insight flashed. "It's not about Dehre, is it? It's about *you*. Why do you hate Rolban so much, Mentàll? What have they done to you?

He snarled, "What *haven't* they done? They are arrogant and fat. They've never rendered aid here. Never. Not even when hundreds of *innocents*," he spat the word, "died. It is the same now. We are worthless. As dust beneath their heels. Now they will take note. Now they will understand that we are a power worthy of their respect and fear."

"Why should they fear us? Aren't we friends now, through the Alliance?" She had to make him see reason. "Soon we'll receive food in exchange for oil. This Alliance is good. Why would you want to break the peace you worked so hard to create?"

He said between clenched teeth, "Do not worry about that, little cousin."

Hendra gathered her courage for one final, dangerous parry. "Is the Alliance a lie? Is that why you're making swords and training…" She stopped with a gasp, for Mentàll's face had darkened with rage, and he advanced on her so fast that she froze in utter shock.

He stopped a spare three handbreadths from her. "You will *never* call me a liar. Never! A liar is a man who pledges promises he never keeps. Who leaves a child and his mother to be eaten by wild beasts. That is what the Rolbanis have done! That is the kind of people they are. This is not about lies, Hendra. It is about serving justice. I will keep my word with the Alliance. But they must keep theirs." Mentàll stepped back, seeming to come to himself. Fists clenched, he turned away.

Hendra trembled with fear. Gathering her last threads of courage, she whispered, "Tell me what they've done. Tell me what they did to you."

He did not answer, and instead strode for the door. She sensed the fire in him, consuming the ice that usually held him in complete, cold control. He didn't like it, she sensed; he didn't like anyone seeing the true heart that still lived inside of him. But she had pushed much too far to stop now. The truth must come out now.

"Tell me why you want vengeance!" she cried out. "What have they done to you?"

In the tent doorway, he turned. "You would not understand," he said thickly. "No one will ever understand."

"I *want* to understand," she said softly. "Help me understand. I can't believe you would deliberately go somewhere you've promised peace, and then cut down innocent children in cold blood."

He visibly blanched. "No innocents will die."

"How do you know?" She pressed harder, "If you're planning war…"

"I am not planning war. I have promised peace, and I will keep it—as long as Rolban keeps their end of the bargain." He paused. "Only the guilty will suffer."

What did that mean? Hendra took little comfort from his words. Clearly, he meant to hurt someone. Clearly, he meant to wreak vengeance on Rolban. But who were his intended targets, and how did he plan to administer his own brand of justice?

"You can't," she whispered. "You have to stop now, before it's too late. The Prophet warned me. He said that those who draw the sword will die by the sword. I don't want you to die, Mentàll!"

"I will not die, little cousin," he said coldly. A bitter smile curled his lips. "I will not die until rights have been wronged, and justice served."

"But..."

"*Enough!*" His voice cracked like a whip. "I have allowed your questions, but no more, do you understand me? No more." The ice was firmly back in place, and his tone sliced like sharpened icicles. "Do you understand?"

"Yes." Her voice trembled. She understood that she would get no more information from him. But the things she had learned disturbed her. Worse, they raised still more questions. Mentàll claimed that he did not plan to start a war, as long as Rolban held up her end of the Alliance. Why did he think they would not?

Much as the thought of betraying Mentàll sickened her, maybe it was time to warn Behran and Methusal.

"I almost forgot," her cousin stated coldly. "I came here for a purpose. Jascr brought news of your match with Wortn."

She gasped. Jascr had finally spoken to Mentàll, as he had threatened last week. She had begun to hope Jascr had forgotten. Foolish of her. Drawing a shallow breath, she stared into Mentàll's chilly, expressionless eyes. She had already made him angry. Would he listen to her now?

She must make him understand. "I do not want to do it."

"You do not want to marry?"

"No. *Never!*"

Surprise flickered. "Jascr is your closest kinsman."

"He has no rights over me!" she insisted. "I live in *your* tents. I live under your protection. I will listen only to you."

"*Now* you will listen to me?" Amusement barely twitched his lips. "First blood is a stronger tie. His authority out-weighs mine."

Panic tore through her, ripping like wild beast claws. What he spoke was true, in Dehrien law. She had to make him see. But how?

The answer came, and it sickened her. Mentàll did not know her shame. Or why her brothers had refused to provide shelter for her when their father had died. She had to confess the truth now.

Feeling ill, she swallowed her dishonor. "Jascr and I share no blood. He is no true brother."

Mentàll's gaze narrowed. "Explain."

"Jascr's mother was not my own. His mother died, and then Father married my mother."

"Yes. I know that."

She drew a shaky breath. "When I was thirteen, my mother introduced me to my real father. He was not Jascr's father."

"Who, then?"

"He's dead now. The only truth that matters is Jascr and I share no blood. What's more, he knows this."

Her cousin considered her words. Still, she could not tell what he was thinking. The horrible, choking terror rose higher. He had to listen to her! He must!

"Please, Mentàll," she begged. She would go on her knees, if she had to. "Please don't let Jascr have power over me again!"

He frowned, and she knew he remembered the past as clearly as she did.

After a moment, he said, "I will not."

"Thank you," she choked out. She crossed her arms, hugging herself, trying to stop her now uncontrollable trembling.

Her cousin frowned, obviously noting her distress. But just as clearly, he did not know how to respond. He said in a lower, gentler voice, "You will marry no one...unless you wish it. We will not speak of this again."

She nodded wordlessly, and Mentàll left as silently as he had come. Hendra crumpled on the floor and wept tears of relief. What would she do without Mentàll's protection? He had saved her life when he'd taken her in four years ago. And he continued to protect her now, even after she'd confronted him with her fears about Rolban. How could she ever tell Behran her suspicions about him? How could she betray her only living blood relative? She owed her safety and all of her loyalty to her cousin.

Another conviction gripped her as she recalled the gentle tone Mentàll had used with her just now. It reminded her of the young man he had once been. Mentàll could not have lost his soul completely if he could still speak to her that way. She had to help him out of this mess before it was too late—for him, and for everyone else. Somehow, she must stop his plot.

But how? How could she do it without betraying him? How could she stop it, if she didn't even know what he planned?

Hendra would not talk to Behran. Not yet. Somehow, she would uncover all of the facts. Then she would stop Mentàll. If he would not listen to reason then—if she was left with no other choice—only then she would betray her cousin.

△ △ △ △ △

"...since Tarst and Dehre have experienced first-hand how kaavl makes great leaders..."

Methusal's eyes popped open in the darkness. She still heard the crystal clear words. It was Mentàll Solboshn's voice. Different voices spoke now...

Where was she? What was happening?

Heart thumping, she sat up. Her roommates' quiet breaths were the only sounds in the pitch black. *Dehre.* She was in Dehre for the IC Kaavl Games.

Her hand clenching the coverlet relaxed.

"What about..." The clear voice spoke in her ear, making her jump. Frightened, she swung her arm, trying to find the source, but no one was there.

What was happening?

She forced herself to focus on her surroundings. The clear voice faded to a whisper.

Her dark room was silent, except for the snores of her roommates. So was the men's cabin next door. No one spoke in either room. Then why did she hear voices?

Methusal pinched herself, just to make sure she wasn't dreaming. It hurt. Good. This wasn't another sleepwalking nightmare. Slowly, she lay down again. Was she going crazy? She'd read stories of people hearing voices in their heads—of course they'd all skipped off the bluff of reason.

The whispers faded. She relaxed, and to her surprise one voice rang clear again. It was Verdnt's. Did crazy people hear the voices of real people? Forcing herself to relax even more, she listened.

"Petr fully agrees now that individuals excelling in kaavl make the best, most honorable leaders for a community. Dehre is the perfect example."

Methusal cringed. In her opinion, Dehre's leader possessed no honor.

Mentàll spoke again. "...the job is half completed. I congratulate your devotion to kaavl and to your community." A pause. "Kitran, have you begun to teach my precepts on emotional energy yet?"

Kitran! Methusal strained her ears to listen more closely.

"Yes, to a few. I'll admit I introduced it as my own idea. At the time, I wasn't sure they would follow a Dehrien leader's teaching. No offense, Mentàll."

"None taken. You have been wise. Has this method helped your kaavl? Do you feel like you are approaching the Ultimate level, like I am?"

"I think so. Some of it is still a bit hard to grasp."

"Do not worry. It will become clear to you soon. Go now and rest. We will have time to talk more in the days ahead."

"Goodnight, then."

A tent flap slapping shut reached Methusal's ears. A minute later the door creaked open next door, and two sets of footsteps softly stepped inside. Kitran and Verdnt.

So, she hadn't been hearing things. But *how* she had heard the conversation must be considered later. More important was Mentàll's claim that he was approaching the Ultimate level, and that the things Kitran had taught Behran and herself about using emotional energy were really *Mentàll's* concepts. And Petr appeared to be on board, as well.

The knot on her head throbbed. Something very wrong was going on here. And Kitran, Verdnt, and Petr appeared to be blindly following Mentàll's teachings. But she could not piece together *what* was wrong, besides kaavl being corrupted by the detestable Mentàll. If only Deccia or her mother were here—their intuition would probably help her figure out what was going on.

Murder, thefts, secret conversations, kaavl in leadership, and the possible corruption of kaavl... How did it all tie together?

Exhaustion finally made her eyelids droop. Methusal drifted on the edge of slumber when voices again awoke her. Once more, the first voice was Mentàll Solboshn's.

"You want to bring the count to *three?*" Cold disbelief cracked in that harsh voice.

Who was he talking to now? She groaned softly. Would the man never sleep? Why did she keep hearing him?

"It's necessary," whispered a second voice. "I warned you before, in the letter, remember? Don't worry. I will take care of it."

"As you took care of the others who were in your way? *Without* my authorization."

"Methusal must *go.*" The words were a sibilant hiss.

Methusal drew in a sharp breath. She must *go?* She concentrated harder, trying to pinpoint the location of the voices. They appeared to come from about thirty lengths northwest. Maybe from the Chief's tent.

"No." A flat, cold order. "You will leave Methusal to me."

"You are a *fool!*"

"She is a mere girl." Contempt sliced through that icy tone. "It will be an easy matter to make sure she keeps her place."

"She is not easily intimidated," insisted the whisperer. The tone was low pitched. He must be a man. "Better to kill her now."

Methusal gasped softly. Pieces of the conversation flew together in her brain. *As you took care of the others who were in your way...You want to bring the count to three...Better to kill her now.* Finally, she understood.

Mentàll was talking to Renn and Liem's killer. The Dehrien must be the thieving murderer's ally. And the killer wanted *her* dead, too. She wasn't sure whether to feel relieved or uneasy that the Dehrien Chief wouldn't allow it. For what purpose he wanted to keep her alive, she couldn't imagine. Unless he truly thought he could use fear to manipulate her into keeping her place. A likely possibility, and in keeping with the Chief's arrogant personality. And if fear didn't work, she had no doubt he could take that ultimate step. Something about that cold man told her he could kill brutally and emotionlessly, should the situation require it. She shuddered at the thought.

If only the killer would quit whispering, so she could identify him. Was he a Rolbani who had come to Dehre with the kaavl team? Or had he traveled to Dehre tonight on his own?

"You will leave her in my hand." A nasty note underscored Dehrien Chief's tone, "Do you understand?"

"She will destroy our plans."

"*Do you* understand?"

A squeak escaped, and then a small scuffling sound. "All right," rasped the other man. "But you had better not let her destroy my plans... Your plans, I mean. Believe me, soon you will want her dead, too."

A tent flapped.

"Bloodthirsty *scienth*," the Dehrien Chief muttered contemptuously.

Nearly silent footsteps glided east across the compound. Methusal strained her ears, struggling to hear where they ended.

The faintest sound of a tent flapping came from far across Dehre. Frustratingly, she had no idea where the killer had gone—just the general direction. She lay very still, listening hard. But she heard nothing else.

CHAPTER TWENTY-SEVEN

Fourthday

VICTORY IS NEAR. Rolban is hungry to embrace her own destruction. They still suspect nothing, which is laughable. Their weaknesses are plain, and have been simple to exploit. Soon Rolban will trust neither Dehre nor Tarst. Suspicion festers, and boils hotter every day. Even if our pawn's takeover fails, thanks to me, new distrust has been sown, bitter and deep. I am confident the ore is ours to pluck, for war between the communities is imminent. Soon Rolban will stand alone.

△ △ △ △ △

The next morning Methusal slid onto the dining bench beside Behran, pack strapped to her back for the journey ahead. She yawned sleepily. She hadn't slept well at all.

The Dehrien Chief's conversations played over and over through her mind. It appeared that her fate was in the Dehrien Chief's hands—not the killer's. That didn't make her feel any better, but at least now she could put a face to her enemy.

However, she still did not know who had killed Renn and Liem. Or who might next be in danger from the bloodthirsty man.

Was the killer on the Rolbani kaavl team? Both Verdnt and Kitran had exited from the cabin next door this morning. Both accounted for. And Behran too, of course. However, just because the killer's footsteps had traveled far across Dehre after visiting Mentàll last night, it didn't rule out the possibility that either Kitran or Verdnt was the killer. The man could have gone across town to visit a woman, and then returned later in the night, while Methusal slept.

While in her heart Methusal didn't want to consider the possibility too closely, she must face the facts: both Kitran and Verdnt were immigrants, had access to the ore, and were tall with dark hair. But there were a number of other Rolbani men who met those criteria, too. It was possible the murderer had left Rolban for a secret meeting with the Dehrien Chief yesterday. But if another Rolbani had come to Dehre, she didn't see him now.

Her mind again returned to the uncomfortable idea that Verdnt or Kitran might be the murderer. While she didn't like Verdnt as well as Kitran, Kitran had been to Dehre often recently. In addition, in the past he'd been a messenger to both Dehre and Tarst. He had many contacts, including other runners, in both places.

On the other hand, Verdnt was from Dehre. He'd left seven years ago, before Mentàll had come to power. They must have trained in kaavl together, though. Still, Verdnt was trying to become Chief of Rolban. Why jeopardize his chances by going on a thieving and killing spree?

She could find no motive for Kitran, either. And she couldn't imagine either of her instructors killing Renn and Liem in cold blood.

None of it made any sense.

Methusal longed to tell Behran about the conversations she'd overheard last night. But then she'd have to reveal her secret hearing ability, and she didn't want to do that just yet, even though the conversation between the Dehrien Chief and the killer scared her. Someone wanted her dead.

She cast a glance down the table. No one paid the least bit of attention to her.

Breakfast did little to settle her nerves, either.

"Porridge!" Aali wrinkled her nose at the goop streaming from her spoon.

"Odd," Behran said with a frown. "They had a small grain crop. I thought it would be gone by now."

"So where did they get this?" She drew a quick breath. "What if it's our stolen seed grain?"

One eyebrow lifted. He glanced at his bowl.

"Of course!" Aali cried out.

She was right. Of course it was Rolban's stolen grain. The killer and Mentàll were allies, as she'd learned last night. Probably the grain theft was only one fruit of their unknown alliance.

"But how did it get here?" Behran asked.

Thinking out loud, Methusal said, "Remember, the thief carries his stolen goods to the plateau and tosses them into the ravine. Maybe he rolls them down the incline, so they aren't damaged. Pots went to Tarst. The grain came to Dehre."

"Right," Behran agreed. "But why would the thief send stolen goods to two communities? He'd need at least two accomplices. It sounds pretty complicated."

"Unless the killer sometimes carries them himself."

"Maybe he's trading for precious stones. Or gold or silver," Aali suggested.

Was this about greed? Although why someone would stock up on gold or jewels, Methusal couldn't imagine. Few people used gold. The communities provided everything people needed, for free. It would look suspicious if someone left town and bought expensive items from other communities, and then brought them home.

Behran said, "And think about this. How would the thief's accomplices get all of the stolen stuff into Dehre and Tarst? Someone would notice a person carrying in suspicious, bulging packs."

"Not if they were messengers."

"You think the accomplices are messengers?"

"Or maybe the thief is a messenger, too." This new thought struck Methusal. "Dehriens aren't afraid of wild beasts. A Dehrien messenger probably wouldn't be afraid to take the grain from the ravine in the dark."

"But who?"

And that was the question. A man who was tall and dark. Timaeus? Kitran used to be a messenger, too. He'd made a lot of visits to Dehre lately to work on the Alliance. So had Verdnt, for that matter. Considering last night's strange conversation between Mentàll and Kitran, she wasn't sure what to think about her enigmatic kaavl instructor any longer.

Behran said. "Ludst is a Dehrien messenger, and he won the Quatr-level. I'll bet he could sneak out to the ravine and carry the grain home without being seen."

Methusal nodded. "Whoever's involved has to be good at kaavl. To escape being caught all this time, kaavl has to be the key."

Behran nodded, and Methusal sent an apprehensive glance toward the Dehrien Chief's white, rippling tent. A Primary level kaavl player could easily put together such a tricky, devious plan. She didn't trust Mentàll one hand-breadth. And the killer in Rolban...it sounded like he had taken some matters into his own hands. Was his agenda different than Mentàll's?

What *were* the two men's plans? Why steal grain or pelts or ore pots? Well, she could see why the grain was stolen, because the Dehriens were starving. But the rest? It made no sense at all.

Hendra slid onto the bench across from them, so the conversation ended. Methusal still wasn't sure how far she could trust the Dehrien girl. While her instincts said she was trustworthy, they also said she was hiding something. Time would tell.

"Morning, Hendra," Behran said with a grin. "Are you coming to Tarst today?"

The blond-haired girl smiled shyly. "Yes. In our games, I finished third, so I get to go."

"Great!"

Hendra glanced toward her cousin's tent. "We'll leave soon," she said softly. "Are you ready?"

Behran lifted his pack in answer. "Is Mentàll married now?"

Methusal followed his gaze to the Chief's tent. Mentàll stood outside with a pack slung over one shoulder. A slim woman with red hair spoke to him. Methusal had never seen anyone with red hair before. It gleamed copper in the sun. The woman rested her hand on the Dehrien's broad shoulder, and spoke close to his ear. Mentàll shook his head, and twitched his shoulder free. The woman pouted and slunk away.

"No," Hendra said. "He has women companions—but never the same one, and never for long. She was his latest, but he wants nothing to do with her now."

The woman should count her blessings, Methusal thought.

"We're ready to go." Kitran spoke from behind Methusal. "Verdnt's feeling under the weather today, so he's volunteered to take you home, Aalicaa. He'll miss the games."

"No!" she wailed.

"Yes. He has a fever, and can't compete. And you're too young to make the trip over the mountains."

"I am not!" But Kitran could not be budged. Aali went into a funk and fell stonily silent, glaring at, but not touching her food until it was time to go.

Verdnt and Aalicaa would travel with the kaavl teams until midday, and then head south for Rolban when they neared the Rolban Mountains. Rolban was located midway between Dehre and Tarst, with Tarst located in a mountain valley to the northeast of Rolban. The whole trip would take seven hours of steady walking, but the last three hours of the trip would be especially tiring. They'd be hiking over rocky, mountainous hillsides.

Behind Methusal and the Rolbani team straggled behind the Dehriens. Ahead, Kitran talked to Mentàll. Darkly, she wondered what they were talking about now.

A quick listen revealed they were talking about the upcoming Games in Tarst.

Last night's conversation haunted her. She longed to talk to someone about it, but if she did, she'd have to reveal her secret—and she didn't want to do that yet. Not with new games ahead. But after...yes, definitely after.

She still didn't know how she had heard Kitran and Mentàll's voices last night. They'd woken her up, for goodness sake. How had that happened? In the past, she'd always needed to concentrate hard in order to hear far off conversations. Last night had been so easy—so effortless—so *unconscious.*

She plodded on, trying to understand what had happened. Maybe that whack to her head had done something. It didn't seem likely. So far, all it had inspired was a dull, throbbing headache. More likely it was all the kaavl she had been practicing recently. Maybe kaavl was simply becoming a part of her. Whatever the case, it had happened. Would it happen again?

"You're so quiet when you walk, Methusal," Retra's admiring comment broke into her thoughts. "How do you do that?"

Methusal looked where she was stepping—one toe pressed down an inch beyond a brittle twig. Her other foot carried forward, avoiding a stray, dry leaf. What was happening here? Yesterday she'd had to work hard to avoid the noisy ground cover. Another example of her kaavl becoming automatic? Was this what it was like for Kitran?

Bemused, she shook her head. "I don't know."

Methusal paid more attention to what she was seeing, hearing and experiencing. But nothing else unusual happened. Kitran cut back to join his group.

"Are you practicing?" His tone was stern. "I want to see a better showing in Tarst than in Dehre."

"Just so long as *they* play fair," Lina muttered.

Kitran's eyes narrowed. "The rules will be made clear before the games begin."

About an hour into the hike they all stopped for a moment to say farewell to Verdnt and Aali, who would continue heading directly east to Rolban, while everyone else would head north.

Methusal approached her cousin, who looked very unhappy. "It'll be okay, Aali."

"No. It won't." Her lips trembled.

"Don't worry. Petr might be mad, but he'll get over it soon. The Dehrien delegation will arrive soon. That'll distract him."

"It's not fair," Aali mumbled unhappily.

Methusal hated to say it. "Maybe if you tried harder to obey him, he'd let you do more things you want to do. Like kaavl. Picking fights and running away is not going to help you."

"Right." Bitterly. "Like how Deccia always does what he says, but can't see Timaeus."

"She will. Petr will see reason." Eventually.

"I hate him! He doesn't care about me at all!" The younger girl burst into tears and ran after Verdnt. The two trekked east to Rolban. They were a sad looking pair, with Aali crying stormily and Verdnt looking white and fatigued.

Methusal felt sorry for Aali, but for the second day in a row had to agree with Deccia's assessment. Aalicaa must learn discipline. If she wanted to advance in kaavl, she must learn to control herself. Petr's stubborn unreasonableness only made it harder.

The remainder of the morning flew by. It was as silent as the trip to Dehre had been yesterday. Methusal practiced fervently, determined to win in Tarst. It didn't sit well that she had been beaten by the arrogant Dehriens, or by Behran, either. She'd still dearly love to beat him at the Tri-level, although truthfully she was glad he'd beat the Dehriens yesterday.

At midday they halted for lunch at a cluster of boulders just south of the Tarst Mountains.

Methusal was starving, and was glad for the rations she'd brought from home. The water, too. The noonday sun beat into her dark hair and her brown leather clothing.

Hendra sat by herself on a boulder a short distance away, and after a little while Behran moved to join her. The blond girl flushed a little, but smiled when Behran spoke to her. Discomfort twisted through Methusal as she watched them. They looked perfect together. The different shades of their blond hair complemented each other, and it was clear from their body language that they were still good friends from days long past.

△ △ △ △ △

Hendra felt happy, but also a little uncomfortable that Behran had chosen to sit with her. For one, she'd noticed Methusal casting a disturbed glance at the two of them, and for another, Hendra felt uneasy to have any man sit so close beside her. Discretely, she added a handbreadth of space between them when she retrieved a meat strip from her pack.

"Dehre is worse than I had expected," Behran said in a low voice, chewing on a grain disc.

"It's the drought. And the aptes and wild beasts." Hendra decided to share her biggest concern. "I'm afraid for the orphans. Our well water is low. Now the river is diverted, so it's closer to Dehre. That should help. But it takes a long time to cart buckets of water back home. We don't get enough to really be able to clean. The children have been sick. I wish the water was closer."

Behran lifted his pack. His arms flexed as he tied it up, and his elbow brushed hers. A cold waterfall of alarm rushed through her, and she froze. Coldness prickled through her nerve endings and sped toward her mind. *No.* Not now. Not with Behran!

Oblivious to her distress, Behran said, "I know. But Dehre can't move closer, because when the Tarst River floods it almost reaches Dehre now."

"Yes." Stiffly, Hendra bent to retrieve a grain disc, and edged even further away from him, hoping that would help. It did not. The skittering panic cooled to ice. She hoped he didn't notice that she'd shrunk away from him. She felt bad about doing it.

Behran watched her now, and the force of his warm male attention and his obvious concern should have made her feel better. It didn't. She just felt colder. More detached. "Don't worry, Hendra," he said softly. "I remember. I won't come any closer."

She wasn't afraid anymore. She didn't feel *anything* anymore. With a choked laugh, she said, "I'm not worried. You're one of the good men."

"And how much experience have you had with one of us?"

None. And she felt certain he knew that. Behran had always been able to see right through her. Why was that, when she'd never told him anything about her home life? And he'd left just before the most awful things had happened. She forced a smile to her frozen lips. "Please...can we talk about the river?"

His deep blue eyes held hers for a long moment. Finally he said, "Dehre needs to dig an irrigation ditch from the river to Dehre. It might be best to dig it west of town, and maybe a reservoir, too. Then loop it back to the river. That way if the river floods, it still won't affect Dehre. It would take a long time to dig, though."

The simplicity of the idea amazed her. "That's a wonderful idea. You should tell Mentàll."

"You tell him," Behran said grimly. "He won't listen to a Rolbani."

"But you're not..."

"I am."

"I will, then."

Confiding her fears about Mentàll to Behran flitted through her mind. Behran was a good man, and she knew she could trust him. Part of her longed to relieve herself of the heavy burden. How easy it would be to give the responsibility to him.

But she would not. She would give her cousin the benefit of the doubt for now.

In Tarst she would spy on him and discover the full truth.

Even though ice froze her emotions, shame still slipped through a crack and twisted her gut. It reeked of betrayal. But what other choice did she have? Then, if she couldn't stop him, she would tell Behran everything.

△ △ △ △ △

"Time to go!" Mentàll's grating voice was a welcome sound, for once. Methusal averted her gaze from the sight of Behran sitting so close to Hendra on the rock.

What was wrong with her? It wasn't like she had those sorts of feelings for him. She pulled on her pack again to turn her mind away from her disturbed feelings, and they all started hiking north again.

Soon they reached the foothills of the Tarst Mountains. The path steadily grew narrower and steeper. Methusal hiked in the middle of the pack. For the most part, the trail followed the Tarst River. At times the slow moving, deep green river rushed faster and frothed white over boulders. Sometimes, when Methusal turned a corner, cool water misted her skin.

Behran lagged behind, talking with Hendra again, which Methusal struggled to ignore. The path widened as they crossed a plateau on the first mountain, and the Dehrien Chief dropped back to fall into step beside her. A sick feeling lodged in the pit of her stomach.

"How are you today, Methusal?" His voice was perfectly charming, but a darting glance upward encountered ice blue eyes. She remembered his conversation with the killer last night.

"Fine." She kept her tone level, and tried to overcome an unwelcome spurt of fear. He would kill her if she got in his way. His actions right now would probably be designed to frighten her; to make her "keep her place." And if she did not... She swallowed.

"Do you have hopes that you will win in Tarst?" Mockery rang clear in the low tone.

She walked more rapidly, wishing he would leave her alone. "Yes, I *do*."

"Temper, temper!" Mentàll chided softly. "Only the self-controlled will win, you know."

"Like you?"

"The fiery Methusal speaks at last."

"Leave me alone. I've done nothing to you."

"You challenged me in Rolban. Threatened, if I recall. Have I won, then?"

"You have won nothing," Methusal snapped. "You're an evil whip. And you'll lose!" More rash words. Would she never learn? If she didn't pretend to "keep her place," Mentàll might decide the killer was right—that he should kill her.

Anger and fear tightened in her gut. She couldn't stand the thought of kowtowing to this man. She'd sooner jump off a cliff than pretend any sort of submission, or admit any fear to the Dehrien Chief. Maybe that was stupid, but she couldn't help how she felt. Unfortunately, it was that same attitude that had caused her so much trouble with Petr, Verdnt, Pogul, Goric, and others.

"You think I will lose?" Mentàll laughed harshly. "No. But you fear me." He lowered his voice. "And that is just as it should be."

"I fear nothing." Methusal hated that she couldn't meet his gaze, to give truth to the lie.

His knuckle lightly traced the edge of her jaw. The shock of it made her gasp, and she jerked free. "Don't touch me!" Tears sprang to her eyes. Although she knew the move had been calculated to frighten her, rather than to be suggestive, that didn't make her feel any better.

He hated her—this had become abundantly clear. Now, to accomplish purposes of his own, Mentàll wanted her to fear him. And she did. She hated that.

"Now we see the truth." The Dehrien Chief's voice hardened into a low threat. "Only a fool would cross the line I have given you, Methusal."

She glared back and spoke again before thinking. "You're not my Chief. You have no authority over me."

"Haven't I?" His teeth bared in a small smile. "Keep your place, Methusal. I will not give you another warning."

The Dehrien Chief strode forward again to take the lead.

A shudder rippled through her. Why hadn't she taken the smart path? What made her want to challenge him?

Well, that was simple enough. She wouldn't let the whip win the final victory over her.

Clearly, she posed some sort of a threat to him. But what was he plotting that would require strong-arming her to submit to his will? It had to be about more than a few thefts.

Last night's disquiet returned in full strength. Mentàll was a dangerous man. Not only to her, but to all of Rolban.

Behran walked beside her now, his deep blue eyes looking curious and faintly protective. It was amazing how two sets of blue eyes could look so different. "What did Mentàll want?"

"He's trying to intimidate me."

"Why?"

"He hates me. I told him I think his Alliance is a trap. It made him angry. He's warned me not to cross him."

"Cross him how?"

Methusal shrugged. "By trying to uncover his secret plan? I don't know. He scares me. I don't trust him, and I don't trust that Alliance."

"The Alliance will do a lot of good for Dehre. Why would he risk it? For any reason?"

"I don't know. I just wish he'd leave me alone!"

"He's changed since I knew him," Behran commented after a moment. "He was always a solitary person, and only interested in perfecting his kaavl. He was always polite enough, but he was reserved. Sometimes he even seemed aloof, like he thought he was better than everyone else."

"Well, he hasn't improved with age." Methusal didn't want to discuss the Dehrien any longer.

The trail narrowed and steepened, so Behran fell in behind her. The troop silently marched on, and as the slow hours passed, Methusal's legs grew fatigued. But no one mentioned a rest stop, so she trudged on without complaining. The sooner they reached Tarst, the sooner she could rest.

While nocturnal wild beasts were not a threat in the mountains, rotarhudges were. They were stout, short-legged beasts with razor sharp teeth. They traveled in packs in the daytime, and were a danger to sleeping wild beasts and humans alike. They were also able to swiftly navigate through the dense forests, unlike the large wild beasts, which was another reason why few wild beasts roamed in the mountains.

She was glad several of the men carried hunting knives, and Ludst Lst, the Dehrien runner, carried a bow and arrows. They should be safe enough. She hoped.

As they hiked through Tarst's high, densely forested mountains, she wondered if Tarst would be like Dehre. Or would the people be friendly, instead?

The sun was low in the sky, and the air turning chilly when the twelve began their final descent into a heavily wooded valley. Sunlight glinted off the tops of lush, green leaved trees as they slipped into the cool shadows of the valley floor. Here the Tarst River flowed dark green and wide. And probably deep, Methusal guessed.

It was dim and quiet, except a few winged beasts perched, chattering, in the branches overhead. The ground cover was mossy and soft, and their footsteps were almost noiseless. So far, no snuffling snorts of rotarhudges.

The beautiful forest would provide new challenges in the championships tomorrow. Inexplicably, she felt her spirits lift. Surely people who lived in this beauty would be more openhearted than the cold, withdrawn Dehriens.

The valley floor curved up on the other side of the river. A high, flat clearing came into view, dotted with tidy rows of clean, well-mended buildings. More buildings dotted the hillside beyond it. Tarst. No bonfires marked the edges of this town. Apparently the wild beasts were not a threat to this secluded valley. The river probably deterred the few that strayed into the mountains.

To the left, on the far, northern slope, she spotted a herd of animals nibbling grass. Urchets. Methusal had only seen a few in her lifetime. The pack beasts preferred the rocky hills and lush vegetation of the mountains. She'd heard that the Tarst had tamed the large beasts of burden. The four-legged, broad-backed animals did look content as they munched on the grass.

Ahead a wide, wooden bridge arched over the mighty Tarst River. Methusal stared in amazement. She'd never seen such a thing before! How had they built it over the water?

Heavy gates had been built on each end—no doubt to keep out stray wild beasts. Inhaling the refreshing, tangy scent of pine air, Methusal stepped onto the wooden bridge. The raw power of the rushing river thundered beneath her feet. She wanted to absorb the sound of it, and drink in the beauty of the mountains surrounding her. And the wonderful scent of the trees. What a magnificent place!

"It's beautiful, isn't it?" Hendra stopped beside her. Wonder shone from her brown eyes.

"Can you imagine living here?"

"I'd love it," the other girl said with quiet fervor.

The rest of the team passed by.

"Hendra." Warning sounded in that low voice.

Hendra jumped. "Mentàll." Worry clouded her eyes.

The Dehrien Chief sent Methusal a cold look. Evidently he didn't believe she was fit company for his cousin. "Come." He waited, obviously expecting Hendra to join him.

"I'd like to talk to Methusal."

Methusal glanced between the two of them, surprised that Hendra would defy him.

Mentàll's icy gaze moved from his cousin to Methusal. The cold hatred in it pierced her soul. He hated *her*. For a second, this fact hit deep. Was it because she was trying to uncover his secrets? Or did he hate her, personally?

"Remember my words, Methusal." His words felt like sharp knives. He turned on his heel and left them.

"I'm sorry for how my cousin treats you," Hendra said, as they followed in the tall Dehrien's footsteps.

"He hates me. Do you know why?"

Hendra didn't directly answer. "Did something happen when he visited Rolban?"

"Yes. I told him I thought his Alliance a trap. He didn't like it. Maybe because it's true. Is it a trap, Hendra?" She carefully watched the other girl's expression.

"He tells me nothing. But his behavior toward you is wrong." Hendra looked troubled. "I know you won't believe me, but I've never seen him act like this before."

"What? Cold? Mean?"

"Mean." Hendra hesitated. "I've seen him intimidate many men. But I've never seen him attack a woman the way he does you. He wants to frighten you. It's wrong, and I'm sorry."

"Do you know why he wants to scare me?"

"No."

"I know you owe Mentàll your loyalty. He's your cousin, and he gives you shelter. And maybe you know a side to him that I don't." Personally, Methusal couldn't imagine anything good living in the Dehrien. And Hendra had admitted yesterday that she didn't know him very well, either. Maybe gratitude made Hendra imagine qualities in her closest kin that didn't exist. She needed to help Hendra see the truth now. Maybe then the Dehrien girl would help her to expose his plan.

"Mentàll is a cold, ruthless man, Hendra."

"Yes, he is cold. And he can be completely ruthless," she agreed. "He'll do whatever it takes to get what he wants."

In other words, he was dangerous. "I think he wants something. Desperately. Do you know what it is?"

Hendra looked away. "No. Nothing specific."

Softly, Methusal said, "If you find proof he's a danger to Rolban or Tarst, will you tell me?"

The other girl's conflicted gaze met Methusal's. "Yes. I will. You have my word."

△ △ △ △ △

The inner section of Tarst consisted of buildings set in an unusual pattern. Two rows of buildings formed each of the four sides of Tarst, and each parallel line was approximately the same length. The town was laid out like a long rectangle. As she stepped past the two rows of outlying shacks, she noticed that the buildings faced a large, inner courtyard paved in flat stones.

A massive building at the far, southern end of the plaza caught her attention. That must be their communal hall.

Her tired steps quickened as they neared the large structure. Already she could tell this place was totally different from Dehre. For one, it didn't stink!

The company halted in the open doorway and waited to be greeted.

"Kitran, old boy!" A fat, balding man jogged into view. "You haven't changed a bit. And Mentàll!" His tone lowered in reverence as he shook the Dehrien Chief's hand. "It's wonderful to see you again. I trust we'll have more time to talk this time?"

Mentàll bowed slightly, "Of course. I regret that my last trip was so hasty."

The little man smiled and nodded, and turned his attention to the remainder of the group. "Kitran, introduce me to your team."

Kitran introduced the Rolbani team, and Methusal found her hand squeezed warmly by the short man. She felt like she towered over him.

His direct green gaze smiled a welcome. "I know your father, Methusal. A fine man, and I see he has produced a fine daughter, as well! I have a daughter about your age, but unfortunately she has no interest in kaavl." He sighed noisily. "What's a man to do?"

Not sure how to respond, Methusal smiled, infected by his warm gaiety. As the man moved down the line, welcoming each visitor, she slowly followed the others inside. With wonder, she surveyed the great interior of the building.

The hall was at least twenty-five lengths long and fifteen wide, with a roaring fireplace imbedded in each of the two longest walls, which suffused heat and light throughout. Rows of tables occupied the center area, and located at the far end were the serving tables and a raised speaking platform.

"Come in, come in!" With an energetic arm, the stout little man waved the remainder of the group inside. "We have a table prepared for you."

Delicious, strange aromas assailed her nose as they zigzagged around throngs of people to a table located near the serving area. One of the great fireplaces blazed to the left. The weary travelers dropped their packs on the benches.

Friendly Tarst faces looked on as they followed Pan to the serving tables. Methusal's spirits lightened. What a wonderful place this seemed to be.

With a plate resting lightly in her hands, she stepped up to the first steaming dish on the serving table. Displayed in an artistic, scalloped pattern were thin cuts of meat seasoned with unknown leaves and savory juices. Methusal speared up two pieces with a serving stick when it was her turn.

At least ten dishes, all different, and each smelling delicious, filled the serving table to overflowing. She was starving, and everything looked delicious. By the time Methusal reached the end of the line, her plate was heaping. She walked carefully, holding the heavy platter in one hand and a mug of dark liquid in the other. She had no idea what the drink was, but it smelled heavenly.

At the table she sat between Lina and Behran. Their plates were piled as high as hers, so her guilt at taking so much food eased.

"Eat!" Pan waved a hand. "I'll make a speech after everyone's been served. Don't let your food get cold!"

Methusal did not need another invitation, and tucked in with gusto. The meats and vegetables were recognizable, but the tastes were not. Everything was absolutely delicious! The foods were seasoned with unknown leaves, herbs, and crushed seeds.

"I wish we could have food like this at home," Lina exclaimed.

"I know." Methusal chewed on one side dish that looked completely unfamiliar. It consisted of long, thin strips of a chewy substance—bark?—soaked thoroughly in a sweet, sticky sauce. It quickly became her favorite, and as she chewed, a thought struck her.

Why *couldn't* they eat like this in Rolban? Maybe the Tarst would share their cooking secrets. Perhaps this was answer to the boring winter food problem in Rolban! Sims had told her that the basic foods had to stay the same, but their preparations did not. Her gaze darted around the room, and she wondered who the cook was.

She sipped at the unfamiliar, tangy drink. It deliciously cooled her taste buds before sliding down her throat.

The last of the Tarst filed to their tables with their loaded plates in hand. A good number of them were shorter and heavier than the Rolbanis or Dehriens.

Pan Patn nimbly sprang up the steps to the speaking platform. "Ahem." The dull roar of voices continued. Loudly, he cleared his throat. "Ahem!"

The dining hall gradually quieted.

"It is my pleasure to welcome the Rolbani team of five, led by Kitran Mehl, and the Dehrien kaavl team of seven, led by the honorable Chief of Dehre, Mentàll Solboshn. We are proud that you have chosen to visit our humble village, and we're glad you will participate in our annual Kaavl Games. May your stay here be profitable and joyous."

Beaming and nodding, he descended from the platform amid hearty applause, and joined the visitors at their table.

He quickly fell into an animated conversation with Kitran and Mentàll.

Methusal glanced at her Dehrien companions across the table, wondering how they felt about the warm welcome. Sneers curled the mouths of several. Hendra sat quietly, speaking to no one.

As the evening passed, Methusal's eyelids grew heavy. The combination of good food and eight hours of strenuous exercise were taking their toll. The warm fire didn't help, either. She stifled a yawn with the back of her hand and closed her eyes. That wasn't enough, so she rested her chin on her palm, and tried to ignore her aching head.

"Looks like your team is exhausted, Kitran!" Pan's jovial tones jolted her from the edge of sleep. She blinked guiltily, but she wasn't the only one who looked tired. Lina and Retra's nonstop chatter had slowed, and both looked glassy-eyed.

"I'll show you to your quarters. Afterward, any who'd like to come can join me for a drink at my house."

Most of the Tarst still sat clustered at their tables, enjoying the evening social hours. They looked a bit surprised to see their visitors leave so early.

Cold night air froze into Methusal's pores as they headed across the courtyard, which was dimly lit by a few small, scattered bonfires. Pan led the group to several small buildings on the west side of town. One cabin was especially small, and Pan pointed to this one first.

"That cabin is for the girls, and the one next door is for the Rolbani men. The next one is for the Dehrien men. Mentàll will have a cabin of his own, since he's Chief of Dehre. It's near my own home, across the square." He glanced at them expectantly. "Why don't you get settled, and then those who'd like to may come to my house. It's the one with the double wide doors." He pointed across the courtyard. "My wife and daughters will be glad to meet you."

Methusal stepped into the small room after Hendra, Lina and Retra. The quarters resembled those at Dehre in layout and size, but there the resemblance ended. Warm furs covered the four cots and the floors, and two lamps warmly lit the cramped room. A bowl of fresh smelling red flowers rested on a small table in the corner, giving the room a delicate fragrance, and a small window near the door was shuttered closed for the night. It felt warm and cozy.

Sinking down onto a cot near the door, Methusal pulled the pack from her shoulders. The fur that covered her cot felt soft to the touch, although it appeared to be bristly wild beast fur. How had the Tarst softened it? They were full of surprises.

"I like it here," Retra commented.

Lina settled down on her own bed with a yawn. "Me, too," she sighed. "Much better than Dehre. Then she cast a guilty look at Hendra. "Sorry."

"It's okay," the Dehrien girl murmured. "It *is* nicer here."

"You can say that again." Retra flopped back on her bed. "No offense, Hendra, but except for you, every Dehrien I've met acts like a whip beast—all scaly and slithery and mean. I don't like them, and I don't like Mentàll, either, even if he did win the Primary level."

"I don't, either." Methusal couldn't stop the shudder that rippled through her. She'd tried to push his threats from her mind, but feeling sleepy like this, it was hard to keep up her armor.

"We've seen the way he treats you," Retra sent her a keen glance.

Methusal laughed shortly. "I wish he'd leave me alone."

Hendra averted her face, obviously feeling uncomfortable with the topic of conversation.

"Why are you so nice, Hendra?" Retra asked. "I mean, if your cousin and everyone else you know are mean...why are you so different?"

Quietly, the blond girl said, "My mother was the warmest, most self-sacrificing person I've ever known. I have friends, too, who work with me at the orphanage. They're nice, too."

"What about your father?" Retra asked.

Hendra's expression closed.

"Retra, you're nosy," Lina said.

"It's okay," the Dehrien girl murmured. "I don't mind telling the truth. He was...cruel. He had fits of rage, and he took them out on us."

"You don't mean..." Horror slid through Methusal.

"He beat us," Hendra said softly.

She felt sick. "I'm so sorry."

"That's why I first learned kaavl. So I could escape from him, like Mentàll did." Pain lurked in her brown eyes. "I'm tired. Lights out?"

CHAPTER TWENTY-EIGHT

A DENSE MIST enveloped the little village the next morning. Methusal awoke before the others. She hadn't slept well. Partly because it was a strange new bed, and partly because she wondered if she'd overhear a strange conversation again. But mostly because she'd had an odd sense that disaster was looming on the horizon. And it was all tied up with the Dehrien Chief. Maybe she was imagining things. After all, she wasn't empathic, like her mother or Deccia.

Still, the Dehrien Chief was up to something. Time was slipping away, and she had the uneasy feeling that soon it would be too late for Rolban...for them all.

Methusal quietly left the cabin and slipped through the thick fog toward the dining hall—at least, she hoped it was toward the large gathering hall. She couldn't see a length in front of her. It was eerily quiet.

The mist pressed cold, damp kisses to her face. It was peaceful and quiet. She felt alone, but not frightened.

A short, bulky shape rose out of the mist. It was a man wearing a fur tunic. Her pulse spiked, and she stopped in her tracks.

An old man. He stood very still, as if waiting for her. Mist swirled about his face, obscuring his features, and his short tufts of white hair blended into the fog. His hair contrasted with his deeply tanned skin. The man held a staff in one hand, and he looked like he belonged in the wild, rather than in civilized tents.

Was he real? Or a ghost?

"You are a seeker." His deep voice took her by surprise. It sounded earthy and strong, as opposed to his body, which looked like an apparition.

He didn't appear to be dangerous. With caution, Methusal stepped forward. The old man's black, lively eyes appeared to size her up. "Seeker?" she repeated.

"Of the truth."

The thick fog seemed to press in harder, enveloping the two of them in a silent cocoon of white. "What do you mean?" How could he possibly know about her investigation?

"You want to know the truth."

Cautiously, she said, "Yes."

"You seek answers in the wrong place."

"Where should I look, then?"

"You look to earth." A gnarled finger rose to the sky. Overhead the mist brightened to a light, crystalline white. The sunshine was fighting to break through. "Beyond the dross of earth lie your answers."

"I don't understand."

The wise eyes turned to her, and a hint of amusement glimmered. "Don't you? Are you not seeking The One, Methusal Maahr of Rolban?"

A light prickling sensation ran over her skin. "How..." How could he know her name? She swallowed hard. "Are you the Prophet?"

He smiled, but did not answer. He did not need to. "Seek him while he may be found, Methusal."

"But how?" Methusal could barely believe she was speaking to the fabled Prophet.

"When he speaks, listen."

"He hasn't... Wait. Maybe he did. I had a strange dream. The One said to follow him."

The old man nodded, as if he already knew.

"But he didn't tell me *how* to follow him, or what to do. He just showed me the dark, trapped end for me if I don't."

"That dream will become clear in time, Methusal. I do not have that word for you yet. But for now, I do have one word."

"You have a word for me? From *The One?*" It still seemed unreal that she was speaking to the Prophet. But to think The One might have a personal word, just for her? She felt slightly dizzy.

"Of course. Is that so hard to imagine? He loves us, and wishes to speak to each of us. If only we would listen." He smiled. "Are you ready to listen, Methusal?"

Listen. In her dream, The One had told her to listen. "Yes. Of course."

"Pray for those who mistreat you."

"Who do you mean?"

"You know of whom I speak."

Methusal felt hot, and then cold. She breathed, "But he's a *danger* to me. And to Rolban!"

"True. I have already given him a word."

"What word?"

"All who draw the sword will die by the sword."

That certainly sounded ominous. "What is he going to do? Do you know?"

"That is for you to determine. And others of faith and courage."

"How? What am I supposed to do?"

The Prophet smiled, but did not reply. He had already told her. Pray.

But what good would praying do? Unless she was supposed to ask The One to smite Mentàll before he could hurt Rolban.

Somehow, she didn't think that was what the Prophet meant.

His smile widened. "So you do understand. But you think my words are foolish."

"They don't make sense to me."

"Accept them or not, as you please. Always, it is your choice." He went very still. After a moment, he blinked and gave her a piercing look. "I have a final word for you, Methusal Maahr."

His deep voice intoned, "Take note. This is only the beginning."

"The beginning of what?"

"Trouble. For all of Koblan."

"The whole continent?" she said in disbelief.

"Mmm." He looked off into the thick white mist, as if trying to penetrate its secrets...or perhaps trying to see into the future.

Her dream flashed to mind again, and she felt alarmed. "War, do you mean?"

"Yes. If it comes to that."

"When? When will the worst trouble come?"

"I cannot say. One year... Maybe three."

"What else can you tell me?" she said urgently.

"Goodbye, Methusal. We will meet again." He melted into the swirling mist.

War? Her dream must have been a prophecy, which astounded her. But who would start the war? Mentàll? A sick feeling twisted through the pit of her stomach. The Prophet had told her of no way to prevent the coming catastrophe. He'd only told her to pray for her enemy now.

But what should she pray for him? That good things would happen for him? Never! Everything within her rebelled at that thought. What, then? For his deliverance from evil? For the redemption of his soul?

Methusal wanted to laugh. It sounded so foolish. Maybe she should pray, but instead for Rolban's deliverance from the Dehrien's underhanded plots.

She'd never tried to pray to The One before. Could it be as simple as in her dream? Just talking to him?

Feeling self-conscious, Methusal cleared her throat. But who was around to listen? "The One." Her voice sounded loud in the thick, quiet fog. She felt a little silly. Was he listening? But she had to try. More softly, she said, "Please protect us from Mentàll's plan, whatever it is. Save us. Stop him, and the thief, before it's too late."

Her words whispered to nothingness in the mist. A prayer, true. But it was for herself, Rolban, and Koblan. Not for Mentàll or for the murdering thief, both of whom were her enemies. Did the Prophet want her to pray for *both* of them? Everything within her rebelled at praying for either of them, including their deliverance from evil. Eternal torment by whip beasts and wild beasts seemed too good for the man who had murdered Renn and Liem.

And if Mentàll was planning further crimes against Rolban, well, she wanted him to suffer every consequence he deserved, too.

Even if The One loved people like them, she could not. She didn't want to listen to the Prophet's words. And yet who was she to ignore God? She did want to do what was right. If only it didn't feel so wrong. Maybe she could pray that they would forsake their evil paths. Yes. That would be a prayer that would benefit all of Koblan. She directed that prayer heavenward, and hoped it would do.

Feeling unsettled, she headed toward the dining hall. Bits of the conversation with the Prophet replayed through her mind. So did his seeming acceptance that The One had spoken to her in a dream.

If by some chance the dream was prophetic, then her new arch enemy, the Dehrien, would play a prominent role in it. A role where he would hunt her to the end, unless she listened to The One. So maybe she had better listen.

Maybe later.

The mist cleared a little, revealing the double-arched doors of the gathering hall just ahead. Thank goodness. At least she'd walked in the right direction. Methusal pushed open a door and a rush of heat enveloped her like a soft blanket. She hadn't realized how chilled she'd become until she stepped inside. She rubbed her hands together. Delicious breakfast smells permeated the air.

The serving line was short because it was still early. Few people populated the tables. The Dehrien Chief's blond hair caught her eye. Pan sat opposite him, and they appeared to be deep in discussion. The Dehrien laughed at something Pan said, but something about that harsh chuckle rang false to Methusal. Calculation hardened his features. He was playing some sort of game right now; she'd bet on it.

"Stop him," was all she could think to the Almighty, should he still be listening to her rebellious heart. "Stop him before it's too late."

She slipped over to the steaming serving tables. The Tarst cooks must have risen early to put together such a feast. Scrambled flying beast eggs, fried strips of apte beast, and soft warm loaves of bread. Berry preserves. No porridge in sight. Quickly filling her plate, she found an empty table and sat alone until her Rolbani teammates joined her. No Dehriens appeared, which probably explained the light-hearted atmosphere.

Everything tasted delicious. She was just finishing her last bite of the sweet, rich bread when Pan Patn trotted up to the table. A wide grin dimpled into his flushed, round face. "Good morning, my Rolbani friends! I see you've had a taste of our morning mist. Never fear. It'll burn off within the hour." His dark gaze darted around the room. "The Dehriens haven't arrived yet?"

"No."

"Enjoy your meal. I think I'll fetch myself a plate!" He trotted away.

The Dehriens straggled in soon after. Finished with her meal, Methusal slipped away on a mission of her own.

She dumped her dirty dishes in a bin and approached a rosy-cheeked, matronly woman who was overseeing a girl replacing an empty plate of eggs.

Hesitantly, she said, "Excuse me."

Bright eyes looked up and a smile flooded the wide, ample face. "Aren't you Methusal? Kitran has told us so much about you! I'm Pan's wife, Aenill. So glad to meet you."

Methusal smiled warmly, surprised by such an enthusi-astic welcome. "I'm glad to meet you, too. I wanted to compliment your cooks. The food is delicious."

Aenill dimpled, clearly pleased. "Thank you. Just old family recipes, tried and true."

"They're wonderful. I noticed that you add different leaves, herbs, and seeds to the food for flavor. Would you mind if I ask what they are?"

"Of course not. Don't you use them in Rolban?"

Methusal shook her head. "We have the same meats and grains, but we don't use many seasonings."

"How awful!" The older woman's brow wrinkled, looking genuinely distressed. "How dull that must be. Come with me, dear, and I'll show you what we use."

Pleased with her good fortune, Methusal slipped behind the serving tables and trotted after Aenill to the pair of wide wooden doors in the back corner of the dining room.

"In here, dear." Smiling, Aenill ushered her inside.

A blast of warmth and baking smells assailed her as she slowly stepped inside. It was a huge kitchen, and bustling with energy.

Three giant cooking stoves and scattered preparation tables furnished the room, and two fireplaces flanked the left and right walls. Pots of a delicious, steaming substance simmered over one, and a large wild beast smoked over another.

Aenill saw her staring at the beast. "The hunters brought it in this morning." She smiled. "It ought to make a good lunch, don't you think?"

Methusal had no doubt the wild beast would taste even better than the one in Dehre. The Tarst seemed to work magic with everything they set their hands to. Clearly, they were an inventive and hardworking people.

The older woman scuttled to the right, where a row of clay pots lined a wooden table. "Here we are, then. They're labeled. Let me get you something to write with." Aenill found a parchment leaf and a sharpened charcoal writing stick, and then left Methusal to copy down the names of the seasonings. When she was finished, Aenill returned and gave her a few pointers, and indicated which herbs and spices worked especially well with different meats and grains.

Methusal quickly wrote down those notes, too. "Thank you. I'll be sure to tell our cook about your ideas. I want to make the porridge at home taste better." She made a face. "Although I shouldn't complain. Next year, we may not have enough."

Aenill frowned. "Why is that?"

"Someone stole a bag of seed grain."

"An entire *bag?* Why?"

Should she tell Aenill her suspicions? Methusal's conscience prickled. She had no proof, but if the Dehriens were up to no good, shouldn't the Tarst be warned? "I'm not sure. But I think it went to Dehre."

"Why do you think that?"

"They served us gruel one evening, and porridge the next morning. Strange thing is, their grain crop pretty much failed last year. So where did they get it?"

"They certainly didn't get it from us. Do you think the Dehriens stole it? By Mentàll's orders?"

Methusal was surprised by Aenill's rapid questions. "I don't know. But I don't trust him."

Aenill's gaze sharpened. "Why not?"

Methusal felt uncomfortable to speak about this topic. "Well..."

Aenill's expression softened, and she patted Methusal's hand. "I can see that it's hard for you to talk about. But if it's important that we know, please tell me."

"Well..." Methusal bit her lip. "He's threatened me several times."

"He's threatened you? How?"

The rattling memories of the Dehrien's deliberate intimidation flooded her mind. "He gets too close to me." For a second her voice trembled. "He touched my face once, just to scare me. And he's warned me not to cross him, more times that I can count."

"I don't like the sound of that. Not at all." Aenill frowned. "Have you told Kitran? Do you need protection?"

"No." Unfortunately, she wasn't sure how far she could trust Kitran, either, after the conversation he'd had with Mentàll the night before last. But she couldn't tell that to Aenill. "If I keep my place, he'll leave me alone. But I can't do that. I'm afraid he's plotting something against Rolban."

"But we just signed the Alliance."

"I know. It doesn't make any sense at all. But I do think he's plotting something, and I told him so. That's why he threatens me every time he sees me. I ask you, why would a man with nothing to hide do that?"

Slowly, Aenill shook her head. "I'll watch him and mention your concerns to Pan."

Methusal nodded and stood. Her tablet necklace, which she'd worn hidden inside her tunic for the last few days—ever since she remembered the Dehrien's unhealthy interest in it—chafed against her skin. It had been bothering her a bit for days, but she'd been able to ignore it until now. It felt like a rough edge was scratching against her skin. She pulled out the heavy necklace and ran her thumb over the right corner. Yes. A small, raised edge of scratched metal prickled against her thumb. Maybe she should wear it outside of her tunic.

Aenill's sharp gaze took in Methusal's unusual necklace. "Isn't that curious." she commented. "It looks old."

"It's a family heirloom."

"Do the peaks stand for the Rolban Mountains?"

Methusal glanced at the tablet in surprise. That thought had never occurred to her. "No. The Rolban Mountains have three peaks. This is actually an "M," for my family's last name."

"Oh. Well, it's lovely."

"Thank you. Do you have a metal scraper? It has a scratch. Maybe I could smooth it out." Methusal did wonder when the scratch had appeared. She usually wore it outside of her tunic, but she had worn it close to her skin in the past. A scratch had never bothered her before. Had the necklace been damaged while the thief had it?

Aenill led the way to a counter near the stove, and rustled through a jar of metal utensils until she found an old wire brush. It only took a moment for Methusal to sand the ore smooth again.

"Thank you." Methusal sniffed the hearty, delicious steam rising from the pots nearby. "What are you cooking? It smells wonderful."

With a smile, Aenill lifted one lid. A thick vegetable stew bubbled inside.

Methusal savored the fragrant aroma. "Matron Olgith should come here and take lessons from you." When Aenill replaced the lid, Methusal eyed the pot, remembering that Rolban's pots had been discovered in Tarst. But the pots had been returned. And she certainly could not imagine Aenill being party to receiving stolen goods. So again, how had the pots turned up in Tarst? And why?

The answers must lie with the thief, his accomplice in Tarst—possibly Kilum, the messenger—and maybe Mentàll. Certainly, no clues would be found in this kitchen. After meeting the kind and open Aenill and Pan, she felt absolutely sure they knew nothing about the thefts.

Methusal folded the list of seasonings and put it in her pocket. "Thank you very much. The spices will make a big difference in our meals in Rolban."

"Oh, goodness! I'm glad to be a help. Perhaps your cook and I could exchange recipes."

"That's a great idea." On the way out the door, one last question sprang to mind. "What was that chewy, sweet dish we had last night?"

Aenill's eyes twinkled merrily. "Tagma bark. Boiled and then steeped in..." she glanced at the pots on the table. "The seasonings in the fifth and seventh jars, in water, overnight. Not too much of number seven, though."

"Thank you again."

Methusal hurried back to her cabin. The games were about to begin.

As good as Pan's word, the cold mist had cleared off and sunshine warmed the little valley.

"There you are!" Retra greeted her. "Kitran's been looking for you."

Methusal tucked the parchment into her pack. "Oh? What for?"

Her teammate shrugged. "I don't know. The games start pretty soon, though."

"I'll see what he wants." She slipped into the warm sunshine. A knock on the men's door summoned Behran, who poked out his head.

"Is Kitran there?"

"No. He wants us to meet him on the playing field." He squinted at the sun. "Now, I guess."

Methusal relayed the news to her roommates and followed the crowd to the playing field with Behran. The Dehrien team was already there, clustered to the left, and Kitran stood waiting to the right. A ridged, sloped hill rose behind him.

Catching sight of them, Kitran gestured abruptly and began a quick, agile ascent up the slope.

He waited for them at the top. "I want you to see the playing field from this view first. It can get confusing on the ground. The trees block part of the course." He pointed to a tall, triangular rock, which was a good fifteen minutes away running time. "That's the halfway point." His hard dark gaze regarded each of his students. "Are you ready? It's your last chance to prove yourselves this year."

As the others nodded, Methusal wondered if Kitran resented the fact Mentàll had beaten him in Dehre. Maybe this explained his subtle pressure on them to win now.

Kitran glanced at the valley below. Tarst individuals were already climbing the steep slopes of the mountains. "The games are about to start. We'll watch from up here, but when your event is called you'll need to go down to the starting line."

Retra and Lina looked nervous. "I guess we should start down, then."

"You can do it," Methusal encouraged. "Remember, it won't be like Dehre. You can win if you try hard enough."

"Do you really think so?" Hope and doubt warred in Retra's expression.

"Absolutely."

"Go get'em!" Behran agreed.

Lina's thin shoulders straightened, and the two hurried down the narrow, twisting path to the valley below.

"Come sit with me, Thusa." Behran invited, and sat on a warm, grassy spot near the ledge. She gladly sat beside him, and her legs dangled off the short drop off. Already the Tarst residents had begun to fill the ledge beneath them. Closing her eyes, she relaxed. The sun felt warm against her face. She desperately wanted to win today.

A shell trumpeted, quieting the gentle conversation of the Tarst dotting the hillsides. Pan spoke through the shell, but Methusal listened with only half an ear as she attempted to fit in a last minute practice before the Tri-level started.

The Tarst leader spoke for several minutes, explaining the rules, and then requested a respectful silence from the audience when the games began. Another trumpet signaled the end of his speech, and the Quatr-level contenders lined up on the starting line.

Six Tarst, two Dehriens, including Hendra, and Rolban's Lina and Retra stood slightly crouched, ready to go. Their postures looked rigid and tense.

Pan grasped the two kaavl disks and stepped up behind them. An attendant held the shell amplifier to the Chief's lips.

"Let the games....Begin!" The crash of the metal cymbals catapulted the contenders into motion. All ten players fanned out into the forest.

It was hard to make out Retra and Lina's progress as they darted through the trees, but Methusal silently cheered as she glimpsed each segment of ground they covered. Both were moving fast and making good time. Hendra fell from view and then Lina emerged, running hard. Lina had captured her!

The players disappeared behind a curtain of greenery when they neared the mark. Breath bated in hope and fear, Methusal watched the remaining players finally burst into view again, pounding toward the finish line. Retra had vanished, but Lina sprinted out in front with Ludst Lst close on her heels. A lone Tarst man brought up the rear.

Behran leaped to his feet, but Methusal held her breath, willing Lina's victory over the Dehrien every step of the way. When Lina crossed the line, Methusal jumped up with the rest of the crowd, screaming and clapping. The Rolbanis had beaten the Dehriens!

Pan announced the score. "Capturing seven, evading nine!"

Behran whistled loudly, grinning from ear to ear. "She did it!"

"Methusal, Behran, go down," Kitran ordered.

The two scrambled down the path. At the finish line they gave Lina congratulatory hugs, and a consolatory one for Retra, who had just jogged up. But she was far too thrilled by her teammate's win to feel sorry for herself.

"You showed that slimy Dehrien!" she squealed, clutching her friend's arm. Even Hendra, who had just walked up, looked pleased for Lina's win.

A sharp movement in the background caught Methusal's attention. Ludst Lst glowered at Lina. Hatred smoked from his gaze. Abruptly, he turned around and stalked off. Disturbed, Methusal glanced at the other Dehriens. Most scowled at the Rolbanis with flared nostrils and glaring eyes. Their attitude was unsportsmanlike, to say the least.

△ △ △ △ △

Methusal nervously toed the starting line as the other contenders stepped into place. Six Tarst, two Dehriens, and two Rolbani participants would compete.

She rubbed sweaty palms against her leather tunic. Beside her Behran looked calm, and he actually joked with a Tarst competitor.

She shook out her shoulders and tried to relax and concentrate. But unwelcome thoughts flooded her mind. What if this was her last competition? It could be, if she decided not to rise to the Bi-level, because she'd rather retire than stay forever at the Tri-level. And if Mentàll's teachings were at the core of Kitran's new precepts... Well, she felt extremely reluctant to follow any kaavl advice given by the Dehrien Chief. Her stomach knotted. This was not helping her to relax.

She took a deep breath and concentrated on her surroundings. Twenty lengths to the first tree. She would circle to the left...

Pan's footsteps approached from behind her.

"The Tri-level is about to begin." His voice was solemn. "Are you ready, contenders?"

Methusal dug her toe deep into the soft earth for a firm push off.

"Then let the game... Begin!"

A cymbal crash and she was off, flying into the forest along her chosen path. The moment her feet left the starting line she fell into a deep calm, and felt utterly relaxed. Her mind had clicked into kaavl easily. Effortlessly. Like the night before last, when she'd overheard those strange conversations.

Silently, she flew over the soft moss of the forest floor. Although the others were quiet, too, each of their movements whispered clearly in her ears.

Someone cut in behind her and stepped up his speed, and she smiled to herself. She pulled a narrow leather kaavl strip from her pocket and swiftly wrapped it around her palm. Time for her first capture.

Sprinting ahead, Methusal flung one end of the string at a tree. It whipped tightly around it, and she darted behind a bush and held the kaavl strip low and taut. Only a split second to spare. A balding, sandy-haired Dehrien charged up and abruptly tripped on her trap.

Snatching his flag, Methusal was pleased to note that it was Wortn, the Dehrien who had tackled her in Dehre.

She quickly caught up with the others. Four remained now. She circled the mark, and then cut left and center, neatly evading a cleverly laid trap.

Each of her senses felt keenly attuned to her environment, and she breathed in great gulps of tangy forest air. She listened for each nuance of sound. Two opponents remained, but they had fallen behind her; probably because they had paused to set traps and capture the other players.

One more person must be captured before the winner could cross the finish line. Methusal decided to set the trap herself, since she was a good five lengths in front of the others. She ducked behind a bush, directly in the path of the player right on her heels. If he wasn't paying close attention, he wouldn't see her. She waited, barely daring to breathe.

A tan clad leg swung into view. She lunged out and brought her competitor down with a flying tackle around the ankles. Snatching his flag, she was up in a flash. But then she froze.

It was Behran! Stunned dark blue eyes met her own. After another split second, she whirled and sprinted as hard as she could for the finish line.

The other contender must have heard the crash, and probably knew it was down to two players. He had the advantage, as he was slightly ahead of her, but Methusal felt consumed by a burning, overwhelming desire to win. Her legs pumped harder and harder, and her feet sprang off of the moss. She could see the finish line ahead, and her competitor; a short, chunky Tarst, his legs pumping for all they were worth.

Her feet flew over the ground. One handbreadth closer to the Tarst. Another...straining, she stretched to the limit of her endurance. The finish line was almost upon them both. She hurtled for it and crossed over, one foot length in front of her competitor.

Gasping, they both jogged to a stop. The Tarst young man stuck out his hand and smiled as best he could through his wheezing pants. "Congratulations."

Methusal returned the handshake. Still breathing harder than usual, she slowly stepped over to receive her award. Pan held up an arm so he could announce her scores.

"Capturing, ten! Evading, ten!"

After a vigorous handshake, he slipped the smoothly curved wooden disk, hanging from a bit of leather, around her neck. The carved flying beast in the center was made of white bone, and felt smooth beneath her fingertips. She turned and waved to the cheering crowd.

Finally, she followed Behran up to their seats.

"Good job." A brief smile cracked Kitran's granite expression.

Retra, Lina, and Hendra greeted her with excited grins.

"You did great!" The Rolbani girls gave her fierce hugs and urged her to sit with them on the ledge.

Methusal glanced at Behran. He was the only one who had said nothing.

His deep blue eyes shuttered when she looked at him. He sat down a full arm's length away from her. "Congratulations."

"What's wrong?"

"Nothing. It's stupid."

"What is?"

He scowled before replying. "It bothers me that you captured me, instead of the Tarst player."

Surprised, she gaped at him. "I had to eliminate the person behind me. How could I know it was you?"

"You seem to know everything else."

"What is that supposed to mean?"

"You always seem to know exactly where everyone is."

"I know where people are, but I don't pay attention to who's who," she said, trying to keep a level tone. Although maybe Behran had a point. If she'd concentrated and paid attention to each person from beginning to end, maybe she could have known who was directly behind her.

"Okay." He stared down at the starting line.

His accusations stung. "I played the game, Behran. If you'd been paying attention, you would have seen me hiding behind that bush. Don't try to blame me for *your*..."

"Methusal!" Kitran's voice cut like a knife. "That is enough."

Of *course* she hadn't cut him from the game on purpose. What kind of opinion did Behran have of her, anyway?

She tried to ignore him as the Bi-level contenders stepped up to the line. But she found herself blinking back tears.

The cymbals crashed and they were off. Only four players participated in this game—two from each community, except for Rolban, which had none, since Verdnt had gone home sick.

Methusal didn't care who won, but she would prefer that the Dehriens lost. But that was not to be. Long minutes later a lone Dehrien crossed the finish line. Arrogance exuded from every line of his body. Efron had come in first, and Tabor, another Dehrien, had come in second. Finally, a first place win for Dehre. And it was an important win.

But the next Game, the Primary level, was the most important of all. It would determine the Kaavl Master for their three communities.

Pan blew the shell twice. "Before the Primary level begins, we will eat lunch in the dining hall."

Behran trotted down from the plateau first. Methusal made no effort to catch up to him. His accusations still stung. The raw, uncomfortable feelings between them bothered her, too.

Lunch consisted of a thick, savory stew and tender cuts of wild beast. No carcass lay on the serving table here.

The Dehriens muttered amongst themselves across the table and ignored the Rolbanis, as usual. Mentàll talked quietly with Pan. A frown marked the Dehrien Chief's usually expressionless face. Methusal wondered what they were talking about. Maybe she should feel guilty for concentrating lightly into kaavl to eavesdrop, but she did not. She cut off a bite of tender rotarhudge meat.

Mentàll said, "I am glad you accept my reassurances. I'm also happy that we share the same view. Strong kaavl leadership is essential to the health of a community." He paused to drain the cup before him. "I would like to continue this conversation later, if possible. Right now I need to prepare for the Primary. The competition is strong."

He gave a short, self-deprecatory laugh, and her insides curled. Instinctively, she knew Mentàll wasn't worried in the least about losing. Not to anyone.

But Pan was speaking now. She forked the last bite of meat into her mouth and listened intently. The Tarst Chief said, "I would be honored. Come to my house tonight after the evening meal. We can have a good talk then."

Beneath her lashes, Methusal slid a glance down the table. A pleased smile beamed on Pan's face. He looked honored that Mentàll wanted to speak to him later.

Why did Mentàll command such respect wherever he went—from Kitran, Petr, and now Pan? The object of her speculation rose to his feet and extended his hand. "I look forward to this evening."

Pan vigorously shook it. "Good luck this afternoon."

"And you, as well." Mentàll murmured. But Methusal caught the flicker of derision that twisted his mouth before he turned away. Clearly, he didn't believe he needed luck to win.

Kitran and Behran had already disappeared, and the Tarst people now streamed from the dining hall. She cleared her plate. The Primary was about to start.

The sun felt warm after the shadowed hall, and she lifted her face to the golden rays.

A dark head, seen out of the corner of her eye, made her glance right. Mostly because the man stood at least a half a head taller than many of the Tarst. His head was down and he had just come from the direction of Mentàll's cabin. In fact, Mentàll exited from the cabin now and strode toward the playing fields, to the north. Her suspicious gaze latched onto the tall, dark haired man. Kitran? What would he be doing in Mentàll's cabin?

But when the person looked up, she saw it was Timaeus. What was he doing here? And why had he been speaking to Mentàll, of all people?

She altered her path to intercept his. But he'd seen her, and was already cutting her way. A smile lit his face. "Methusal! I didn't think I'd see you. Have you competed yet?"

"Yes. I won first place at the Tri-level. Thanks for asking. What are you doing here?"

"Petr had a message for Mentàll. The merchant delegation arrived this morning, and he feels honored that Mentàll will be arriving tomorrow." The memorized words flowed easily off his tongue.

"I thought the delegation would come tomorrow. On Sixthday."

Timaeus shrugged. "Change of plans, I guess. When Verdnt got back, he carried a message from Mentàll, asking if the delegation could come a little earlier. That way they could spend two full days in Rolban before they had to go home."

"Oh." She absorbed this news. Her thoughts turned to Rolban, and she felt a small pang of homesickness. "How is Deccia? Have you been able to speak to each other? And what about Aali? How much trouble did she get in with Petr?"

Timaeus chuckled. "Aali's been banished to her room for a week, I think. Petr's at his wits' end with her. But that might have been a good thing for Deccia and me."

"Why?"

"I think he's realized how lucky he is that Deccia respects him so much. Anyway, he's agreed that we can talk to each other again. But only for a little while each day."

"That's great!"

"I guess so. It would be better, though, if she wasn't constantly working. Verdnt's kept her chained to the classroom ever since he got back. He barely lets her out of his sight." Jealousy tinged his tone.

"Why? Doesn't school end today? And I thought he was sick. Why is he working at all?"

"He's not sick anymore. He felt bad yesterday, but this morning he seemed fine. He says Deccia needs to start planning lessons now, so she can teach her own class next year. And he expects her to help with his classes, too. If you want the truth, I think he's keeping Deccia busy on purpose."

"Why?"

"So she doesn't have any free time."

Methusal remembered that Verdnt had appeared to be interested in Deccia, and that Petr had practically promised her hand in marriage to the teacher. Was Verdnt jealous? Was he trying to keep Deccia and Timaeus apart?

She glanced toward the green hillsides, which were rapidly filling up with people. The Primary would begin soon, but she still had one last, hurried question. "What is the delegation like, then?"

"Okay, I guess. They seem a bit... I don't know..."

"Hostile?" she supplied.

"Yes. How did you know?"

"Most Dehriens have been, so far."

"Mmm. Anyway, Deccia doesn't like them, that's for sure. She has a bad feeling about them." Timaeus glanced at the angle of the sun. A black flying beast cut across the sky.

"Really." Methusal took her twin's hunches seriously. Usually they were right, just like Hanuh's. Deccia's instant distrust of Mentàll was one clear example.

"I'd better go," he said abruptly. "I want to get home before dark."

"Have a good trip. We'll be home tomorrow."

"Right. See you." He loped for the bridge.

She watched him go, and absently noted the flying beast circling above his head. Had it followed him? In general, flying creatures seemed to like humans. That was one reason why the one she'd tended several months ago had docilely submitted when she'd splinted its broken wing. Thank goodness for that, because the power of its other wing could easily have knocked her silly.

The game was about to begin, so Methusal hurried north. Unease lodged in her spirit as she pondered the information Timaeus had given her. Why had the delegation arrived a day early? And why was a sense of urgency nipping at her—as if she needed to figure everything out right now? Before it was too late.

She climbed up to the Rolbani level and found a spot next to Hendra. A short distance away, Retra and Lina sat beside Behran. The conflict with Behran continued to bother her. The fact surprised her, because they'd been at odds for years. Their previous spats had been silly, though, for the most part; Behran had teased her like an obnoxious pest, and she had unfortunately responded in a similar manner. This afternoon's discussion had felt too real and personal. It bothered her that Behran was upset with her.

"Look at the flying beast," Hendra said, with a soft note of awe. "It's coming in so close."

Methusal had been so lost in thought that she hadn't noticed. She drew in a quick breath when the beast swept by, only two lengths away. It circled up lazily, high in the air, and then swooped down again.

Its bright black eyes seemed to be fixed upon *her*.

Surprised, she eyed it more closely. Was it the same beast that had followed Timaeus? Had it followed her to the bluff?

On impulse, she chirped three high, clear notes. With a rush of wings, the beast dove straight for her.

Methusal flung up her arm to protect her face, and Hendra gasped.

But with feather soft delicacy, the beast sank onto her arm and folded its wings. It was heavy. Methusal opened her eyes. The beast stared at her, its head cocked to the side. And then she saw the lump on the top edge of one folded wing. She smiled. "You're a long way from home."

"Is he your pet?"

"No. I splinted his injured wing. Now he's healed." Methusal carefully stroked the beast's smooth, shiny black feathers. Contentedly, the creature gazed back at her.

"Mentàll had a flying beast when I was eight. Its wing was broken, too."

"He mentioned that, the first time I saw him. He said it died soon after." Methusal bit her tongue so she wouldn't ask if he had played an instrumental part in its death.

Hendra's expression shadowed. "It was weak. It couldn't fly, so Mentàll fed it. One day my father found it and killed it with his bare hands. Right in front of us."

Shocked, Methusal said, "Why?"

"To punish my cousin."

"What had he done?"

Hendra shrugged, and looked off into the distance. "I never understood why my father did anything," she said quietly. "Racmun spirits made him mean. He made up reasons to punish us, and then he'd lie to my mother about it. He said we had done things we hadn't. He lied about everything. I never trusted him, and now Mentàll hates liars so much that anyone on the Dehrien Council who's caught in a lie is thrown out."

She fell silent for a moment. "I don't know if my mother believed Father's stories or not, but she was afraid to stand up to him. No one was safe from his fists. Not me, and especially not Mentàll."

"That's awful, Hendra."

Softly, she said, "Yes. I was afraid to care for any animal after that. I was afraid he would kill it, too."

"He probably would have. He sounds like a cruel man." Maybe Mentàll had learned his own brand of cruelty from his uncle.

Below them, the slug shell trumpeted. With a small squawk, the flying beast sprang upward. After circling once, as if to say goodbye, it took off with long, lazy strokes for Rolban.

For a moment, Methusal envied the beast's freedom. It had no responsibilities; just endless freedom to go wherever it wanted. No mysteries to solve. No worries. No enemies would ever catch him, high and free in the blue sky. The world belonged to the beast, but Methusal was glued to the earth, and all of the overwhelming problems she could not escape.

She longed for a sign that everything would be all right. If only Kitràn would win the Primary now. With all of her heart, she hoped he'd win. Anyone, except for Mentàll.

Chapter Twenty-Nine

The three Primary contenders stood on the starting line, evenly spaced apart. Kitran was in the middle. Sunlight glinted off of Pan's bald head as he rhythmically stretched his arms forward and overhead to loosen up. Both Kitran and Mentàll, however, stood motionless.

The extraordinary kaavl skills of those at the Primary level far surpassed Methusal's own. Watching three of Koblan's best competing against each could prove educational—especially since she'd never had the opportunity to watch a Primary Game in Rolban, since Kitran was the only one who had achieved that level. Methusal was eager to see their skills in action.

Pan's assistant was in charge of the kaavl disks and amplifying shell during this game. He bellowed, "The final event has arrived. In our experience, one can go no further than the Primary level. The winner of this event is surely Kaavl Master of our land! May we have silence, please? Are the contenders ready?"

Three nods, and the disks were placed in the assistant's hands.

"Then let the game... Begin!"

And the three were off. What followed once they came under cover of the trees was the most intensive sort of hunter-hunted game Methusal had ever witnessed. Unfortunately, she could only catch glimpses through the leafy foliage.

Traps were set and then sprung, and the winner accumulated pieces to add to his own trap collection. The three men endlessly circled each other as they slowly approached the triangular halfway point. No one was captured. Each of the competitors seemed to possess a sixth sense which told him the exact location and activities of his opponents. No one walked into a trap, and each cunningly stayed out of range of the others.

The three disappeared beneath a thick canopy of trees when they neared the halfway mark. Long, nail biting minutes elapsed before they crept into view again, heading toward the finish line. Kitran was not among them.

Behran leaned forward at the same instant Methusal did. She anxiously searched the forest floor.

Only a minute passed before the truth became clear. Kitran walked into view, his flag noticeably absent from his waist.

Disappointment crushed Methusal's hopes. Rolban would be last. The title of Kaavl Master would go to either Pan or Mentàll, and a horrible, sickening feeling engulfed her. Mentàll would win.

The certainty of this premonition made her feel a bit sick. Worse, the brooding weight that had lifted upon her arrival in cheery Tarst now settled over her spirit again. If only Pan would win. Then everything would be all right.

Below, the figures danced in slow motion. Mentàll circled back, to the right, and then threaded backward through the trees once more. Both men paused to listen. Then, stealthily, Mentàll crept closer and knelt behind a rock.

He flicked stones to his right, in an effort to divert Pan's attention.

Surely the Tarst Chief wouldn't fall for that old trick. However, Pan circled—right toward his opponent!

Pan hesitated, clearly listening, and glanced quickly about. Mentàll remained absolutely still, waiting for him to move. The Tarst Chief sidled to his left.

In one fluid movement, Mentàll rose to his feet and silently stepped closer. Now he was hidden behind a tree. Pan took another cautious step, and Mentàll darted quickly and purposefully behind him. Too late, Pan saw him. With a short dive, the Dehrien Chief attacked, sweeping Pan off his feet. The Tarst flag was now Mentàll's own.

Graciously, he extended a hand to help Pan up. Mentàll was the winner, and undisputed Kaavl Master.

Crossing the finish line a moment later, Mentàll presented the assistant with two flags—Pan's and Kitran's—before receiving his award, and scores of two perfect tens. Not only had he won, but he had captured both of his opponents.

Applause rippled from the hills.

Methusal did not clap. The apprehension that had seized her began to fade. She felt drained. Really, what difference did it make who won? It was just a game—just a title. Mentàll would be Kaavl Master for a year, and then new games could crown a new victor. Someone else might win next year. Maybe. That thought did not comfort her.

Feeling slightly depressed, she glanced at Behran and found him watching her. Was he still mad at her? Methusal barely noticed as the Quatr-levelers stepped by to descend from the Rolbani viewing level.

When Behran remained silent, Methusal glanced at the forest floor again.

"I'm sorry," he said softly.

She quickly glanced back. He had moved closer, and his strong, sharp features cut a black profile against the setting sun.

"Do you forgive me?" he asked.

She searched the shadowed eyes and found regret.

Her depression lifted a little. "Yes, of course I do."

"Good." A matching smile flickered.

"And if I'd known it was you..."

"Don't worry about it."

A companionable silence elapsed.

"Looks like Mentàll is Kaavl Master," he commented.

The dark, nebulous feelings again stirred. "Just what he needs."

"What do you mean?"

"His opinion of himself is already inflated all out of proportion."

"You really dislike him."

"He scares me."

Several moments passed, and then he quietly asked, "Has he bothered you lately?"

She shook her head. "Everyone thinks he's such a great leader, but he's not what he appears to be. He's a whip, and I don't trust him. I can't wait until he leaves for Dehre."

"Pretty strong words against a Kaavl Master."

But she had stronger, if only she dared to tell him about the conversations she had overheard the other night. Maybe she should tell him. But she wasn't ready—not yet. Instead, she changed the subject. "I saw Timaeus just before the Primary. Petr had a message for Mentàll."

"Anything new since we've been gone?"

"A little." She repeated what Timaeus had told her.

"Mmm. Interesting about the delegation. I hadn't heard that news when we left Dehre."

"Me either." Another moment passed. "So, what are we supposed to do until the dinner hour?"

He shrugged and rose to his feet. "I thought I'd talk to a few Tarst, and see what they're like."

Methusal followed him down the slope. "I like their village. It feels a lot like home, only it feels warmer and friendlier."

His shoulders jerked in a shrug. "Probably because they spend a lot of time together. If we Rolbanis did that, we'd probably be closer, too."

Methusal glanced at his straight back. An inflection had bitten through his tone that she didn't understand. The moment his foot touched the valley floor, he gave her a curt wave. "See you later."

She frowned. What was bothering him now?

Slowly, she followed in his footsteps. She felt lonely, and wished Deccia was there to talk to. A glance at the sun told her it was another two hours until the evening meal. What should she do?

Silent footsteps whispered up behind her as she approached the outer line of shacks, and a quick, sinking feeling in the pit of her stomach alerted her to the person's identity. Her steps quickened. But a hard hand bit into her arm, jolting her to an unwilling stop.

"If it isn't the fair Methusal." Pale eyes glittered down at her. The Dehrien Chief was so close that she could see the pale gold stubble sprouting from his hard, angular chin. Puffs of hot, rank air caressed her face.

Futilely, she jerked and twisted to free her arm, but Mentàll's grip only tightened. His teeth bared into a snarl. "I will let you go when I'm finished speaking to you, Methusal."

He was *furious*. Fear sliced through her. Clenching her teeth, she stood perfectly still, forcing herself to meet his gaze. But she couldn't stop the waves of loathing and terror licking through her.

"You do not listen well, do you?" he hissed.

"I'm not afraid of you."

"You spoke lies to Aenill."

So, that's what this was about. "I told her about the stolen grain. And that I don't trust you. You're a whip and a liar."

His grip on her arm tightened so hard that she cried out. "I do not *lie!*" The ice behind his eyes cracked, and in that instant Methusal saw complete hatred. He shook her arm once, hard, before his inhuman self-control slipped back into place again. "I never lie. I do not need to."

"Let me go." Tears burned her eyes. To her surprise, he thrust her arm free, and she rubbed it, hating that one tear trickled down her cheek. She shoved a palm across it, obliterating it, and gathered up her splintering courage. "You're an evil, selfish man," she spat. "I told Aenill I don't trust you. You're cruel, and I know you want to hurt Rolban. I told you once, and I'll tell you again—I'll do everything I can to stop you."

"Do not threaten me, Methusal," he gritted. "You will regret it."

"How can a mere girl threaten you?" she mocked. "Aren't you the Chief of Dehre?"

Red tinged his cheekbones. "The Alliance means food for my people. A girl with her lies and foolish imagination could ruin the lives of hundreds of people."

"You want more than food! You're a threat to Rolban. Who knows, maybe Tarst, too," she said rashly.

He gave a thin, derisive smile. "You are a fanciful girl."

"Then why terrorize me? How can a mere *girl* disrupt all of your mighty plans?"

He gave a harsh laugh. "You cannot, arrogant though you are. It is time someone put you in your place. Your father cannot. Your own Chief cannot. But I will. Your footprints will not tread dirt on the Alliance I have created."

Another threat. Jaw clenched, she said, "If the Alliance was truly for the best, I wouldn't oppose it."

"How do you know it is not? You are a fool to pass judgment on a matter far beyond your comprehension."

"Don't talk down to me," she snapped. "I know you're plotting against Rolban. That's why you threaten me. You want me to be so scared of you that I'll cower in fear, and let you accomplish whatever you want."

"You are paranoid, Methusal. Keep your wild imaginings to yourself. Think of the lives you will ruin with your lies."

"Your lies, you mean."

The ice broke again, just for a second, and Methusal shuddered at what she saw. In that instant, she saw that he could easily kill her. She stepped backward.

"That's right, Methusal," he snarled. "Choose the prudent path. Flee while you can."

Without a word, she turned and trotted south, her heart racing with panic. She *was* a fool. Why couldn't she control her mouth? She'd be smarter to spy and report facts to the proper authorities. Threatening the Dehrien was stupid. What if he did try to hurt her? He was clever and powerful, and could no doubt accomplish that goal in any number of vile, untraceable ways.

She certainly wasn't "keeping her place." Would he decide to kill her now? Methusal felt sick. Why hadn't he killed her already? Maybe because she knew no facts. That was pathetically obvious. She couldn't stop him, because she had no idea what was going on!

Methusal slipped inside her cabin and slammed and locked the door behind her.

The slatted window shutters gave her a good view of her tormentor, who strode by her room. He didn't even look in her direction.

Gradually the rapid, panicked beating of her heart slowed, and she released the lock with shaking fingers. Her roommates wouldn't appreciate being locked out.

She sat down cross-legged on her cot and slumped back against the wall. More than ever, she wished Deccia was here—someone she could talk to about Mentàll, and how frightened she was becoming. But she was alone, and her options clear. She had to avoid the Dehrien Chief. And avoid being alone at all times—at all costs.

Methusal glanced about the gloomily lit cabin. She was alone now. But he had already threatened her. Surely he wouldn't try to kill her now. He'd wait until she made another move against him. ...Or maybe he'd attack tonight, like the wild beast he was.

Shivering, she lay down and drew the warm fur over her. Maybe she'd nap until dinner time. Her last thought before sleep overtook her was that Mentàll had frightened her into hiding out in her cabin.

△ △ △ △ △

Hendra hugged her crossed arms to chest. She felt sick inside. She'd just seen her cousin seize Methusal's arm. His menacing body language told the rest of the story. He was threatening her again. Her new friend had put on a brave front, but then she'd run for her cabin and slammed the door.

Hendra swallowed hard. Clearly, Mentàll was up to no good. Why else would he threaten the Rolbani girl? He must know she was investigating him; which was more than could be said for herself. Last night Hendra had fallen into bed early, too exhausted to spy on her cousin.

Knowing the Dehrien delegation had already arrived in Rolban made Hendra feel even more apprehensive. Tomorrow Mentàll would arrive in Rolban, too, and so would his best kaavl players. It was now or never. Tonight she must discover what was going on if she wanted to protect Rolban. She was sure the delegation would do nothing until Mentàll arrived.

Hendra watched her cousin enter his cabin and shut himself inside. Tonight she'd listen at the table for hints, and then shadow him wherever he went and listen in on his conversations. If he was plotting against Rolban, surely he would give last minute instructions to his team tonight. At least, she hoped he would.

The Rolbani girl was already suspicious. But without proof, Rolban couldn't pick up arms. Not legally, anyway, because it would break the Alliance. Hendra would do everything she could to discover the truth. Not only to protect Rolban, but to save her cousin from self-destruction.

△ △ △ △ △

Methusal felt refreshed an hour later when the soft foot shufflings and giggles of her roommates woke her up.

"She's awake," Lina whispered.

"Good! It's hard, trying to be so quiet."

Hendra smiled when Methusal sat up and yawned sleepily. "It's time for dinner. Do you want to come with us?"

Methusal nodded, and stifled another yawn. Her skirmish with Mentàll flooded her mind, but she shoved it into the back of her thoughts. Sleep had made one thing clear. The man was a menace. Maybe she wouldn't be able to prove that he planned to make a move against Rolban. Maybe she should try to make it home before the Dehrien Chief arrived. Then she could speak to her father and Petr...that thought brought her up short. As if Petr would listen. The whole thing seemed hopeless.

"We're having freshly grilled slug monster tonight," Retra said, hopping down the stairs.

"Slug monster!" The brisk twilight air revived Methusal's disturbed spirits. "Where did they find that?" Slug monsters were a rare delicacy.

Lina shrugged. "We don't know, but the cooks said to get there early if we want a good piece."

Spirits rising, Methusal trotted into the warmly lit dining hall. A delicate, tantalizing aroma wafted from the serving tables. Already a long line stretched halfway around the room. Evidently slug monster was a special treat for the Tarst, as well.

"Look, there's Behran," Hendra said, and with a small smile, quickly moved to join him at the end of the line. Behran's face lit up when he greeted the Dehrien girl, and a sharp twist of an unidentified emotion stabbed Methusal. Her steps slowed as she approached the two.

Behran's warm smile, and his total attention was focused upon Dehrien girl. He had never looked or acted that way with Methusal. Did he have feelings for Hendra? Another, sharper twinge stabbed her, but she glanced quickly away.

Already the line behind her stretched through the open doorway, and every face looked hungry and expectant. The line slowly moved forward. Hendra and Behran fell silent as they neared the serving tables.

The tables were laden with bread, bowls of torn up logne leaves sprinkled with nuts, and two trays of slug monster. The tender white meat was thinly sliced, so everyone could have a taste of the delicacy. Aenill served from the platter to make sure no one took more than his or her fair share.

"Methusal!" The Chief's wife greeted her warmly when she stepped up to the tray. "Congratulations on your win to-day." Her eyes twinkled as she forked two slices of meat onto her plate. "Kitran was right to boast about you."

The kind words made her smile. "Thank you. But I almost came in second. If I'd been a moment slower, it would have been a Tarst victory."

Aenill nodded, pleased by her response. "Denl is a good boy. Maybe next year he will win."

The crowd behind pressed her on, so Methusal continued to the next table, where she tossed several forkfuls of leaves and a bread bun onto her platter. She was sad to see there was no sweet tagma bark tonight.

Since Behran and Hendra lingered to wait for Lina and Retra, Methusal was the first to arrive at the visitor's table.

Conversations ebbed and flowed around her as she steadily chewed her way through the meal. She didn't feel much like talking.

The slug monster was delicious. Its tender, firm meat held a hint of a sweet/sour taste—unlike anything she had ever tasted before. In Rolban, the slug meat automatically went to the Chief and those he invited to eat with him. None had been captured while her father was Chief.

"Look!" Retra elbowed her.

Pan stood at the shell amplifier on stage, and four stout Tarst flanked him. Each of the four men wore bleached white breeches and a red tunic, and had slicked his black hair back to a point at his nape. Except for slight variations in height, they looked like exact copies of each other. Each held over-sized kaavl disks in their hands.

"Ahem." Pan coughed discreetly. "Ahem!"

Silence fell in the Great Hall.

"Thank you. In honor of our special guests, our dance singers have prepared a salute to the Kaavl Games. Please welcome the talented Tarst Quartet!" He jogged down the platform stairs amid foot stomping, thunderous applause.

Dance singers? Rolbanis didn't dance much. Children occasionally made up little dances, but that was all.

The identical men slashed their metal disks together and began to hum. The low sound intensified, and then broke up into a series of staccato blasts. Another resounding crash of the disks, and they began to march. Each man's humming differed slightly in pitch, which created a pleasant, harmonizing effect. The humming grew rhythmic, and slowly the four stepped to the time of their own music.

Each successive dance pattern grew more complicated than the last, corresponding to its song. The tune was varying, complex, and indescribably beautiful. Spellbound, and spirit unexpectedly lifted, Methusal wished they would never stop.

Gradually, though, their steps slowed and the metal disks lightly brushed together. Three soft, staccato blasts, and it was over. Everyone in the dining hall rose to their feet and cheered and whistled. Even the implacable Dehriens clapped.

Slowly, Methusal sat down again, enthralled by the music still pulsing through her soul. She felt as if she could have listened to the quartet forever.

"Weren't they great?" Retra's eyes shone.

She could only nod, because she didn't want to break the spell of the moment.

Next, Pan introduced a fleet of jugglers. More acts followed, and the evening sped by. The Tarst Quartet performed a final encore. Then it was late.

Dreamily, Methusal said goodnight to Behran and Kitran, and wandered with Retra and Lina to their own cabin. Hendra had disappeared.

"That was the best entertainment I've ever seen," sighed Retra, flopping onto her cot.

"Maybe we could talk to Petr about having more singing and dancing in Rolban," Methusal suggested. She snuggled down in her warm fur. Her spirit still felt bright from the wonder of the evening. Surely even Petr would love it.

"We should!" Lina agreed. "I didn't realize what we were missing out on until we came here."

Methusal squeezed her eyes shut, wanting to savor the feeling of peace that still permeated her soul. She didn't want to think about Mentàll. Maybe it was foolish, but just for a little while she wanted to believe that everything would be all right. That her worries only existed in her imagination.

Methusal drifted into a dream world perched in a cloud. Nothing but blue sky and white, puffy clouds surrounded her, as far as her eyes could see.

Until night encroached.

Speeding shadows darkened the landscape. The clouds turned gray, and then black.

Thunder rumbled through Methusal's soul, and a cold, stiff breeze chilled her skin.

The time for peace had ended.

CHAPTER THIRTY

IN THE PITCH BLACK, Hendra crouched in the shadows of the Tarst Chief's cabin. Warm lights spilled from the small side windows onto the grassy earth. She'd seen her cousin enter minutes earlier. Voices murmured indoors, but frustratingly, she could not hear what they said.

Maybe if she crept closer to the front of the house she could hear better. That's where they were standing. The only trouble was, at that spot two large windows beamed bright light outside. Someone might spot her.

But hadn't she played it safe for long enough? People's lives could be in danger.

She had to chance it.

Hendra slipped around a bush and tiptoed to the front corner of the house. She pressed her cheek to the rough wood. Sure enough, the voices were a little clearer. Maybe if she moved just a *tiny* bit closer to the window...

"Got you!" Pain bit into her arm and someone yanked her upright, onto her tiptoes.

Hendra gasped with terror.

Ludst Lst's cruel face grinned down at her. "Well, if it isn't little miss meek and mild." He dragged her closer to him. She gasped again, and horror spiraled. He was too close. Every instinct in her screamed to flee. She wrestled frantically to free herself.

He smiled, as if pleased by her terror, and pushed his face closer her own. "Would Mentàll be happy to find you out here?"

"No," she gasped. "Let go. Let me go *now!*" The large hulk of him terrified her. The fact that he could overpower her horrified her. The fact that he was a man, and even worse, one with no scruples or morals, threw her into an uncontrolled panic.

She couldn't catch her breath. Hysteria blanketed her mind. "Let me go," she cried out. Terror screamed through her mind, and she choked on a gasp. She couldn't bear it! *Not for one more second.*

Her knees buckled, and she collapsed into blackness.

△ △ △ △ △

Voices whispered, mixing with the wind whipping through Methusal's dreams.

"Do you think that's necessary?"

"They are behind the times. Both have agreed that stronger kaavl leadership is needed."

"But taking over their government?"

"No, no. Of course the agreement calls for nothing so drastic. I would merely provide counsel to their leaders. Counsel they desperately need."

Methusal fought sleep. She struggled to wake up. Mentàll. Pan...

Voices. With a gasp, she sat straight up.

Mentàll and Pan were meeting tonight. Maybe right now? She rubbed her eyes, and yawned so hard her jaw crackled. Her brain felt fuzzy.

Had she just heard Pan and Mentàll talking?

Yes. She had to hear their conversation again. She *must.*

She could. She must relax to hear... Sleep curled like tiny, anesthetizing tendrils through her mind. As she relaxed the voices filtered in again.

"If they agree they need counsel so badly, why do I have to sign this document?" Pan sounded confused.

"Petr and Kitran know what is best, but the elders do not." The Dehrien Chief's cool, persuasive voice slid into Methusal's ears. "You see," parchment rustled, "Petr sent this letter of authorization. You can read his wishes in his own handwriting."

Letter of authorization?

Methusal tensed, and the last threads of sleep vanished.

"It is Petr's handwriting," Pan agreed.

The Dehrien Chief said, "You must understand that Rolban has strayed far from the Old Kaavl Master's teachings, Pan. Kaavl is only used for entertainment there. They desperately need kaavl back in their leadership, but the elders will not allow it. Only a few understand how urgently it is needed. Rolban needs *me* to show them how to get back on the right track, Pan. And Petr agrees. Petr cannot sign the treaty, but he wants you to do so. His letter makes his wishes clear. This treaty, together with the Alliance, will force the Rolbani elders to listen to reason. It is for their own good."

"I don't know..." A nervous flipping of pages tickled Methusal's ears.

"It is only for three weeks, at first," the Dehrien Chief said. "Then I will assess their progress."

Assess their progress? Whose progress? Petr's? The Council's? And how?

Methusal sat up on one elbow. What exactly was going on?

Clearly, Mentàll wanted Pan to sign a treaty that would affect Rolban's government. So did Petr. In fact, he'd apparently sent a letter via Mentàll to give to Pan, which told Pan to vote in favor of Mentàll's new, second treaty.

Other bits of information lingered, too. Mentàll wanted to force Rolban to accept his counsel for three weeks. But why?

The rest of the conversation faded as she tried to understand.

The Alliance Petr had signed!

The second clause stated that one community must abide by a law passed by both of the other communities. So, if two communities passed the same law—or treaty—then the third community must obey the law too; whether they agreed with it or not. In this case, Mentàll was trying to convince Tarst to sign a treaty with Dehre which would force Rolban to accept Mentàll's counsel for three weeks.

The whole thing seemed crazy. What did Mentàll really want? And Petr's lust for power had clearly blinded him to common sense. Her heart beat rapidly. Erl had tried to warn the Rolbanis about that clause!

A door banged shut. "Did he sign it?" whispered a man.

"Yes, the fool. Now Rolban is mine."

Methusal's palms beaded with perspiration. Rolban was *his?* What did that mean?

Her heart pounded. Mentàll obviously meant to use that agreement to gain complete power over Rolban. That was the only conclusion that made sense.

She rubbed her clammy hands together. Rolban had to be warned, and Kitran, too. Surely Kitran wasn't the thieving murderer. In her heart she couldn't believe it, and right now she needed to trust someone. Rolban had to be warned about Mentàll's schemes before the Dehrien Chief arrived.

Then a horrifying thought hit her—the Dehrien merchant delegation had already arrived in Rolban! What if they weren't there to negotiate trade deals? What if they were waiting in Rolban for Mentàll to arrive? What was the final piece of his terrible plan? Rolban could be in danger right *now*. And her parents, Deccia, Sims...

Quietly, so she wouldn't disturb her roommates, Methusal pulled on her moccasins and an extra tunic. Hendra was still missing.

Methusal strapped the pack to her back and slipped silently into the dark, moonless night. Led only by the soft glow through the shutters of the men's cabin, she silently slipped to the Rolbani men's cabin. The bonfires in the courtyard had burnt out, and the moon hadn't risen yet, so the night was an inky black. A sharp knock brought Behran to the door. A small triangle of orange light spilled into the shadows.

"What's going on?" His gaze took in the pack on her shoulders, and his brows flew together. "Are you going somewhere?"

"Get Kitran! Quick."

Behran withdrew from sight. "Kitran..." His voice was muffled.

Methusal waited. The velvety darkness that enveloped her felt like a living thing. Suffocating...evil. Her heart beat harder. A few faint, shuttered lights glowed from across the courtyard. Their occupants were snug inside, protected from the dark night. Besides those muted lights, everything was pitch black. And silent.

"What is it, Methusal?" Kitran's voice sounded unnaturally loud in the stillness. He stood on the top step of the cabin. The orange light backlit his body, so his face was in shadows.

"I need to speak to you about Mentàll. It's urgent." She hoped she was doing the right thing by trusting Kitran.

"I can barely see you." Methusal heard the frown in Kitran's voice. Grass softly rustled nearby. "What's this all about?"

But an overpowering urge to flee had seized her, and her feet itched to run *now* as hard and fast as she could. Her words tumbled out in a jumbled heap, and made little sense.

"Slow down. Tell me again about the treaty. And how do you know about it?"

A rising, uncontrollable terror tightened her throat, but she forced the words around her uncooperative tongue. "I said, Mentàll had Pan sign..."

"Sign what?" The words hissed from the darkness behind her and she jumped. Cold, hard fingers bit painfully into her shoulder. "If you are making accusations about me, Methusal, perhaps you should make them to my face."

A squeak flew from her lips when a vicious jerk sent her staggering backwards two steps and turned her partway around. His form was outlined in jet black, larger than life against the midnight sky.

It was so dark. The Dehrien's body now partly shielded her from Kitran's limited view. Kitran could barely see her before. Surely he couldn't see her at all now.

Her lips trembled, but she fought a rushing, paralyzing panic. "Let me go."

"I don't think so, Methusal," Mentàll murmured. His grip tightened, threatening to squeeze muscle from bone, while his other hand clamped over her mouth, preventing her from crying out.

The Dehrien Chief's voice lightened as he addressed Kitran. "Evidently this young woman has been eavesdropping. That is unfortunate. Obviously, she has misunderstood what she heard."

"Then the treaty she was talking about..."

"Exactly what you and I have discussed. I am willing to show it to Methusal so she can see that her concerns are groundless. The agreement is for the good. Something a young girl might not understand."

Anger surged at his condescending tone. She violently wriggled and twisted, trying to free herself.

Kitran seemed satisfied with Mentàll's explanation. "The agreement is for the best, Methusal. Let Mentàll explain it to you, and you'll see."

"Right. Come along, *Methusal*." Her name was a chill rasp in her ear. Desperately, she bit down and caught a pinch of skin on his palm. His hand jerked away.

"But he plans..." Her cry was stifled when Mentàll's large hand clapped across her face again, painfully gripping it.

"I will have her straightened out in no time, Kitran. Goodnight."

The night was so inky that Methusal knew Kitran couldn't see her desperate, lunging attempts to free herself from Mentàll's rib squeezing embrace. One arm crushed her chest, holding her feet inches above the ground, while the other held her jaw painfully immobile.

He carried her, kicking and squirming, across the square. She thought she had a chance when he released her mouth to open the door to his cabin, but she had let out no more than a strangled cry when he thrust her hard inside, sending her sprawling across the wooden floor.

She'd only gained her knees when she was propelled upright and shoved into a chair. A kaavl strip quickly lashed her wrists together behind her.

"Now," Mentàll stared down at her, and a thin, humorless smile curved his hard lips. A ball of leather was clenched in his right hand. "Do I need to use this? Or will you keep quiet on your own? No one will come, you know. A Chief can do what he likes."

"This isn't Dehre!" she spat. "The Tarst aren't animals!" Terror whirled inside her. He could kill her now.

"Perhaps not, but no one will dare question me." The pale eyes glittered.

You're a monstrous beast! But she clamped her mouth shut, glaring instead of speaking. Any fight or fear she showed now would only goad him on.

Mentàll abruptly knelt before her, and hard fingers gripped her chin. She tried not to flinch back, but his face was so close to her own that she could see the little streaks of red in the whites of his pale blue eyes. His familiar, nauseating breath filled her nostrils.

He murmured, "What am I going to do with you?"

Instinctive revulsion made her shrink back.

A faint smile curved his lips, and hard satisfaction glinted. Clearly, he had just obtained his goal. In one swift movement, he rose to his feet. "You fear me. Good. That is as it should be."

She hated that she had revealed weakness to him. Now he knew how to intimidate her. "That's because you've tied me up!" she snapped. "And you're threatening me."

"You expect me to set you free?"

"I expect only the worst from you. You are an abominable whip!"

"Watch your tongue." Threat chilled the low tone.

Methusal shuddered, but managed to keep her chin up.

"You should learn respect for authority."

"I have no respect for you, slug monster!" she managed to spit.

With predatory purposefulness, he stalked closer, which forced her to crane her neck back in order to meet his gaze. Swelling fear made her heart pound in response to his calculated intimidation.

A handbreadth from her, he hissed, "What other names would you like to call me?"

She swallowed. "None."

"So your tongue can be tamed. Respect, in its basest form."

"I was wrong before. You're not a whip. You're a wild beast. Completely uncivilized and vulgar."

"I warned you." When he went down on one knee beside her, terror galloped through Methusal. Why couldn't she control her mouth?

When his thumb brushed her lower lip, she closed her eyes in horror. What would he do to her now? She was a fool!

Her voice trembled. "You're threatening me in the basest possible way."

"Perhaps I am attracted to you."

A disbelieving laugh choked out. "You *despise* me."

"Yes. But you are beautiful. And a challenge. I never turn away from a challenge."

"Don't...don't touch me anymore," she gulped out. It hurt to capitulate; to allow him to win this battle of their wills.

When he stood, she gasped softly with relief.

"Then what good are you to me?" Anger edged that harsh tone. "You are a liability."

"Let me go!"

He gave a rusty laugh. "I cannot, Methusal. You will cry warnings to your friends, and my plan will fail."

"Then what will you do to me?" She hated the tremor in her voice.

"What would you do in my place?"

"Keep me tied up," she said promptly. "Run immediately to do your plan. Preferably now, so the wild beasts can eat you up on your way to Rolban."

He gave another harsh laugh. "The wild beasts do not frighten me, Methusal." His long legs passed by as he slowly paced the small room. What was he plotting now? What would he *do* to her?

Terror rose again, and her eyes darted about the plushly decorated cabin, seeking a way to escape. There was none. She was alone and helpless.

He noticed her desperate, agitated movements, and gave a grim, cold chuckle. "Go ahead and look. You cannot escape. You will have to accept my attentions for a little longer."

Methusal turned her head so he could not see the tears filling her eyes. She refused to let him know how terrified she was. Her earlier, foolish words had been a show of bravado. Now in the lengthening, awful silence, her overactive imagination conjured up scene after scene of the despicable things he could do to her. And she had a sickening fear that she would never escape him afterward—if he let her live. He was powerful and could get away with what he pleased, now that the second treaty was signed. He certainly wouldn't let a mere girl foil his ambitious plans. She squeezed her eyes shut to prevent the tears from spilling over.

What would he do to her? Kill her? Violate her? Violate and kill her?

Hysteria rose in her throat as the silence lengthened, until finally his footsteps approached her chair.

"I have decided... Look at me, Methusal!" That harsh voice whipped, and fear made her eyes pop open. She glared at him through her tears, hating him with an overwhelming hatred.

"Aah, Methusal." His smile looked vicious. "You despise me. So be it. I have made my decision, and you should thank me for it, although I doubt you will."

Vainly, she tugged at the cord binding her wrists as Mentàll turned and paced toward the door. "I have decided you will become my wife. You will stay here tonight with me, and Pan will marry us in the morning. By then, you will not be fit for another man. Then you will travel with me to Rolban, where you will do everything I say, or I will destroy your family, your friends, and everything you hold dear." He approached her again. "You have no other choice—besides death, of course."

Death....Or a lifetime of bondage to Mentàll. Which would be worse? A hysterical gurgle welled in her throat. Surely this was a dream. A nightmare, except he'd caught her...too soon, wasn't it? The events in her dream hadn't happened yet. If only she could wake up...

Unthinking, panicked words flew from her mouth. "Why marry me? Surely I'm not worthy of the great Mentàll."

"But your name is."

"My name?"

"Maahr." He watched her carefully. "You are a direct descendent from the Old Kaavl Master, Mahre."

"Yes." Little point in denying the truth. "So what? Why would that make you want to marry me?"

"I do not *want* to marry you," he snarled. "But I would, for that fact alone. Or you may choose death, if you prefer." Mentàll stepped away and pulled a long, sharp blade from a narrow leather pocket sewn into the thigh of his breeches. The metal glinted in the light, and she stared at it, transfixed. An illegal sword. Would he truly kill her?

Silly question.

"I am waiting." His voice and eyes were cold, and she gasped out the first words that flew to mind.

"Remember what the Prophet said to you?"

His eyes narrowed.

"He said, 'All who draw the sword will die by the sword.'"

"So, your spying goes deeper than I suspected."

"Aren't you worried?"

"I will not need to pull my sword. The work is done."

"You've pulled it on me now. If you draw blood, you will pay."

"Who will make me pay? Your Prophet? His God?"

"Everyone's God. Yours, too."

"The One abandoned me when I was five. He will not step in now." Fury flashed through those cold eyes. And pain. Methusal had seen feral pain too many times in wounded animals not to recognize it now. Instead of accepting help, the dangerous ones lashed out, ready to kill. What had happened to the Dehrien when he was such a small boy? What had turned him into the man he was today? A man with no love, and no mercy.

"Decide, Methusal! I have run out of patience."

She grasped for another straw. "Everyone will know you killed me!"

"No, Methusal. They will not." He knelt before her again and pressed the cool, smooth side of the blade against her neck. She could barely think. The only bizarre thing that ran through her mind was that Hendra was wrong. Her cousin was not worthy of her respect or trust. He wasn't the man she believed him to be. He was a monster.

Mentàll's voice lowered to a menacing whisper. "You do not give me enough credit. Of course your body will be found—torn to pieces by the wild beasts. A foolish girl wandered alone from camp. Look." He fingered the strap of her pack. "How fortunate you're already packed to go. And I'm not the only one who has seen you wearing this tonight."

She stared, stricken, into the Dehrien Chief's eyes. He had her. It was true. He could have her dead body carted into the low mountains, and the wild beasts would devour her by morning. No one would ever know that Mentàll had killed her.

But *would* he truly kill her? That illogical question surprisingly flitted through her mind.

Only Hendra's steadfast hero worship of her cousin allowed the tiny glimmer of doubt. That, and the fact that if he'd wanted her dead, surely she would be dead by now. He'd have killed her, like Renn's murderer wanted, rather than repeatedly threatening her. She stared into his eyes, trying to read the truth behind the frozen ice.

Unthinkingly, she whispered, "Would you truly kill me?"

Cold, assessing surprise flashed, and for a split second she saw something that made her wonder. But his expression swiftly hardened, concealing his true motivation. He drew still closer, and she struggled not to shrink away.

His voice sounded like hissing, popping ice. "You doubt me?"

Methusal didn't respond. She was scared to death.

"No? Wise of you." He tapped the blade against her neck. "What is your decision?"

Death? Or life—a living, tortuous hell? Somehow, the decision wasn't as easy as it should have been. A slow minute ticked by. She felt frozen, unable to move or think.

The Dehrien Chief grasped a heavy handful of her dark hair and pulled her face near his own. His pale eyes were narrowed, and teeth bared. "My patience is running out, Methusal. Live or die. Decide now, or I will decide for you. Much as I could desire you, I do not need an unwilling wife."

Methusal desperately moved her lips, but no sounds emerged.

The blade turned, edge imperceptibly stinging into her neck. It was razor sharp. One quick move and he could slit her throat. The blade pressed harder. Terror seized her.

"Live!" The word gasped out, and instantly the pressure on her neck eased.

"Good." He drew back, releasing her hair, and inserted the blade again into its almost invisible pocket. He gave her a thin smile, although he did not look particularly pleased. "I am glad we understand each other." His hard gaze impersonally ran down her body, making her shiver. "Obey my first order to you, as my wife to be. Disrobe and wait for me beneath that fur." She followed his gaze, through an archway to another room which contained a wide pallet, pushed flush against the far wall. "I will wait outside while you do that... As I *am* a gentleman, despite what you might think to the contrary."

Mentàll quickly untied her wrists and stepped toward the door. "You have two minutes. If you try to escape, you will die." His words were horrifyingly conversational. He closed the door behind him.

Shaking, Methusal leaped to her feet, and dashed for the large window at the back of the cabin. Locked! Her fingers fumbled with the lock, but it would not open. Was it rusted shut? She sprinted to a smaller window across the room. That one had no latch. Tears of frustration streamed down her cheeks, and she clenched her trembling hands together, trying to calm herself. Surely, there must be a way out.

She gulped back a heaving sob and flew to the back window again. It had to open! Violently, she rattled the unyielding lock. It did not budge.

Chapter Thirty-One

Hendra's eyes fluttered open. Cold air and total blackness enveloped her. In a flood, the memory of Ludst's attack returned. Panic slammed through her heart, making it race. But she was alone. He was gone.

Slowly, she sat up. She must have fainted. That had never happened before. Dirt crunched beneath her fingers and when she looked heavenward, stars spangled across the sky. A large structure loomed nearby. Pan's house?

Gathering those few bearings, she realized it was late now. All of the lights were out, except for the ones in Mentàll's cabin.

Quickly, she staggered to her feet and brushed the dirt and leaves from her clothes and hair.

Had her cousin already given his last orders to his men? Had her weak, hysterical fainting spell cost her the opportunity to discover his true goal?

Hendra ran toward her cousin's cabin and discovered that her right knee hurt. Maybe she'd fallen on a rock. It didn't matter. She had to find out what Mentàll was doing. Maybe he was still speaking to his men.

Hendra crept closer to the large cabin, but discovered that the front window had been shuttered. She'd spotted another window at the back, though. Trying to ignore the now sharp, stabbing pain in her knee, she hurried to the other window. It was high, because the house was built on a platform, but she was tall enough to see straight in and through to the very front of the house.

She gasped. Methusal sat in a chair with her wrists bound behind her back. Mentàll knelt before her with a sword pressed against her neck.

Mentàll suddenly stood, resheathed the sword, and smiled down at Methusal. It wasn't a nice smile. In fact, it made her blood run cold.

What fate had he chosen for the poor Rolbani girl?

Terror engulfed her. She wouldn't let him hurt Methusal. Even if it meant sacrificing her own life, she would not let him commit a despicable act that would irreparably damn his soul.

To stop him, though, she'd need reinforcements. She darted around the corner of the house, but before she'd gone a step, a hand seized her arm.

Hendra cried out, and the man clapped a hand across her mouth. "Shhh," he hissed in her ear. "It's Behran." He released her.

Heart pounding in panicked thumps, she spun to face him. The faint, rising green light of Ryon made his features clear. It *was* Behran. So why did she still feel so afraid? She *hated* feeling terrified every time a man touched her.

"What...what are you doing here?" she gasped.

"I'm spying, same as you are," he said dryly.

Hendra took a deep breath, trying to calm her jumping nerves. "I was just about to get you. Mentàll..."

"I know," Behran said grimly.

They both heard the sharp click of the front door closing.

"What's that?" Hendra whispered.

"I'll check." With quick stealth, Behran crept to the front corner of the house and peered around. A moment later he was back. "Mentàll's outside."

"Why?"

"I don't know. But now's our chance to rescue Thusa."

A rattle came from the back window, and they rushed to the back of the house. Methusal struggled with the lock, her eyes wide and terrified. She whipped a glance over her shoulder and banged on the window with her fists.

"Shhh!" Behran's sharp whisper cut through the night. Methusal froze, obviously listening.

"Look for the pin in the bottom ledge of the window," Behran hissed. "Pull it out, quick!"

Methusal snatched out the rounded knob that held the window locked shut. She shoved the window up.

"Hurry!" Hendra urged.

Methusal threw her pack onto the ground. Then Behran steadied Methusal as she wriggled out the window, and helped her safely jump the three quarter length drop to the ground.

Behran wrapped her in a tight hug. "Thank goodness," he murmured. "I saw Mentàll pulled a sword on you. Are you all right?"

"He...he ordered me to take off my clothes and wait..." Methusal's voice broke into a sob. "I was afraid. I was so afraid, Behran!"

Her words felt like punches to Hendra's heart. She felt like vomiting.

"Thusa!" Behran held her tighter.

Reluctantly, it seemed, Methusal pulled free. "We have to leave *now,* Behran. We have to warn Rolban. I know what he's planning."

"We'd better move fast, then. He'll hunt for you the minute he knows you're gone."

"I'll slow him down," Hendra blurted. "I'll take your place, Methusal." She trembled at the very thought of what she was offering. If Ludst had terrified her earlier, how much more petrifying would it be to face her cousin when he was furious beyond all reason? Not only that, but he would realize that she had betrayed him. He would cut her from his life and he'd banish her from Dehre forever, too; the punishment for treason. But none of those things was the reprisal she feared most.

"No!" Methusal exclaimed, visibly horrified. "What if he..." Her face looked pale in the faint green light of the rising moon, and remnants of terror lingered in her wide eyes.

"He won't hurt me." Hendra didn't know that for sure, but she had to do the right thing. She had waited far too long to take a stand.

"Hendra. Don't do it," Behran said softly. His fingers touched her shoulder, and she flinched. She hated it, but she couldn't help it. He noticed, because she saw his faint frown.

"I have to do the right thing," she told them both in a steady voice.

The other two silently stared back.

"Do you need help to climb inside?" Behran finally asked.

The window was at shoulder level. "I'll need a step."

Behran knelt down and linked his hands together. "Put your foot here."

"Thank you." It was surprisingly hard to take that step of trust and place her foot in the hands of a man. But nothing would stop her now. Hendra took that step, and Behran held her steady so she could hoist herself into the window and slither on through. When she turned to latch the window, the two Rolbanis were gone.

Heart beating hard with fear, Hendra surveyed the room. The lamps cast an orange glow on the huge, raised pallet beside her. Furs covered it. This is where Mentàll had asked Methusal to wait for him. So Hendra would wait in her place. First, though, she blew out the lamps so he wouldn't see her immediately. Another tactic to give Methusal and Behran more time to escape to Rolban.

Only the rising green light of Ryon bathed the room. Hendra lay silently and waited.

If she hadn't heard it with her own ears, she would never have believed Mentàll meant to violate Methusal. How could the man who had defended her honor so long ago have sunk to such depths? Had lust for power and his inexplicable hatred for Rolban ruined him? Had she ever known her cousin at all?

Would he harm her?

The old terror darkened her mind and sucked the oxygen from her lungs. But she would not faint again. She waited, unmoving, determined not to lose the little courage she had mustered. She would face her deepest fear.

The cabin's front door slammed shut and she heard Mentàll's quick footsteps. They weren't silent, which meant his perpetual kaavl concentration was off. He was angry. She sensed it the moment he entered the room.

He stared into the dark for a second, obviously disoriented. "Get dressed!" he snarled, striding closer. "I will not..." The words cut short.

Mentàll was only an arm's length away. Hendra stared up at him, terrified by his rage, and by the knowledge that he had just discovered her identity.

"Hendra!" His voice whipped, low and terrible. "What are you doing here?"

"What have you done?" she whispered.

Her cousin swore. "You have betrayed me!" He snatched his pack off of a nearby chair and spun to leave.

"Stop," she cried out. "Don't do it!"

"I *must!* You are a fool, Hendra!"

"It's wrong to murder innocent people! Now Rolban will know you're coming."

"*Be silent Hendra, or I won't be able to answer for my actions!*"

"Don't. Please don't do it, Mentàll!" Her voice broke. Had she been wrong? Was he no longer the man she had known her whole life?

But he left, slamming the door behind him.

△ △ △ △ △

Behran grasped Methusal's hand and propelled her at a dead run out of the Tarst village.

The two ran down the hill to the Tarst River bridge. There they wasted precious time opening and shutting the gate to get to the other side. Then they ran on, tripping and stumbling through the forest, over rocks, and up into the mountains. Methusal's lungs were burning when they finally slowed and dropped down behind the first ridge.

"Here's a stream. We'd better drink our fill, because we won't find more until we reach Rolban." Behran knelt by a glimmering, inky pool. "Hurry. Mentàll will have a search party out in no time—if not already."

Methusal knelt beside him. From deep in the forest came a sudden, eerie howl. It shivered down her spine.

She glanced at the dark horizon. Wild beasts. They were out now, prowling the low lands. She tried to shake off her unease. They hated high altitudes; partly because of the thick trees, and also because of the vicious rotarhudges. And those beasts should be sleeping now. Surely she and Behran were safe, high up here in the mountains.

She cupped her hands and slurped up handfuls of cold, sweet water.

"Let's go." Behran's low voice was urgent, and Methusal quickly followed him downhill, slipping and sliding down the pebbled slope. The going was hard, and it was impossible to be quiet. If Mentàll was close, he would have no trouble tracking them.

The moon dipped behind a cloud, and in the sudden darkness she slipped and clutched at Behran's shoulder to break her fall.

"Careful." His strong hands steadied her. Their pace slowed until the sliver of a moon broke free again and illuminated the landscape. The two continued their bouncing jog downward.

They silently concentrated on putting as much distance as possible between themselves and Tarst. Gradually Methusal found herself relaxing into kaavl, and she listened for any sign of pursuit. But the night was still and silent. She knew better than to lower her guard, though. Mentàll would follow them. Too much was at stake. He couldn't allow them to escape and warn Rolban.

Guided by the position of the moon, the two continued their steady trek south, through mountainous hills and valleys. As the hours passed, Methusal's legs grew shaky and fatigued from exertion and lack of sleep. The howl of the beasts grew louder as they trekked closer to the lowlands.

When she felt she couldn't continue further without rest, Behran unexpectedly stopped and motioned for silence. They stood at the edge of a jagged, sloping cliff. At last, far below them stretched the plains. On the far horizon, an inky blot hinted at the familiar Rolban Mountains.

Behran scrambled down several lengths and sidled onto a narrow ledge which hugged the cliff face. "We'll have to wait here until day breaks."

Following, Methusal thankfully sank down beside him. But she didn't relax until her straining ears failed to pick up any sounds—either behind them, or on the plains below. Neither Mentàll nor the wild beasts were close by at the moment. They would be safe on the ledge. The wild beasts couldn't climb up here. And at dawn the animals would slink back into their caves.

"Hungry?" Behran offered a piece of dried meat he had pulled from his pocket.

"Thanks." Chewing quietly, she glanced at his shadowed figure. "How did you and Hendra know I was in trouble?"

"I don't know about Hendra. When I ran into her, it looked like she was spying on her cousin. But I heard you talking to Kitran and Mentàll about the second treaty. When he ordered you to his cabin and you didn't put up a fight, it made me worry. So I went and listened at one of his windows."

"So you heard...?"

"Everything." His voice was grim. "I was going to get you out, one way or another. I wouldn't let him...take advantage of you." This last was said through clenched teeth.

"Thank you." Tears prickled.

Several quiet moments passed, and then Behran said, "What is Mentàll planning? What is the second treaty about?"

"I overheard Pan and Mentàll talking about a new treaty. It could be enforced because of one of the clauses in the Alliance." Quickly, she explained how Kitran and Petr seemed to be in favor of a new agreement requiring Rolban to accept Mentàll's kaavl instruction for three weeks. And how Petr had sent Pan a letter which basically said he wanted Pan to sign the second treaty. She also explained that after Pan had signed the treaty Mentàll told one of his men, "Rolban is mine."

"His?" Behran said sharply. "Why would Pan give Mentàll complete power over Rolban?"

"He didn't. At least, I don't think he did. He agreed that Rolban should submit to Mentàll's kaavl counsel for three weeks."

"Again, how does that make Rolban Mentàll's?"

"I think he plans to take over Rolban. Permanently." Which would mean killing every last Rolbani, because no one would allow a Dehrien to rule their community.

A long silence elapsed. "How?" Behran sounded grim.

"I don't know. But I do know he has a sword. We have to warn everyone before Mentàll gets there."

"The Dehrien delegation is already there. Maybe Mentàll plans to use them to help defeat Rolban."

That frightening idea made sense. In fact, it reminded her of her previous suspicions about the merchant delegation. What if every man on that delegation was hiding an illegal sword in his clothing, just like Mentàll was?

"But why take over Rolban?" Methusal wondered. "They have their own community."

"Simple," Behran said. "Dehre doesn't have much—they're always fighting the wild beasts and never have enough grain. The drought has made everything ten times worse. Hendra is worried about the orphans starving to death."

"That's awful."

"Mentàll probably told the delegation that living in Rolban would solve all of their problems. Of course, he convinced them Rolbanis are despicable, and deserve to be thrown out of their home."

"And they'd believe that?"

"Wouldn't you, if you lived like they do? Things weren't that bad, even when I lived there."

Everything made sense now. Her father had been right. Petr should have negotiated for a better Alliance, but his ego had tripped him up. He'd been too desperate to chalk up a diplomatic victory before the elections. Worse, he had been willing to forge an illegal treaty with the Dehrien Chief so he could potentially gain even more power. Now Rolban was trapped. Legally and morally, it was bound to uphold both agreements, unless proof of deceit was delivered in time to justify a preemptive, defensive attack.

Behran seemed to be thinking along the same lines. "We have to warn them," he said harshly. "We have to do everything we can to stop the massacre."

"I know." But she didn't verbalize her deepest fear—what if they were too late? What if the delegation had already taken over Rolban?

"How did you hear Pan and Mentàll's conversation, anyway?"

Methusal froze. She felt Behran's eyes bore into her...or maybe that was just her imagination.

"Well," she hesitated, in order to collect her thoughts. Did she trust Behran enough to confess the truth? Would it mean losing her advantage over him in future competitions? *If* she competed again.

Behran gazed now at the green-tinged, shadowed plains below. Emotionally, Methusal felt like she was teetering on the brink of something big. Should she take that leap of faith and trust her most guarded secrets to her fiercest competitor?

Her hands felt suddenly clammy, and she wrung her fingers together. Yes. Yes, she should. Taking a deep breath, she emotionally stepped off that cliff. She blurted, "I can hear things sometimes... All the time, I guess."

"What do you mean?" His intent gaze rested upon her.

"I can hear far away conversations, if I concentrate."

He sat very still, listening.

She paused. "Remember the legends of Mahre? How he could hear sounds an hour away by foot? I can do that, too, but to a smaller degree. I'm not sure how I do it. I just concentrate, and it's *there*."

"You mean you can eavesdrop on conversations wherever you want?"

"I don't! Well, rarely. Only when necessary."

"So you use your hearing ability like Mahre did."

"Right. I listen to animal noises...leaves falling... Things like that, so I can practice pinpointing their origin."

"Wow!" He gave a low whistle. "No wonder you're so good at the games. Does anyone else know?"

"No. I didn't want to give away my advantage."

"It wouldn't have helped if I'd known."

"Anyway," self-consciously, Methusal returned to the subject at hand, "lately—the last couple of nights—conversations on the other side of town have woken me up. I wasn't even concentrating—I was asleep, for goodness' sake.

When I woke up, I still heard the voices if I relaxed. It's happened three times now, and Mentàll was speaking every time."

"What did you hear?" Behran sounded a bit awed.

"That first night was in Dehre, and Mentàll, Verdnt, and Kitran were talking. I didn't understand what they were talking about then. But it all makes sense, now that I know about the new treaty. Kitran was telling Mentàll that Petr was in favor of it."

Behran whistled again. "So Kitran and Petr have been selling out Rolban?"

"No," she countered, "I don't think so—not exactly, anyway. Remember, they were agreeing to receive three weeks of Mentàll's counsel—no more."

"But why? Why would Petr want to receive lectures from Mentàll about how to put kaavl into leadership? He knows the elders are against it, and if they found out he was for Mentàll's treaty, his chance of being reelected Chief would be wiped out. The elders would censor him, and no one would vote for him. Why would he risk it?"

The same question had been bothering Methusal, too. Petr desperately wanted to be reelected. He'd only agree to Mentàll's plan if he was certain it would help him.

A glimmer of understanding hit. She spoke slowly, trying to form her nebulous thoughts into words. "Petr wants to be reelected, right? And I'm sure Mentàll knows that. What better way to be reelected than if Petr can prove he's the best leader in Rolban? Mentàll must have convinced him that kaavl would make him that leader."

"But how?"

"Remember, Petr and the others practically worship Mentàll. And kaavl has made *him* great, supposedly. He promised to show Petr how this works—*if* he could get the second treaty signed.

"So Petr must have liked the idea of the new treaty. No one would actually *know* he was in favor of it, if everything turned sour. He didn't sign anything, except for the letter to Pan, which I'm sure is supposed to remain a secret. So he's protected either way—if it doesn't work out, it's not his fault, and if it does, he gets reelected, because everyone will see how kaavl has transformed him into an outstanding leader. Maybe Petr hopes the elders can be convinced that only kaavl players should be Chief. I'm sure Mentàll painted it as a win win situation to Petr."

"What about Verdnt? He's a kaavl contender, too."

"I know, but Petr beat him in the games. Petr would point out that the best kaavl contender will make the best leader. Since only Kitran is above him, and he isn't interested in politics, that leaves only Petr to be Chief. Simple."

"So Mentàll was manipulating him," Behran concluded. "Petr would welcome Mentàll and his hordes with open arms.

"He's already welcomed them." Heavy foreboding again settled in Methusal's spirit. "I heard one other conversation, too." She told him about Mentàll's conversation with the man she believed was the murdering thief. "I don't know who it was. Kitran, or Verdnt, or another Rolbani that snuck into Dehre without being seen. Maybe a messenger. I don't know."

"We'll probably find out soon enough," Behran said grimly. "You should have told me this a lot sooner, Thusa."

"I know. I'm sorry."

They both fell silent as Ryon rose higher overhead.

"It should be light soon," Behran said. "Unless I miss my guess, Mentàll will track us down then, on the plains."

"Probably. He knows we'll have to wait until dawn to cross it." She hugged her knees to her chest and tried to block out a new, growing sense of urgency that urged her to throw caution to the winds and race home now. "Mentàll was armed."

"I know. I saw the sword, but where did he get it?"

"I don't know. But it was hidden in a thin pocket on the thigh of his breeches. I didn't even know it was there until he threatened me with it." She touched her neck gingerly, remembering the sharp pressure against it. Her neck stung. "Looks like Dehre didn't melt down all of their weapons like the Great War Peace Agreement ordered."

"But they did," Behran countered. "Remember? I lived there. The only metal objects we had were kitchen utensils or hunting knives. And those were vital. They wouldn't melt those down for swords."

"But it wasn't a hunting knife he pulled on me. If they didn't melt down their tools, then where did Mentàll get the metal for his knife?"

The answer became clear to both of them at the same time. "The metal stolen from Rolban!" Methusal also remembered her heavy ore tablet necklace. It had probably been stolen, too, and accidentally left in the ore mine. Somehow Renn had found it, which had put his life in danger.

Then why did Rolban's two missing pots end up in Tarst? Both were made from ore. It was the one link that made no sense.

"There's a traitor in Rolban," Behran said softly. "Renn must have found something incriminating. The thief had to stop Renn from reporting it, because that would have jeopardized his bigger mission."

"To arm Dehre, so they could take over Rolban." But she wondered about the stolen grain and pelts. Were they only diversions, so no one would suspect that ore was the primary target? Were the pots left in Tarst as a diversionary tactic, too—to point blame away from Dehre?

"The delegation is probably armed." Behran's voice was grim. "It might be tough to get them out of Rolban before Mentàll arrives."

What if they had already started their attack? But wouldn't they wait for their leader? Urgency to hurry home overfilled Methusal. She scanned the eastern horizon. Surely the sun would rise soon.

Worrying had side-tracked her mind from kaavl, and she knew, by the jerk of his shoulders, that Behran heard the rock tumbling down the cliff the same instant she did.

He hissed, "What's that?"

Methusal concentrated and listened for the slightest sound. Footsteps scuffed above them. Six systems of movement rustled close by, and lighter, softer footsteps were further away. Seven.

There were seven in the Dehrien kaavl team. That included Hendra. But wasn't Hendra on their side now?

A softly spoken word reached Methusal's ears.

"...here?"

"Yes. At first light we will have a clear view as they cross. We will catch them then."

Mentàll's voice caused a shiver to ripple down her spine. He was a cruel, dangerous, cunning man. Could she and Behran outwit him?

"Dehriens," she whispered. "They'll track us at first light."

"We'd better start now, then, before they can see us."

"What about the wild beasts?"

"Our lives won't be worth more if Mentàll catches us."

Methusal shivered, but knew he was right. Their luck had run out. This time Mentàll wouldn't hesitate kill her, if he caught her. In that light, the decision to run now didn't seem so foolhardy.

"How do we get down?" she breathed.

"Follow me." Behran swiftly rose to his feet. He must have been mapping out a plan of escape while they had waited on the ledge, for he moved with confidence. Trustingly, she followed, forcing herself to relax and concentrate fully. It was a long way down. One foot slip, and she'd be dead.

The ledge narrowed to a handbreadth just when the moon swam behind another thick cloud. Methusal halted and pressed herself against the hard, angular rocks jutting from the cliff. Her heart bumped hard and she closed her eyes, refusing to look down—not that she could see much in the dark, anyway. To her right, Behran's breaths sounded calm and even.

As soon as the moon peeked out again, they continued. The ledge tapered to nothingness, and Behran carefully led the climb down the craggy bluff. Thankfully, hand and foot-holds were plentiful. Only once did Methusal lose her footing and hang, swinging by her fingertips. A stifled scream tore from her lips.

"Move your right foot to the left." Behran's voice came, calm and reassuring. "Now up a bit. There, you've got it."

Methusal's heart pounded so wildly that she felt like it might explode from her chest.

Left foot now secure as well, she took time to wipe her damp palms, one by one, against her tunic. Then she continued her descent, trying to ignore the tremors rippling through her. She had almost fallen to her death.

Right hand...left hand...right foot...left foot...right hand...

"You're almost down." Encouraging words, and then Behran's strong hands lifted her down the remaining drop.

Boulders lay jumbled before them now and gently sloped downward to the plain floor. Behran led the way, scrambling over the smaller rocks and around the larger ones. Methusal intensified her kaavl and stepped carefully after him. She couldn't allow anymore slips in foot or concentration—a twisted ankle now would mean certain death. She sent an apprehensive glance at the eastern horizon. A faint yellow glow backlit the eastern Rolban Mountains where it curved north to meet the Tarst Range.

No sound of pursuit—or wild beasts—so far. Her feet touched the dry, cracked surface of the plain. If they hurried, they could reach Rolban in a little over an hour.

She walked more rapidly to match Behran's long strides. The waning moon bathed the tagma bushes in cool green light. A small beast skittered under the bushes ahead. The plain was still, as if the wind held its breath, watching and waiting to see what fate would befall them. The sun slowly rose, lightening the sky with pale, rosy gold and pink fingers.

It seemed too quiet. Too still. Methusal's flesh crept, but her straining ears heard nothing. Only the faint hiss of a breeze to the west, softly rustling the dry leaves...

Instinct made her catch at Behran's sleeve, catapulting them both into a frantic, foot pounding sprint. Those weren't leaves. The scratch of claws flying over the earth filled her ears. She willed her legs to work harder to keep up with Behran. The hot, snarling breath of the beasts seemed to reach out and envelop her very soul.

CHAPTER THIRTY-TWO

Sixthday

FEET BARELY TOUCHING the ground, Behran and Methusal flew desperately over its hard surface. The sky was now lightening rapidly, pushing the night shadows from the land. It was a race against time. The beasts' sensitive eyes could not bear the bright sunlight. Soon they would have to give up the chase. But when? When would they give up the hunt?

Methusal gasped, and slowed slightly when a stitch seized her side. The scratch of tens of razor sharp claws ripped over the earth. *They were almost upon her....*

Terror urged a burst of speed from her flying legs, and her mind rapidly assimilated the terrain before her. A stumble now would mean an agonizing death, ripped to shreds by the long, sharp fangs of the wild beasts.

"They're gone." Ahead of her, Behran slowed, panting. A quick glance over her shoulder revealed the furry backs of the beasts as they fled for the gloomy protection of their rocky caves. A few howled, as if in pain.

Her steps slowed to a fast walk and she doubled over, gasping. Pain, like a hot fire stick, seared into her side.

"You okay?"

She nodded, unable to speak. Her well-conditioned lungs wheezed, not used to sprinting all out so far, or for so long. Finally, with a wince she straightened. "I thought...I thought we weren't going to make it." Her back prickled. The threat of goring, shredding claws still felt like an itch down her spine.

Behran unexpectedly caught her hand and gently squeezed it. "But we did." His gaze held hers for a steady, reassuring moment. Reluctantly, it seemed, he released her hand.

A little of the fear melted away. Unexplained happiness warmed Methusal's soul.

They were almost home now. Only a half an hour remained.

Moments later Behran asked, "Do you hear anything?"

Methusal listened. The relief of escaping from the wild beasts had almost made her forget about Mentàll.

Nothing.

They were still too far away to hear without using her kaavl gift of carrying. She first directed her attention back to the rocky cliff, and then practiced a carry by placing the center focal point of her hearing on that spot. It was as if she actually she stood on the rocky cliff and heard everything just as clearly as if she stood there right at this moment.

Ahh, there they were. They'd just jumped down from the final boulder onto the plain. Moccasins scratched over the soil. They were running. Soon they would be within Methusal's normal range.

"They're coming fast. Six of them," she reported, and the two sprang back into a hard sprint. But pain again seared Methusal's side. Gasping, she jogged to a halt. Behran checked his pace.

"Go on," she urged. "I'll trick them off course. Then I'll make a run for it when this pain lets up."

"No. I won't leave you alone."

"Rolban has to be warned. That's the most important thing right now. I'll be okay. Promise."

"Mentàll is Kaavl Master! No, I won't..."

"Hurry!" She shoved him as the sounds of their pursuers filled her ears. "We're out of time!"

Behran gave her one last agonized look, and then took off at a dead run, leaving her quickly behind. Limping in his footsteps, Methusal hastily formed a plan. A game, actually. A kaavl game—except she competed against six Dehrien opponents, one of whom was Kaavl Master. No time to capture. Only evade.

Walking as fast as she could, Methusal cut west, deliberately leaving a faint trail behind her. Next, she cut north for a time, and then south and west again. Faint, scuffling noises tickled her sensitive ears.

Mentàll's contemptuous voice said, "They're running scared. You two go north and east, you two west. You'll go south with me. Regardless, we'll meet at the Rolbani gate in fifteen minutes. Is that clear?"

It was clear to Methusal that only Mentàll and one Dehrien were tracking her now.

She lunged into a sprint for Rolban, but pain seared her abdomen again. She gasped, frustrated. She had to continue to escape capture for a few more minutes.

Deliberately, she left a faint trail in the hard ground beneath her moccasins. A tagma root lay exposed several lengths ahead. She quickly scooped up a handful of loose stones and leaped lightly and with perfect balance onto the narrow, gnarled root. Carefully thrown rocks stirred the dust, continuing her old path. Hopefully it would mislead the Dehriens.

Toes clutching the wood through the new, soft moccasins, Methusal ran to the other end of the exposed root and hopped onto another one. No foot marks betrayed five lengths of her path now. She leaped onto a flat rock, and then onto a smaller, rounded one. There her options ran out, and she set off again for Rolban, her feet flying over the dusty earth. The pain in her side had eased. Only another minute of rest and she should be able to sprint for home.

Her ears strained to hear her foes. One followed her latest diversion, but the other Dehrien was hot on her trail. Probably Mentàll. He was chasing her, just like in her dream. Was her dream a prophecy? Had it predicted what was happening now?

But hadn't the Prophet said it applied to a future time?

It soon became clear he wasn't fooled by her feeble diversionary tactics. Within a minute, Mentàll would reach her. Panic churned in Methusal's heart, but she forced herself to remain calm.

Another tagma root poked up, stretching south and left, but this time she ignored it. Several small stones formed a path to a tall, bushy tagma plant two lengths to the right. If she jumped from stone to stone, careful not to let them skid, she could make it.

Feet moving as swift as thought, Methusal put the plan into action and hopped, landing on the pads of her toes. So far so good....

Mentàll was almost upon her.

She ducked behind the prickly, leafy bush at the last possible second and crouched, her breaths silent, as Mentàll jogged into view.

He stopped, barely a length from her bush, and carefully glanced about. First at the tagma root, and then at the stones beneath his feet. He stood very still, as if listening.

Frozen, hardly daring to breathe, Methusal waited, formulating a plan of escape. Then she heard the faint slither of a whip beast come from the direction of the root. Mentàll heard it too, for his blond head quickly swiveled that way. He took one hesitant step that way, and then another. Quickening his stride, the Dehrien trotted after the false lead.

Methusal leaped to her feet and sprinted for Rolban. The pain was gone now. If she was lucky, she had a few seconds before Mentàll realized his mistake.

Her mountain home drew closer and closer, but she still had to round the southern end, because the gate to the community faced south. That was when she would be most vulnerable, because there was little vegetation to use for cover at the base of the mountain.

Rounding the corner, she heard two systems of movement sprinting up behind her. One minute until they caught her. The memory of Mentàll's razor sharp knife urged her tired legs to pump faster. She could see the wide open gate now. Only a few more seconds...

Something caught at her arm and jerked her violently sideways, and then down to her knees. Quicker than thought, someone dragged her behind a huge boulder. A firm hand pressed against her mouth, cutting off her frightened cry. "Sshhhh!" Methusal struggled to see her captor.

Behran! He held a finger to his lips and cautiously peered around the side of the boulder. He sprang to his feet. "Come on!"

Confused, Methusal staggered after him up a narrow path that twisted up the southern side of the steep mountain. The path was hidden by massive boulders. Crouching low, she sprinted from boulder to boulder.

Near the top he ducked into a shallow cave. She blinked to adjust to the gloomy shadows.

"Thusa!" A little body hurtled forward and hugged her fiercely. "I thought Mentàll was going to get you!" Aali's face was dirty and tear streaked. When her cousin pulled back she clutched Behran's hand, as if afraid to let it go.

"What's going on?" Fear made Methusal's words sharp.

"It's awful!" More tears streaked her cheeks.

"What is?"

"If only I hadn't gone sneaking, like Father said!" She choked on a tremendous sob. Terror gripped Methusal. Something was terribly wrong.

"Come sit down." Behran took charge, and gently led Aali to the back of the cave, where the three squatted. "The delegation took Rolban hostage late last night." His voice was quiet.

"*What?* But why didn't they wait for Ment..."

"It's all my fault!" Aali wept. "Father told me to stay in my room and I wouldn't. I didn't trust those merchant people. So when Father fell asleep, I snuck down the hall to the guest chambers and listened outside one of the doors. I thought for sure it was probably too late and they were sleeping. But they weren't. And I didn't think..." More sobs, and a wet sniffle. "I didn't think I'd hear something *incriminating!*"

"What did you hear?" Methusal fought to keep her voice as calm and level as Behran's.

"A loud voice—it sounded familiar, but I don't know who it was, because other people were talking at the same time. Anyway, he *insisted* they should take over Rolban right now. Now was the time, he said, while everyone was sleeping. He said Mentàll would be glad, because then he wouldn't have to do the messy work. The man said he hated us Rolbanis. That we were horrid and prideful and deserved to be put in our place."

More gulps. "Then another voice argued that they *had* to wait, because those were Mentàll's instructions, and they'd be foolish to cross him. He said Mentàll wanted a peaceful, legal takeover. Then a mean looking, dark-haired man threw open the door and saw me!" With a heavy, shaky breath she whispered, "I think it was Jascr. He won the Bi-level in Dehre."

"Then what?"

"He grabbed me and put his hands over my eyes and mouth and dragged me into the room. He wanted to kill me, but the others wouldn't let him. He said the first man was right. They *had* to take over Rolban right now. Because if I went missing or told anyone, their whole plan would be ripped. The others agreed. So they tied me up, threw me in a closet, and jammed it shut. I heard their plan. They said they'd go from compartment to compartment and break in and tie up the Rolbanis. It would be easy while everyone was sleeping."

"And we don't have locks to keep anyone out," Methusal interjected grimly.

"Yes, they said they'd capture every single Rolbani, or kill us, if necessary." Tears streamed down her cheeks. "Then they rampaged out."

"So they took over Rolban while you were in the closet?" Methusal blinked rapidly, trying to hold back horrified, welling tears. What had happened to her parents and her sister?

"I finally got out, but it was too late. They had a bunch of people corralled in the dining hall at knife point—actually most had *swords*. The Rolbanis were gagged and their hands were tied, but their feet were tied loose enough so they could shuffle a little. I knew a secret passageway outside, so I snuck out and hid outside all night. Luckily, I stopped Behran before he ran in and got captured."

"Mentàll!" Methusal suddenly turned to Behran. "Do you think he'll find us up here?"

"Listen."

And she would have remembered that, too, if she had been thinking clearly. But Methusal heard no footsteps climbing up the mountain. "Nothing," she reported. "So he must be inside already."

"Probably," Behran agreed. "But he'll search for us soon, so we'd better come up with some ideas, and fast."

"A plan!" Aali looked up. Her eyes brightened through the tears. "Can we rescue Rolban?"

"We have to try," he said grimly. "We're the only ones left."

"Except for Kitran, Lina, and Retra."

"It'll be a while before they get here. Have they captured everyone?"

"I don't think so. I've heard fighting."

"So hopefully it's still chaos inside. We need to move now."

"What can we do?" How could they possibly rescue Rolban from twenty warriors, plus Mentàll, plus five kaavl competitors—a total of twenty-six Dehriens to their three? Of course, hopefully some Rolbanis were still free, but how many?

"We need to free the people in the dining hall," Behran said.

"But how would we get by the Dehriens and untie them?"

"I don't know. Maybe a few are free. We have to try. That would help even out the odds. Then we can hunt down the other Dehriens in the halls, one by one."

Methusal turned to Aalicaa. "You said you know a secret passageway to get in. Where does it come out inside? Is it anywhere near the dining hall?"

"Yes. Just down the teaching hallway a bit—it comes out in the first classroom. It's hidden in a closet behind a loose board."

"Here's an idea," Behran said. "We'll go hide in Aali's passageway now. It's not safe here. Mentàll's sure to send out a search party for us soon. While we're inside you can listen, Thusa, and tell us what's going on in Rolban. We'll take it from there."

Aali sprang to her feet. "We'll need weapons, Behran. The Dehriens have long, wicked looking, skinny knives."

"That they hide in their breeches," Methusal finished grimly. But Aali paid no attention to her comment, and scrabbled about outside, gathering up fistfuls of rocks.

"We can use these!" she shrilled.

"That's probably the best we can do," Behran agreed. The three scooped up what they could, and tucked them into their pockets, tunics, and in Methusal's pack, and then Aalicaa led them outside and up a short distance to the sheer face of a cliff. A length overhead, balanced on a narrow stone ledge, was a tall, flat rock. The top edge of the tilted rock rested against the cliff.

"It's behind that rock. Be careful going up, 'cause there aren't many holds," Aali explained, stepping nimbly ahead of them.

The other two watched her climb first, and then carefully followed. The fingerbreadth holds were almost invisible to the eye. Methusal followed first, and clung desperately to the smooth, rocky bits, determined not to slip like she had on the Tarst Range.

Quickly, so she couldn't dwell on her fear, and before her hands became slick with nervous perspiration, she stepped up once, twice, and pulled herself onto the ledge and behind the tilted rock. The rock concealed a small black opening in the cliff. Gingerly, she patted her hand inside it. Satisfied it didn't drop off immediately inside, she crawled in.

Behran followed. The pitch black tunnel spiraled downward. Their hands and knees quietly scuffed along on the gritty floor. Methusal had to keep her head down and level with her shoulders in order to keep it from scraping against the top of the passage. The tunnel smelled of dry, dusty earth and crumbling rocks, and her nose itched, wanting to sneeze.

"Sshhh! We're almost there." Aali's hissed warning was unnecessary, because they'd remained as silent as death for the entire trip. "It widens out here, so we can sit."

Thankfully, Methusal crawled up and sat beside her cousin. The low ceiling brushed her scalp, so she kept her head bent, but she was glad to rest her aching knees.

"Can you listen from here, Thusa?" Behran whispered.

"I could. But it would be easier if I had an idea where to focus my hearing. I think I'd like to go to the school room and then listen from there."

After a short rest, she went on all fours again and carefully crawled down the dark, remaining stretch of passageway. The tunnel grew steadily narrower and lower, until finally she scooted along on her elbows, dragging her body behind. A turn, and she saw a faint sliver of light ahead.

She inched forward until she felt the rough back of the loose board. Her fingers slid over a knob, and she pushed the board out a bit so she could see out. It was her own classroom. Just a few days ago Verdnt had taught their class in this very room.

A sudden lump filled her throat. If only! She'd give anything to be sitting in there again, bored. She blinked. Now wasn't the time for tears.

She listened intently. The classroom was empty, which was a piece of good luck. The dining room would be the source for her first carry.

An uproar of some sort was going on. People were shouting, and crashes...

"Six of us have escaped!" Petr Storst roared. "You can't keep us locked up in here!"

"I suggest you calm down. Or would you prefer I order each of you killed, one by one?" It was Mentàll's voice, and it sounded as cool and cutting as the knife he carried. "You are right, Petr. A few have escaped, but you have not. It is in your best interest to do what I say. You would not want your lovely daughter Deccia to be killed first, would you?"

A horrible, sickening silence followed that question. Deccia! Chilled, Methusal held her breath.

"I thought not. Keep calm, and I will keep your daughter safe while we hunt down the escaped prisoners." A short pause elapsed. "Don't like that?" Mentàll snarled, "*Get* to like it."

"You betrayed our trust!" Petr bellowed. "The Alliance was a sham!"

"Do you intend to cover your own sins, Petr?"

Petr roared, "You are a whip and a liar!"

"Tell your people the truth. Did you not send me a letter, asking me to come to here? You asked me to take temporary control of Rolban, didn't you?"

Rolbanis gasped.

With a satisfied twist in his harsh voice, Mentàll continued. "Yes. You wanted me to show you and Rolban how kaavl, applied practically, can create the best leaders. And the best Chiefs. Tell the truth. What was your purpose in sending your authorization letter to me? You want power in Rolban. Forever. Thank you for the payment of grain, by the way."

Methusal gasped. *Petr* had given the seed grain to Mentàll?

"*No,*" Petr shouted. "You tricked me! You tricked us all! Why create an Alliance, if you meant to make war on us?"

"It was a tool." Hard triumph edged the Dehrien Chief's voice. "A way to take over Rolban peaceably, which was my goal from the beginning. Your authorization letter, combined with the new treaty, made it happen. A civilized victory by the pen, rather than the sword. Unfortunately, that was not to be, since your Rolbani traitor started a war before I arrived. But I own Rolban now, and that is all that matters." He gave a short laugh. "You should have listened to the honorable Erl Maahr, Petr. But your pride and lust for power won. They are qualities I knew I could count upon."

"Why you..."

Methusal could barely wrap her mind around what she had just heard. It confirmed some theories she had already formulated. Petr had actually agreed to give Mentàll power in Rolban for three weeks. And he'd given Mentàll grain as advance payment for his kaavl instruction, too! And then Pan had signed the second treaty, allowing Mentàll's plan to roll into action. It was all very hard to believe. Mentàll must be a whip charmer to finagle that sort of blind trust and cooperation.

"You!" Mentàll barked. "Watch the girl. Everyone else, keep the prisoners separated."

Methusal had no idea how many Dehriens were guarding the dining room. Or how many were hunting down the escaped prisoners.

She fanned out her hearing again, and located the pockets of disturbance in the community. Most seemed centered in the living areas and around the supply room. A few people ran up the stairway to the plateau above...and several more fought it out in the Great Hall.

Since there wasn't room to turn around in the tunnel, Methusal slithered backwards. The rough stone floor caught at her tunic and scratched her stomach.

"Thusa!" Her foot had run into Behran's leg. "What did you hear?"

Grateful to be able to sit up again, she quickly relayed the news.

The other two were silent for a moment.

Aali's voice trembled. "Father betrayed us?"

"It's not so clear cut. He didn't know Mentàll planned to take over Rolban permanently." That was the best Methusal could say for her close-minded, selfish uncle. His lust for power had blinded him.

"We can sort that out later," Behran said grimly. "Mentàll is the true enemy. And so is the traitor who started the war today."

"That same traitor killed Renn and Liem." Again, Methusal wondered which Rolbani had turned against his own community.

"Right now we need to focus on freeing Rolban. At least six of the others are free. We'll need to move fast, while they're still creating a diversion."

"What can we do, Behran?" Aali whispered eagerly.

"Distract the Dehriens in the dining hall. Maybe a few more Rolbanis can escape. And we need to capture or incapacitate as many Dehriens as we can."

"I wish we had weapons!" Methusal whispered fiercely.

"We could throw rocks at them," Aali supplied helpfully. "Maybe we can knock out a few. Or we can throw rocks and run away, so they'd chase us. If a few Dehrien guards leave, then the people in the dining hall might have a chance of escaping."

"But..."

"Wait!" Methusal said. "I have an idea. One of us can climb to the plateau and throw rocks down through the portals in the dining room ceiling. That ought to distract the Dehriens. In the meantime, the other two could create a diversion in the hall with our rocks. That should confuse them enough so that the people inside can take the offensive."

"They're tied up," Behran pointed out.

"Well, they could try to do something. They've surely been thinking about how to escape all night."

"Okay. Dangerous, but definitely worth a try."

It had a chance—a slim one—of working. One chance was better than none.

"Maybe Aali should stay here," Methusal worried. "It's too risky."

"No. I have to help, Thusa!" Aali's passionate plea ended with a half gulp, half sob. "I have to help. It's all my fault! I have to do something."

"Whether we like it or not, we need her help," Behran said. "We'll give her the safest job, and I'm guessing that'll be on the plateau. Did you hear what's happening up there, Thusa?"

"Yes. Not much. If she's careful, she can probably get into position without being seen."

"I know a path up. It'll be safe. And there are a bunch of rocks up there. I won't need to bring any with me. Take mine, Thusa."

"Good. Listen. Count to one hundred, slow from my mark, and get into position on the plateau. At one hundred, start tossing down rocks. Count like this: one one thousand, two one thousand, three...got it?"

"Yes," Aali's voice was tense, but keen. "It won't take a long time to get up there, if that's what you're waiting on."

"No. We need time to get into position, too."

"Good luck, Aali."

"Mark from now."

Aalicaa scrabbled back down the passageway, toward the outside entrance.

Fear pinched Methusal. They were actually going to pit their wits against Dehrien swords. The odds seemed overwhelmingly stacked against them.

"Thusa." Behran's gaze held hers. "When we throw our rocks, Dehriens will probably chase us. If they do, we'll split up and steer them away from the dining hall. From then on, we're on our own. We'll try to capture as many Dehriens as we can." Killing was out of the question, since they had no weapons.

He sounded so calm and brave. Methusal swallowed, and tried to quell her prickles of fear.

"Are you ready?" A strong hand reached out of the darkness and gripped her arm. "We can do it."

"I know." Her voice sounded more positive than she felt. She was sorry when his comforting hand let go, leaving her alone.

"Let's go, then. Count to eighty, from now."

Methusal led the way, first crawling, and then slithering down the passage. Already her palms felt scraped raw from the sandy, gritty floor. Finally, the opening loomed ahead. She peered out.

"It's safe."

It was now or never. No more time for fear. She wiggled into the silent, dimly lit classroom. A lone lamp flickered against the far wall, near the door. She took a few rocks from her pack and shared them with Behran, and then tiptoed toward the exit, hugging the wall in order to stay clear of the desks in the center of the room. She paused at the door and listened.

A scuffle sounded to the right, around a bend in the hall, but it came from the opposite direction from the dining hall. They wouldn't be seen.

"Clear." Her whisper was a mere breath, and the two turned simultaneously into the hall.

CHAPTER THIRTY-THREE

ALL CLEAR for the moment. Behran and Methusal rushed on tiptoes to the edge of the dining hall entrance. There, Methusal held up her hand and listened. The Dehriens inside were snarling orders, apparently trying to separate out the most defiant Rolbanis.

"I'm going to the other side." She sprinted across the opening before Behran could speak.

Safe, she crouched and watched Behran's fingers tick down, one by one. Five...four...three...two...

A bellow erupted from the dining room, and then the sharp snap of rocks ricocheted off the stone floor. It sounded like the pitter patter of hail raining down wrath from the skies. A man cried out, and a Dehrien ran out in a panic.

Behran was ready, and swiftly tossed him down and whipped a strip of leather about the man's wrists. He stuffed a large stone in his mouth, cutting off a startled bleat for help, and then rapidly trussed his legs and dragged him down the hall and into the first classroom.

It had all happened so fast that Methusal's jaw was still agape when Behran emerged and crouched into position again, his grin cocky. Methusal smiled back. One down. She pulled one of her two leather kaavl strips from her pocket and clenched it in her teeth, and then quickly gathered more rocks in her hands. A nod from Behran, and they lunged forward and into the dining hall, hurtling rocks.

Overhead, Aali's supply of stones appeared to be dwindling, so their attack was perfectly timed, catching the

Dehriens completely off guard. One of Methusal's well aimed rocks hit a large Dehrien in the ear, and another in the neck, and Behran had stunned two by the time the plainsmen realized they were being attacked from another front. Several charged, vicious snarls contorting their faces. Their blades flashed, reflecting the brilliant sunlight pouring through the portals. Methusal turned and ran for her life just as a triumphant cry ripped the air. From the Rolbanis—or the Dehriens?

She didn't have time to dwell on it, because a swift Dehrien was hunting her, and she couldn't help but imagine the long, wicked knife poised to stab through her shoulder blades.

The hall ahead branched to the right, and she plunged down the new passageway. Two observations pierced her panicked fog: first, the familiar passageway cut sharply left two steps ahead, and second, a step to her right was the deeply recessed door leading to the laundry room. The Dehrien wasn't close enough to see round the first corner yet...so she ducked instinctively into the doorway and snatched the leather strip from her clenched teeth. She doubled it through her fist.

Standing motionless, every nerve taut, her heart pounded double time. The footsteps were almost upon her— had he guessed?—and then a sprinting Dehrien leg flashed into view and a dark head craned to the left, sure she had rounded the next corner.

Her kaavl strip flicked out and curled with a snap around his ankle. She jerked the line hard, and braced back at the same instant he pulled. The Dehrien staggered and pitched forward. His knife arced toward the ceiling as his hands flung out to protect his face from striking the stone floor.

The sharp, tinny clatter of the knife catapulted her into motion. She grabbed the enemy's arms and whipped her last kaavl strip around his wrists before he collected his wits. His ankles were secured with the strip still coiled around one foot, and only then, when she finally paused, did she hear more feet scuffling toward her. Her sensitive nose wrinkled, recognizing the scent. Dehriens. The Dehrien opened his mouth, and she snatched the last large rock from her half open pack and shoved it in his mouth.

She leaped for the concealing entry she had just hidden within, and shoved the door open. Arms doubled in strength through sheer panic, she dragged her trussed prisoner into the laundry room and then hurtled her body against the door, clicking it shut at the last moment.

She crouched near the door, ears straining to hear what was happening. But the Dehriens ran by in silence.

Only when the sounds faded did she relax for a second. Think! What should she do next?

She needed more kaavl strips and the Dehrien's knife, if it was still in the hall. She'd find more kaavl strips at home.

Plan half formulated, she slipped into the silent passage. The knife had vanished. She sprinted to a quiet residential hall, and finally hurtled into her own compartment.

Back pressed against the smooth door, she gulped to catch her breath. Safety. At least for the moment. Her eyes swept the familiar, much loved room. The normal, everyday sights—shutters flung open to receive the morning sun, Papa's cup on the table, and the door hanging to her room dimpling softly in the breeze—filled her with an odd feeling of unreality. Chup Chup waddled up, chirping to be petted. She knelt and stroked the apte's soft fur. In this quiet, normal place it didn't seem possible that Rolban was overrun by Dehriens.

But a shout down the hall jolted her from the half-formed fantasy. It was real. Very real, and if they wanted a chance of winning, she needed to get moving. Now. Reluctantly, she left Chup Chup and gathered the leather kaavl lines in her room. Were her parents in the dining hall, still captured, or had they been one of the six to escape? She refused to think that they might be dead.

Pockets filled, and cumbersome pack left in her room, Methusal pressed her ear to the door and concentrated intently. Most of the grunts and screams were centered in the dining hall and Great Hall now, but she still heard systems of movement near the supply room, and still others winding through nearby living quarter passageways. She drew a deep breath and transferred her kaavl strips to her clenched teeth.

The supply room would be her next battleground. Fear slid through her, but she glided out of her compartment before it could tempt her into riding out the battle in her room, where it seemed so safe.

Once in the hall, her concentration and senses focused, and tuned finely into her environment. No room for doubt or fear now. She slipped effortlessly into a kaavl state of mind and slipped toward the supply room, attuned to every slightest noise. Dehriens could lie in wait just as easily as she could.

Odd noises came from the supply room. Carefully, she sidled along the wall. The door tilted at a crazy angle sideways, anchored only by Old Sims' lock. The hinges had been ripped right off, and she heard the Dehrien inside snorting and noisily smacking his lips as he devoured Rolban's food.

Methusal glanced up and down the hall, planning her attack. A bit of leather slipped from her teeth to her palm. Stealthily, she tiptoed to the edge of the door and anchored one end of the strip to one of the broken door hinges, located a handbreadth up from the floor. Now was the tricky part.

Swiftly she tossed the other, balled end of leather across the doorway and under the angled door jutting into the hall. Hardly daring to breathe, she listened for movement within the supply room. But the disgusting, slurping noises didn't falter. The Dehrien seemed too intent upon his meal to notice anything. She boldly darted across the opening and ducked and rolled behind the broken door. Heart pounding, she grabbed the other end of the kaavl strip, wrapped it around her palm, and pulled it tight.

This time the gorging Dehrien did seem to sense that something was wrong, because the disgusting slurping noises stopped. Footsteps approached the door.

Please don't let him see the trap, she prayed. She crouched, unmoving, against the wall. Perspiration slicked her fingers as feet scuffed closer. He paused in the doorway and she was about to bolt, sure he had seen her, when the bulky Dehrien shuffled suddenly forward, jerking the line deep into her palm.

Her shoulder slammed into the unstable door, and her arm was almost yanked from its socket. The man fell and cracked his head sharply against the far wall of the passage. He lay in a crumpled heap and didn't move. She freed her smarting hand from the leather bit.

Tugging with all of her strength, she dragged the huge man as far as she could into the supply room and then heaped up bags of grain and tagma berries around him, so anyone looking in wouldn't see him right away. Then, with a gag of an old sack, and after lashing his feet and wrists securely, she was off, so buoyed by her success that she barely noticed the stinging ache in her shoulder. She'd captured two Dehriens already!

Utterly relaxed, and each sense sharply focused, she pulled a few more kaavl strips from her pocket and clenched them in her teeth, ready for the next encounter. She tiptoed down the hallway, listening for the next disturbance. Around the corner and down a bit....Aahhh. Ahead, she saw a door ajar. Someone inside was panting heavily. Dehrien? Or fellow Rolbani? But why would a Dehrien hide?

The thought of teaming up with a fellow Rolbani gave her the courage to swiftly peek inside.

"Methusal!" Someone gasped with relief, and a hand plucked at her sleeve, jerking her inside. A flickering lamp in the corner illuminated a wild-eyed Verdnt. His dark hair was a mess. "I'm glad you're here! I need your help."

"Why?"

His quick breaths sounded panicked. "You've been gone, so you don't know, but there's a *traitor*, and he's betrayed Rolban."

"I know."

"You know?" His voice tensed. "How?"

"It's a long story. Who is it?"

He let out a breath. "Barak. He's hunting me now. Help me capture him."

Barak! He perfectly fit her theory that the murderer must be a big, dark-haired immigrant man with access to the ore mine.

But Barak was the one who had caught her on the stairs when she'd been pushed. Of course, that meant he'd also been close enough to push her. She didn't know what to think.

And Verdnt seemed so certain.

Heavy footsteps interrupted her thoughts.

"That's him!" Verdnt hissed. "Follow my lead."

Committed to her new course of action, Methusal tensed in readiness. When Barak's towering form lumbered through the door, Verdnt and Methusal both leaped on him. They had the edge of surprise, and the large man barely had time to fight. They'd trussed and gagged him within moments, with the help of Methusal's kaavl lines.

"Whew!" Verdnt sat back on his heels. "Glad you came when you did. I'm not sure I could have done it alone."

She smiled, relieved the traitor had been so easy to capture. "I..."

"It *is* fortunate, isn't it?" The cold words cut from the far corner of the room. Methusal whirled and terror seized her heart. She'd know that voice anywhere. Her tormentor stepped out of the shadows. The dim, flickering light cut his angular face into hard planes.

"Mentàll!" she whispered, and cast Verdnt a desperate glance. But he didn't move. A small smile played upon his lips.

And then she knew. Barak wasn't the traitor. Verdnt was! Verdnt had spoken to Mentàll in Dehre. Verdnt was the thief. *He* had murdered Renn and Liem. She felt sick.

Horrified, she shot a glance at Barak, who lay helpless on the floor, and then back at Verdnt. Her teeth clenched. "You killed Renn!"

Raising a black brow, Verdnt gave her a terrible smile. "Yes."

"So we meet again, fair Methusal." Her head jerked around at Mentàll's approach. She wasn't fooled by the cool smoothness of his voice.

"So we do." Stonily, she met his gaze, determined to mask her fear.

"I hoped we would meet again."

I'll bet you did. But she remained silent. Fear fed her anger and hatred for this man.

Mentàll suddenly turned his head. "As usual, you have done an excellent job, Verdnt. You have captured the leader of the resistance and the lovely Methusal, as well. You deserve a promotion."

A smirk twisted the teacher's lips, and he bowed his head, accepting the praise.

Methusal burned to hurl "Traitor!" at the man, but kept her temper tightly in check. Her situation was precarious enough, and right now she needed to focus on the Dehrien Chief. He was the biggest threat. She lifted her chin to look him straight in the eye.

"Bring me a report on the battle, Verdnt." That pale gaze held hers as Verdnt's hasty footsteps headed for the door. "It will be my pleasure to detain our prisoner for a few moments."

"Yes sir!" The door closed quietly, leaving her alone with the Dehrien Chief.

"You broke our bargain, Methusal." His cool voice sounded deceptively calm, and the hairs on the back of her neck prickled.

"An agreement made under duress." Not the slightest flicker of an eyelash betrayed her terror churning just beneath the surface.

"An agreement, nonetheless." He stood motionless. Tightly reigned power and violence exuded from every pore. But one eye twitched before he deliberately reached out and grasped a lock of her hair, tugging it tight with a jerk. "It is regrettable that I shall have to kill you, Methusal." Anger glittered. "But you made your choice clear in Tarst. You have chosen to remain my enemy."

"We will always be enemies," she spat. "Because you are a murdering wild beast! You started this war, and you're responsible for Renn and Liem's deaths!"

"No. Verdnt chose to kill Renn and Liem. I made an Alliance and a treaty. Victory by the pen rather than the sword."

"Did you really think this would be a bloodless coup?" Overwhelmed with rage, Methusal grabbed her hair and tugged it free from his hurting hands. "You armed your 'merchants' with swords! People are dying. Don't you hear them screaming? This is all *your* plan. And it's all *your* fault!

You ordered Verdnt to steal metal. Renn found out. So Verdnt killed him."

"War was not my first choice. The swords were for back up, should I need them."

"Right!" she scoffed.

"I have killed no one. No blood is on my sword."

"No?" She grabbed for the blade, and it bit into her palm. Blood smeared the cutting edge. "Now you have the life blood of my family on your hands."

His lip curled in distaste. He swiped the blade once, hard, on his breeches. "Rolban has *everything*." Palpable fury shook his voice. "Everything. And my people starve."

"You don't want *food*. You want power over Rolban. Admit it! And you want to steal what is rightfully ours. People are dying for your greed."

"You are a fool!" he snarled, grabbing her tunic and hauling her up on her tiptoes. "I hold your life in my hands." He gave her a hard shake. "And still you dare to attack me?"

"I'm not afraid to speak the truth." She struggled to ignore the panicked beating of her heart. "And you shouldn't be afraid to hear it."

Verdnt burst back in the room. "More Rolbanis have escaped!" He shot a vicious look at Methusal. "We need to eliminate our liabilities, and move quickly."

"Kill me, you mean," Methusal said. "How simple for you to slit the throat of a girl. But I should expect no less from a traitor..." her gaze swiveled to the Dehrien Chief, "...and a liar." Why she felt so determined to antagonize them, she didn't know. But she did want them both to feel as furious as she felt. And if she must die, then first she'd try her best to extract some answers.

"Tell me." She drilled a gaze into Verdnt. "How did you do it, you clever man? How did you steal food and pelts and get them to Dehre? And let's not forget Tarst."

Verdnt glanced at Mentàll. The Dehrien Chief unexpectedly released Methusal, but that didn't make her feel any safer. No expression flickered on Mentàll's stony face.

Pride visibly swelled Verdnt's chest. He couldn't resist this opportunity to boast. Just as she had hoped. Maybe if she could keep these two sidetracked for a few more minutes, the Rolbanis could turn the tide of the war. Even better, maybe she could turn them against each other.

"It was simple," Verdnt said. "I stole what I wanted, and dropped it into the ravine. My accomplice collected it on the plain."

"Who?"

Verdnt's lip curled with arrogance. "Ludst Lst."

The Dehrien runner. "And what about the pots in Tarst? How did they get there?" Methusal pressed.

A contemptuous, nasty smile twisted Verdnt's lips, but he said nothing.

"Why send the pots to Tarst?" she pushed. "To make us think they were guilty? To throw suspicion off of Dehre?"

"You're not even close, Methusal. For a smart girl, you're stupid when the facts are staring you right in the face." His glance included Mentàll. "You all are."

Mentàll blinked.

"What does that mean?" Methusal said.

"Rolban's treasure is what matters, don't you see, Methusal?"

"What treasure?"

"Why, the ore, of course, and the *Second Book of Kaavl*. Isn't that right, Mentàll? Isn't that your true reason for taking over Rolban—to find the second book, just like I want to do? And let's not forget vengeance. I forgot your truest motivation."

Methusal looked from one to the other, confused now. Vengeance? And what did he mean about the *Second Book of Kaavl*? She could read nothing on the Dehrien Chief's cold face, but Verdnt looked prideful and self-satisfied. "I thought the Dehriens took the book during the Great War. Why would it be here?"

Verdnt sidled forward and yanked at her tablet necklace. The cord bit painfully into her throat. "The clue is here, of course."

The pressure on her neck scared her, and made her feel vulnerable. She swallowed, and tried to sound cool. "Show me the clue." She'd never seen anything but the "M" before.

"Here." Verdnt twisted the necklace over and pointed to the scratches near the bottom edge on the back. The first few were indecipherable, but the last was a capital "R." Two mountain peaks had been scratched above it. She'd noticed the scratches before, but had never thought much about them, because she'd thought one of her child ancestors had made them. But obviously Verdnt thought the "R" referred to Rolban. Did he think the mountains did, too? The Rolban Mountains technically had three peaks, not two. Few people realized this, though, since the most distant peak was a little lower than the others, and couldn't be seen unless someone hiked up to the glaciers. She didn't mention this fact to Verdnt.

"Let me see." She tugged the tablet free of Verdnt's clutches. "Why do you think these scratches point to the location of the book?"

"Mentàll told me the legend thirteen years ago, when I first arrived in Dehre. When we were both training for the Kaavl Games. Should I tell the tale, or will you?" He turned to the Dehrien.

Mentàll's face remained expressionless. "Tell your tale. All of it."

Verdnt smirked. "Legend says, Methusal, that your ancestor foolishly brought the book to the battle line during the Great War. That line was inside of Rolban's borders. The Dehriens invaded the camp on the plateau, stole the book from Jotham Maahr, and took him prisoner. The Dehriens wanted to hide the book somewhere for safe-keeping, until they could recover it after the war. The book disappeared then.

"The Dehriens used Jotham as bait to lure the Rolbanis away from home. They killed him outside the coastal city of Quasr. Legend says he scratched the location of the book on his tablet necklace, which he wore until he died. The Dehriens took the necklace, but on their way out of Quasr they were captured by Rolbani forces. All were killed except for one, who carried the tale home to Dehre. The necklace was returned to the Maahr family. Now you wear it."

Methusal couldn't believe her ears. "I've never heard this story before. Why should I believe it?"

"It's a Dehrien legend, Methusal. A tale told to children. Until I stole your necklace, I didn't believe it, either."

So *that* was why her necklace had been stolen. Also, her link to the *Second Book of Kaavl* was why Verdnt had used the necklace to frame her for Renn's murder.

"Have you found the book?" Neither man spoke. "Well, have you?" she demanded. "It belongs to Rolban."

Mentàll flicked her a freezing glance. "It belongs to the Kaavl Master."

"You, I suppose. How convenient. But you're a thief. Just like the Dehriens were murdering thieves back then!"

Mentàll turned his attention to Verdnt. "Where is the book?" His low words sounded deadly.

Verdnt shrugged. "Did I say I'd found it? And would I give it to you, if I had?"

The Dehrien Chief's shoulders tensed. Methusal watched, fascinated, as the full force of his fury turned upon his partner in crime. He snarled, "You are a *traitor!*"

"Never." Verdnt gave a sly laugh. "My loyalties have never wavered."

In one swift movement, the Dehrien Chief grabbed Verdnt by the throat and shoved him hard against the wall. "Where do your loyalties lie?" he hissed.

Verdnt didn't attempt to fight Mentàll. Instead, he seemed to wilt. "Myself, of course. Dehre is second."

Mentàll stared at him for a long moment. "You are a liar *and* a traitor!" The harsh voice shook. "And you started this war without authorization. Why?" His grip tightened, and Verdnt's face turned purple.

He gurgled, "The war had to start sometime." He choked and gasped. "The Rolbanis were vulnerable. We had our best warriors here. It was better to start the takeover then, before their best kaavl players returned."

Mentàll shoved him away, and Verdnt crumpled to the floor, clutching his neck. The Dehrien Chief's cheekbones were etched red. It was the only visible evidence of his rage, except for the hatred and fury in the gaze with which he skewered Methusal. He came closer. "Give me that necklace."

Methusal was scared to death. In this mood, he'd probably rip it from her neck. Now wasn't the time for bravado. She took it off.

He examined it briefly and shoved it into his pocket. He turned to Verdnt. "We have a war to win. Can I trust a traitor to fight beside me?"

Verdnt stumbled to his feet and bowed his head obsequiously. "I want Rolban defeated, too." But Methusal saw the sly twist to his mouth.

Mentàll grabbed him by the tunic and propelled him to the door. "You first, then."

Had they forgotten about her? And what did the rift between the two of them mean? It sounded as if Verdnt might have an agenda the Dehrien Chief knew nothing about.

"I'm not finished with *you* yet." Mentàll snarled at her, and the door slammed shut. A bar lock scraped across the door outside and slid into the wall, anchoring it shut. She was alone in the sudden silence. Her heart thundered against her ribs. At least she was still alive.

She rushed to the door and futilely rattled the latch. She had to get out!

She looked through the hole just beneath the opening handle and twisted her head left and right, trying to see where the bar lock was located, although she suspected it was above the door handle. An unknown person swept by outside and sent a cool waft of air into her eye. She blinked and withdrew. Poking a finger out didn't reveal any information either, and she sprang to her feet to inspect the door hinges. Maybe she could take them off.

A roar swelled from the dining room, and she examined the hinges, knowing the battle was intensifying. They needed her. If only she could pull these hinges apart...

"Mmm! MMmmmm!" The enraged growl came from behind her. Barak! Dismayed, she spun around. How had she forgotten about him? Quickly, she untied him and pulled off the gag.

"Rah..Blllb!" The large man violently shook his head, and spit out a small piece of leather.

"I'm so sorry, Barak," she cried. "Verdnt fooled me into thinking you were the traitor!"

"Rmmmph!" The crop tender lumbered to his feet, fists clenched. A scowl darkened his face. "That traitor fooled a lot of people."

He was at the immovable door in two strides. After inspecting it for a second, he stepped back a few paces. "I can't..." he hurtled his body at the door. It shuddered mightily. "...wait..." A few quick steps and he retreated to the far back wall. Concentration pulled at every line of his heavy face. As he leaped toward the door, running full tilt, one word belted out with each stride.

"...to...get...my...hands..." A shuddering crash, and the door folded like a leaf under his mighty shoulder, and Barak erupted into the hall. "... on him!" he finished triumphantly. Wow! Methusal stared at the door, and then at Kitran's brother.

"Can you take care of yourself?" he said roughly.

"Yes." Apparently that was all the confirmation he needed, for he plunged down the passage, toward the shouts and screams in the dining hall. Pandemonium of some sort seemed to be going on there.

Alone again, Methusal wasn't sure where to go next. The dining hall? Or maybe... But she didn't have time to consider her options, because a commotion down the hall, from the direction of the supply room passage, sent her ducking back into the room.

When the footsteps unexpectedly paused, she peered out again and forced herself to relax into kaavl. She needed to focus now, more than ever.

Where had they stopped? If only she could *see* around the corner and into the next passageway. Her gaze fastened on a lamp facing directly down the supply room passage. If she was standing right there, she could see down...

Suddenly she saw Mentàll, Verdnt—who gripped Aali's arm—Old Sims and five Dehriens standing just beyond the lopsided supply room door. The picture was as crystal clear and rich in detail as if she actually *saw* them this very minute. Even as she watched, Mentàll's lips moved. Now, just to focus in and listen...

But the moment she realized what had just happened, the image vanished. Had she actually *seen* down the passage?

Shaken, she slipped into kaavl again and listened.

"We caught these two throwing rocks on the plateau, Mentàll."

"Let me go!" Aali shrilled. A scuffle reached Methusal's ears. Verdnt cursed.

"Be quiet." Mentàll's voice sounded venomous. "An old man and the Chief's little daughter. This could be fortunate."

"Let's kill the old man now," Verdnt urged. "We don't need him."

"No!" Aali screamed. "I won't let you! You can't, I say! Let me *go!*"

A harsh slap, but her young cousin cried out again, undaunted. "Let us go, you horrible bea..." Her shout was abruptly muffled.

"We need to make a plan," Verdnt bit out.

"Be quiet!" snapped the Dehrien Chief. "Hold them still while I think."

Methusal's palms felt sticky with nervous perspiration. She *had* actually seen down that hall, and it was clear Aali and Old Sims were Dehrien prisoners. She had to do something! But what? Clearly she could not take on seven Dehriens by herself. And Aali and Old Sims wouldn't be much help. She listened intently. If only she could hear their plan...

"...plateau?"

"Yes, but it's tricky." Verdnt's voice.

"Get moving, then." Footsteps whispered back down the passage.

They were going to climb up to the croplands. But why? Did they plan to kill Aali and Sims up there? That didn't make sense.

Methusal gave up trying to figure it out for the time being, because she realized that regardless of Mentàll's plan, she needed help. And she knew just where to find it. She hoped.

CHAPTER THIRTY-FOUR

METHUSAL RAN toward the dining hall, kaavl strips in her teeth, and rocks in her hands for protection. Pandemonium reigned in the dining hall, passage, Grand Staircase, and Great Hall. Rocks flew and knives flashed as men fought in hand to hand combat. Screams and hoarse shouts reverberated in the rocky halls. From the number of people up ahead, it looked like at least two dozen Rolbani men had escaped. She didn't see any women or children, and guessed they were probably still captives in the dining hall.

She crouched low and ducked and twisted among the wrestling throngs of people, heading for her classroom. A flying knife grazed her arm, but she barely felt it. A lunging, slithering crawl between the legs of two fighters, and then she was through, rolling down the narrow passage on the other side of the dining hall.

She leaped into the dark sanctuary of the first classroom, hoping no Dehriens lay in wait for an unwary Rolbani. She hoped, instead, to find friends. If not, she'd use Aali's passage so she could go help those on the plateau.

"Thusa!" A hoarse whisper caught her attention.

Cautiously, she tiptoed toward Aalicaa's tunnel, located in the far corner of the room.

"Here." Behran leaned over Deccia, who lay sprawled against the far wall. In the dim light, her face looked pale.

Horrified, Methusal dropped to her knees. "What happened?"

"She'll be okay." Behran's gaze rested on her for a moment, reassuring her. "Her arm is sprained, and right now Timaeus is finding a sling. She also has a knife wound in her side. It's not too deep. Timaeus already treated that."

Methusal was glad that runners always carried healing coltac leaves with them, just like she did. "Are you sure you're okay?" she anxiously asked her sister.

Deccia offered a wan smile. "I'm fine. But I'm glad Behran got me out of that fight. It's wild, isn't it?"

Just like Deccia, to turn the attention away from herself. Methusal turned as Timaeus ran into the room carrying thin strips of leather for Deccia's sling. He was white around the lips, and his tense expression showed just how worried he was. Methusal and Behran scooted away so he could tend to Deccia.

"What's going on at the other end of Rolban?" Behran asked, pulling Methusal up by the hand to stand beside him.

"Not as much as here."

He interrupted. "You're bleeding!" Dark blood smeared his palm.

"It's nothing." A glance decided this. "Only a little cut." A quick dig through her pocket brought up squashed coltac leaves, which weren't of much use. "I'll deal with it later."

But he gently held her arm up to the light spilling through the doorway before he would agree. "I guess we can't do much now. Timaeus is out of coltac leaves, too. You say the other passages are pretty much cleared?"

Methusal quickly explained that Verdnt was the traitor and murderer. Deccia gasped.

"I *knew* Verdnt had done something wrong!" she said. "Before you went to Dehre, Verdnt said something strange. He said that he and Mentàll are friends. Present tense. Like they're still good friends.

"I didn't think anything of it. Verdnt had lived in Dehre for a long time, after all. But after he said that, he looked at me kind of oddly and said they *used* to be friends. Something felt off. I think he knew it. After that he wouldn't let me out of his sight. Like he'd said something he didn't want repeated."

Verdnt's many deceptions would have to be figured out later.

Quickly, Methusal told them about the situation on the plateau while Timaeus finished tying on Deccia's sling.

"Aali!" Deccia's face paled even further. Timaeus gently took her hand in his large, sun darkened one.

"But why would they go to the plateau?" Behran sounded puzzled. "I'd think they'd want to use Aali and Sims as hostages to turn the battle in their favor. What good are hostages on the plateau? The battle is inside."

"I think I know." Finally, Methusal understood. "They want to reach the front gate. They'll show their hostages in full dramatic glory there. But they don't want to go through the fight in here to reach it. They'd be overwhelmed if they did."

"I know there's a path down from the plateau to the plains. It's by the stream," Timaeus said. "Is there another path, too?"

"One, but it's pretty faint, and really steep," Behran said. "Aali used it to climb to the plateau from her secret passage. Verdnt may know about it, too. Remember, he's been spending a lot of time on the plateau, and he carried Liem's body down to the plains. It just depends where the Dehriens want to come down. Aali's trail comes out closer to Rolban's main entrance. Verdnt could show them the way, if he knows it."

The traitor! Methusal's temper kindled. The *murderer*. The injustice of it all made her clench her fists. He was despicable. Rolban had accepted him as one of their own. Not only that, but they'd given him the honorable job of teacher, and let him run for Chief.

"We have to *do* something!" Deccia's fearful eyes beseeched them all.

"Seven Dehriens to our four," Behran said. "We can do it if we plan it right, and if you use your kaavl, Thusa."

"But how?"

"Traps?" Timaeus suggested.

"Don't forget, one of those seven is Mentàll," Methusal reminded them. "He won't be easy to fool. Plus, they all have weapons, and we have none."

"They're probably climbing down the cliff now." Deccia sounded worried. "We'd better hurry up and think of a plan to rescue Aali and Sims."

None of them spoke the other obvious thought: and save Rolban. The drama of the new hostage situation could distract the Rolbanis from the fight and give the Dehriens a chance to gain the upper hand again. That couldn't be allowed, regardless of the hostages.

"Let's go," Methusal agreed.

"We need a plan, Thusa." Behran put a restraining hand on her arm. "Let's throw out ideas."

"Pop them off one by one as they climb down the cliff," Methusal suggested promptly. "Someone could throw rocks from Aali's passage. There's a great view at the top, and it's protected."

"Good. That might get a few Dehriens, if we hurry. What else?"

"We could hide and wait for them outside the entrance, among the rocks," Deccia suggested. "Maybe throw stones at them first, and then attack them with knives, if we have any."

"I have one," Timaeus said.

"Who wants to throw rocks from Aali's cave?" Behran asked. "We'll need someone who's a good shot."

"I'll go," Timaeus spoke up.

"Right. Then after they're down the cliff, follow and help us out down below, if you can." Behran pointed. "Aali's passage is behind a loose board in that closet, Timaeus."

Timaeus peered into the dark hole, and looked a bit surprised to discover its existence. Before going in, he handed a short, wicked looking dagger to Behran. "I have two. Take this one."

With a final hand squeeze for Deccia, he wriggled in and his feet quickly slid out of sight.

"When we hide outside," Methusal said, "we'll need to stay clear of the Dehriens' line of vision while they climb down the mountain. I'll be the scout."

"Good." Behran turned to Deccia. "Do you feel up to helping, or would you rather stay here?"

"I'm coming." Resolve hardened her voice.

"Come on, then."

The sisters followed Behran to the door. He poked his head out and looked left and right.

"It's still a mess near the dining hall and down the stairs," he reported. "We'll have to make a run for it. Put up your arms to protect your heads."

The three ran and forced their way into the fray, and were buffeted, almost falling, all the way down the stairs. The Great Hall was a scene of bedlam, too, and they dodged back and forth, speeding for the entrance.

"Over here." Behran burst outside first. The brilliant, early morning sunlight washed his blond hair gold.

Methusal ducked into the cool shadow of a boulder just to the left of the great gates.

The three crouched and waited to see if anyone would follow them out. No one did. A faint breeze whispered across the cave entrance, swirling up leaves from the ground. Methusal drew a breath of relief.

Behran craned his neck back and looked up the mountain. "I don't see them. Do you hear anything, Thusa?"

While she strained her ears, directing her focus for the mountain slope on the other side of the gates, Deccia quietly collected together a large pile of rocks and stray sticks.

"They're about halfway down the other side," Methusal reported finally, "but too many rocks are falling. I can't tell if Timaeus has hit any Dehriens yet. I'm going to go hide over there and see what's happening. I'll signal back to you."

"Okay." The hesitancy in Behran's voice made her glance up. His blue gaze caught hers and held it for a moment. "Be careful."

"You, too." She offered a cheeky grin. She didn't want to think about the possibility of going up against the Kaavl Master, one on one. Methusal had escaped from him once, but only by the narrowest of margins. The man terrified her.

"Good luck, Thusa." Deccia touched her arm. Her gaze looked calm, but determined. "We can do this."

Taking a deep breath, Methusal dashed across Rolban's entrance and ducked behind a boulder, which was overshadowed by a small ledge. She pressed her back against the rock, hoping Mentàll and the other Dehriens hadn't seen her.

The strange visual carry she'd experienced in the hall flew to mind. Could she repeat it here? Then she wouldn't have to poke her head out to see up the mountain.

Concentrating hard, she stared straight ahead at a small rock, which was perched on top of a boulder. If she could just carry visually from that point, she could see right up the cliff...

Nothing happened. She was trying too hard. She needed to *relax*. In that instant, she knew where Kitran and Mentàll, in all of their strivings for the Ultimate level, had gone wrong. The secret to kaavl wasn't in manipulating emotions or states of consciousness. It was practice, yes, but even more than that, it was relaxation—lettin

g kaavl flow without restriction through her entire being.

This unexpected insight made her giddy. The hairs on the back of her neck stood on end. Was this what Mahre, the Old Kaavl Master, had learned? Methusal felt like she was on the brink of an incredible discovery, but the scrabble of feet overhead snapped her attention back to the present.

The Dehriens were close. She had to risk it. Carefully, she craned her neck so she could see just past the ledge over-head. There. Even as she looked, a huge rock hit Ludst Lst's head. He was the messenger who had so cruelly won the Quatr-level in Dehre. He gave a startled cry and fell, tum-bling fatally down the steepest, rockiest portion of the cliff.

Now five Dehriens remained, and Aali and Old Sims.

Movement to the left caught her eye. Belatedly remem-bering her duty, she signaled the information to the others. Behran darted over, but hid closer to the entrance. Now they just needed to wait. She quickly stockpiled stones and stout sticks for weapons. As she listened and waited, she formulated a plan.

Closer...closer. Now! She pulled a kaavl strip from her pocket. They would walk right in front of her. If she could capture the last man without any of the others noticing...

She peered out, glad that she was almost completely concealed on all sides by large boulders. There was just enough room to drag a man into her small space.

Mentàll, Aali, Verdnt, Old Sims, and a Dehrien passed, and she tensed, ready. Another...and her string flicked out, expertly snapping around the last Dehrien's leg. He fell with a startled "OOoomph!"

She shoved a rock into his mouth and whipped the line around his legs. One, two, three passes. Now for his hands... But as she fumbled for another line, a slight snap sounded behind her and an arm clamped around her neck, jerking her violently up on her tiptoes.

Choking, she grabbed at the steely arm. "Le..."

"Thought you could fool me, Methusal?" The Dehrien Chief's voice was soft in her ear, and he wrenched her closer. "You can't hide from me."

He yanked her between two rocks and out onto the plain. Her toes barely wisped over the ground, "I might not kill you after all. You are much too entertaining. Now, come on!" This jerk was vicious. "You'll help win me Rolban, fair Methusal."

Unaware of anything, except for Mentàll's ore-like arm about her neck, she clawed at his sleeve, straining for a small gulp of life giving air. They had almost reached the gates now, and the world was going gray. Methusal had a brief impression of the Dehriens and hostages watching. Desperately, with all of her strength, she wrenched at his arm.

Finally, a cool draft of air slid down her throat, easing her searing lungs and giving a spark of coherency to her slowed thoughts. Behran and Deccia needed help!

Tears filled her eyes, and she fought desperately, fighting like a wild thing. She had underestimated Mentàll. But he couldn't win this easily—she wouldn't let him.

The Dehrien Chief easily subdued her frenzied thrashings by tightening the arm around her neck and clamping a hand on both of her wrists. She gasped. The world swirled, slowly going black. Mentàll shouted something...warnings, maybe, to the Rolbani people, as he carried her inside.

Suddenly everything went very quiet, and Mentàll's grip loosened, allowing her feet to touch the ground. Greedily, she gulped in great breaths of sweet air. It took a few seconds to take in what was going on around her.

Mentàll was speaking. "As I have told Petr and Erl, Tarst has signed a treaty with Dehre. It gives me complete legal control over Rolban for three weeks. You are illegally fighting and killing my men, who arrived here for peaceful purposes.

I am willing to produce the document and discuss the matter with your elders."

A low murmur broke out. The scene before her looked frozen. Dehriens and Rolbanis alike stood motionless, staring at Mentàll.

Erl Maahr stepped forward. "It is clear you've violated the Alliance, Mentàll. We will not honor your new treaty."

"Oh, but you are mistaken, honorable Erl Maahr. I have not violated the Alliance. Verdnt started the war. That is regrettable. He is a traitor to both you and me."

Verdnt stared at the Dehrien Chief. His expression was difficult to read. Was it contemptuous? Victorious?

The Dehrien Chief smoothly continued, "I have killed no one. What is more, the Alliance and the new treaty together give me complete legal power to take over Rolban."

"We're not honoring a treaty giving you power over Rolban!" Petr Storst roared from the Grand Staircase.

"Then perhaps you will explain to your fellow citizens why you agreed to give me that power, Petr."

"I agreed to no such thing, Mentàll! You twist my words." The Rolbani Chief thrust forward, struggling to descend to the Great Hall.

"Stay where you are, Petr." Mentàll's voice sounded deadly. "I am prepared to kill Aalicaa, Methusal, and the old man, one by one, should it prove necessary."

"We won't stand for this!" Barak strode forward, fists clenched. "Is this the way you win wars? Threatening the lives of women and children?" He spat in contempt. "That is what I think of you. You are not a man at all."

Methusal felt the sudden rage that tensed her captor. "Stay where you are!" he snarled. To her surprise, the hand holding her wrists loosened for a split second. In that instant she wrenched her wrists free—a childhood defensive move, long forgotten, and yet still automatic. As was her next move.

Quicker than thought, she reached over her head and grasped Mentàll's wide right shoulder and the sleeve of his tunic. Then she rolled her right shoulder forward, while at the same time bending forward at the waist. The noble Dehrien Chief flipped over her shoulder and landed on his back with a guttural "Oooooph!"

Chapter Thirty-Five

INSTANT CHAOS ERUPTED, and Rolbanis surged down into the Great Hall.

Methusal found herself lashing a kaavl strip around the gasping Mentàll's wrists, and another about his feet. A rush came behind her, and then the prick of a knife. Just as suddenly it fell away. She spun to find Behran slugging it out with a cold-faced Dehrien.

To the side, she spotted Deccia clinging to Verdnt's back, who still held Aalicaa captive. Her good arm was wrapped around his neck, trying to choke him. Even as she watched, his grip loosened and her gritty cousin broke free and spun around to pummel him with her fists. He whipped out a knife, and Methusal gasped in horror.

The next moment seemed to pass in slow motion. Aali's mouth formed an "O" of horror, Verdnt's blade arched up...and then Timaeus dove in and threw his hunting blade through the teacher's heart. Verdnt's eyes bugged out, and he crumpled to the ground.

Aali stared in horror, and burst into tears. Deccia staggered around her instructor and pulled Aali into a hug. The hug included Timaeus, too, when he'd staggered to his feet.

Methusal felt numb. Frozen. She'd never seen anyone killed before. Even though Verdnt deserved to die for killing Renn and Liem, the finality of it—the violence of it—the ending of a life seemed too awful to comprehend.

Old Sims was free now, too; tossed aside by an unknown Dehrien. Methusal glanced around, wondering what to do next, and then she heard a hoarse shout. All of the Dehriens fled for the gate, chased by knife wielding Rolbanis. Barak led the pack.

"Out!" He roared, and others picked up the furious cry.

The hall was clear of Dehriens within seconds, except for Verdnt and the bound Dehrien Chief, who had gained his feet. Barak shoved him back onto his knees, and then pushed him down to the floor. "Spin all the pretty speeches you want," he growled, and raised his sword. "You plotted war. Now you will die."

Horror seized Methusal at the thought of seeing the Dehrien Chief murdered in cold blood, right before her eyes. Wasn't Verdnt's death enough? Hadn't Mahre said the strongest should show the greatest mercy?

Barak lifted his sword higher, readying for the plunge.

"Barak, no! Stop," she cried out.

Barak hesitated.

"He's defeated. That humiliation alone will kill his pride a thousand times every day."

"She's right," Erl agreed. "Throw him out. Never return, Mentàll."

Barak hauled Mentàll to his feet, his arms still tied behind him. The Dehrien held himself erect, holding onto his tattered pride. His smoking, furious glare seared into Methusal. He didn't look grateful that she'd just saved his life. No. If looks alone could kill, she'd be dead right now.

She suppressed an involuntary shiver, and returned glare for glare, refusing to reveal her fear. She felt compelled to speak. "You've lost, Mentàll. But your life has been spared. Don't forget the words of the Prophet, 'Those who live by the sword...'"

"You will not instruct *me*, Methusal," he spat.

"Can anyone instruct you? Or are you so prideful that you think you are above The One?"

"You will pay, Methusal. One day you will *pay!*" he snarled. "You can be sure of it."

A chill slid down her spine. He hated her. And he would do what he promised, if given the chance. He'd kill her...or worse. She had earned an enemy for life. "You don't scare me." A blatant lie, and they both knew it.

He bared his teeth at her. "Then you are a fool."

"Throw him out, Barak," Erl ordered.

"If you return, we won't treat you so kindly," Petr said harshly. "Our guards will kill you on sight."

Barak dragged Mentàll to the gate and gave him a mighty shove, so the Dehrien fell to his knees. Barak kicked dirt at him. "Eat dust, like the whip beast you are."

The other Dehriens rushed to help him up, but the Dehrien Chief raised a hand, stopping them.

Standing beside Deccia, Timaeus murmured, "'For everyone who exalts himself will be humbled, and he who humbles himself will be exalted.'" Methusal had never heard that saying before, but it was certainly appropriate for the situation.

Rolban's gates clanged shut.

△ △ △ △ △

Hendra limped around the corner, toward the Rolbani mountain community. Her knee hurt more with each step. For a while now, she'd heard the screams of the wounded. Her heart bled with guilt and misery. It was all her fault. She'd waited too long. If only she had told Behran and Methusal her suspicions when they'd been in Dehre. Then none of this would have happened.

She turned the corner and saw a sight she couldn't believe. A group of Dehriens milled around outside the gate, and a blond giant of a man lay sprawled in the dirt. Mentàll!

She almost ran forward, but stopped herself. He would not want to see her. But what if he was dead?

Hendra ran closer, ignoring the pain in her knee. Her steps slowed when she saw her cousin's large frame shift. He climbed to his feet. He seemed to be tied up, and Tabor, his second-in-command, sawed the cords free.

Mentàll shuddered with clear fury. He lunged forward and shook the gates of Rolban with all of his considerable strength. The ancient bars actually rattled, and Hendra shrank back. Never before had she seen him lose control of his temper.

Footsteps whispered behind her, and she spun. Kitran and the Quatr-levelers had finally arrived.

The Rolbanis inside the mountain must have seen the kaavl players, too, for a giant, dark-haired man bellowed, "Back!" and poked a sword through the gate, perilously close to Mentàll's chest. Her cousin backed up, his nostrils flaring. Rage stained his cheeks red. He flicked a glance over his shoulder and saw the newly arrived Rolbanis. Lips contorted in a vicious snarl, he took one step backward, allowing them to pass. As he did so, his gaze veered to Hendra, as if sensing her presence. His gaze clashed with hers, and Hendra trembled with what she saw there. Condemnation and fury...and dismissal. She had betrayed him. Now Mentàll hated her. He would throw her out of her home forever.

Tears gathered in her eyes. She deserved it. The Alliance was dead, and it was her fault. She should have spoken up sooner. How many people would now starve in Dehre? How many children?

Tears burned her eyes, and Hendra crossed her arms, hugging them to herself. She had lost the last member of her family. Not only that, but she had betrayed her friendship with Behran, too, by not speaking up soon enough. She was a failure to both Dehre and Rolban.

Never had she felt so alone. She did not belong with the Dehriens anymore. She glanced at the locked gate. And she did not belong with the Rolbanis. She belonged exactly nowhere.

△ △ △ △ △

Barak hustled Kitran, Lina, and Retra inside and the gates clanged shut. The three looked stunned and confused.

"What happened?" Kitran demanded. "Hendra warned me something was wrong. We came at first light."

Erl gave a weary head shake. "The Dehriens just tried to take Rolban by force. Thanks to some quick thinking by our young people, we were able to hold them off."

Everyone took a deep breath and looked around, coming to grips with the battle and their sudden victory. Moans sounded from upstairs. Now to tend to the wounded, and to free the remaining captives in the dining hall. Most people turned and stumbled for the stairs. Methusal followed, but a sudden movement and expletive beyond the gates sent her spinning around.

Hands and feet now untied, the Dehrien Chief towered behind the gate, his face apoplectic. A sheaf of parchment leaves shook from his hand. "I have a treaty here, Rolban! Honor it, or start a war! Tell them, Petr and Kitran."

Erl Maahr turned slowly, acknowledging the outburst. He glanced from Petr to Kitran. "He's mentioned this before. What treaty is he talking about?"

Both looked uncomfortable. Petr sputtered, "He can't be trusted. I never agreed to give him control over Rolban, whatever he says."

"I'll call a Council meeting," Erl said. "Too much has happened in the last twelve hours for any of us to understand what is going on."

"Nonsense!" Petr roared. "We owe him nothing. And contemplating his phony agreement is ridiculous! We're not going to hand control of Rolban over to him!"

"No," Erl agreed, "But I still want to understand what has happened. As Elder in Chief, I'm calling a Council meeting. I want you, Kitran, Methusal, Behran, Aalicaa, Deccia, Timaeus, Barak, and all the elders to meet me in the Council room in five minutes. Timaeus, go spread the word."

"Yes, sir." Timaeus sprinted off.

Erl Maahr turned to the livid Dehrien Chief. "We have no intention of honoring your treaty, Mentàll. But we will review it during our meeting, just to put closure on this whole incident."

The fingers clutching the white parchment sheets convulsed. Mentàll smiled tightly. "By all means. I have Petr's letter of authorization, too."

Since Behran was closest to the gate, he accepted the papers from the Dehrien Chief. The look that passed from older man to younger, from Dehrien to former Dehrien could have cut through stone. Contempt was clear from Mentàll, and a grim unwillingness to back down from Behran. After a long moment, Behran turned his back on the Dehrien and gave the papers to Erl.

Methusal followed her father upstairs, and was startled to discover that she was shaking a little. She pressed her hands together to stop the trembles.

An arm squeezed suddenly around her shoulders. "You okay?" Behran's gaze searched hers. Quick tears filled her eyes, and she relaxed into his body, feeling some of the tension drain away.

"Yes." She gave a short, choked laugh. "But I can't believe it's over."

"I know." His voice was grim.

The two followed Erl, Petr, and the other elders into the overflowing Council room.

"A lot has happened in the last twelve hours." Erl cast Petr a hard look. "Much needs to be explained."

Petr looked pale. His great form crumpled into the Chief's chair.

"Now," Erl glanced around the packed room. Most Rolbanis stood wedged in, shoulder to shoulder. "What are the facts?"

"Tell what you overheard, Thusa," Behran spoke up. All attention turned to Methusal.

Behran's arm, still tight around her shoulders, gave her a feeling of calm and serenity, so the words fell clearly and easily from her lips. She told about Mentàll's harassment, the three conversations she'd overheard, Petr's letter of authorization, the second treaty, and discovering Verdnt to be a traitor. She never mentioned her extraordinary hearing.

"Is that true, Petr? Did you make an agreement with Mentàll without consulting this Council?" Erl's voice sounded bleak and hard.

"I didn't know he planned to trick us," Petr blustered. "Maybe Methusal's wrong. Maybe she misunderstood what she heard. Kitran and I only wanted to put kaavl into Rolban's leadership. Mentàll is so advanced in kaavl that we thought he could teach us its benefits. We certainly never meant to give him real power in Rolban!"

A loud grumble accompanied this plea.

"You forget your letter of authorization," Erl said harshly, looking up from the parchment. "This clearly states that you wanted to give Mentàll control over Rolban for three weeks while he taught you kaavl leadership. You also asked Pan to sign the second agreement."

"Whip! And you gave him our seed grain!" Barak bellowed. "Payment, right? That's what the Dehrien said. Is that true?"

Petr's face blanched. It almost matched his white beard. He said nothing.

Voice shaking, Kitran said, "I knew nothing about a letter of authorization. Or the grain. I agreed with the second treaty, but I trusted Mentàll. I didn't think he would try to take over Rolban."

"Neither did I!" Petr's bluster sounded half-hearted.

"You shouldn't have written that letter," Ben Amil returned angrily. "You know the elders don't want kaavl incorporated into leadership. Conspiring against the majority vote was wrong, Petr."

Erl raised his hand. "I'll pass the parchments around the room. Let's examine the documents and put an end to this whole affair."

Behran's warm, comforting arm dropped from Methusal's shoulders. He moved closer to examine the parchments, too.

Apprehension flooded her again. What would happen now? What if the papers did give the Dehrien Chief legal control over Rolban? Surely her father and Petr wouldn't give it to him!

"Why would Pan sign this thing without consulting with all of us first?" Erl muttered, after rereading a document. "I thought our relationship with the Tarst was better than this. Would he take the word of Petr and Mentàll above all reason?"

"Papa." He looked at Methusal, but didn't seem to see her.

"Mentàll fooled him, just like he did Kitran and Petr. He won all of the Kaavl Games, and he's charismatic, I guess. He's Kaavl Master, and he convinced them he's the best leader in the land. Not only that, but he claims he knows the secret to achieving the Ultimate level."

Erl Maahr stilled. "Does he?"

"I don't think so. The things he teaches seem to contradict the *First Book of Kaavl*."

Erl read the final parchment and passed the treaty on to Kitran. "We'll need to go downstairs and speak to Mentàll," he said in a quiet voice.

Fear flared. "Why, Papa?"

"The documents are legal. I need to address a few issues with the Dehrien. Now."

"But..." Methusal and the others followed him down to the Great Hall, where Mentàll still stood outside. His demeanor looked calmer now, but Methusal wasn't fooled.

"Aah! My fellow Rolbanis. I hope you are ready to discuss this rationally."

"I have read your treaty, Mentàll."

"So you see it is legal and binding."

"It appears to be so," Erl agreed. "But your act of war nullifies the Alliance."

"*Verdnt's* act of war does not nullify the Alliance," the Dehrien Chief returned.

"Semantics. Your citizens attacked..."

"No. *Your* citizen led the attack." A thin smile curled Mentàll's lips. "The insurrection was a mutiny, not an act of war."

Erl flushed. "*Your* delegation held us hostage in the dining room."

Methusal heard an ominous ringing in her ears. Would her father fight this battle only with words? Clearly he wanted to find a legal reason to break the treaty. Honor demanded it. Panic beat inside her. Surely something could be done. They would not give the Dehrien power in Rolban just on a legal technicality.

On impulse, she tugged the treaty from Kitran's hand and quickly scanned both pages. Then she read the second page again. A ray of hope hit her. And none too soon, either, if the superior smirk on Mentàll's face was any indication.

"Papa," she said urgently. "Listen to this."

Erl frowned. "What?"

Methusal read, "'Rolban agrees to accept three weeks of counsel from Mentàll Solboshn, Chief of Dehre. Mentàll has the right to demonstrate all acts of leadership during this three week period. Rolban will accept his decrees as law during this interval, so the benefits of kaavl leadership can be understood by every Rolbani. At the end of three weeks, control of Rolban will return to Rolban's Chief, under one condition.'" She glanced up at the Dehrien Chief, who stared back with a cold glint in his eyes.

She smiled at him. "Here's where your ego tripped you up, Mentàll." His cold look sharpened to flint. "'A Rolbani must first beat him at the Primary level.'" She eyed Mentàll through the gate. "Your defeat can be arranged. If someone beats you now, would you agree to destroy this treaty?"

Arrogance oozed from Mentàll's every pore, just as she had hoped it would. He smiled through his teeth. "Of course. I am nothing, if not fair."

"Good." Methusal turned to her father. "All we have to do is rematch Kitran and Mentàll. Then we can legally break the agreement."

Behran spoke up. "Not necessary. It seems clear someone else has already beaten Mentàll at kaavl."

The Dehrien Chief flicked a condescending glance at him. "Who?"

"Methusal."

Both Methusal and the Dehrien stared at him in astonishment. Then the Dehrien Chief spluttered into derisive laughter. "We've played no game. And Methusal is far from the Primary level."

Behran smiled. "You're wrong, Mentàll. The ultimate game just took place, on a regulation playing field. Methusal won her life. She beat you, fair and square."

"When? If you remember, gentlemen, I caught the fair Methusal and held her *hostage* just a few minutes ago! Hardly a kaavl win." The Dehrien Chief's nostrils flared.

"True, but remember she freed herself and captured *you*—a win by any account. And she beat you earlier, when we crossed the plain to Rolban. That was the true test, because it was on a regular playing field, with her wits pitted against yours. She won, remember?"

"That is ridiculous!" Mentàll shouted. Fury outlined the cords of his neck. "She's not at the Primary level! She's unfit to compete against me!" Spit flew in all directions.

"Apparently not." Erl's mouth glimmered in a small smile. "Either she's at the Primary level, or you are not. Whatever the case, she beat you, fair and square."

Mentàll shook with rage. "She wasn't even close enough to catch! How can that be kaavl? It was only a race!"

"But she *was* close enough to catch." Old Sims' voice wavered nearby. "My eyes may be old, but I saw the whole thing from up on the plateau. So did Barak. No question about it. She completely outsmarted and danced kaavl rings around you, Dehrien."

Mentàll's cheeks pulsed in fury. "This is an abomination! You haven't heard the last of this!"

"We have." Erl said in a low, firm voice. "Your word now binds you. We are all witnesses. The treaty is nullified." He pulled the papers from Methusal's hands and thrust them through the gate. "I expect you to abide by your word and leave. Now."

Mentàll let out a terrible roar and ripped the papers to shreds, and ground them beneath his heel. Shaking, he spun and strode toward the cluster of Dehriens. Only Methusal heard the threat he snarled beneath his breath. "I will make *you pay, Methusal!*"

But with Behran's strong hand gripping her shoulder, the old fear did not quite touch her. She was safe. Mentàll was on the outside now.

Hendra followed her fellow Dehriens westward. Methusal realized that by helping her, Hendra had betrayed her cousin. What would become of her? How would Mentàll treat her?

The Dehrien girl did not look back. Apparently she did not want to plea for amnesty to the Rolbanis. She wanted to return home and face whatever punishment might face her. Methusal sent a prayer heavenward that The One would protect her, because she had been very brave.

Behran watched Hendra go, too. A pensive expression tightened his features.

"I'm sure there's more to the story." Erl sounded weary. "Let's go to the dining hall and sort out the rest, if we can."

So while most Rolbanis cleaned up, and others helped D'Wit tend to the wounded, the Maahrs, Amils, Storsts,

Kitran, and most of the Council elders congregated at the longest dining table.

"First order of business," Ben Amil said. "Petr's break in faith with Rolban's citizens. I move that we schedule a trial. Facts will be judged by a group of your peers, Petr. I think it's safe to say that you'll lose your power as Chief. And you will lose your bid for reelection."

Petr's face crumpled, but he said nothing.

"In fact," Ben turned to Erl, "since every man running for Chief has been disqualified or is dead...Erl, be prepared to take office on Firstday. We'll hold a vote, but I'm sure you'll win."

Hanuh and Methusal smiled at Erl.

Another member of the Council spoke up. "I'm confused. So much as happened. Would someone tell the whole story, from beginning to end?"

Erl looked at Methusal. "I think Methusal, Deccia, and Aali can do that."

Methusal and Deccia started the tale with their suspicions about the robberies and murders, while Aalicaa threw in pertinent bits, and then Methusal repeated the story of her trip home from Tarst.

"...and Aali got us in through her secret passage," Behran interjected. "If it hadn't been for her, I don't know how we would have made it inside without being caught. And she and Sims distracted the Dehriens in the dining hall, too, when they threw rocks down onto them."

Petr looked at his daughter with pride and with humility. "It seems I've made many mistakes, Aalicaa. It's a hard lesson for a man to learn, to realize he's been prideful and close-minded to his peers," he glanced at Erl and Ben Amil, "and inflexible in raising his daughters. Aalicaa, you have my blessing to pursue kaavl. Make me proud."

"Father!" Aali burst into tears and flung her arms around his neck. "Thank you, Father. But I don't deserve it, I don't! It's because of me sneaking that they took over Rolban so soon. I should have listened to you."

Gently, Petr said, "Then we've both learned that we need to follow the rules. I hope it's a lesson neither of us forget."

Aali shook her head, face still buried in her father's shoulder, but when she pulled away she was smiling, and happily clutched Methusal's arm. "You'll help me learn kaavl, won't you, Thusa?"

"Of course."

Kitran spoke up. "I feel like most of what happened is my fault." His voice was heavy, as if he had a lot to get off of his chest. "I'm sorry. Mentàll fooled me, and I'll admit he played on my pride to get what he wanted. He's cunning, and I'm beginning to see how he planned the whole takeover. With Verdnt as his eyes and ears here, he knew exactly how to play on my weakness—and Petr's—to achieve his own ends. My weakness is a passion for kaavl, at the expense of common sense, and Petr's was a desperation to be reelected, and to stay Chief for as long as possible."

Petr's eyes narrowed, but he said nothing. Kitran went on, "Mentàll claimed to be great in kaavl—and he is. I could see that for myself. When he told me it was because he'd found the way to the Ultimate level, I was ready to believe him. Then, when he told me how to *reach* the Ultimate level...I was overwhelmed. And I started to believe everything he said."

"Anyway," Kitran drew a harsh breath, "Mentàll told me that only kaavl can produce the best, most honorable leaders. He thought it was really important, and I began to agree. Kaavl does make the mind sharper. Maybe wiser, too. And both Dehre and Tarst have strong kaavl leaders. I began to think Rolban was wrong to ignore how vital kaavl could be to leadership. It wasn't long before I convinced Petr of it, too."

He looked at his partner in crime. Petr stared at the table, his mouth twisted in clear humiliation. The great man had been humbled. He had been fooled, yes, but it had been his decision to go along with Mentàll's self-serving plan, and to write the letter of authorization, and to steal Rolban's seed grain and give it to Dehre. Fooled or not, he was responsible for his actions.

Kitran doggedly continued. "Mentàll must have planned out every detail. He gained my confidence first, and then used my influence to get to Petr. He tricked both of us into thinking the second agreement would be a good thing."

He gave a short, bitter laugh. "All the secrecy around the second treaty made me feel uncomfortable, but I tried to ignore it. Facing up to the true fact—that I'd been taken for a fool—was too hard to face. But on that long trip home this morning, I realized I'd made a huge error in judgment. And I'd convinced Petr to make the same mistake. I'm terribly sorry."

Hanuh touched his arm. "Mentàll is a cunning man, Kitran. He would have found another way to trick us. Count it as a lesson. I think we've *all* learned from this."

Kitran clenched his fist. He did not look comforted. In fact, fury blazed in his eyes. He clearly hated the Dehrien Chief for tricking him.

"I'm sorry, too." The words sounded wrenched from Petr's throat. He would soon face trial. As punishment, he'd be stripped of power, and probably disqualified from ever running for Chief again. Maybe even worse was facing unpleasant truths about himself. Such as how his lust for power had almost destroyed Rolban.

It seemed clear to Methusal that kaavl alone couldn't make a truly great leader. Only wisdom, fairness, honor, and integrity could. Kaavl couldn't produce strong character, because character came from a pure heart, which was made evident by the honorable decisions of a man. Mentàll, the Kaavl Master, portrayed none of those qualities.

Timaeus stepped up during the reflective silence and put a hand on Deccia's shoulder. "Are you ready to look over your classroom, *instructor?* We've just finished clearing out Verdnt's things."

With the chief teacher gone, Methusal realized Deccia would have to start teaching full-time next year. It was a lot of responsibility, but she had no doubt her sister, in all of her quiet strength, would do a wonderful job.

No one had mentioned Verdnt. Maybe because the hurt of his betrayal ran deep. He'd been the first Dehrien to immigrate to Rolban, and had lived there for over seven years. They had trusted him.

How long had he betrayed them? Always? Or starting four years ago, when Mentàll had come to power?

Maybe answers could be found in his compartment. Methusal decided to speak to her father about that a little later.

Deccia glanced up at Timaeus, and a soft smile lit her face. "I'm ready." A final, serene smile for Aalicaa, Methusal, and her father, and she departed with the man she loved. Unmistakable joy leant a spring to her step.

"We've all learned a lot," Erl said after a little silence. "One thing is clear. The Dehriens—or rather, Mentàll—can't be trusted. They're back to the same tricks that started the Great War. We'd better warn Tarst."

"Later." Ben stood. "Today, we'll celebrate the heroes of Rolban."

"Many of whom are our children." A relaxed Hanuh Maahr looked proudly at her daughter, and Methusal smiled.

Two weeks ago, so many things had been different. Renn had been murdered, and her necklace on his body had implicated her in the crime. Now she finally understood why Verdnt had framed her. Her necklace was the key. Verdnt had stolen it because both he and the Dehrien Chief had wanted the *Second Book of Kaavl*. Verdnt had thought her necklace was a clue to its location. It appeared he'd been mistaken. Maybe she'd never know how Renn had ended up with the necklace in his pocket. But she guessed Verdnt had planted it on Renn's body, in order to point suspicion toward her.

And now Mentàll possessed her family heirloom. She wondered if she'd ever get it back.

So many things had changed since the night Renn had died. She had changed the most. Two weeks ago, all she'd cared about was becoming Tri-level kaavl champ. Since then, she had accomplished that, and so much more.

But best of all, she had discovered there was more to life than kaavl—family, community solidarity, and more. She glanced at Behran out of the corner of her eye. Rolban would never be the same after this, and neither would she. For the first time in her life, she realized just how lucky she was to live in Rolban.

Slowly, the party broke up and Methusal wandered down the hall to her compartment to change for lunch. Pain twinged in her shoulder, which reminded her of capturing the Dehrien in the supply room. But after moving it a little more, she decided it wasn't that bad. A small price to pay for victory over the Dehriens. She'd also need to put coltac juice on the cut on her arm.

Lost in her thoughts, she jumped a bit when Old Sims fell into step beside her.

"I'm glad you're back, my girl. Didn't realize what a help you've become to me until you left for that long trip."

"Oh, Sims!" Methusal impulsively hugged him. Her discoveries in Tarst flooded her mind, and she grinned. "Have I got a surprise for you!"

△ △ △ △ △

During lunch, Erl agreed with Methusal that Verdnt's compartment should be searched for more clues about the conspiracy. Verdnt had admitted that Ludst Lst was one accomplice, but what if he'd had more? All facts needed to be brought to light now, for Rolban's safety.

Erl searched Verdnt's desk, Ben searched the bedchamber, Petr the main compartment, and Methusal the trash. She discovered the mother lode. One page of dense, cramped handwriting was addressed to a "Presidente."

"Papa," Methusal said urgently. "Look."

Erl took the letter and read out loud:

Presidente,

Victory is near. Still, they suspect nothing. I have planted clues so that Rolban will trust neither Dehre nor Tarst. Already those seeds are bearing fruit. Even if our pawn's takeover fails, distrust has been sown, bitter and deep. I am confident that when the full course of time has ripened, the ore will be ours to pluck. Their weaknesses are plain, and have been simple to exploit. The plan is a success. My fellow Zindedi in Tarst has done his job well, and I will give him this letter soon. As for your deepest, closest spy, he remains silent and undiscovered, waiting

*and watching, as you wish. When the battle is finished,
I will convey the full details to you.*

*I remain your dedicated servant,
Verdnt*

"Who is this Presidente?" Petr wondered.

"And where is Zindedi?" Methusal wanted to know.

Lines of worry deepened in Erl's brow. "I'm not sure, but Zindedi must be a land across the sea. No such people live on Koblan."

"Verdnt and his accomplice came here to create distrust. They want us to be at war with the Dehriens *and* the Tarst?" Methusal asked.

"Yes. And apparently they want our ore."

"Verdnt said that to me," Methusal agreed. "He said Mentàll wants the ore, too."

"Maybe Mentàll is the pawn Verdnt referred to in the letter."

"Do you think Mentàll was working for Verdnt? For Zindedi?" Although Methusal didn't think much of the Dehrien, she felt fairly sure he was only acting for himself, to accomplish his own goals. She couldn't imagine him knowingly being a subservient pawn to anyone. Then again, what did she really know about the Dehrien? He'd proven he was a wild beast. Maybe he was capable of anything.

Petr blustered, "I wouldn't put anything past that Dehrien whip."

"One thing is clear," Erl said. "Verdnt's accomplice lives in Tarst. I need to contact Pan. We'll need to talk about the Alliance and Zindedi."

"What about that deep spy Verdnt mentioned?" Methusal said. "Do you think he's here in Rolban?"

Grim lines tightened her father's mouth. "We will be on guard, and we'll warn other communities to do the same. Clearly, the Zindedis have been planning this for years. They planted Verdnt in Dehre thirteen years ago. And he moved here seven years ago. His death won't stop their plan, whatever it is. Multiple spies could infest communities all over Koblan."

Methusal remembered again what the Prophet had told her about the coming trouble. Would that take place in a few years? Or sooner? Maybe she hadn't listened closely enough to the Prophet before, but she would now. He'd known about Mentàll and his sword. He'd told her to pray for her enemy, but she had not.

Would it have made a difference if she had?

In a quiet voice, she said, "I think we'd better hurry, Papa."

Erl frowned. "Why?"

"According to the Prophet, this is only the beginning of trouble."

△ △ △ △ △

That night, Methusal sat with Behran on the crop plateau. They were safe from all predators there—both man and beast. The tally had come in—five Rolbanis had been killed during the short war, and seven Dehriens. They were lucky they hadn't lost more people.

Stars pierced the black velvet sky, and the plain below glowed green, bathed in the pale light of Ryon. Methusal had just finished telling Behran about Verdnt and Zindedi.

"I'm still confused about a few things," Methusal said. "It seems clear from Verdnt's letter that the Zindedis are the ones who wanted the ore. Did Mentàll, too?"

"He wanted power. I'm not sure about the ore, except for maybe to make weapons."

"Yes. And he's arrogant enough to think he can have anything he wants."

Behran gave a short laugh. "It'll prick his pride to learn he was only a pawn."

"Or maybe Verdnt was *his* pawn." For the first time, Methusal wondered why the Dehrien had really wanted to take over Rolban. Because his people were starving? Because he wanted to find the *Second Book of Kaavl?* Had his delegation been sent to conquer Rolban, or to be used as back up if his unknown plan didn't go like he'd hoped? In reality, twenty-six Dehriens would be hard-pressed to conquer Rolban, unless he'd planned to send for reinforcements.

Little made sense. What had been Mentàll's primary motivation? What had he really wanted to do in Rolban?

Slowly, she said, "Verdnt said Mentàll wanted vengeance. For what, do you think?"

"It doesn't matter now. It's all over."

"I hope so." Her mind returned to the strange visual carry she'd experienced during the battle that morning. She decided it was time to trust this fact to her fiercest competitor.

"Wow," Behran said afterward, and fell silent.

Methusal felt uncomfortable. "I guess I'll have to wait and see if it happens again."

"It probably will." Behran's voice was quiet, but proud. He didn't sound envious at all. "Are you going on to the Bi-level, then?"

"Yes, since Kitran has rejected Mentàll's theories. What about you?"

"I'll never be able to beat you again."

"How do you know?" She glanced at his familiar features. "I think we've barely scratched the surface of kaavl. But I know we can learn more together."

"Maybe you're right." His midnight blue eyes held hers. She felt his warm hand enfold hers. He interlaced their fingers. Her breath caught—a little surprised, and a little bit not. A sweet joy surged through her, tingling to her fingertips.

From rival to friend, to possibly more. The future stretched out before them, bright with promise and hope. Adventure lay ahead...and challenges. Of that, she felt certain. But no shadows.

Surely, no shadows.

Epilogue

Carachki, Zindedi
(Two weeks later)

"A letter, Presidente." Bowing, the skinny young man placed the envelope on the desk, and scurried out.

"At last." The Presidente of Zindedi plucked it up with a smile. "The pot has boiled."

Across the room, the General stopped muttering to himself. "What, brother?"

The Presidente flicked him a tolerant glance. "Are you prepared for the mission?"

His amber eyes, so like the Presidente's, finally focused. "Mission? Yes! I am ready for battle." He licked his lips in anticipation.

The Presidente smiled. "Good. Make sure your mind doesn't deviate too far while you are on the battlefield."

His brother smiled widely, his teeth gleaming yellow in the sun that shone through the window. "On the battlefield, you have no one better than me. And off the bloody field, my fancies are my own."

The unholy light in his brother's eyes made the Presidente smile. "Go ahead. Be as ruthless off the field as on. Just so long as it sharpens your appetite for battle."

The General's eyes hardened into the eager blood lust the Presidente knew so well. And the Presidente knew his brother would deliver Koblan to him, just as he had united Zindedi in one short, horrific war two years ago.

The Presidente slit the envelope and withdrew the single page. Unease shot through him. It wasn't Verdnt's neat handwriting. The words were dark and crudely formed. He checked the signature. It was from his spy in Tarst.

"Read it out loud," the General urged.

"Verdnt is dead." The Presidente read the words again, hardly able to believe them.

"Forget him," the General said. "What about the war? Is Koblan weakened, and primed for our attack?"

The Presidente read more. "Verdnt started the war, and our Dehrien puppet joined the cause, as expected. But..."

"But what?" The General strode over and tried to grab the paper.

The Presidente shot him a vicious glare and bared his teeth. The General lowered his hand. "Read it. I want to hear."

The Presidente complied; mostly so he wouldn't have to repeat it later.

The war ended in two hours. Rolbanis fought fiercely, and Methusal Maahr used kaavl to capture the Dehrien Chief. Rolbanis found one of Verdnt's letters. It stated he wanted to stir up war between Rolban, Tarst, and Dehre. Zindedi was mentioned.

The Presidente pressed his palm to his forehead. "The fool!"

"Read!" his brother said impatiently.

The Presidente continued, feeling his horror mount.

They are warned. Any attack should wait until their defenses become lax again. I will report when this is so. Verdnt also mentioned an accomplice in Tarst. As you know, I planted Rolbani objects in Tarst, at Verdnt's instruction, to try to create suspicion between the communities. We hoped war would engulf all three villages, and thereby weaken all of Koblan. I'm afraid I will be suspected, since I'm one of three messengers who travels between Rolban and Tarst. I am moving south, to Wyen. I will still messenger, and will send reports to you. But Verdnt's mission has failed. Your deepest spy, however, remains safely undetected.

Build a large army before you try to take over Koblan. As you know, only Verdnt and one other Zindedi learned kaavl. In any war against Koblan, kaavl will prove your most formidable foe. You will need to carry many arms to defeat it. ...If that is even possible."

"If that is even *possible!*" the General snorted. "Mind games are no match for swords or our firearms."

The Presidente crumpled the letter. "Now we have only one man in Rolban!" With a vicious thrust, he flung the paper across the room.

"We need no one," the General countered, his eyes gleaming. "Only arms. And lots of men."

The Presidente grabbed the ink well on his desk and hurled that across the room, too. It made him feel better.

"Think, brother." The General stared at him. For once, his words were the sane ones. "Make your plan."

The Presidente slowly ran a hand through his prickly hair. His fingers dug painfully into his scalp. The discomfort helped him think. "I'll activate our other spies," he growled. "And we will manufacture more arms. When we take Koblan, I want it to be fast and hard. No escape for any of them!" With a swift, violent arm, he swept everything from his desk onto the floor. The objects made a series of satisfactory crashing noises.

"More arms than we have assembled now?" the General asked.

"Much more! I underestimated one small village on Koblan. Perhaps I have underestimated them all." He named the number of arms and ships he wanted prepared.

The General looked visibly taken aback. "But that will take months. Years. Do you really want to wait..."

"Do it! We will win this next war. The Koblan continent, and even this Methusal with her kaavl tricks, will bow in submission to me before this war is over!"

"Very good, Presidente. We will train every day. When we attack, Koblan will have no escape."

"Make sure it is so, brother. We need that ore. And we will get it." The Presidente spun in his chair and stared outside at the city skyline stretching north from his two story window. Zindedi. He controlled it all...the entire continent. But it was not enough. His brother, the General, lusted for blood. Well, he lusted for power.

When a year or two slipped by, and Koblan was not attacked, the continent would relax. He felt confident of that.

Koblan was not a united continent. The Presidente snorted. *Weak fools!* He would win Koblan easily; of this, he had no doubt. And his deepest spy would surface to help him achieve the crowning victory. Then, with Rolban's ore to make more weapons, and Koblan's inhabitants as free slave labor, his power would have no limit.

A smile curved his lips. He could easily wait two years to win a jewel like Koblan. With her, he would rule the world.

∆ ∆ ∆

Author's Note

I sincerely hope you enjoyed *Kaavl Conspiracy* as much as I enjoyed writing it. There are three more books in this quadrilogy. The next book, *Kaavl Quest*, will be published in July 2016.

One final note. As a small press author, getting my books before readers is a real challenge. You can help! If you liked this book, please consider writing a short review on Amazon, B & N, or the retailer's website where you purchased the book. Each review encourages Amazon and other online retailers to promote the book to more readers. Each and every review counts, and means so much!

I'd love to hear from you! Please drop me a note at jennettegreen@jennettegreen.com.

Best wishes always,
Jennette

www.ingramcontent.com/pod-product-compliance
Lightning Source LLC
Chambersburg PA
CBHW020241120726

47904CB00001B/53